TASTE OF HONEY

EILEEN GOUDGE

TASTE *of* HONEY

A CARSON SPRINGS NOVEL

Bookspan Large Print Edition

VIKING

VIKING

Published by the Penguin Group

Penguin Putnam Inc., 375 Hudson Street, New York, New York 10014, U.S.A.

Penguin Books Ltd, 80 Strand, London WC2R 0RL, England

Penguin Books Australia Ltd, 250 Camberwell Road, Camberwell, Victoria 3124, Australia

Penguin Books Canada Ltd, 10 Alcorn Avenue, Toronto, Ontario, Canada M4V 3B2

Penguin Books India (P) Ltd, 11 Community Centre, Panchsheel Park, New Delhi—110 017, India

Penguin Books (N.Z.) Ltd, Cnr Rosedale and Airborne Roads, Albany, Auckland, New Zealand

Penguin Books (South Africa) (Pty) Ltd. 24 Sturdee Avenue, Rosebank, Johannesburg 2196, South Africa

Penguin Books Ltd, Registered Offices: Harmondsworth, Middlesex, England

**This Large Print Book carries the
Seal of Approval of N.A.V.H.**

For my godsons, Jason and Ethan Lazar,
who serve as constant reminders
that family comes in all shapes and forms.

ISBN 0-7394-2683-4

Printed in the United States of America
Designed by Carla Bolte

In lieu of the usual acknowledgments—those of you deserving thanks, you know who you are—I would like to take this opportunity to make mention of the fact that something extraordinary occurred during the writing of this book: September 11th. I was heading upstairs to my office when the news came. Along with millions of others across the land, I watched in horror as the twin towers collapsed. Living in New York City made it especially poignant. In the days that followed I couldn't walk out my door without seeing the photos of all those missing loved ones, and weeping at the almost certain knowledge that they would not be found alive.

I was luckier than most. I could retreat daily to the safety of my fictional town, Carson Springs, where the destinies of my characters weren't controlled by terrorists, or even acts of God. It was me moving the chess pieces about the board, a sense of empowerment that seized hold in my everyday life as well, saving me from the worst of the anxieties that plagued us as a nation. A reminder that we are all, ultimately, captain of our souls, if not of our fates.

I would like to pay tribute to all who were lost on that terrible day. They are the true heroes and heroines. Mine exist only on paper, while the memories of those slain live on in the minds and hearts of their families and friends.

*My child, eat honey, for it is good
and the drippings of the
honeycomb are sweet to
your taste.
Know that wisdom is such to
your soul;
if you find it, you will find a future,
and your hope will not be cut off.*

—Proverbs 24:13–14

Prologue

Our Lady of the Wayside, 1973

Gerry Fitzgerald, poised before the altar in her dark gray habit and white veil, fixed her gaze on the squares of cloth spread over the scuffed floorboards at her feet. They seemed to float almost, like magic carpets: the white one a symbol of the material world she was renouncing, the black one of her journey through darkness to Christ. Within minutes she would be a professed nun, the years of rigorous tutelage and constant questioning behind her. Yet as she stood there alongside her fellow novices, she all at once felt deeply afraid. Her heart began to pound and each breath brought the sodden weight of the August heat that lay over the chapel like a freshly boiled jar—Mother Jerome steadfastly refused to install air-conditioning—pressing down on her lungs.

She brought a trembling hand to her veil, which she would soon trade for the black one of the professed nun, her mind spinning back to her very first interview with Mother Jerome. *This will be a test, my dear,* the kindly old mother superior had warned, *not of your strength or courage—you have more than enough of those to spare—*here, she'd smiled—*but of the quality of your faith, which is the most difficult test of all.*

She'd been just shy of her eighteenth birthday. The next nine months as a postulant had been filled with constant reminders; to walk without bouncing on the balls of her feet; to hold her hands clasped to prevent them, in Sister Eunice's words, from flapping about like two birds; and, most difficult of all, to keep custody of her eyes. She'd learned to bite her tongue and to rein in her ready laugh. Two more years as a novice had taught her the patience of Job. She'd learned to let answers come naturally rather than constantly seeking them out, and to give without asking or expecting anything in return.

And hadn't she humbled herself before Him, praying until her knees were a constant ache? Risen before sunrise seven days a week for morning office? Toiled without complaint scrubbing floors and toilets, pulling weeds, working in the apiary at the risk of getting stung? She'd even borne in silence (except for occasional mutterings under her breath) the criticisms of sharp-tongued assistant superior Sister Eunice. All that remained now was to take her final vows. Why then was her heart pounding so? What was this taste like old pennies on the back of her tongue?

She watched Ann Marie Lozano, on her right, lower herself onto the black cloth, facedown, arms stretched out on either side of her. Dark-haired, birdlike Ann Marie, newly renamed Sister Paul, who'd been desperately homesick that first year and often whimpered in her sleep even now. As she lay motionless a white sheet was placed over her: a shroud symbolizing death to the material world. Listening to her recite her vows, Gerry heard only a series of muffled cheeps that seemed to mimic those of the swallows nesting in the terra-cotta roof overhead. Gerry cast a glance over her shoulder at Ann Marie's family nearly filling the second pew, her mother and father and six brothers and sisters, all small and dark like her, with eyes that seemed to take up half their faces. They were beaming as Father Gallagher and Mother Jerome said their blessings over Ann Marie.

After Ann Marie, Peggy Rourke's trim, taut form was a living crucible stretched out on the cloth. Peggy's calling was the envy of every thirteen-year-old girl: The Blessed Virgin Mary had actually appeared before her, clad in a shimmering blue robe and bearing a bouquet of white roses. That this vision had occurred in the days following Peggy's mother's death made it all the more awe inspiring. Wherever she went Peggy seemed to carry with her a faint but somehow pervasive scent of roses. Though it hadn't escaped Gerry's notice that in her humble insistence on always being the last in line, taking the smallest portion, and as-suming the hardest task, Peggy succeeded only in drawing more attention to herself.

Under the white cloth that covered her from head to toe, Gerry could see her trembling. She felt oddly reassured. If Peggy Rourke, their resident Bernadette, had butterflies, then who was she to question her own faith?

It's not just nerves, and you know it, another more sinister voice whispered in her head. A voice that spoke the truth, for her belly seemed hotly alive, not with butterflies, but with a buzzing swarm of bees.

Gerry raised her eyes to the carved reredos over the tabernacle, at the center of which, crudely applied to wood with mineral colors and cactus juice by some long-forgotten artisan, was a painting of Jesus on the cross, heart displayed like a medallion on His chest. When she was little, she'd misread *sacred heart* as *scared heart* until Sister Alice set her straight in front of the whole class her first year of catechism, to the tittering delight of her classmates. Yet it seemed appropriate somehow. How could Jesus *not* have been scared? He'd been human after all, a man with doubts and fears. A man who might even have given in to the occasional temptation . . .

Gerry grew lightheaded, swaying on legs gone watery as the thing she'd pushed to the back of her mind came bursting forth. *You're a liar and a hypocrite,* scolded the waspish voice in her head. *And you have the gall to stand here, pretending to be worthy of the vows you're about to take.*

It wasn't as if her mother and sisters

hadn't tried to warn her. Mavis, who'd remained dry-eyed throughout Gerry's father's
funeral five years before, had wept when her
youngest daughter announced she was going into the convent. Even Sam, her best
friend Sam, who rarely raised her voice, had
shouted that she'd be a racehorse shackled
to a plow. As usual, Gerry hadn't listened,
even when her own inner voice chimed in.
Such doubts were normal, she knew. And
how could she ignore this *pull*?

But something had happened along the
way: She'd sinned. Not like the sins whispered in the confessional—doubts and small
lapses, a word spoken out of turn—but one
so deep and dark she'd told no one. Not
even dear, good-hearted Sister Agnes. For
the novice mistress would have been duty
bound to bring it to the attention of Mother
Jerome, who'd have immediately summoned Gerry to her office.

That's not all, she'd have been forced to
tell them. *There's more.*

But a missed period didn't necessarily
mean anything, did it? It wasn't the first time
she'd skipped a month, and was probably
the result of not eating enough to keep a bird
alive, as her mother would've said. Hadn't

Sister Agnes warned that fasting could interrupt the cycle and even bring on nausea?

But what if it was something else? Something she didn't dare voice, not even to herself. Gerry felt it start to take shape, the murky brown fear in the back of her mind, and was swept with a chill that blew through her like a Norse wind. She rocked back on her heels, taking slow, even breaths until the buzzing lightness in her head receded and she could trust her legs to remain steady. Close to her heart, where she'd once felt the warmth of God's love, there was only emptiness. How could He love her in the face of what she'd done?

Even with her head lowered, she became acutely aware of Father Gallagher's eyes on her. But when she at last dared meet his gaze, it passed through her as if she were invisible. An icy bolt shot through Gerry's heart. What was going on behind those eyes? Eyes malice free and blue as the sunlit Sea of Galilee depicted in the stained-glass window over the tabernacle. There was a time she'd believed Father Gallagher—Jim—to be as close to God as was possible in a mortal being. But now she knew that he walked the earth like any man: on feet of clay.

If he led, I willingly followed.

She couldn't blame Jim. It was her own weakness that had caused her to stumble from the path. And now here she was, putting one foot in front of the other simply because it was the only thing she could think of to do.

Gerry glanced at her novice mistress out of the corner of her eye. Sister Agnes was seated in the first pew to her right, flanked by Mother Jerome and horse-faced Sister Eunice, a plump little muffin of a woman whom she'd grown to love like a mother, and who had instructed her in everything from the chanting of the Divine Office to mulching flower beds and making Mulligan stew. Now she caught Gerry's eye and smiled in encouragement, her round cheeks glowing and deep-set blue eyes sparkling with a warmth that penetrated even the coldness at Gerry's center.

I should have confided in her. Sister Agnes never judged, only gently corrected. She saw God in everything, even the humblest of His creations: the bees delivering pollen to the hives, a perfect piece of fruit, even the homeliest wildflowers, equal in her eye to the lilies of the field. *She'd have understood.* Like a lighted window, she'd have guided Gerry through the darkness.

But no one could help her now. These past weeks had been a sort of half sleep in which she'd floated dreamily, a sleep from which she'd only just been awakened as if by a rude slap. Now the moment of reckoning was near. Once she took her final vows there could be no turning back, no second thoughts. It wasn't just that she'd be living a lie, there would be no more—*God forgive me*—of the hot, furtive pleasure she'd found in Jim's bed. Never again would she feel that delicious heat between her legs, building and building until she was consumed by it.

Gerry watched with growing panic as the sheet over Peggy was removed and she rose gracefully to her feet, swaying slightly, her face a pale pink cameo framed by her starched white wimple and veil. Peggy, who'd sooner offer her throat to be cut than open her legs to a man. As Father Gallagher stepped toward Peggy, Gerry allowed herself a glimpse, just one, like a stolen sip of wine: a fleeting impression of dark hair dipping in a comma over a smooth white brow, a small straight nose, a sharply defined upper lip curled in a bow over the fuller bottom lip. His white and gold vestments shimmered jewellike in the light streaming through the stained-glass window as he directed his beneficent gaze on Peggy before turning to face Mother Jerome.

"Reverend Mother," he said in a solemn tone, "do you accept Sister Bernadette," a nod toward Peggy, "as a member of your congregation for the rest of her religious life?"

Mother Jerome, as ancient as the breviary she clutched in one hand, its pages worn to a whisper, once more struggled to her feet. A small woman hunched with arthritis, she nonetheless carried herself with a grace earned from years as a Living Rule. In a cracked voice that somehow carried up into the rafters, she responded, "We do, Father, and with God's grace she will remain faithful to her vows all the days of her life. May her soul be one with Christ, united with Him for all eternity."

Father Gallagher returned his solemn gaze to Peggy. Was it only six years ago he'd been assigned to their parish, fresh from the seminary? His demeanor was that of someone far older and wiser, as if he occupied a higher plane than those around him. How did he stand there looking as if nothing were out of the ordinary? As if the things they'd done together in the darkness of his bedroom were but a fever dream. Remembering, she felt blood surge up into her face, making it throb.

"Do you, Sister Bernadette, promise obedience, chastity, and poverty to God for the rest of your days?" he went on.

Jim, he said to call him Jim. As if the name she whispered in the close-smelling darkness were a separate entity from the priest known to the outside world as Father Gallagher, a man who ceased to exist outside the narrow confines of his bed and therefore carried no responsibility for what happened there. There were times she herself wondered if she hadn't imagined the whole thing. Only her guilt, nibbling at her with sharp rodent's teeth, told her it was real, guilt she alone was left to bear.

The newly anointed Sister Bernadette, formerly known as Peggy Rourke, raised her blameless blue eyes to his. "I do," she said in a voice husky with emotion.

Mother Jerome hobbled over, listing to one side, to remove Peggy's veil, allowing a fleeting glimpse of short wispy locks the pale orange of marmalade—hair that from now on was to be cut eight times a year, only on holy days—before fitting the black veil of profession over her head. When the mother superior presented her with a plain silver cross on a sturdy black cord, Peggy placed it around her neck as if it were the finest of jewels. Gerry caught the rapturous glow on her face as she floated back to her pew, where she knelt and bowed her head in prayer.

Now it was Gerry's turn.

She could feel every eye in the chapel on her. Mother Jerome and all the sisters. Ann Marie, Peggy, and their families. She glanced over her shoulder at her mother, sitting ramrod straight in her pew several rows back, her thick hair that had once shone as bright as new pennies springing from its combs like a tangle of rusty wires. Mavis, who'd cried that she hadn't buried a husband only to lose a daughter, but who'd eventually come to accept her decision. Beside her sat Gerry's fourteen-year-old brother Kevin, who must have shot up at least three inches since she'd last seen him. He looked close to tears.

What would they think if they knew?

Her knees threatened to buckle. Oh, God. She was doomed, not only to hell, but also to endlessly replay those memories: the whisper of his breath against her neck, the brush of his lips over her bare flesh. Each day, throughout her morning and evening prayers and the chanting of the Divine Office, when she ought to have been filled with the Holy Spirit, she'd been overflowing with thoughts of Jim instead. His skin, pale and smooth as marble. His slender hands with their shy touch that took her breath away. The feel of him thrusting into her, that little gasp he gave, as if caught by surprise.

Help me, Lord.

They say God is in the details, and in the end that was what brought it all to a head. In the collectively held breath that seemed to fill the chapel, swelling up into the rafters, she heard the soft mutter of ancient Sister Helena passing wind. Gerry didn't have to look around to see noses wrinkling and lips pressed together in helpless mirth. Suddenly the answer to her dilemma became clear: She had no more control over her fate than poor old Sister Helena had over her bowels. However hard she fought it, however much she prayed, her course was set. She had no choice but to navigate it.

With a small strangled cry Gerry turned and fled. The oak pews on either side melted into a waxy blur lined with startled faces. She caught sight of her best friend, Sam, in a sleeveless green shift, her wide hazel eyes seeming to register relief.

Then a fire seemed to engulf Gerry, incinerating everything in her wake, a rush of heat that seared her lungs, leaving her gasping for air. She stumbled and nearly fell. The double doors to the vestibule swam into view. What was waiting beyond those doors? What kind of life would she have? For it wouldn't be just her. There'd be—

The baby.

The realization swooped out of nowhere, like a bird smacking headlong into a windowpane: She was pregnant. At least two months. Deep down, hadn't she known all along?

In a wild panic, she hurled herself at the heavy oak doors, scrabbling blindly for a knob. Not until the following day would she notice the bruise running in an inky smudge down her right shoulder all the way to her elbow. The only thing she was aware of that bright August morning, as she dashed through the vestibule and spilled panting into the ivied cloister garden, with its statues of saints staring blankly back at her from amid the lush greenery, was that life, *her* life— wildly divergent from any she'd imagined— was about to begin. And there wasn't a blessed thing she could do about it.

Chapter One

Present day

Gerry slipped a hand into her coat pocket. The envelope was still there: folded and re-folded, the letter inside dog-eared, its contents long since committed to memory. In the two days since it had arrived in the mail she'd carried it everywhere, fingering it as compulsively as she once had her rosary beads. *Her name is Claire.* Not a name she'd have chosen. In her mind it would always be Aileen. Aileen Fitzgerald, after her great-grandmother from Kenmare.

An image surfaced in her mind: a small

red face peeking from the folds of a blanket, topped by a tuft of pale brown hair. An old pain flared to life, and her ears were filled with a rushing noise that momentarily dimmed the warbling of the carolers. On the thronged sidewalk, in the flickering glow of countless bobbing candles, their voices drifted toward her as if through layers of cotton: *Silent night, holy night . . . all is calm . . . all is bright . . .*

The knot of people in front of her inched forward: men and women, each clutching a lighted candle and bundled up against the unaccustomed cold, many with babies in their arms or toddlers on their hips. She spotted Sam's sister, Audrey, with her husband, Grant, the tin of coconut snowballs Audrey gave Father Reardon every year tucked under one arm. And who could miss Marguerite Moore, in a crimson jacket, sailing at the head of the line like a brightly decked barge? Or the elderly Miller twins, Rose and Olive, dressed in identical green velvet coats and matching cloche hats.

It was a tradition that had been a part of Christmas festivities in Carson Springs since the days of the early Spanish settlers, this candlelight procession up Calle de Navidad that ended with evening mass at St. Xavier's.

Gerry remembered when she was small, trudging dutifully at her mother's side, wanting only to be inside where it was warm and she could keep an eye out for Santa. Tonight it was the only thing keeping her sane. She straightened her shoulders, joining the chorus in her sure, strong alto.

Round yon virgin, mother and child . . . holy infant, so tender and mild . . .

The familiar lyrics acted like a tonic, and her fears seemed to evaporate along with the frosty plume of her breath funneling up into the night sky. The knot in her chest loosened, and she felt a surge of wild hope: that she and Claire would meet and find they had more in common than not, that they would find a way to put the past behind them and move forward, like a broken leg that's healed badly but is still strong enough to walk on.

Yeah, and a few hours from now Santa and his reindeer are going to land on your rooftop with a sack full of goodies. She gave in to a small, wry smile. It was Christmas, the time of the year one was allowed visions of dancing sugarplums. Tomorrow, when the wrapping paper was cleared away, she would get real, as her daughter would say.

She caught sight of Andie, a dozen or so

yards ahead, gabbing with a group of friends from school, their faces rosy in the candlelight. She looked happy and relaxed, and Gerry couldn't help thinking of how long it had been since she'd been that way at home. Justin, dragging his heels at Gerry's side, followed her gaze and sighed.

"Mom, how come Andie gets to be with *her* friends?"

Gerry turned to him, answering mildly, "Because all of yours are with *their* parents. And because," she threw in, "you'd be leaving your poor old mother all alone on Christmas Eve."

Justin, not seeing the humor in her reply, merely eyed her plaintively, his narrow freckled face, framed by the hood of his sweatshirt, making her long for the Christmas Eves when he'd been a baby in his snowsuit and she'd carried him in her arms up Calle de Navidad. "It's just . . ." His voice trailed off, and he looked down at his Air Jordans that were two sizes bigger than last year's. He was small for his age, but his feet seemed to have a life of their own.

"I know," she said gently.

"It's nothing against *you,* Mom."

"I know."

"It'd be different if Dad were here."

"You miss him, don't you?"

He gave her a sheepish look. "Sort of . . . but only a little." His brand of loyalty, she knew. He must think he was sparing her in some way.

"Look at it this way," she said. "Think of all the fun stuff *he's* missing out on."

A dark and decidedly unchildlike look flitted over her eleven-year-old son's face. "Yeah, like what?"

"Christmas with you guys, for one thing, and—"

"Snow?" A corner of Justin's mouth hooked up in a wise-guy smile.

"Okay, but a time-share in Tahoe isn't exactly what the guy who wrote 'Jingle Bells' had in mind," she said dryly.

Her son fell silent, his unspoken words hanging in the air: *He could have invited us anyway.* Not that Justin would have preferred spending Christmas with Mike and Cindy, just that it would've been nice to have been asked. Gerry knew exactly how he felt. Hadn't she spent the better part of fifteen years waiting for Mike to do right by her?

"Mom, watch it."

Gerry's eyes dropped to the candle pre-

cariously atilt in one hand, molten wax a
hair's breadth away from dribbling onto her
knuckles. She tipped it so that the wax drizzled onto the sidewalk instead. "We'll have a
wonderful Christmas, just the four of us—
you, me, Andie, and Grandma," she said in
what she hoped wasn't too hearty a tone.
"You'll see."

The procession inched forward. Justin
took a shuffling step, only the toes of his
sneakers protruding from the jeans puddled
about his feet—gravity-defying jeans that
rode so low on his hips the back pockets
were roughly in line with his knees. "Is
Grandma spending the night?" he asked.

"If it's okay with you." Her mother lived
only a few miles away, out by Horse Creek,
in the ramshackle Victorian Gerry had grown
up in, but her eyesight had gotten so bad
she no longer drove, and it would save Gerry
from having to pick her up in the morning.
The only thing was that Mavis would have to
bunk in with Justin since his was the only
room with two beds.

"Sure." He shrugged, though she knew he
was secretly pleased. "Except Buster won't
like it."

"It won't kill him to sleep on the floor for

one night." Their elderly Lab was far too spoiled as it was.

"You should've let her come," he said with mild reproach.

Now it was Gerry's turn to sigh. Mavis was still recovering from a bout of pneumonia that had left her with hardly a scrap of meat on her bones—though naturally she claimed to be fine, insisting she had the constitution of an ox. If she'd still had her car, she'd have driven here on her own. "It's too cold," she said. "We wouldn't want her to get sick again."

"She hates being left out even more."

From the mouths of babes. Maybe she *was* being overly protective. But somebody had to play the bad guy. She only wished it didn't always have to be her. Mavis was peeved. Half the time Andie didn't speak to her. And Justin . . . well, he'd only be a little boy for so long.

They were nearly at the crosswalk. On their right lay Muir Park, with its adobe walls over which a dark crown of treetops rose. Directly across the street a spotlight showcased the two-hundred-year-old mission with its fluted bell tower and rows of campanario bells ringing in the Yuletide. On the sloping lawn out front the procession had slowed before the life-size crèche. One woman was snapping pictures. Gerry recognized former classmate Gayle Warrington, no doubt gathering material for another of the brochures she was always putting together in her tireless effort to boost winter tourism in Carson Springs. Gayle, who'd been school spirit commissioner and now owned a successful travel agency. Gayle, happily married for more than thirty years, with an elderly mother she looked in on at least once a day and two perfect children—a son in premed at UCLA and a daughter at Columbia Law. Gayle, who even at twenty would have sold pencils on the corner of Old Mission and Juarez rather than give up her own child.

"Mom?" Justin was giving her that look: the one that reminded her he was too old for some things, and not nearly old enough for others. "It'd be okay if we made believe there's a Santa Claus. Just, you know, in case Grandma forgets I know there isn't."

Her eyes prickled suddenly, and it was all she could do to keep from reaching for his hand. What would he say if he knew he had another sister? What would *Andie's* reaction be? Her children would be confused, maybe even hurt. They'd want to know why she'd kept it a secret for so long. Mostly, they'd want to know why she'd given her baby away, her own flesh and blood. And what could she tell them? What viable excuse could she give?

I was a different person then. Scared out of my wits. Nearly three years in a convent had left her hardly equipped to care for herself, much less a baby. But how could she expect them to understand?

At that moment she spotted Sam up ahead, hand in hand with Ian. Gerry caught her eye and waved, edging toward them. In her red jacket and knitted cap, Sam, six and a half months along, made her think of the pregnant young moms you saw in the playground, pushing their toddlers on swings. Never mind that she was forty-eight, every bit as old as Gerry, with two grown daughters old enough to have children of their own. Gerry noted, too, as she drew near that the candle Sam carried was in a decorative punched-tin holder. She smiled. Wasn't that just like Sam. In high school, when their classmates were donning love beads and letting their hair grow to their waists, she'd worn hers short and taken up macramé.

Sam greeted her with a kiss on the cheek. "We missed you at the Tree House," she said. Every year the procession was kicked off with gingerbread cookies and hot mulled cider at the Tree House Café.

"I had trouble finding a place to park," Gerry told her. The truth was that by the time she'd rounded up Andie and Justin, they were too late. Sam would have understood, of course, but such explanations always left Gerry feeling slightly inadequate. She turned to Ian, who, perhaps in honor of the occasion, was sporting a tiny cross in one ear. "Hey, Dad. How's it going?"

He flashed her the grin that had no doubt brought stronger women than Sam to their knees. He was thirty-one, nearly fifteen years Sam's junior, and her eldest daughter's stepson to boot. Gerry liked to tease Sam that she'd gone from *Family Circle* to the *National Enquirer* all in one leap. One thing was for sure: Nothing had been the same since Ian.

"Sam's great," he said. "I'm a nervous wreck."

"I've had practice, remember." Sam slipped an arm through his, and smiled up at him reassuringly. "It's like riding a bike. You don't forget."

Gerry opened her mouth to remind her that it'd been more than a quarter of a century since she'd last ridden this particular bike, but just as quickly shut it. Except for the straining buttons on her jacket, Sam was as slender as ever with the energy to match. Women half her age would be begging to be put out of their misery while she was valiantly bearing down. All Gerry said was, "Just give her a leather strap to bite down on, and she'll be fine."

Ian pulled Sam close. The top of her head fit neatly under his chin, over which he smiled at Gerry. "I'm counting on you to be my understudy," he told her. His blond ponytail curled rakishly from beneath the navy knitted cap he wore pulled down around his ears.

"He's afraid he'll pass out," Sam said with a laugh. "I told him it only happens in movies."

"What she actually said," Ian corrected, "was that if I valued my life, I'd better not dare."

"That sounds more like it," Gerry said with a laugh. Sam tended to soft-pedal, but rarely hesitated to speak her mind.

"He's been delegated to cut the cord," she reported matter-of-factly. "Inez says it's what fathers do these days."

Gerry and Sam shared a look: It wasn't like that in *their* day. Times had certainly changed. She remembered when Sam had had Alice; it had practically taken an act of Congress for Martin to be permitted in the delivery room, where, come to think of it, *he* had fainted.

"Gross." Justin made a face.

Ian gave him a solemn look, man to man. "Just wait till it's your turn, buddy. You'll see. I'd fight a tattooed, beer-swilling biker before going up against a pregnant woman."

"The voice of wisdom." Sam poked him in the ribs with her elbow, and stepped away as the procession moved forward into the street, calling over her shoulder, "Why don't you stop by the house on your way home? I made my marzipan coffee cake. If you guys don't help me out, I'll be big as a house by the time this baby is born."

"Sounds good," Gerry called back.

How did Sam do it? she wondered. Having a baby when most women their age were planning graduations and weddings. She recalled those bleary days of stumbling about in a sleep-deprived trance, a diaper over one shoulder that did more to cover old spit-up stains than prevent new ones, the nights of pacing the floor as she'd struggled in vain to quiet a shrieking baby. No, she wouldn't have traded places with her friend in a million years.

Still . . . when she was around Sam, she felt it: regret beating like a tiny heart beneath the layers of old excuses and protective reasoning. She'd watch her friend bring a hand to her belly, wearing that secret little smile shared by expectant mothers the world over, and find herself steeped in the memory of her first pregnancy, the wonder of those stirrings. As Sam's belly grew so had Gerry's desire, long since put to rest—or so she'd believed—to be reunited with her eldest child.

Three weeks ago she'd hired a private investigator. She hadn't expected to hear back so soon. In fact, she'd half expected no news at all, which in some ways would have been a relief. When it *had* come, the shock had had the effect of a tornado on a haystack.

Underneath this calm exterior she was thousands of whirling bits. Which was why she hadn't told anyone, not even Sam. First she had to get her head on straight, decide how to handle it.

The image rose once more: bright blue eyes peering from the folds of a blanket, a feathery tuft of hair. She felt a profound sense of sorrow sweep over her. That baby girl was gone forever. Gerry would never again hold or cuddle her; she could only hope to know the woman her baby had grown up to be. She slipped her hand into her pocket, once more fingering the envelope and seeing in her mind the address neatly typed at the bottom of the letter inside: Claire Brewster, 457 Seacrest Drive, Miramonte. That's what had gotten to her the most, that all this time she'd been so close, just half a day's drive up the coast. She recalled the weekend, six years ago, that she and Mike had spent in the quaint seaside town, strolling along the wharf, with its rows of tacky tourist shops, where they'd warmed themselves with bowls of thick chowder and peered through cloudy windows at saltwater taffy being made. To think she might have passed right by Claire and not have known it.

The caroling drifted to a close. They were mounting the steps that led up a steep slope to the mission, perched in theatrically lit splendor atop the grassy knoll overlooking the park. Another, smaller spotlight was trained on the crèche, artfully banked in poinsettias—dozens and dozens, in every shade ranging from pale pink to blood red—that gave the illusion of a tropical island inhabited by Jesus, Mary, Joseph, and the Three Kings. She was reminded of the Christmas Eve some years back when the manger had been found empty, the baby Jesus missing and a live infant left in its place: a tiny boy just hours old. The mystery hadn't remained unsolved for long. Within hours his remorseful mother, a popular junior at Portola High, had shown up to claim him, and after much ado the authorities released him into her parents' custody. The following morning, Christmas Day, the infant Jesus reappeared in the manger, none the worse for the wear. These days she often saw Penny Rogers around town with her little boy, who looked happy and well cared for. Gerry always made a point of being friendly.

Inside, the church was packed, with standing room only. She quickly lost sight of

Sam and Ian, and had to keep a close eye on her children lest she be separated from them as well. Andie cast one last longing glance at her friends before joining her and Justin. Together, they made their way up the narrow flight of stairs to the choir loft, where they were lucky to find three seats together.

Gerry preferred the loft. From her bird's-eye view, she could see the whole sanctuary: the ancient hand-hewn timbers and paneled walls darkened with age, the niches displaying painted wooden statues of saints, and the alcove, accessed by a decorative wrought iron gate, where the stone baptismal font stood. A deep peace stole over her. It didn't matter that she'd failed miserably as a nun and even now often railed against Catholic doctrine. Within the comforting embrace of these old walls, steeped in smoke and incense, the ancient rituals never failed to work their magic.

Her gaze fell on her old friend Father Dan Reardon, resplendent in his purple vestments at the altar: a priest with a ploughman's build and the gentle heart of a child. In the golden glow cast by the candelabra at both ends of the tabernacle, he might have been the larger-than-life star of some biblical epic. Wasn't it Fran O'Brien who'd once sighed that for a man as handsome as Dan to be off-limits was downright cruel? Gerry happened to agree, though she knew that the constant stream of female attentions he received were as lost on him as the *Mona Lisa* on a blind man.

Following a soaring rendition by the choir of "What Child Is This?" led by Lily Ann Beasley on the organ, they all stood for the opening prayer, the sounds of shuffling feet and riffling pages as soothing as the wind rustling through the trees outside. Gerry settled into the familiar rhythms of call and response.

The Lord be with you.
And also with you.
Lift up your hearts.
We lift them up to the Lord.
Let us give thanks to the Lord our God.

The first reading was from Micah, prophesying the advent of the promised one in Bethlehem. The second, from Hebrews, told of the second covenant. But it was the gospel reading, from Luke, with its reference to the infant Jesus in Mary's womb, that spoke to Gerry most.

Father Dan seemed to be looking straight

up at her as he lifted his head from the prayer book that lay open on the pulpit before him. But she was imagining things. How could he possibly have singled her out? She shivered even so, glancing at Andie and Justin on each side of her. No, she wasn't a complete failure. She'd raised two beautiful children, after all.

The thought did nothing to dispel the certain knowledge that she'd failed her first-born. Why couldn't she have done the same with Claire? Looked after her and loved her? Gerry bowed her head in prayer: *Dear Lord, if there's a way to make this right, help me find it.*

Before long, she and her children were descending the stairs to join the congregants making their way to the altar. As she knelt to take Communion, it occurred to her that it'd been months since her last confession. What was the point if she was going to keep on committing the same sins over and over. Her extracurricular activities might be frowned on by the Church, but in her opinion—albeit hard-won—there was nothing wrong with two grown-ups enjoying a bit of companionship and mutual satisfying of appetites.

The thought of Aubrey's supple fingers

playing over her naked limbs rose unbidden to warm her cheeks. His breath that smelled faintly of the Gauloises he smoked. His—

A bolt of lightning shot down through her belly. Her Christmas present to herself, she thought, if she could steal away, would be an hour or two with Aubrey in the big oak bed at Isla Verde.

The sermon was short and to the point. Father Dan told the true story of a married couple who'd won several million in a lottery and given every penny of it to charity. More like a football coach rallying his team than a priest reminding them of their Christian duty, he urged everyone to do as the couple had and find room in their hearts for those in need.

Then they were all shuffling to their feet for the final hymn: "Angels We Have Heard on High." A lusty contralto soaring behind her caused Gerry to steal a glance over her shoulder. She was surprised to find the voice belonged to Vivienne Hicks, the mousy town librarian. Vivienne's head was thrown back, the cords in her neck standing out. Where had this talent came from? Why hadn't Gerry noticed it before? It was as if her world had been turned inside out like a pocket, revealing all sorts of things she'd never known were there.

On her way out, she dipped her fingers in the holy water and made the sign of the cross before stepping out into the cold. In the belfry above, the campanario bells were pealing. She glanced at Andie and Justin, their frosty breath punctuating the night air. Soon they would have to know. She would have to find a way to tell them. But first she needed to meet with Claire. At the thought, a small sharp tug like a pulled stitch caused her chest to tighten.

Suppose she doesn't want to meet me?

By the time they reached the car, parked all the way over on El Paseo, she was chilled to the bone. Gerry wanted nothing more than to be curled up in front of the fire at Sam's, but it would've been unthinkable to skip their annual stop at the People's Tree. Even the kids didn't complain when, a mile or so down the road, she turned off Willow onto Old River.

The tree, a towering Spanish cypress featured on postcards at Shickler's Drugs and no doubt in Gayle Warrington's brochures, stood smack in the center of Old River, a short distance from the junction where it met up with Highway 33. A number of years ago, when the road was going in, the town council had called an emergency meeting two weeks before Christmas to decide what to do about the tree. The obvious thing would have been to cut it down, since to jog around it would've meant either blasting into the steep embankment on one side or bringing the road down into the dry creek bed on the other. Yet to the people of Carson Springs, its venerable trees were just this side of sacred. The vote had been unanimous in favor of letting it stand, and the road was merely widened to allow access on either side. In honor of the decision, and because it was Christmas, after all, someone had anonymously hung an ornament. Soon other ornaments began to appear until the whole tree was covered. A tradition that, in the decades since, had become as deeply rooted as the tree itself.

They parked and got out. The road was deserted. Almost perfectly centered, the People's Tree, decked in all its finery, rose tall and dark and majestic. Justin scampered up the ladder that had been set up alongside it, taking his time finding a branch for his ornament: a Styrofoam ball studded with colored pushpins that he'd made himself. After it was hung, he leaned back to admire it, a hooded silhouette against the star-lit sky.

"It's not the same without Dad."

Andie sounded so wistful, Gerry's heart went out to her. "I know," she said, silently cursing her ex-husband.

"I'm not sorry, though. About Tahoe. I wouldn't have wanted to go anyway."

"I'm sure he would have asked if . . ." She let the sentence trail off. For her kids' sake, she made a point of sticking up for him, but at that moment couldn't think of a single valid excuse.

"Whatever," Andie said with an elaborate shrug.

"There'll be other trips," Gerry said.

"No, there won't. She doesn't like me." *She,* meaning Cindy.

Gerry was about to dish out the usual pap about Mike's new wife's adjusting to stepchildren, but thought better of it. "I wouldn't take it personally. She doesn't strike me as the motherly type."

Cindy was clearly more interested in spending Mike's money than in spending time with his kids. But she wasn't the problem. Mike was the one with his head up his ass.

"Do you think they'll ever have kids?" Andie asked with a note of trepidation.

"I doubt it." Cindy was still young enough, in her midthirties, but far too self-absorbed.

Andie tilted her head to look up at Gerry. "Did you and Dad want more?"

It was as if Andie had somehow picked up her thoughts. Gerry could feel the folded envelope in her pocket glowing like a coal through the heavy wool of her coat.

"We talked about it." She kept her voice light. "With kids as great as you two, how could we not?"

Andie's face was a pale oval, her curly black hair barely visible in the surrounding darkness. The divorce had hit her hardest for some reason, maybe because, growing up, she'd always been Daddy's little girl. "Why didn't you?"

Gerry shrugged. "Things weren't so great with us by then," she said. "I guess we both knew another baby would've been the wrong way to try to fix things."

Andie looked thoughtful, and Gerry had a sudden piercing image of the woman she would grow up to be—beautiful and strong and fearless. Then the moment passed and Andie was yelling up at her brother, "Come *on,* Justin. I'm freezing my buns off down here!"

Justin shouted back, "I'm coming, I'm coming!"

He was descending the ladder when he slipped, skidding down several rungs. Gerry's heart bumped up into her throat, but before she could rush over to catch him, his foot found purchase and he pulled himself upright, the only casualty an ornament that caught the breeze and went sailing off into the dry creek bed below—a small paper cherub, its wings glimmering faintly in the spiny grasp of the Joshua tree in which it had landed.

"Mom, no," Andie squealed.

But Gerry was already slipping her shoes off and scrambling down the rocky embankment. Twigs and small sharp stones dug into the tender soles of her feet. Why was she doing this? She couldn't have said. When she reached the creek bed, glittering white in the starlight with a thin rind of frost, she saw that the Joshua tree was taller than it had looked from the road, the cherub snared in its highest branch. She searched amid the weeds along the embankment, ignoring the small voice in the back of her mind warning of rattlesnakes and other small creatures of the night, until she found a stick long enough to knock it loose.

"Mom, leave it," Andie called. Justin joined in, "Hey, it's no big deal!"

But she couldn't leave it. For some reason the thought of that cherub stranded far from its brethren was too much to bear. She swung at it with the stick, reminded of when she used to swat at piñatas as a child and feeling a little foolish dancing about under the stars in her bare feet. It took several tries, but she finally managed to free it.

Moments later, her children watched in silence as she climbed to the top of the ladder and secured it to a branch alongside a lumpy angel fashioned from pipe cleaners and tinfoil.

"You're not like other mothers, you know," Justin observed as they were making their way to Sam's in Gerry's Toyota Corolla that had nearly 180,000 miles on it and was due for either an overhaul or the junkyard. His voice was tinged with admiration.

"What he means is, you're weird," Andie said helpfully.

"I'll take that as a compliment." Gerry smiled.

They bumped and lurched along the unlit, potholed road, the People's Tree in the rearview mirror glimmering faintly like something more imagined than real. It was Christmas Eve, her children safe and sound. What more could she ask?

Sam had done more than bake a cake. They arrived to find plates of homemade cookies, a bowl of buttered popcorn, and enough hot cocoa to have warmed Washington's troops at Valley Forge. Her little house in the Flats glowed inside and out. A fire blazed in the hearth, and the Christmas tree, decked with antique ornaments passed down through generations of Delarosas, sparkled with dozens upon dozens of white pinpoint lights.

"Either you've gone stir-crazy or I've stumbled onto the set of a Kathie Lee Gifford Christmas special," Gerry teased.

"The former, I hope," Sam replied with a laugh. She'd changed out of her church clothes into a forest-green velour caftan that made her look queenly as she moved about in her graceful, if slightly swaybacked, waddle. "I just hope this baby comes before I run out of projects. Promise me one thing: If I take up needlepoint, you'll have me committed."

"Deal." They shook on it.

"Speaking of projects, wait till you see what Ian's done with the nursery."

They left Andie and Justin with Ian, who was showing them a new computer game, and Sam ushered her down the hall. Gerry stepped inside the nursery to find the antique spool crib trimmed in calico bunting, and the white wicker changing table neatly arrayed with supplies. But it was the wall across from the crib that caught her attention and made her gasp. It was covered in an elaborate mural depicting a host of nursery-tale figures. Ian had to have been working on it for months.

Gerry whistled in admiration. "You should charge admission."

"Not a bad idea. We could use the money." Sam didn't sound worried. With the rent from Isla Verde and the commissions Ian earned, they did all right. "On the other hand, money isn't everything."

Gerry felt a pang of envy. She had no wish for a late-in-life child, nor did she have any desire to settle down—one marriage had been more than enough—but the look on Sam's face as she gazed at Ian's labor of love made her think how nice it would be to feel that way about someone in her own life. The thought of Aubrey once again flashed across her mind, but they were friends— okay, *intimate* friends—and nothing more was ever going to come of it.

"Damn straight. Two weddings and a baby. Some would say your cup runneth over." Sam's youngest, Alice, had gotten married last summer—to Ian's father. And Laura's wedding was little more than a month away.

"Either that, or there's something in the water." Sam gave a little laugh as she adjusted a lamp shade tilted askew. "Which reminds me, Laura wants to know if you're bringing Aubrey."

Gerry felt herself flush. "And here I thought we were being so discreet."

Sam arched an eyebrow, her green eyes dancing. "Are you kidding? The most famous conductor in the world moves into our little neck of the woods—into *my* house, for heaven's sake—and you think half the town isn't going to know you're sleeping with him?"

"I guess they're tired of gossiping about you and Ian."

They shared a laugh reminiscent of when they'd been girls together, primming for dates—Sam, with her straight chestnut hair in curlers and Gerry attempting to iron her unruly black mane flat, the two as different as night and day but somehow more closely attuned than most sisters. Lately, Gerry had been thinking a lot about those days.

She was silent, gazing at the mural. After a moment Sam placed a hand on her arm. "Hey, are you okay?"

"I heard back from Web Horner the other day," Gerry said.

"The private investigator?"

"As if there could be more than one guy with that name."

"What did he say?"

"He found her." Even saying it aloud, it didn't seem real. "Her name is Claire Brewster. She lives up the coast, in Miramonte." That doppelgänger feeling was back: a whole other life that might have been hers being lived out on parallel tracks.

"Oh, Gerry." Sam's face glowed. "That's wonderful."

"Is it?"

Sam said firmly, "*Yes.* It is."

"Then why do I feel like I'm about to make the second biggest mistake of my life?"

"I gather you still haven't told the kids."

"I haven't even talked to Claire."

"Maybe it's time you did."

"I've waited this long. What's a few more days?" *Or weeks.*

Sam's expression grew steely. "Is this the same woman who forced Father Kinney into rehab when everyone else was turning a blind eye?"

"It's easier when you know you're in the right."

Gerry looked around her, at the padded oak rocker over which a delicate crocheted blanket was draped, its squares of blue and pink and white as pale as a misty dawn, and at the lamp on the table by the crib with its little train that chugged around the base when switched on.

"It's funny how things hardly ever turn out the way you expect. Six months ago I couldn't have imagined having a baby . . ." Sam's voice was soft. "But now I can't imagine *not* having it." She squeezed Gerry's arm. "Promise you'll call her."

"I promise I'll think about it."

Gerry glanced at her watch as they were heading back down the hall. "We can't stay. My mom's waiting for me to pick her up."

"You just got here! Besides, you're not leaving me with all this food."

"You didn't tell me you'd baked enough to feed the Mormon Tabernacle Choir." Gerry sank onto the sofa in front of the fire. She was halfway through her second cup of cocoa when she remembered to glance once more at her watch. It was half past nine. How had it gotten to be so late? Reluctantly, she hauled herself to her feet. "Come on, guys," she called to Andie and Justin. "We'd better get a move on. Grandma's going to wonder what's keeping us."

Sam retrieved their coats from the closet, throwing a jacket over her own shoulders and slipping on a pair of shoes. She walked with them outside, murmuring to Gerry as she was kissing her good-bye, "Don't wait too long. Only fools and kings have that luxury."

"Oh, how lovely!" Mavis held up the scarf she'd unwrapped. "It'll go perfectly with my navy suit." She leaned down to hug Andie, cross-legged on the floor by the sofa. "Thank you, darling girl. You couldn't have picked a more perfect gift."

Some things never change, Gerry

thought. Mavis had murmured the proper appreciation for *her* gift, a pink cashmere sweater from Nordstrom's that had cost far more than Gerry could afford, but hadn't lit up like she was now. It wasn't that her mother didn't love or appreciate her, she knew, just that they always seemed to miss the mark somehow. Like the glossy cookbook Mavis had given her this year. Gerry had no doubt she'd meant well, but it only served to remind her of what a lousy cook she was.

She sipped her coffee, one of the few things she could do well. The sense of possibility to which she'd awakened only hours ago seemed to have dwindled along with the pile of presents under the tree.

"It's a hundred percent silk. Look, it says so on the label," Andie pointed out.

Mavis fished a pair of reading glasses from her baggy green cardigan and bent to peer at it, her once-red hair, now the color of old pennies, nestled against Andie's glossy dark curls. "So it does." She smiled and straightened. "I have something for you, too." She handed Andie a small box so clumsily wrapped it pained Gerry to look at it. Her mother's hands, bunched with arthritis, made even the simplest tasks a Herculean effort.

Andie opened it, and gave a gasp of delight. Nestled inside was an antique amethyst brooch set in a filigree of yellow gold—one that Gerry recalled her mother wearing on special occasions. "Oh, Grandma. It's beautiful." She glanced up with a look of uncertainty. "Are you sure?"

"Sure as I am that it'll show off your pretty young neck better than this old wrinkled one of mine." Mavis's eyes, blue as the Bay of Kenmare, where she'd been born, shone with love. "It was my mother's. She was a great beauty in her day. You're the living image of her, you know."

Gerry had always been told that Andie looked just like *her*. When had she become the likeness of her great-grandmother? She watched Andie fasten the brooch to the front of her sweatshirt, thinking how pretty it would look with the silk blouse from Mike and Cindy, though she couldn't help wishing her mother's gift hadn't shown up her own more prosaic gifts to Andie: an outfit from The Gap and a gift certificate for Zack's Stacks.

"I love it." Andie threw her arms around

her grandmother's neck and kissed her loudly on the cheek.

When the last present had been unwrapped, Gerry rose from the couch, rubbing the stiffness from her limbs. So far, so good. Their second Christmas without Mike, and the first that his absence hadn't been felt like a pulled tooth. Now the only thing left before the turkey went into the oven was to call her brother.

Kevin picked up on the second ring. "We were just on our way out the door," he told her. "Art and Thomas's annual Christmas brunch."

"Should I call back?"

"Hell, no. You think I'd rather be nibbling on brioche and discussing the latest in window treatments when I could be schmoozing with my favorite sister?" He laughed, and she pictured him in his Noe Valley loft that'd been featured in the July issue of *Architectural Digest.* On his way to becoming famous in the food world, he was still her freckle-faced kid brother with jug ears and carrot hair that refused to lie flat. "What's up? Mom driving you crazy yet?"

Gerry covered the mouthpiece so Mavis wouldn't hear her say, "She's on her best behavior."

"The day is young."

"She misses you. We all do."

"Hey, I invited her to spend Christmas with us. I even offered to pay the fare." Kevin asked their mother every year, which always managed to prompt a flare-up of her arthritis. "I'm beginning to think she has a wee bit of a problem with the fact that her darlin' boy's a queer," he added in a mock brogue. The laughter in his voice didn't quite cover its bitter edge.

"Go easy on her, Kev. She's doing her best." Why did she always feel she had to defend their mother to Kevin when he was so clearly in the right? "Speaking of your significant other, how's Darryl?"

"Fine and dandy. Just closed on another big deal." Kevin's lover was in commercial real estate.

She wondered if he minded not having kids. He'd always been so great with hers, and Andie and Justin adored him. Of course, it didn't hurt that he sent lavish presents on their birthdays and on Christmas, like the razor bike Justin was at this very moment trying out in the driveway.

"Wish him a merry Christmas from me." Kevin and Darryl were happier than most heterosexual couples she knew. "And, hey, thanks for the gift certificate. I've already seen about eight hundred things I want to buy with it." The certificate was from Gump's, a pricey store in San Francisco. Kevin had been thoughtful enough to include a catalog as well.

"As for *your* gift, you sure know how to make a gay man's heart beat faster."

"I'm glad you like it." Gerry had found the thirties martini set nestled in satin inside a frayed leather case at Avery Lewellyn's antique barn. It'd had her brother's name written all over it. "Listen, I better go," she said. "I should put the turkey in the oven."

"Don't forget to cover the breast with foil."

"What? And risk ruining my reputation as the world's worst cook?"

Kevin laughed long and heartily.

As she hung up, Gerry's thoughts strayed to Claire.

Is she with her family? Gerry knew nothing about the couple who'd adopted her other than that they were Catholic, in keeping with the rules of the agency. Was it fair to intrude? A call from her had to be the last thing any of them were expecting.

When the turkey was in the oven, she returned to tackle the living room, where wrapping paper was strewn over the carpet like tumbleweeds. The logs in the fireplace had burned down, their embers throwing off a drowsy heat. The tree, divested of its presents, looked oddly forlorn. She glanced about at the walls painted a Shaker blue, the country pine tables and chairs. A Nantucket lighthouse basket sat on the mantel, a long-ago gift from Sam, and in the corner by the rocker a fishing pole was propped—a symbol of Mike's relationship with his son. He'd given it to Justin last summer, promising to take him fishing at the lake, but nothing had come of it. She glanced out the window at her son zigzagging down the driveway on his new bike, Buster tagging after him, barking wildly. How could you not love such a kid?

"I'll help." Mavis pushed herself up off the couch with what seemed an effort. They'd filled one trash bag and were starting on another when she paused and said, "I'm having a wonderful Christmas. Thank you, dear."

"We love having you." Gerry meant it.

"I know I'm not the easiest," her mother went on matter-of-factly, smoothing a wisp of rusty hair that had sprung loose at her temple. "It's hard being old. The worst part is feeling so useless."

Gerry squatted down to fish a wad of wrapping paper from under the couch. "Useless? You never sit still!" There was bridge on Tuesdays, and the senior center on Wednesdays. Thursday mornings it was pool aerobics at the YWCA, and Fridays her sewing circle.

Mavis shook her head. "It's not the same."

Gerry felt a rush of concern. There was more color in her mother's cheeks these days, but she was still so frail. "Did you look at that brochure?" For months she'd been working on her mother to sell the house, move into one of those nice new condos out where the old Hensen ranch used to be. Mavis would be around other people her age, the hospital only minutes away.

Mavis flapped a hand dismissively. "What's the point? I'm not going anywhere."

"That old house is too big for one person," Gerry insisted. "Not to mention it's falling down around your ears." The argument was tired, old ground they'd been over many times.

"Well, then, when I'm dead and gone, you can give it a good kick and save yourself the cost of a funeral." Her mother grinned. She might be crumbling like her house, but she still had a full set of teeth and all her mar-bles—enough to trump Gerry from time to time.

Gerry couldn't keep from smiling. "You shouldn't joke about a thing like that," she said.

Mavis lowered herself gingerly onto the couch. "Why not? People die all the time—especially old people." She cocked her head, peering up at Gerry. "Now why don't you tell me what's *really* on your mind? You didn't get those dark circles under your eyes fret-ting over me."

"What do you mean? I'm fine." Gerry glanced around. Justin was still outside, and Andie on the phone with Finch. Gerry could hear her down the hall, comparing notes on Christmas gifts. It seemed Finch had been given a horse of her own, in addition to the two Laura and Hector owned, and it was all they could talk about.

"Nonsense," Mavis scoffed. "Something's wrong. It's no use trying to hide it."

Gerry hesitated a moment, then word-lessly went over to the front hall closet and retrieved the folded envelope from the pocket of her good winter coat. She walked back and handed it to her mother.

Mavis fished her glasses from her cardigan and bent to read the letter, holding it so close it was practically touching her nose. After an eternity she lowered it to her lap, letting out a long sighing breath. "Well, I can't say I didn't see this coming."

"I wish I'd done it years ago." Gerry spoke with defiance.

"You had your children to think of."

"*She* was my child, too." A sleeping dragon stirred to life in Gerry's chest, beating inside her with leathery wings. "I never should have given her away."

"You had no choice."

"You didn't give me one! You couldn't handle another baby in the house, not after raising two of your own." If Mavis had conveniently forgotten, it was as vivid in Gerry's memory as the images on the 8-mm reels stored in her mother's attic—home movies that presented a far sunnier picture.

Mavis's eyes were steely behind the thick lenses of the glasses that sat slightly askew on her nose. "If you'd wanted to badly enough, you'd have found a way to keep her."

Gerry dropped her head, pressing her

loosely fisted hands into the hollows of her eyes. She sighed deeply. "You're right." Blaming her mother was the easy way out.

She looked up to find her mother regarding her, not without compassion. "You were so young. With no job, and no prospect of one. What would you have done with a baby?"

"Loved her." The words emerged in a hoarse whisper. She hadn't known then what she did now, that love was the only prerequisite, that the rest took care of itself.

"You did what you thought was best."

"How could I have known what was best?"

"None of us ever do, dear. The best we can do is keep on putting one foot in front of the other and hope it'll all work out somehow."

She looked sad just then, and Gerry thought of her father, dying inch by inch, and of the sacrifices her mother must have had to make—sacrifices she couldn't have dreamed of as a young, dewy-eyed bride. Gerry remembered him only as sickly, a yellowing husk of a man who'd sit hour after hour in front of the TV, only occasionally glancing with mild interest at his wife and children. He died when she was thirteen, the year she received her calling.

"Am I crazy for doing this?" she asked.

"Crazy? No." Mavis shook her head, saying gently, "It's what any mother would want." There was a touch of yearning in her expression. Claire was her grandchild, after all.

"I'm not her mother. I gave up that right."

"What about Andie and Justin? Have you told them?"

"Not yet."

"They'll want to know why they're only just hearing of it."

"Mike—" Gerry stopped herself. She couldn't blame this on her ex-husband, either. "I should have told them when they were little. It just . . . well, I didn't see the point."

Mavis handed the letter back, her fingers closing over Gerry's, light as the crumpled tissue paper gathered from under the tree. "They'll understand."

Gerry wasn't so sure.

"I . . . I should check on the turkey," she said, feeling a sudden need to escape.

In the kitchen the turkey was browning nicely, and a pan of peeled potatoes floated in milky water on the stove. She eyed the four lonely plates stacked at the end of the counter, waiting to be set out on the dining room table, and brought her head to rest against the cool door of the refrigerator. What was wrong with her? Why was she being such a coward about this?

Quickly, before she could change her mind, she reached for the phone on the wall. She was trembling as she punched in the number on the letter in her hand.

She won't be there.

And what if she *was*? Then what?

The ringing at the other end seemed to go on forever before the line clicked and an answering machine came on. She froze. A pleasant female voice at the other end thanked her for her call and instructed her to leave a message. But what on earth would she say? *Hello, you don't know me, but I'm your mother. Look, I realize it's been a while, but I was kind of hoping we could pick up where we left off.*

She was about to hang up when a voice came on. "Mom? Is that you?"

Gerry felt her heart lurch into her throat. How had Claire known who it was? She felt almost delirious with the wonder of it. But before she could reply, Claire—she was almost certain it was Claire—went on breathlessly, "I was just about to put the pie in the oven. I'll be there no later than five, okay?"

Oh, God. What now? Gerry forced her voice past vocal chords that felt like old rusted pipes. "Is this Claire? Claire Brewster?"

Silence at the other end, then the voice asked cautiously, "Who *is* this?"

For a panicked moment Gerry couldn't quite catch her breath. Then her heart dropped back into place, and a voice she hardly recognized as her own replied calmly, "I'm your mother."

Chapter Two

"Forget peace on earth. I'd settle for peace right here at home," Claire said with a sigh.

Byron smiled. "Don't hold your breath."

"I mean, they've been at each other's throats for so long it's gotten to be a joke: the Montagues and Capulets of Seacrest Drive. Do they even know what they're fighting about anymore?"

It was Christmas Day, minutes before the call that would change her life, and she was enjoying a quiet hour alone with her boyfriend. The irony of the fact that her parents lived next door to Byron's wasn't lost on either of them.

Byron laughed his easy, uncomplicated laugh. He sat slouched on a stool at her kitchen counter, watching her roll out dough for an apple pie. "It's fundamental. One sees white, the other sees black. The only thing they have in common is a fence."

"And us."

"Well, we're out of it, at least," he said with a shrug. Byron refused to take any of it very seriously.

Claire paused in the midst of what she was doing to give him a long searching look. She took in his frizzy brown hair tied back with an elastic band, his speckled green eyes in the sharp-featured face that in childhood had made him look brash and a bit of a know-it-all (a whippersnapper, her mother had called him, and still did), which he'd grown into like he had the hand-me-downs of his well-heeled older cousins. His flannel shirt looked as if it'd been plucked straight from the dryer, and in place of a wristwatch he wore a braided leather thong. Byron was everything her parents abhorred, and she loved him all the more because of it.

"Which is why," she said dryly, "we're forced to sneak around behind their backs." She'd spent the morning at her parents', opening gifts, and as soon as the turkey had gone into the oven had seized the pie excuse to make her getaway. Byron had made his own escape, timing it so he arrived a few minutes after her.

"Who's sneaking? We're merely exercising our rights as free-thinking adults. Speaking of which . . ." He arched a brow, giving her a suggestive look.

"You'll have to wait until the pie is in the oven," she told him, holding up arms dusted to the elbows in flour.

"In that case, I'd better give you a hand." He unfolded from the stool and stepped around the bar, all six feet of him—long in the shank and wide across shoulders—catching her about the waist from behind. He nibbled at her neck, pushing a hand up under her sweatshirt to cup a breast.

"Since you're so free with your hands," she said, ducking out from under his arm, "why don't you make yourself useful?" She handed him a peeler and pointed him toward the bowl of apples by the sink.

He cocked his head. "You really get off on this, don't you?" It wasn't a question.

"I find it relaxing, yes," she said.

"Tarts over torts?" he quipped.

Another sore subject: the long hours at the office tending to real estate transfers and tax shelters and intergenerational trusts when she could be poring over cookbooks and trying out new recipes. She envied Byron's certainty. All he'd ever wanted was to be a doctor. Even with a year of residency under his belt and two and a half more years to go, he hadn't lost that fire.

"Believe me, I'd love nothing more than to chuck the whole thing." She didn't tell him how seriously she was considering doing just that. Why dump it on him now? It was Christmas, and he was only in town for the day.

"It can't be all that bad."

"It's not." She pressed down with her rolling pin.

"At least one of us is solvent."

"Barely." She was still paying off student loans of her own.

"I'll make it up to you, I swear. When we're married, I'll keep you barefoot and pregnant in the kitchen." His speckled green eyes danced, and she couldn't help smiling at the thought.

"Is that a threat or a promise?"

"Until then will you settle for a starving resident up to his ears in debt?"

"Which reminds me, I have something for you." She set aside her rolling pin and wiped her hands on her apron before stepping around the open-sided counter to retrieve a small wrapped package from the living room.

"Hey, no fair," he protested as she handed it to him. "We agreed, remember? No presents this year. Now I look like a jerk."

"You don't need me for that," she teased.

It was a Nokia cell phone in a jazzy shade of iridescent purple, billable to her—a bit of a stretch on her budget. When he dutifully objected to the cost, she argued that it was only temporary. "When we're married . . ." It was how every sentence about the future seemed to begin these days. Words that had come to have as much meaning as children saying *When I grow up . . .* For, oddly, the closer they got to it, the further away it seemed.

"Thanks." Byron kissed the end of her nose. His eyes were lit up like when he was ten, the Christmas his Uncle Andrew had sent him a walkie-talkie from Hammacher-Schlemmer. "I wish I had something for you."

"There's always next year."

"We could look at rings," he said hopefully.

"Engaged to be engaged is not the same as being engaged," she reminded him in the sound lawyerly tone with which she reassured clients who had reservations about her youthful appearance (everyone was always saying she looked closer to eighteen than twenty-eight). They'd agreed a long engagement would be impractical, two and a half years just shy of ridiculous. Besides, everyone knew they were getting married, why advertise the fact?

He put his arms around her once more, burying his face in the crook of her neck and crooning in a husky, off-key voice, "'She can bring home the bacon, fry it up in a pan . . .'"

"And don't you forget it," she interrupted, handing him an apple to peel.

The truth lay somewhere in the middle. Yes, she could fend perfectly well for herself . . . but she couldn't remember a time when she hadn't leaned on Byron.

She recalled the day, in the seventh grade, when she'd gotten her first period. She hadn't known what was happening. Her mother had spoken of it only in vague terms, making reference to "when you're a woman." And at Immaculate Mary the sisters' idea of sex education was a brief talk—more about the dangers of being promiscuous than anything—that had left her more confused than informed. Byron found her huddled on the back stoop, face pressed into her knees.

"What's wrong?" he'd asked, lowering himself onto the stoop beside her.

"I think I'm dying," she'd croaked.

Byron cocked his head. "What makes you think that?" He never got worked up like her parents, which was why she hadn't gone to them with this alarming new development.

She lifted her head. "I'm bleeding." She added in a strained whisper, "Down there."

Byron nodded solemnly and it was only years later that she realized what a Herculean effort it must have been for him to keep from cracking a smile. "You're not dying," he said gently.

He told her it was only her period, except the word he'd used was *menstruation*. Both his parents were professors at the university (his mother taught women's studies and his father headed the English department), and all three Allendale children—Byron, Keats, and Shelley—had been taught from a very young age about bodily functions and to refer to them by their proper names. No one ever said *snot;* it was *mucus.* And when little Shelley, only five at the time, needed to go potty, she would announce loudly that she had to urinate. In explaining things to Claire, Byron had been as natural and unembarrassed as if teaching her to play pinochle.

Now, watching a curly strip of peel unravel from the apple in his hand—a Granny Smith that in his long, loosely jointed fingers might have been a greengage plum—she thought, *He'll make a fine doctor.* He had the touch, but most of all the knack for putting people at ease.

Just then the phone in the living room trilled.

Byron shot her a questioning look. "Want me to get it?"

"No, it's okay." It was probably her mother wanting to know when to expect her for dinner—as if they were having company, as if it even mattered what time they ate. Claire pictured her parents on hold, like a freeze-frame that would commence rolling the minute she walked in.

The answering machine clicked on, and she snatched up the phone. But it wasn't Millie. After a moment of confusion, when the caller identified herself, Claire felt the blood drain from her head.

She cast a panicky glance at Byron, who motioned back, wanting to know if he should pick up the extension in the bedroom. She shook her head. No, she'd handle this on her own.

At the same time, her mind spun in frantic circles: My mother? My *mother*?

The narrow, high-ceilinged room yawed and she gripped the nearest chair—her grandmother's, its lyre back gleaming darkly. From the apartment below came the earnest thumping of a piano: nine-year-old Katie Wexler practicing scales.

"This *is* Claire Brewster?" The woman was polite but insistent.

"Yes . . . yes, it is." Claire felt all at once airborne, like a scrap of paper caught in a sudden updraft.

There was a sharp intake of breath, then: "My name is Gerry. Gerry Fitzgerald." When Claire didn't respond, she said anxiously, "They told you about me, didn't they?"

"Only that I was adopted," Claire replied woodenly.

An awkward silence fell. Then Gerry ventured cautiously, "I . . . I was wondering if we could meet sometime. Just for coffee. I could come to you." She hesitated, adding, "I'm sure you have questions."

"Truthfully, I haven't given it much thought." A lie. Hadn't she thought about it every day for the past twenty-odd years? She glanced again at Byron, who'd drifted over wearing a concerned look. Why was she acting this way? More importantly, what did this woman *want*?

"I'm sorry. I know this is a shock." Gerry sounded flustered. "Would you rather I called back another time?"

"Yes. No. I mean . . . it's just . . ." Claire began to tremble.

"Or you could call me. Why don't I give you my number?"

"I think that would be best." A strange calm descended over her, and she reached dreamily for a pencil to copy down the number. But she must have been pressing too hard because the lead snapped and went skittering off the pad. She blinked and straightened. Her heart was beating much too fast and the sense of being airborne stronger than ever. Suddenly she wanted to know everything there was to know about this woman, this Gerry Fitzgerald. Glancing down at the unfamiliar area code, she observed in the same mild voice, "You're not from around here."

Downstairs the piano scales thumped to a halt, then after a moment started up again. *Da-da-DEE-da-da-da-DEE-da.* The sound seemed to be coming from inside her head.

"I'm not far—just east of Santa Barbara." Some of the tension went out of Gerry's voice. "A little town called Carson Springs. Do you know it?"

"I've heard of it."

"The movie *Stranger in Paradise* was filmed here."

"I've seen it." It was one of the classics run regularly on AMC.

"I'd love to show you around sometime."

The room continued to pitch and yaw. Claire's arms and legs felt boneless, and she was conscious of a vein pulsing in her temple. She sagged into the chair so heavily it creaked in protest.

"I . . . I'd like that," she found herself saying.

Gerry perked up even more. "What about after New Year's?"

"I don't—"

"No rush. Why don't you think it over and get back to me?" The nervousness had crept back into Gerry's voice. When Claire didn't respond, she waited a polite moment or two before inquiring gently, "Is there anything else you'd like to know?"

Where do I begin? She had enough questions to keep them on the phone for hours . . . but all at once she couldn't think of a single one. Claire reached into the swirling maelstrom inside her head and snatched hold of the first solid thing. "Do you have kids?"

"A boy and a girl. Andie's fifteen, and Justin's eleven going on twelve."

The pride with which Gerry spoke made Claire wince for some reason. "Look. I . . . I can't talk right now. I have company." She cast another glance at Byron, standing a few feet away wearing a worried frown.

"Yes, of course. I didn't mean to intrude." There was a beat, then she added quietly, "Merry Christmas."

"Same to you." Claire eyed the notepad in her hand. Somehow she'd managed to jot down Gerry's number, though she had no memory of doing so. "Good-bye," she said, hanging up.

For several long moments she just stood

there, staring at the wall in front of her on which a grouping of framed photos hung. There was one of her at age six, missing a front tooth, with her arm looped around her collie, Lady, the year before Lady died. And another one of her parents, taken a few years back, poised at either end of a large sheet cake with Happy Anniversary written on it in pink and blue icing. Alongside it was a much older black-and-white wedding photo of a youthful-looking Millie wearing a light-colored peplum suit and tricorn hat, arm in arm with a handsome, dark-haired sailor in navy whites who bore only a faint resemblance to Claire's father.

"Claire? Are you okay?" Byron's voice seemed to come from far away.

Hadn't she always known this day would come? Growing up she'd fantasized that her real mother had been forced to give her up after being booted out into the cold by unforgiving parents . . . or that she'd been the much-wanted baby of star-crossed lovers torn apart by circumstances beyond their control (a favorite scenario involved her father as a CIA operative who'd been captured overseas, leading her mother on a desperate search). Whatever the fantasy, it always ended the same: with her real mother appearing out of the blue to reclaim her.

But this was even more shocking in a way: a perfectly ordinary-sounding woman asking pleasantly if she'd like to meet for coffee. A woman with two other children who'd never had to lie awake nights wondering about their mother.

Claire turned to Byron. The thumping of the piano downstairs had mercifully come to a halt, and she could hear doves cooing on the sill.

"That was *her,*" she said in a voice soft with wonder.

Byron didn't have to ask who she was referring to. Since she was little, he'd been the only one she could confide in. Now he put his arms around her, rocking her gently from side to side. "I gathered as much. Are you okay?"

"I think so," she said with more conviction than she felt.

"What did she want?"

"For us to meet."

He drew back slightly. His green eyes, flecked with gold and brown like specks of mineral glinting up from a riverbed, studied her calmly. "You're going to, aren't you?"

"I don't know." She could hardly think straight.

"Aren't you curious?"

Curiosity didn't begin to cover it. But . . . "You know my parents. It'd kill them."

She'd been five when they told her she was adopted. They'd kept it vague, saying only that she'd been the answer to their prayers, the child they'd never thought they would have. When Claire asked who her mother was, Millie's eyes had welled with tears. "*I* am," she'd said in a soft, trembling voice that carried a faint note of defiance.

Claire had known, even at so young an age, that the subject was closed. That was how it was in their house, everyone always tiptoeing around one another's feelings. As careful as they were about knocking first and saying please and thank you. They didn't know where their own needs began and someone else's left off.

At the same time, she loved them dearly and knew they loved her. If at times the house on Seacrest had seemed the loneliest place on earth, her parents weren't to blame. They'd been in their forties and set in their ways by the time she came along. She'd had to learn to adapt to them rather than the other way around.

"When are you going to stop thinking of them and start thinking of yourself?" Byron asked.

"Probably when they're dead and gone." She managed a tiny laugh.

"I don't see the harm in just meeting her."

"It's not as simple as that."

"Look, I know they love you," he said, just then sounding exactly like his father when Dr. Allendale was making a perfectly logical point that somehow left you feeling two feet tall. "But that doesn't give them the right to keep you at their beck and call."

"They never ask for anything!"

"They don't have to. It's always just expected."

Claire looked about at the apartment she'd taken such unreasonable pride in. The furnishings were spartan—an antidote to the house she'd grown up in, where there was no such thing as too much—her collection of antique bottles glittering jewellike along the sills in the pale winter sunlight slanting in through the windows. Where had she gotten the idea that she was independent? What fool's paradise had she been living in? Byron, damn him, was right: Her parents' gratitude kept her tied to them as much as any demands.

"You can't make them happy," he said. "You'll only end up making yourself miserable."

She felt a surge of resentment. Byron's weren't exactly model parents, either. Gaylord and Persa Allendale had been so busy making sure their children were informed, educated, and evolved, it hadn't occurred to them to just let Byron and his siblings *be.* If hers, on the other hand, were overprotective, it was only because she was all they had.

"I don't have to decide right now," she said. But wasn't her mind already made up? She couldn't go behind her parents' backs. And to drag them into it would be needlessly cruel.

Byron didn't argue. He just looked at her sadly, as if she'd disappointed him somehow.

They finished making the pie, and moved on to other topics while waiting for it to come out of the oven: Byron's fellow residents at Stanford Medical and the current rotation he was on—pediatrics, a department headed by an autocratic older woman he'd come to loathe; a particularly thorny trust Claire was working on involving several generations of beneficiaries; and last but not least how many weeks, or months, before they'd see each other again.

When they finally got around to making love, Claire's heart wasn't in it. She couldn't get her mind off Gerry. *Are we anything alike?* And what about her father? Was Gerry still in touch with him? Would he want to see her as well?

When it was time to go, Byron walked her to her car, a five-year-old Escort with fewer than twenty thousand miles (didn't that say it all?). She kissed him good-bye.

"Call me," she said. He was leaving first thing tomorrow, which would put him on the road about the time she arrived at work. They would tell each other stories about their respective Christmas dinners, which always seemed funnier in retrospect.

"How can I refuse? I'm a kept man." He grinned, brandishing the cell phone.

She watched him saunter off to his car, an old blue Hyundai with a scratch on its rear end from accidentally backing into her father's garbage cans, before climbing into hers. The pie, wrapped in a clean dish towel, at once filled the confined space with the rich scent of cinnamon and freshly baked apples. She thought about stopping at Kitty's on the way, but her friend would be busy with her own Christmas dinner. Claire pictured three-year-old Maddie on a step stool patting out dought for biscuits while Kitty puttered about the kitchen, rearranging the table Sean had set. Kitty's two sisters, Daphne and Alex, would be there, too, along with her nieces and nephew. But however much they'd welcome her, she'd only be intruding.

Five minutes later, she was pulling up in front of her parents' house. All the houses on Seacrest looked basically alike: boxy, shingled post-Victorians with gabled roofs and deep porches flanked by square pillars at either end. What made this one different was its lack of specialness, of any detail that would make it stand out. The neatly trimmed boxwood hedge stood at perfect angles to the front yard, in which only the most inoffensive plants grew: juniper and bayberry and hydrangea, and here and there a severely pruned rosebush. Behind the front door, hung with an evergreen wreath, the uniformity was even more pronounced. Here time was measured in teaspoons, the thermostat perennially fixed at sixty-eight, and coffee never consumed after eleven A.M. She steeled herself as she climbed out of the car and started up the path—the grown daughter of doting parents who'd never spoken a harsh word, nor raised a hand against her—feeling more than a little guilty for her thoughts.

Claire noted the pulled window shades that gave the feel of a darkened stage with the curtain about to go up. A feeling that only intensified when the front door swung open before she could even knock, as if her mother had been standing watch.

"Sorry. It took longer than I thought," Claire said, stepping up onto the porch. It was only a little after five, but she knew how Millie fretted when she was even a few minutes late.

"You're here now. That's all that counts." Millie held her pale blue cardigan clutched about her thin shoulders like an old peasant woman's shawl. "Dinner's ready. We're just waiting on you."

Claire handed her the pie. "I'll go wash up."

The house smelled of roast turkey and stewed onions. In the living room the wrapping paper had been cleared away and only a scattering of needles remained under the tree. Claire padded over the thick patterned carpet that cushioned her like an egg in its crate. As she washed her hands in the guest bathroom down the hall, with its matching powder-blue rug and toilet seat cover and seasonal hand towels embroidered with reindeer, muffled voices drifted toward her, familiar and comforting.

The dining room table was set with Grandma Brewster's good Spode china and silver. Millie, an only child herself, was particular about such things, while Lou, the youngest of five boys—one of whom had died in infancy, another in combat in World War II—would happily have eaten off paper plates every day of his life. The china sparkled as if new, and Claire saw that the extra leaf had been added to the table. With the three of them clustered at one end it looked like a raft in danger of capsizing.

As they bowed their heads in prayer, Claire felt a gratitude that had little to do with the meal. *This* was her family. People who loved her. Who knew that she was allergic to down pillows, that she loved Mozart and sailing and anything made with coconut.

"White meat, anyone?"

She eyed in dismay the platter her father was passing her way, with its slices of dry, splintery breast. "I'll have the dark meat, please." She wouldn't choke on it, at least.

Until she'd left for college, Claire had done most of the cooking. Not that her mother wasn't as conscientious in that regard as she was in all aspects of her housekeeping. It was just that everything she cooked came out exactly the same: bland and tasteless. Even now that she had her own place, Claire visited several times a week, often staying to prepare a meal. Her efforts were always lavishly praised, even the more experimental dishes—like last week's quinoa casserole, the remains of which she'd discovered in the garbage can this morning when she'd taken out the trash—for the simple reason that it kept them from having to eat alone.

She helped herself to a thigh, watching her father, a large man whose meaty frame had in recent years surrendered almost entirely to gravity, heap his plate. His jowls melted into his chin, which had joined the downhill slope of his chest, ending in the substantial roll overflowing his belt. She'd really have to speak to him about his weight, though ironically it was her mother, who barely ate enough to keep a bird alive, she worried about the most. Millie didn't look at all well.

Claire helped herself to the brussels sprouts. "How's the picture on that TV, Pop?" Her gift to her parents this year had been a brand-new television to replace their ancient Zenith.

"Crisp as a new dollar bill," he said, chuckling a little as he added, "Now I'll know which team is scoring a touchdown."

"The old one was good enough," Millie said sharply, then caught herself, casting a sheepish glance at Claire. "Not that we don't appreciate it, dear. Just that we'd rather see you spend the money on yourself. We have everything we need, don't we, Lou?" She lifted the lid from a covered casserole. "Stuffing anyone?"

Lou passed his plate. "You find a spot for the toaster oven?" he asked Claire.

"Not yet," she told him. "I'll have to rearrange a few things first."

Her parents exchanged a look, and she knew what they were thinking: What could she have to rearrange? After a year her apartment was almost as bare as when she'd moved in.

Millie cleared her throat and said brightly, "Did you notice your father's wearing his new tie?"

"It looks nice on you, Pop," Claire replied dutifully. Every year at Christmas his former district manager sent the retired managers of Food King a spectacularly hideous tie— this one in a loud zigzag pattern that made her think of the picture on the old Zenith.

"Forty-two years," he said, shaking his head, a forkful of mashed potatoes poised just short of his smiling mouth. "Some days I still can't believe it's all behind me."

"You and Mom should take a trip," Claire told him. For years she'd been trying to get them to book a cruise, like the Alaskan one old Mrs. MacAfee down the street had gone on last year and been talking about ever since.

"Sure, one of these days," Lou said in a tone that suggested he was as likely to climb Mount Everest.

"I've been thinking," Millie said brightly, as if it had only just occurred to her. "Why don't we rent a cabin up at Pine Lake next summer? Just like the old days."

Claire felt her heart sink. Even as a kid, she'd hated being stuck in those drafty old cabins far from her friends, whiling the evenings away playing Parcheesi with her parents. "Sounds good, Mom, but I'm not sure I'll be able to get the time off. You know how it is . . ." She shrugged, hoping Millie wouldn't press the point.

"Any more talk of a partnership?" Lou flashed her a look that told her he understood and was doing his best to get her off the hook.

Claire's mind flew back to last week's Christmas party, when one of the senior partners had taken her aside, confiding there was talk of making her a junior partner. They'd discuss it after the holidays, Glenn had said with an expansiveness that probably had much to do with the two double scotches under his belt. Normally he didn't give her the time of day. But instead of its having the desired effect, she'd suddenly and quite unexpectedly felt as if the walls were closing in on her. Was this what she wanted, she'd wondered, to spend the rest of her life juggling wills and trusts and squabbling relations . . . and the likes of Glenn Willoughby?

"No," she found herself saying now. "And even if they offer it to me, I'm not sure I'll take it."

"Am I hearing right?" Her father cupped a hand to his ear, smiling the way people did when they knew you were only kidding.

Claire braced herself. She'd planned on breaking it to them, just not this soon. She hadn't even told Byron. "Actually, I'm thinking of leaving the practice altogether."

"You mean you've had an offer from another firm?" Lou looked intrigued.

"Not exactly," Claire said, picking at a loose thread in her napkin. "The thing is . . . I don't particularly like being a lawyer."

Millie stared at her in disbelief. Her face, round and dimpled in its youth, now seemed to fold in on itself like dough that had been left to rise too long. "You're not serious," she said.

You don't know the half of it, Claire thought. What would her mother say if she knew about Gerry? "I haven't decided yet," she said, feeling cowardly.

Her father chuckled weakly. "For a second there you had me going."

"All those years of school—how could you even think of letting them go to waste?" Millie's voice held an edge of reproach. It wasn't just Claire's time and effort. Didn't they have a stake in it as well?

Claire felt a surge of rebellion. Sure, they'd helped supplement her part-time income from Tea & Sympathy. But law school had been *their* dream, not hers. A dream fueled mostly by envy. Hadn't Lou's older brother Ernie, a hot-shot litigator who was nothing more than a glorified ambulance chaser, in her opinion, been rubbing her father's nose in his success for years? The day she'd graduated from USF, Uncle Ernie had been the first person Lou called.

A heavy sense of defeat settled over her. What was the use in arguing? It had always been this way. At school, when she'd wanted to sign up for gymnastics, her parents had said it was too dangerous, she could break her neck. The summer she graduated from high school, when she'd begged to go backpacking in Europe with her friends, they'd put their foot down as well. Her mother's favorite saying was better be safe than sorry. And safe they were—like caterpillars in a jar. Moving out on her own was the biggest leap she'd ever taken, and look how far it had gotten her.

"What would you do?" her father asked, humoring her. "You'd have to earn a living somehow."

"I don't know. I haven't really thought it through," she told him. The truth was that no viable alternative had presented itself thus far; if one had, she'd have left months ago.

Her parents exchanged a look that said, *She'll come to her senses.* Who in their right mind would give up everything they'd worked so hard to achieve? And didn't she have the kind of life others envied? A successful career, an apartment of her own, not to mention a loving family just a stone's throw away.

Claire felt something inside her give way. She looked down at her plate, at the cranberry sauce that had seeped into the mashed potatoes, tingeing them an unappetizing pink around the edges, and the gravy congealing atop her turkey thigh.

"By the way," she said, struggling to keep the emotion from her voice, "someone called this afternoon. A woman named Gerry Fitzgerald."

A deathly hush fell over the table. There was only the ticking of the heating ducts along the baseboard and the faint hum of the kitchen fan Millie had forgotten to switch off.

At last her father let out a ragged breath. "I guess we should have seen this coming."

"She wants to meet me." Claire felt a rush of remorse. She should've kept her mouth shut. Dear God, what could she have been *thinking*?

Millie made a shrill noise that fell short of being a laugh. "And you think that's *all* she wants?"

"What do you mean?" Claire's head, which suddenly felt too heavy, swiveled slowly toward her mother.

Millie sat stiffly upright, a hand pressed to her chest as if to stanch a bleeding wound. "I knew it," she said with a queer note of triumph. "Oh yes. She's been waiting all these years. Waiting until she could get her claws into you."

Claire couldn't help smiling at the imagery. "You make it sound as if I'm about to be eaten."

"You'll see," Millie went on in that same odd, high-pitched voice. "It won't stop there. She'll call and write and visit. And . . . and pretty soon she'll want you all to herself." Her eyes, the faded blue of airmail envelopes tied in bundles, glittered with unshed tears.

"Mom, that's ridiculous."

"You say that now. But just wait."

"Mother has a point." Lou didn't look entirely convinced; she knew he was only sticking up for Millie.

"It's just *coffee,* for heaven's sake," she cried in frustration.

"A woman who never bothered to give you the time of day," Millie went on as if Claire hadn't spoken. "A woman with no regard for anyone but herself. Was she thinking of *us* when she called? Of *you*? Of what this would do to *our* Christmas?"

Claire felt miserable. "I'm sure she didn't see it that way."

"We wanted more children." Millie's voice trembled. "But we were blessed with just you. Do you think I haven't gotten down on my knees every day to thank God for sending you? And now this woman who tossed you aside like an unwanted kitten wants you *back*?"

"Mom, you're making too big a deal of it. Really. I'm not going anywhere." Claire tried to strike a lighthearted note, but she felt sick inside.

She cast a desperate look at her father. They locked eyes for an instant, and she saw that he understood, that he knew Millie was blowing the whole thing out of proportion. But he only sighed, and dropped his gaze.

"Food's getting cold," Millie said stiffly. The subject was closed.

They got through the rest of the meal somehow, but it was an act of pure will on Claire's part. Even the apple pie was like choking down glue. When at last she rose from the table, it felt as if an ice age had passed. "Mom, why don't you put your feet up? I'll do the dishes," she offered.

"Thank you, dear. I believe I will." Millie, paler than usual, pushed herself to her feet with what seemed an effort.

Lou cleared the table while Claire washed up. Half an hour later the dishwasher was humming and the leftovers tucked away in the fridge. Leaving her father in front of the TV, where a football game was in progress, she tiptoed down the hall to check on her mother.

At her tap on the door, Millie called softly, "Come in."

Claire found her stretched out on the bed, the crocheted afghan at the foot pulled up over her shoulders. In the light filtering in from the hallway, she looked small and frail.

Claire thought of a line from *Julius Caesar: O pardon me, thou bleeding piece of earth.* Hadn't she stabbed her mother in the back the way Brutus had Caesar?

"I'm on my way out," she said. "I just wanted to make sure you were okay."

Millie's eyes glimmered in the half light. "I'm just a little tired is all."

"You should've let me help with the cooking," she said.

"You do too much as it is."

Claire planted a kiss on her mother's cheek, which felt smooth and dry as sanded wood. "Thanks again for dinner." She hesitated before adding, "I'm sorry if I upset you."

"*You* didn't upset me." Millie's tone made it clear where she placed the blame. But hadn't Claire secretly wanted to hurt her? Wasn't she the real villain here?

Frustration rose in her. "Mom, this isn't about you. Why can't you see that?"

"Oh, I see all right. I see the handwriting on the wall."

"Nothing will change. You're still my parents."

"Yes, your parents." Millie's voice was thick with tears. "The ones who fed and clothed you and looked after you when you were sick. The ones who sat up worrying themselves half to death when you stayed out late. What has this woman ever done for you? Tell me. What can she give you that we can't?"

Claire gazed down into her mother's face, at her mouth slack with anguish and the deep lines etched about her eyes. "It's not about what she can give me—I want to know *why*," she said.

"You'll get more than you bargained for."

"Maybe. But it won't change how I feel about you and Dad." She reached for her mother's hand, holding it lightly clasped. It felt cool to the touch, the bones underneath like something loosely wrapped in tissue paper. "Goodnight, Mom. Sleep tight."

"Would you shut the door on your way out?" Millie sighed, turning her head toward the wall. Claire was stepping into the hall when she added in a barely audible voice, "The pie was good."

Claire eased the door shut, pausing to rest her forehead against the jamb. A headache was starting in one temple and her eyes felt hot and achy. *What now?* But the house gave nothing back. As she made her way past the living room, there was only the muted sound of the TV. Outside, a strong wind was blowing in off the ocean. She could hear it whining in the eaves, sending leaves scuttling along the gutters her father hadn't gotten around to cleaning—she'd have to look into hiring a yard boy.

"Bye, Dad," she called. She could see only the back of the recliner where he sat, the bald dome of his head flickering with re- flected light from the TV.

"Bye, honey." He didn't get up. "Drive safely."

She retrieved her jacket from the oak hall stand, catching a glimpse of her face in its beveled mirror: her prominent cheekbones with their sprinkling of freckles, her gray- green eyes and Cupid's bow mouth drawn into a straight line. Who did she resemble? Her mother or her father . . . or neither? Was it from some long-lost ancestor she'd gotten her curly brown hair and the dimple in her chin?

She stepped outside to find that the wind had scoured away the fog, leaving the sky empty except for the stars glittering like fist- fuls of flung sand. Stopping to gaze across the hedge at the lighted windows next door, she thought of Byron. She'd never needed

him more than she did now. But the Allendales would be lingering over their supper,
she knew, engaged in an animated discussion about a hot-button topic such as stem
cell research or global warming or gun control. Better to wait until tomorrow.

Her thoughts turned once more to Gerry.
Claire imagined a stout, gray-haired matron
at the head of a table surrounded by family—Claire's sister and brother, grandparents, aunts, uncles, cousins—and felt a
warm trickle of anticipation. Was this a gift
she'd been offered, like in a heartwarming
Christmas tale . . . or the proverbial poi-
soned apple? She shivered at the thought,
pulling her collar up around her ears as she
headed down the steps.

"Of course you should call her."

Kitty stood at the kitchen counter of her
rambling old house that doubled as a tearoom, elbow deep in dough, the air filled with
the delicious scent of something baking in
the oven. A pot of tea was steeping under a
quilted cozy at Claire's elbow.

"Give me one good reason." It had been
two weeks since Christmas, and she was
still no closer to a decision.

Kitty turned to give her a mildly admonishing look. "You don't need one. She's your mother."

"Who gave me up at birth."

"Don't you at least want to know why?"

More than you know, Claire thought. "What about my parents?"

"What about them?"

"It would kill them."

Claire instantly regretted her choice of words. That was all Kitty needed, to be reminded of what had happened to her own parents. Three years ago, in what had to be Miramonte's most sensational murder to date, Lydia Seagrave had fatally shot her longtime husband, Vernon, then shortly afterward killed herself. The scandal—a crime of passion, it was rumored (Kitty rarely spoke of it, though Claire had a feeling she knew more than she'd let on)—had had the effect of a bomb dropped on their quiet community.

But Kitty wasn't thinking of her parents now. "Once they realize she isn't a threat, they'll come around."

She made it sound so reasonable that for a moment Claire almost believed her. She leaned back in her chair, watching Kitty bustle about, the familiar rhythms as graceful as a ballet. Kitty's cloud of gingery hair was pulled back with an elastic band, and stray wisps floated about her elfin face as she pounded at the dough with her fists, sending up pale puffs of flour into the shaft of sunlight slanting in through the window. In her baggy cotton tunic and trousers, her child-size Chinese slippers and socks, she might have been a benign genie from an *Arabian Nights'* tale.

"What makes you so sure?" Claire asked.

"Because I know a thing or two." It wasn't just that Kitty was older by a dozen years, she was also the wisest person Claire knew. "And because they want what's best for you."

"Sometimes it feels more like a ball and chain."

Claire wouldn't have admitted that to another living being, not even Byron. But practically from the first day she'd come to work here she'd been able to tell Kitty anything. Mainly because Kitty never judged or criticized, or offered advice unless asked.

"I used to feel that way about mine." She paused, wearing an odd, faraway look, her floury hands coming to rest on the ball of dough. "But you know something? They did the best they could. I didn't see that until I had Maddie. Now I only pray I won't screw up too badly."

Her gaze softened as it fell on three-year-old Maddie, the child she never thought she'd have, bent over a sheet of butcher paper at the table across from Claire, a crayon in each chubby fist. After years of trying, it must have seemed a miracle when she became pregnant. That she'd gotten Sean out of the bargain as well proved that good people occasionally *did* get what they deserved.

Claire looked past Kitty into the front room with its collection of mismatched tables and chairs. In less than an hour the bell over the door would be tinkling, the tea kettles whistling, and New Year's resolutions a thing of the past. The first time she'd walked through the door in answer to Kitty's ad, she'd felt right at home. Kitty was the main reason, of course. Over the past five years they'd become closer than most sisters.

"I owe them," Claire said.

Kitty eyed her thoughtfully. "Maybe, but not the way you think."

"What if I'm opening a Pandora's box?"

"Too late. The lid's already off." Kitty pushed at the dough with the heels of her hands, flattening it into an oblong. "If you don't take a peek inside, you'll never know what you're missing."

"What about her kids?"

"Once they get to know you, they'll see you for the wonderful person you are." She turned to give Claire a warm if distracted smile, wiping absently with her wrist at a smudge of flour on her chin. "Would you hand me that?" She pointed at a Pyrex bowl heaped with a mixture of chopped nuts, brown sugar, and cinnamon.

Watching her sprinkle it over the dough, Claire found herself confiding, "You know something? Sometimes I wish I still worked here. Life was a lot easier then."

Kitty laughed. "That's because you weren't the boss. Here it is only half past eight—" she cast a rueful glance at the clock on the wall— "and it feels like I've been on my feet all day."

"I'd trade with you in a heartbeat," Claire said, meaning it. "I'm so sick of my job I could scream."

"What about another branch of law? It's not too late to switch."

"How can I think about changing careers with this thing hanging over me?"

"Mommy, look!" Maddie crowed. "I drawed a bunny rabbit."

Kitty wandered over to have a look. "Is that a carrot in his mouth?"

Maddie giggled, the image of her mother with her elfin face and cloud of strawberry curls. Only her determined little chin and lower lip that thrust out when she was mad were Sean's. "Not a carrot. A *ba-nana*."

"I didn't know bunnies ate bananas."

Maddie nodded vigorously. "Yeah, they do."

"Well, in that case, we'll leave one for the Easter bunny this year." She kissed the top of her daughter's head and went to check on the pie. The scent of pumpkin and spices filled the kitchen as she eased open the oven door. From outside came the buzz of a chain saw: Sean trimming the elm tree out back.

Kitty rolled the dough into a fat sausage. "You don't need my advice," she told Claire. "Your mind was made up when you walked in. You only want me to second the motion." Her voice was as matter-of-fact as Maddie's insisting that bunnies ate bananas.

"I wish I were as certain," Claire said.

She watched Kitty pinch the ends of the dough and then slice it into cinnamon-swirled wedges. She'd scarcely finished arranging them in a pan when the timer pinged. In a seamless motion she took the pie from the oven, and slid in the tray of buns.

"Want me to put those out front?" Claire asked, indicating the baked goods cooling on the counter. Though she no longer got paid for it, she often pitched in when she was around. And it looked as if Kitty could use a hand. Willa was late as usual and the young woman who'd taken Claire's place on vacation until next week.

"Would you?" Kitty shot her a grateful look.

In the sunny front room, Claire lined the wicker baskets in the display case with clean sheets of parchment before arranging the baked goods in neat little piles: muffins of every kind—blueberry, cranberry-orange, pumpkin, apple streusel, peach—cookies fat as doorknobs, golden turnovers edged in crispy brown lace. There were currant scones, slices of orange pound cake drizzled with syrup, and a recipe of hers that Kitty had adapted: lemon-coconut bars made from the Meyer lemons that grew out back.

Stepping back to admire the effect, she thought once more how wonderful it would be if she *could* spend every day like this, steeped in tantalizing fragrances, surrounded by the familiar faces of regulars who'd come to seem more like family. Like old Josie Hendricks, the retired schoolteacher who was one of the first to arrive each morning. And Gladys Honeick, proprietress of Glad Tide-ins, the beachwear shop two doors down, who last year had tied the knot—where else but here?—with another longtime customer, crusty newspaper owner Mac MacArthur.

Dream on, a voice scoffed. Kitty would be the first to admit you'd never get rich this way. Some years she barely broke even.

Claire returned to the kitchen to find that Willa had arrived like a change of season, rubber thongs slapping as she ambled to and fro, fetching eggs and flour and fruit from the pantry. The plus-size Filipina favored tight clothing and splashy prints, like the hot pink sweater embroidered with sequined butterflies she had on now; and though she talked incessantly, mostly about her boyfriends, she never seemed to run out of breath.

Willa directed her sunny smile at Claire. "You keep hanging around here, pretty soon you'll be as fat as me."

Claire laughed. "I don't see that it's hurt *you* any."

Willa giggled. "Oh, I didn't tell you about my *new* boyfriend. Deke Peet, how's that for a name? We met at the Rusty Anchor . . . you know that place out on Highway One, with the neon sign that blinks? . . . it's kinda skeevy but they have good bands on the weekend . . . that's what me and Teena was doing there, you know, lookin' to shake it up a little on the floor . . . so, anyways, this guy, *big* guy, looks like he just rode up on a Harley, comes up and asks supersweet if he can buy me a beer . . ."

Claire let the tale spin out a bit more before reaching for her jacket, slung over the back of a chair. "I'd love to stay all day, but I should be going. I have to be at work."

"On Saturday?" Kitty raised an eyebrow.

"I have a client coming in from out of town. Everything has to be ready for him to sign first thing Monday morning." She paused to ruffle Maddie's hair on her way out, and the little girl tipped her head back to beam up at Claire. "Thanks . . . for everything," she called softly to Kitty.

Kitty turned, and the smile she gave Claire was so warm and accepting it brought tears to her eyes. "I should be thanking you," she said. "Any time you want your old job back, it's yours."

Minutes later Claire was pulling into her assigned space behind the building, neatly trimmed in juniper, that housed the offices of Hodgekiss, Jenkins, and Brenner. Her heart was heavy as she unlocked the door to the lobby. If she didn't have the guts to return Gerry's call, how could she expect to quit her job and find a new career?

In her office she lowered herself into her chair. Her desk was tidy, files and documents stacked in order of priority in the tiered wire holder, the trust she'd been drafting neatly tucked into its folder. Beneath its plastic shroud, her computer gleamed like a great glassy eye. An *evil* eye. For on this crisp January day, while others were strolling along the beach with their pant legs rolled up or sitting down to a cup of tea, she was settling in at her desk with nothing to look forward to but a file as thick as her thumb.

Abruptly, she reached for her Palm Pilot. She'd entered Gerry's number, thinking it would be easier to ignore than if stuck to her refrigerator. Now, as she punched in the name, Claire felt herself break out in a light sweat.

It's still early. She might not even be up.

Claire eyed the phone as if it were a snake coiled to strike. She was sweating freely now, beads of moisture collecting on her upper lip. Thank God none of the partners were in today; they wouldn't recognize her—cool, always-in-control Claire Brewster, whose nickname around the office (though no one had ever said it to her face) was the Ice Maiden. How much easier it would be to forget the whole thing, pretend Gerry had never called. Her life would go on as before, smooth and untroubled.

But she knew that wouldn't be the case. As Kitty had pointed out, the lid was off Pandora's box.

She snatched up the receiver and punched in Gerry's number. It seemed to ring for an eternity. She was about to hang up when a familiar voice answered merrily, "Hello?"

Claire sagged back in her chair. "It's me, Claire."

There was a little hitch of breath at the other end. "Hi. I was hoping you'd call."

"Am I catching you at a bad time?"

"No . . . not at all."

"I've thought it over."

"Yes?" The trembling expectation in Gerry's voice was almost more than she could bear.

Claire closed her eyes, and took a deep breath. "I'd like for us to meet."

Chapter Three

"Move over, will you?" Gerry gave Aubrey a playful nudge. "Being famous might get you in to see the pope, but it doesn't entitle you to more than half the bed."

He rolled onto his side, propping himself on his elbow facing her. The soul of dignity on the concert stage, he might at this moment have been Lady Chatterley's gamekeeper: eyelids heavy and mouth suggestively curled, his silver hair as rumpled as the bed.

"Speaking of the pope," he said, "what would His Holiness think of this?" His sweeping gesture took in the twisted sheets and blankets, the puddles of hastily discarded clothing on the floor.

She tossed her head back with a laugh. "That I'm sure to go straight to hell."

"It doesn't worry you?"

"Do I look worried?"

"Quite the contrary, my dear. You look like a woman in need of—"

Gerry flung a pillow at him, which only made him more determined. He grabbed hold of her and kissed her, leaving her decidedly short of breath. Damn the man. They'd be in bed all day if he had his way, and though she'd have liked nothing better, she had children to get home to, Saturday errands to run, and a house that wasn't going to clean itself.

"Don't tempt me," she growled.

But what would be the harm in a quick one for the road? Andie and Justin were off with their respective friends and not expected back until late this afternoon. She'd be home long before then. Why did she always feel as if time spent on herself was time stolen from her family?

A family that might soon include Claire. Goose bumps broke out on her arms and chest and she shivered, drawing the sheet up over her breasts. Her daughter was flying down this Friday, and they'd arranged to meet for lunch at the Tree House Café. Her stomach turned a slow cartwheel at the thought. It had been exactly one week since Claire's call, and she'd managed to stay on an even keel. But now, stripped of her defenses, away from the demands of work and the world, she could no longer keep her anxiety at bay.

Will I like her? Will she like me*?* She couldn't very well expect the poised-sounding young woman she'd spoken to, a perfect stranger really, to fill the emptiness left by an infant girl held clasped to her heart just long enough to tear a hole in it . . . or fill the shoes of the daughter whose birthday she'd silently marked year after year, wondering what she looked like, how she was doing in school, if she was happy and well cared for.

And what about Andie and Justin? They still knew nothing about Claire. Every time she'd start to tell them, she'd chicken out. But time had run out. Tonight she was going to sit them down after dinner and break it to them as gently as she could. A line from the Book of Mark came to mind: *Be not afraid:*

only believe. She had to believe it would all work out somehow, that God was indeed watching over her. Otherwise, how could she go on?

She scooted over and wound her arms about Aubrey's neck, pulling his head down and holding it nestled against her shoulder. He radiated warmth, and breathing in his scent—dried sweat, soap, a hint of the Gauloises he smoked—she felt her muscles relax. After a moment he lifted his head to smile at her, his eyes—the black-brown of polished teak—seeming to caress her in some way. Eyes that one particularly rhapsodic female reporter had described as reminiscent of nineteenth-century Romantics. Gerry thought the woman might have been referring to more than his romantic appeal, for there was something tortured in them, too, a sense of some unspeakable tragedy buried in the deep, dark woods of those eyes.

She recalled their first meeting at last summer's music festival. Her first glimpse of Aubrey had been from afar; he'd been standing on the amphitheater podium in his tuxedo, baton poised. A line from a poem had come to mind: *He was a gentleman*

*from sole to crown, clean favored and impe-
rially slim.* Tall and straight, with that startling
silver crest, and a presence that even from a
distance commanded the eye. As his baton
came swooping down on the opening chords
of Mahler's Symphony no. 4 and the music
rose as if from a rent in the heavens themselves, she'd broken out all over in goose
flesh. The crowd of hundreds spread on
blankets over the grass fell silent. There was
only the soaring music and its echo in the
valley below. Aubrey, on the podium, looked
like a man in the throes of either agony or
ecstasy.

Afterward, Sam had taken her to meet
him backstage. Sam knew him better than
most—he was leasing Isla Verde and they'd
met early on to iron out details of the contract—though from the stories percolating
around Carson Springs, you'd have thought
half the people in town were on intimate
terms with him. There'd been talk of his
wife's tragic death in a car accident some
years back, and wild speculation about the
women he'd been seen with since (information derived mostly from tabloids). The moment their eyes had met, Gerry had seen
what all the fuss was about. Aubrey

Roellinger was even more charismatic up close, with an angular face, high forehead, and emphatically Gallic nose that might not have worked separately but came together in an irresistible whole. The overall effect, coupled with his distinctly European air, was of a tree falling on the roof of a house safely locked against intruders.

"A pleasure to meet you," he'd said in his faintly accented English. He took her hand, which she'd half expected him to bring to his lips and was vaguely disappointed when he didn't.

"You gave me goose bumps," Gerry had replied, then laughed. "I meant when you were conducting." Their eyes met and lingered a beat too long, as if sharing a joke . . . or an invitation.

They'd gotten together for lunch a few days later, and dinner the night after that. Within weeks they were lovers. The arrangement suited them both perfectly. Mike had cured her of ever wanting to get married again, and Aubrey had made it clear he wasn't looking for a wife. Neither had any interest in more than this: a friendly meeting of minds and bodies and a mutual satisfying of appetites. That they shared a number of interests and enjoyed each other's company out of bed as well as in came as a bonus.

Now, snuggled beside him, Gerry smiled at the irony of it: Here she was in Sam's house, in the bedroom her friend had shared for twenty-five years with her husband. Knowing that Sam was perfectly happy where she was didn't take away from the strangeness of it. She'd been relieved, their first time, to see that Aubrey had kept it pretty much as it was, and she now looked about appreciatively at the white-washed walls hung with watercolors of native flora, and the old pegged floors scattered with Navajo rugs. The only thing missing was the Mission oak dresser Sam had taken with her to her house in the Flats, in its place a handsome antique linen press with pullout shelves that served as drawers.

"Poor Gerry." He nuzzled her hair, his breath warm against her scalp. "Am I keeping you from your appointed rounds?"

She smiled at his formal way of speaking. A lifetime of living abroad had left him with only the faintest of accents, but his way of putting things was decidedly Continental. "I'm not exactly the Pony Express," she told him. "On the other hand, you're no white knight on horseback."

He drew back with a look of mock surprise. "You mean those stories in the tabloids aren't true?"

"If they were, I'd be a twenty-five-year-old blonde with tits by Mattel."

He threw his head back in a hearty laugh. "I prefer you exactly as you are. Tits and all."

"Good, because they're not getting any younger."

She cast a wry downward glance at her breasts. All her life she'd wished they were smaller. As a teenager she'd strapped them into bras that would've dented the fender of any car reckless enough to hit her; as a novice she'd sought desperately to keep them from jiggling under her habit. And now, just as she was getting used to being a bombshell, damn it all if they hadn't begun to sag. She sighed. It was just as well Aubrey wasn't one of those youth-obsessed older men—not, she was quick to remind herself, that forty-eight was *old*—because she had no intention of getting a boob lift, face work, or even a dye job. As if to emphasize that, she lifted her head off the pillow and shook her hair so that it fanned out around her head: a tumble of black curls lightly dusted with silver, more suited to a gypsy fortune-teller than mother of three.

"Now, where were we?" she purred.

Aubrey kissed her throat, tracing her collarbone lightly with his tongue. She shivered, feeling him grow hard as she pressed up against him. God Almighty, where did it come from? Not half an hour since they'd made love, and already he was raring to go again. She smiled to think what he must have been like as a teenager. No wonder he left the women in his audiences breathless and shifting in their seats. They must sense he was a master with more than his baton.

The flutter of his breath against her neck traveled in an exquisite line to her belly and below, where he was gently stroking. She parted her legs, allowing him to explore freely. It didn't matter that just minutes ago she'd been thoroughly sated; all at once it was as if she hadn't made love in a year. What was this effect he had on her? She hadn't felt this way with Mike, or Rory King, or even hot-blooded Anthony Oliveira, who'd oozed sex from every pore and with whom she'd done it in parked cars, restaurant bathrooms, and on one memorable occa-

sion an abandoned ranger station atop
Mount Matilija.

She closed her eyes and gave a soundless little gasp as Aubrey's finger thrust up
into her. Oh, those hands! Like a sorcerer's—long and supple, conjuring magic.
Every woman, she thought, should have an
Aubrey Roellinger at least once in her life, if
only for one night.

His feathery strokes built and built until
she was crying out, begging him to take her.
"Not yet," he whispered in her ear, waiting
until she was on the verge of coming before
he abruptly withdrew his hand and rose to
mount her. She wrapped her legs about him
as he did, using them to pull him into her.
There, heart to heart, pelvis to pelvis, with
the sun warming their naked bodies and the
old oak bed creaking with their weight, they
rocked together with a sure, practiced
rhythm. There was no hurry, for she'd forgotten where she'd needed to be and what it
was she'd been in such a mad rush to do. All
that mattered was here, now . . . *this*. When
he drew back to give her a lazy smile, she
felt herself tumble into those hooded dark
eyes. Seconds later she came in a blaze that
traveled all the way down into her toes.

"Jesus, Mary, and Joseph," she gasped.

His exquisitely timed thrusts became short and fierce. Then all at once he shuddered and reared back with a hoarse yell: that of someone with no kids down the hall, no nosy neighbors on the other side of paper-thin walls. She sank her teeth lightly into his shoulder. Even the texture of his skin thrilled her, like biting into a firm olive tasting faintly of exotic lands. She couldn't seem to get enough of him, which scared her a little. For if, no *when,* this was over, she'd be climbing the walls.

They collapsed, utterly spent. She could feel him pulsing inside her, like a heartbeat, then he rolled off onto his back. She felt the mattress underneath her grow damp. *At least I don't have to worry about getting knocked up,* she thought. Before the first time, they'd had a frank discussion. She'd told him she was on the Pill, and he'd told her she was the first woman he'd been with since his wife. They'd agreed to unprotected sex only after a clean bill of health from their respective doctors. Gerry had no intention of either getting a sexually transmitted disease or ending up like Sam, a middle-aged mom changing diapers and pacing the floor at two A.M.

"I don't know how I'm ever going to get up off this bed." She exhaled deeply, stretching her limbs and staring up at the unmoving shadow of a tree branch on the ceiling. "My legs feel like boiled spaghetti."

"No rush. I'm not leaving until tomorrow," he said, reminding her that he'd be in Philly most of next week. He traced the outline of a breast. "We can stay in bed all day if you like."

"In that case, I hope it has wheels. How else am I going to get to the store?" Gerry reluctantly pulled herself upright. When he chuckled, she asked, "What's so funny?"

"You," he said. "You make me laugh."

"And all this time I thought it was my smoldering sex appeal."

"That, too." He smoothed a hand up the inside of her thigh, sending a quiver through her like the aftershock of an earthquake. "You have marvelous legs, you know."

"Good for running the fifty-yard dash. Did I ever tell you I won a medal in track?" For a fleeting moment she indulged in the memory—the feel of the track beneath her pounding feet, the finish line seeming to rush toward her as she raced to meet it.

"Really?" He looked as if nothing she told him would surprise him.

"Way back in high school. Needless to say, sports weren't high on my list once I went into the convent."

He cocked his head, smiling. "I still can't quite picture you as a nun."

"I was a lot less fun then. I thought nuns weren't supposed to laugh."

"I can see why it didn't last." He brushed her mouth with his fingertips. "Forgive me for sounding trite, but that's like asking the sun not to shine."

"That wasn't the only reason."

She could feel him waiting for her to say more and wondered if she should. But one of the reasons they got along so well was because they kept it light. He didn't need her crying on his shoulder any more than she needed a shoulder to cry on. Which was why she almost never talked about her ex-husband and knew next to nothing about his wife. On the other hand, Claire would soon be part of her life.

Gerry studied him in the sunlight that poured in through the tall casement windows. Every small wrinkle and crease was illuminated, giving his face the world-weary look of a man who, for all his successes, knew something of the dark side, where few people ever walk. An unexpected tenderness washed over her, and she brought a hand to his face, absently rubbing her thumb over the silvery stubble along his jaw.

"What happened was I got pregnant."

He eyed her curiously. "I'd have thought your opportunities would be somewhat limited." His tone was dry, as if he were conscious of the judgment others had heaped on her. If she hadn't loved him before, she almost did then.

"The father was our parish priest."

Aubrey shook his head. "*Mon Dieu*. And the child?"

"A little girl. I gave her up for adoption." Gerry was surprised by the power it still had over her, even after all these years. "I didn't think I'd ever see her again, but . . ." Her voice caught, and she ducked her head.

Aubrey drew her gently against his chest, stroking her back and murmuring in French. It had the effect of a lullaby. Gradually, the knot in her throat eased.

"I hired a private investigator to track her down," she went on. "We've talked on the phone. She's flying down to meet me—this coming Friday, as a matter of fact."

She lifted her head and in that unguarded moment saw the look of pain that flitted over his narrow, Gallic face. His wife, she recalled, had been seven months pregnant when she died. He would never know his child. But if he envied her the chance to know hers, he was far too much a gentleman to let it show. All he said was, "You must be anxious."

Gerry gave a shaky little laugh. "You don't know the half of it."

"I can imagine."

"What if she doesn't like me?"

"How could she not?" He reached up to tuck a stray wisp behind her ear.

"You should hear my kids. Last night Justin told me he hated me."

"I thought it was your daughter we were discussing."

"She probably hates me, too."

"Why do you say that?"

"I gave her away, didn't I?" Gerry felt a familiar tightening in her gut.

"You had your reasons, I'm sure." He didn't ask what they were, and she loved him for that, too.

"Children don't care about reasons."

"She's not a child anymore."

"You're right." Claire was twenty-eight.

"How did she sound over the phone?"

"Nice," she said. "A little reserved, but who wouldn't be?"

"Well, then, you see? You have nothing to worry about."

"I'm Catholic. Worry is my middle name." She swung her legs off the mattress, nudging with her big toe at the clothes heaped on the floor. "Be sides, there's more to it than you think. As far as my kids know, I was pure as the driven snow when I married their dad." She pulled on her black silk panties.

"Mon Dieu." He shook his head again.

As she reached for the black lace bra hooked over a knob of the armoire, she caught a glimpse of herself in its mirror, her tumble of silver-and-black hair and the color standing out along her cheekbones. "I didn't see any reason to tell them," she said. "Until now."

Aubrey remained silent, an odd look on his face—as if they'd only just met and he was trying to figure out what to make of her.

She went on, "I mean, one minute they're babies and the next thing you know they're wanting the keys to the car." She reached around to hook her bra. "Where did the time go? Why didn't I see this coming?"

"I'm the wrong person to ask," he said.

Noting the strained smile he wore, she immediately regretted having dumped all this on him. He had his own problems. She paused in the midst of pulling on her jeans. "I'm probably boring you to death."

"Quite the contrary. I'm glad you feel you can confide in me."

He sounded sincere enough, but his gaze was on the framed photo of his wife atop the dresser, a swan-necked woman in a low-cut blue dress, her flaxen hair coiled in a bun, her pearly shoulders gleaming. In her bright blue eyes, fixed somewhere beyond the camera's range, she might have been catching a glimpse of her destiny: a death that had reverberated throughout the music world, for Isabelle Hubert had been an accomplished musician in her own right. Gerry had one of her last recordings, a Franck violin concerto so exquisite she couldn't listen to it without tears coming to her eyes.

She tugged her sweater over her head and leaned down to kiss him on the cheek. "Thanks. You're sweet."

"I'll call you from Philly," he said.

She felt a small flutter of apprehension. They only talked on the phone when arranging a time to get together. Was this his way of saying he wanted more or was he merely being polite?

"You know where to find me." She struck a breezy tone, letting him know that while she'd appreciate a call she didn't see it as anything to get overly excited about.

On her way into town, her thoughts turned once more to her kids. How would they take the news about Claire? Andie could at least relate. Several girls in her class had had to drop out this past semester, all but one of whom were planning to give their babies up for adoption. On the other hand . . .

She'll probably see this as one more reason to blame me for everything that's wrong with her life.

Gerry pushed the thought from her mind. The day was simply too beautiful to waste, the sun shining and the valley spread out before her like a gift waiting to be opened. Descending into the Flats, where the steep, winding road grew level and straight, she gazed out at row upon row of orange trees bordered by fieldstone walls, many patrolled by geese—more effective than watchdogs, she'd heard—that strutted amid the dappled shade like pompous little generals. Alongside the road, wildflowers climbed from ditches—curly dock and creeping jenny, dog fennel and Dutchman's pipe, with the occasional beavertail cactus or Joshua tree thrusting up like a spiny fist—while in the distance grassy hills gave way to the snow-capped mountains whose fanciful names— Sleeping Indian Chief, Moon's Nest, Two Sisters' Peak—had so captivated her imagination as a child. How could Claire *not* fall in love with this place?

She swerved to avoid a scruffy-looking mutt that had wandered into the road. Old Dick Truesdale's—he really ought to keep his dog chained up. But repeated complaints by concerned neighbors had fallen on deaf ears; the poor guy hadn't been the same since his wife's death. And from the looks of his overgrown yard, littered with the shriveled brown fists of fallen oranges, and ramshackle house beyond—an older frame structure missing a good deal of its shingles whose walls seemed to lean inward like old drunks holding up each other—he wasn't doing a very good job of looking after himself, either.

At least I have my kids . . .

Minutes later she was turning onto Old Mission, with its quaint Spanish-style shops trimmed in colorful tiles. The tile-roofed arcade that stretched along one side of the street was bustling with shoppers, and she remembered that the January white sale was still on at Rusk's. In the park across the street, white-haired Clem Woolley, toting a bundle of his self-published tome, *My Life with Jesus*, was holding forth to the Vietnamese head gardener, Mr. Nuyen, a solitary little man as silent and ageless as the grounds he tended. She knew only that he'd come here just after the war, and was said to be so enamored of his new home he hadn't spent a single night away from it since.

Gerry, lost in her thoughts, nearly missed the entrance to Del Rey Plaza, then had to circle the lot several times before she found a spot. Now where was that grocery list? She searched her purse before moving on to her pockets. It must have fallen out at Aubrey's.

The reminder of how she'd spent the afternoon brought a flush of remembered pleasure. What would these people pushing their grocery carts think if they knew? She spotted Marguerite Moore climbing out of her light blue Le Sabre in front of Safeway. Last summer when Marguerite had gotten wind of Sam and Ian's affair, she'd been like a bloodhound on the trail, no doubt secretly wishing a man, any man—never mind one as young and attractive as Ian—would give *her* a reason to change her sheets in the middle of the week.

She caught the narrow glance Marguerite shot her. Marguerite and her ilk had been looking down their noses at Gerry for years. For one thing, she didn't conform to their standards for how a middle-aged woman should behave. Nor did she dress in the secular equivalent of a habit and veil, as befitting a former nun. Today's outfit, form-fitting jeans that left nothing to the imagination and a stretchy top showing more than an inch of cleavage, had Marguerite eyeing her with open contempt. Gerry waved cheerily as she passed. *I wonder what the old cow would think if she knew what I have on underneath.*

Inside she cruised down the aisles, tossing boxes and cans and jars into her cart with scarcely a glance at their labels. She was too preoccupied with thoughts of Claire. Had the Tree House been the best choice of

venue? Should she have chosen somewhere less crowded, where they wouldn't
draw unwanted attention from the likes of
Marguerite?

Gerry didn't see Fran O'Reilly until they'd
nearly collided. She glanced up to find fiery-
haired Fran hastily stuffing a box into her
cart with a faintly abashed look. It was a moment before Gerry realized that the owner of
Francoise's was embarrassed to be seen
buying Pop Tarts.

"Yeah, I know," Fran said with a self-
conscious laugh. "Me with my culinary degree."

Gerry laughed. "I'm not one to judge, believe me. In my house I'm known as the Lean
Cuisine Queen."

"You don't have a reputation to uphold."
Fran cast a mock furtive glance at Marguerite, trundling up the aisle.

You got that right, Gerry thought. Whatever reputation she'd once had, it had long
since been trashed. "Your secret is safe with
me," she said, placing a finger over her lips.
"Speaking of which, how's business?"

She recalled when Fran had first moved
here, a single mom from Brooklyn who'd
traded her secretary's salary for a shot at a

lifetime dream. That'd been—what? Eight, nine years ago. Since then wiry little Fran, who made her think of a red squirrel always darting about, had made a real go of it. Her hole-in-the-wall creperie was so popular there was always a line spilling onto the sidewalk.

Fran brightened. "Actually, I'm looking to expand. If you hear of anything, let me know. It has to be at least double the square feet, where the rent won't eat me alive."

"What about the Dalrymple place? I heard it was on the market." In her mind, Gerry saw the older shingled cottage with roses climbing up the front and shards of terra-cotta roof tiles scattered about the yard. "I don't imagine they'll get top dollar. It's pretty run down."

"Yeah, I know. It was the first thing I looked at. It'd be perfect—zoned for commercial use, too. Except it's a little too far off the main drag. I'd lose the lunch trade." Fran looked thoughtful, as if she hadn't completely ruled it out.

They chatted briefly about the high price of real estate before Gerry shoved off.

Fifteen minutes later she was on her way home. Turning down Green Willow she waved at Tom Kemp, bent over his hedge with a pair of clippers like a tall question mark. She remembered when Martin's former partner had been crazy about Sam, and wondered if he was still carrying the torch. Did love truly spring eternal? She wouldn't know. The men she dated were disposable. Only Aubrey was different, in a way she hadn't quite been able to pinpoint.

She turned off Green Willow onto Mesa, slowing at the sight of two boys cruising along on their bikes. A little farther down, Marcy Walters's little girl was playing hopscotch on the sidewalk while her brother pedaled in furious on his Hot Wheels. It used to drive Mike crazy that he couldn't park his Lincoln Town Car in the driveway without worrying that some kid would scratch it. But everything Mike had hated about this neighborhood she loved—its older Spanish-style homes standing hip to hip, many still trimmed in Christmas lights; and the neighbors who waved to you and knew everything that went on. She wouldn't have traded it for Mike's fancy new house in the hills any more than she'd have given up the job she loved for one that paid twice the salary.

Pulling into the driveway, the first thing Gerry noticed was Justin's bike blocking the door to the garage. Her mellow mood dissolved. Damn it. *How* many times had she told him—

Go easy, a voice interjected. *You don't want to set the wrong tone.*

Inside she found her son slouched in front of the TV, lost in a video game. He barely glanced up when she walked in. "Where's Andie?" she called, dumping an armload of groceries on the kitchen counter.

"Huh?"

"Your sister. You know: five foot two, curly dark hair. Last seen wearing a red sweatshirt and jeans."

"I dunno—with Finch, I guess." His eyes remained glued to the screen, on which amazingly lifelike race cars zipped through tunnels and around bends.

"Did she say when she'd be back?"

"Nope."

Gerry sighed. When Andie and Finch were together they lost all track of time; she'd be lucky if Andie made it home in time for supper. But hadn't it been that way with her and Sam? At that age they'd been inseparable. Gerry had probably spent more time at Sam's house than at her own.

Justin still hadn't budged. "Hey, buster, I

could use a hand here. If it's not *too* inconvenient." Their elderly Labrador, snoozing by the fireplace, lifted his gray-muzzled head. "Not you," she said. Buster dropped his head back onto his paws with a grunt.

Justin shot her a sheepish glance. "Uh, sure, Mom. In a minute."

Gerry sighed again. The manic soundtrack emanating from the living room made the days she and her sisters used to hang out in the penny arcade at Palisades Park, playing Gypsy Fortune-teller and Rifle Shoot, seem basked in a golden glow. Though she was certain her son, perched on the sofa in his baggy jeans and even baggier Lakers T-shirt, would have scoffed at the idea.

She went back for a second load. Her mother would say she was too easy on the kids, that you couldn't run a tight ship without cracking the whip now and then. But Gerry wasn't interested in running a tight ship. Hadn't she done that with Mike? Juggling a job and kids with a constant round of lists, chores, and activities: cocktails with clients, dinner parties for people she barely knew, an endless stream of country club affairs.

If it hadn't been for the Dawsons, who

knew how long it might have gone on? She cringed at the memory, even though it had been her salvation in a way. Paul and Nancy Dawson, a couple she knew from church, had expressed interest in joining the club. Gerry, seeing no reason such nice people wouldn't be welcomed with open arms, had offered to sponsor them. Unfortunately, the board members hadn't seen it her way. The Dawsons, she learned when the vote came down, weren't quite tony enough for the Dos Palmas crowd.

"They knew the risk," Mike had said when she came to him in tears. "This is a private club, not some church organization."

That had only stoked Gerry's ire. "I get it. They're good enough to organize a drive for earthquake victims in Nicaragua, but not loll about by the pool showing off their tans."

Mike shrugged. "There were lots of considerations."

"You mean like the fact that Paul doesn't play golf, and Nancy isn't on the museum board?"

"That had nothing to do with it, and you know it. Stop blowing this out of proportion. They just . . . well, they didn't fit in."

"Maybe I don't fit in either," she'd shot

back. She knew perfectly well she wouldn't have gotten in on her own. Not that she'd have cared; Mike was the one who'd been so hell-bent on joining.

The very next day she told him he could screw the club. But if she'd secretly hoped he would come around to seeing it her way in time, the plan backfired. Mike saw no reason to stop spending his weekends at Dos Palmas just because she was foolish enough to stay home. It was around that time he'd met Cindy—newly divorced, and an ace golfer to boot. Cindy, with her tiny voice and even tinier waist, her baby blues that could fell a man at fifty paces. Once they became an item, it was all over but the shouting. They'd been married a year, and Gerry wished them well. She had nothing against Cindy; Mike either, for that matter. It all made perfect sense. If anything, she wondered what he'd ever seen in *her*.

With the groceries unloaded and put away, she filled a large pot with water. When it was boiling furiously, she dumped in a packet of noodles and went hunting for the jar of Ragu she was sure she had. One of the great innovations of the twentieth century, she thought, was spaghetti sauce in a jar. Mixed with a pound of hamburger you had the perfect meal.

Dinner was almost ready by the time Justin ambled into the kitchen to help. She put him to work setting the table, trying not to notice when he laid the forks and knives in the wrong place and left the milk carton out. Andie walked in the door just as they were about to sit down.

Gerry watched her daughter shrug off her jacket and toss it over one of the hooks by the door. Her cheeks were ruddy with more than cold; it looked as if she and Finch had hit the makeup counter at Rusk's. And was that a new earring? It was hard to tell with so many in her ears.

"You're just in time," she said.

Andie meandered over to the table. "What's for dinner?"

"Spaghetti." Gerry spoke calmly, though it was perfectly obvious what they were having. "Did you and Finch have fun?"

"We were at the ranch most of the day. Then Hector had to go into town, so we caught a ride with him." Andie dropped into her chair, eyeing the spaghetti without much interest. "I tried on some stuff at Rusk's."

"That's it?"

"Oh, yeah. We saw Laura's dress. She had to go in for a fitting."

"Was it nice?" Gerry remembered that Laura and Hector's wedding was just weeks away. She hadn't gotten them anything yet. What did you get a couple who'd spend their entire lives on horseback and camping out under the stars if they could?

"Yeah. Not frilly or anything. More like a long slip." Andie buttered a slice of bread. "And she's wearing a wreath instead of a veil."

This wedding would be very different from Alice's, that was for sure. Instead of a church wedding followed by a fancy spread on the lawn at Isla Verde, there'd be only a handful of nearest and dearest attending the rustic hilltop ceremony. Gerry wondered what kind of wedding Sam and Ian would have if they ever decided to tie the knot. Knowing Sam, she'd combine it with the baptism for efficiency's sake; why not kill two birds with one stone? She smiled at the thought.

"Weddings are stupid," Justin said. He was sulking because she'd told him he couldn't bring his friend Nesto.

"Only a stupid person would say that," Andie replied loftily.

"Says who?" Justin glared at her.

"Ask anyone."

Gerry dropped her fork onto her plate with a clatter. "That's enough, you two." She felt weary all of a sudden. How could she bring Claire into the mix when half the time they barely got along with each other? "I'd like it if once, just once, we could get through dinner without your squabbling."

Andie and Justin were subdued throughout the rest of the meal. They stuck to harmless topics: the new teacher who'd replaced Mr. Geiger at Justin's school, the Little League tryouts in just a few weeks, the car wash Andie and Finch were organizing to raise money for Lost Paws. By the time she got up to clear the table, Gerry was feeling more optimistic. Nevertheless, she waited until the dishwasher was humming and the kids settled in the living room with their bowls of ice cream.

"Guys. I have something to tell you." She sank down on the sofa.

Justin lowered his spoon with a worried look. "Something bad?" The expression on his face was the one he'd worn when she'd told him she and his dad were getting divorced.

"Not at all," she said. She felt sick. Hadn't

these kids been through enough? Why didn't she just write a book? *Fifty Ways to Screw Up Your Child.* "Just something you need to know." She looked from Justin to Andie, who'd gone very still. Gerry would have given anything just then to have them little again, when they'd still believed in the tooth fairy and the idea of an unknown sister wouldn't have seemed so strange. "Remember my telling you about when I was at the convent? The reason I left?"

"Because you weren't cut out to be a nun, right?" Andie eyed her warily.

"That was partly it." Gerry took a deep breath. "I was also pregnant."

There was a long, stunned moment in which no one spoke.

Andie's mouth fell open. She stared at Gerry as she might have at an intruder that had just burst in through the front door.

Justin merely looked confused. "But . . . you weren't married to Dad then."

Andie whipped around to glower at him. "Don't you *get* it? She wasn't married, *period.*" She turned her blazing eyes on Gerry. "I can't believe you didn't tell us."

"I didn't see any reason for you to know." Gerry spoke calmly, as if by her very tone she could make them believe there was a perfectly rational explanation for all of this.

"So why are you telling us now?" Andie's eyes narrowed.

"Something's come up."

"What?"

Gerry felt as if a bone were stuck in her throat. This was worse than when she'd told them about Mike because at least then they'd had some idea of what to expect. This was like dropping a bomb on a village peacefully going about its business. She swallowed hard.

"You have a sister . . . and she wants to meet you."

Andie stared at her, the color draining from her face. "I don't believe it."

"Her name is Claire," Gerry went on in the same purposefully upbeat tone. "I didn't know where she lived until just a few weeks ago. It turns out she's just up the coast. She's flying down next week to meet us."

"I don't believe it," Andie repeated, shaking her head.

"What's she like?" Justin asked hopefully.

Gerry could have kissed him.

"Nice. I think you'll like her."

"You make her sound like a puppy." Andie's voice was heavy with scorn.

"Is she staying here?" The bowl of ice cream on Justin's lap had melted to a brown soup.

"Not this time," Gerry said. "We thought it'd be best if she stayed at a motel. Until we get to know each other a little."

Andie moaned. "Tell me this isn't happening."

"I'm sorry to spring it on you like this." Gerry reached over to place a consoling hand on Andie's knee, but she jerked away as if scalded. "I should have told you. I *wanted* to. But . . . it all happened a long time before you were even born." She didn't add that Mike had been adamant she not tell them.

"Why didn't you keep her?" Justin looked so innocent just then—like when he was a little boy wanting to know why Grandpa Ed had to go to heaven—it very nearly broke her heart.

She smiled at him tenderly. "I was young. And you're right—I wasn't married to your dad then. I was afraid I wouldn't do a very good job raising her."

"Couldn't Grandma have helped?"

Gerry had often wondered the same thing, but ultimately it had been *her* decision.

"She was working two jobs and taking care of Uncle Kevin. It would have been unfair to her, too."

"What if it'd been one of us?"

All eyes, even Buster's, turned to Andie when she spoke. There was something in her voice—something so lost and plaintive. Suddenly Gerry knew the real reason she'd kept it a secret for so long: She'd known this was the root of it, the common denominator of the equation. For hadn't she asked it of herself, too?

"It was different when I had you. I'd have cut off my arm before giving either of you away." She spoke firmly, leaving no room for doubt.

"You're only saying that now." Andie wasn't going to be bought off so easily. "But if it'd been *me* instead of her you'd have done the same—given me away."

Gerry's heart constricted. "Oh, honey. You know I—"

But it was too late. Andie jumped to her feet and dashed from the room. A moment later Gerry heard the door to her room slam shut. She let out a ragged exhalation, the air in her lungs feeling like it was being squeezed through too small an opening.

Make that Fifty-one Ways to Screw Up Your Child, she thought. Her gaze dropped to the bowl of ice cream Andie had left on the floor, which Buster was happily lapping up.

Justin, slumped on the sofa, said tonelessly, "He can have mine, too."

Later that evening, as she lay reading in bed, Gerry heard a tap on her bedroom door. "Come in," she called.

Andie poked her head in. "Justin's in his room crying. I just thought you should know." Her voice was matter-of-fact, like a TV newscaster announcing that two hundred people had been killed in plane crash. But the look on her face told a different story.

"Come here." Gerry patted the bed beside her.

After a moment's hesitation Andie nonchalantly strolled over. She'd changed into leggings and an old T-shirt of Mike's—regulation nightwear these days. Standing next to the bed, her curly mop pulled back with an elastic band, she might have been a tall crane poised at the edge of a pond.

"Do you feel like talking about it?" Gerry asked.

Andie gave her a deeply injured look, as if

to say, *How can you even ask?* Then with a sigh she sank down on the bed. Gerry remembered when her children were little and would burrow under the covers, snuggling against her like puppies, one under each arm. In those days it had seemed she would never get enough sleep, but now she'd have done anything to turn the clock back. She tucked a bookmark into the novel she'd been staring at without really reading by an author with the unlikely name of Daphne Seagrave.

She tried a different tack. "I'm sorry I upset you."

Andie shrugged. "Justin's the one crying. Not me."

Gerry sighed. These days she thought of her daughter in terms of Before and After, for it seemed she'd lost more than a husband in the divorce. The sunny, affectionate girl who'd chattered incessantly, helped out around the house, and often hugged her for no reason had vanished, leaving in her place this hard-faced, unforgiving teenager.

"Would it help," she said gently, "if I told you I'm just as nervous as you are about meeting her?"

Andie lifted her head. In the shadowy light from the night-table lamp, her eyes looked bruised. "The difference is you have a choice. We don't."

"Fair enough," Gerry acknowledged, and saw a flicker of surprise in her daughter's face. They'd been butting heads for so long. "Still . . ." She risked a small smile. "Aren't you a little bit curious at least?"

"Maybe." Andie plucked at a loose thread in the bedspread. After a moment she asked in a voice so low Gerry had to strain to hear it, "What made you decide to look for her?"

Gerry's gaze shifted to the framed movie poster on the wall by the dresser: *Breakfast at Tiffany's* in Italian, which she and Mike had bought when they were on their honeymoon but which now seemed a souvenir from another lifetime.

"I'm not sure," she said. "I think it had to do with Aunt Sam. Seeing her pregnant. I don't know—it just hit me, that's all."

"You didn't think of her when you had *me*?"

"Every single day." She laid a hand over Andie's, stilling its fretful plucking. "But it wouldn't have done any good to go looking for her then. Even if I'd found her, I doubt her parents would have let me see her. Besides, your father . . ." She let the sentence trail off.

"Dad knew?"

She nodded. "I told him before we were married." Mike had been understanding at the time. It wasn't until the children were born that he'd made his true feelings known. He didn't want them to think less of her, he'd said. Too ashamed to argue, she'd gone along.

Andie's mouth twisted in a smile that was more a grimace. "It's weird, isn't it? Here I was thinking it'd be Dad and Cindy who'd surprise us with a kid. I never expected it from *you*."

"I guess we're all a little shell-shocked."

"So where do we go from here?"

Gerry reached up to brush a curl from her daughter's forehead. "The main thing you need to remember is that I love you and Justin very much. Nothing will ever change that."

She caught the gleam of tears in Andie's eyes. "Finch talks about it sometimes, what it was like growing up without parents. I always felt so lucky . . ." She turned away, her back to a brick wall Gerry felt helpless to breach. "I'm going to bed now. Do we have church tomorrow?"

"Would you like to go?"

Andie, for whom Sundays had become a

battleground, nodded ever so slightly before getting up and heading for the door.

Gerry climbed out of bed. "I'll check on your brother."

Andie paused in the doorway and turned, a wedge of shadow falling over her face. In the soft glow from the hallway the illuminated half gleamed like a newly minted coin. "He misses Dad."

"I know." Gerry kissed her on the forehead. "Goodnight, sweetie. Sleep tight. Don't—"

"—let the bedbugs bite," Andie finished for her, smiling a little and shaking her head as if at the antics of a child. In that moment she looked so grown-up Gerry felt an urge to snatch her back from the brink of adulthood the way she might have from the path of a speeding train.

They arrived just after the introductory hymn, sliding in next to Anna Vincenzi in the second to the last pew. Anna smiled and passed them each a missal. She looked her usual frumpy self in a shapeless flowered smock, yet something was different about her. Then Gerry realized what it was: She was used to seeing Anna with her sister, stoically pushing Monica about in her wheel-chair, Monica treating her as if she were a flack in the entourage that had once shad-owed her every move. Today Anna was with her elderly mother instead. It must be one of Mrs. Vincenzi's good days.

"Page thirteen," Anna whispered while her mother stared vacantly ahead, a hollow-eyed wraith, the black mantilla draped over her snowy head only adding to the effect.

Gerry glanced over at her children. Justin, his face still a little puffy, was quietly thumb-ing through his missal. Andie, dressed de-murely for a change in a long-sleeved top and corduroy jumper, was subdued as well. Gerry saw her pull something from her pocket and was surprised to see it was the rosary beads Mavis had given her when she was confirmed.

The congregation rose for the penitential rite, and Gerry chanted along with the oth-ers, "I confess to almighty God, and to you, my brothers and sisters, that I have sinned through my own fault," she struck her breast lightly with her fist, "in my thoughts and words, in what I have done and what I have failed to do. . . ."

The familiar rhythms of the mass wrapped

around her like a warm blanket, and when it was time for the Eucharist, she felt as if she were being roused from a light doze. She made her way down the aisle, past pug-faced Althea Wormley in a hideous yellow hat several seasons out of date; David and Carol Ryback with their sickly son, Davey; elderly identical twins Rose and Olive Miller. At the altar, when she lifted her head to take the Host, she found Father Dan's kind blue eyes on her, as if he were looking into her soul—and liking what he saw. She felt a rush of gratitude. In all the years she'd known him, he'd never judged or condemned her. While others whispered behind her back, Dan seemed to understand her passions and needs. Needs he'd surely wrestled with himself. With all the women batting their eyes at him, he'd have to be either gay or made of stone not to at least be tempted.

She closed her eyes, and there was only the rustle of vestments smelling of starch and incense. The murmur of his voice as he dispensed his blessing along with the Host was like cool water trickling over her head.

The sermon that followed had to do with today's reading from Corinthians. In his deep voice Father Dan read, "'If the foot should

say, "Because I am not a hand, I do not belong to the body," it does not for any reason
belong any less to the body. . . . ' " He lifted
his head, wearing his easy smile that
seemed to carry a knowing wink. "Who
among us hasn't pulled that one? Our boss
asks us to do something and we say, 'Oh no,
not me. That's not *my* job. Go talk to Mr.
Jones down the hall.' Or a wife asks her husband to watch the kids—" his gaze fell on
Janet Stickney and her brood, five red-
haired boys ranging in age from two to
twelve—"and he says that's *your* responsibility. I'm too busy earning a living." He waited
for the titters to die down. "The point is we've
all been guilty of setting ourselves apart, of
thinking it's somebody else's problem, not
ours. Paul says there are many parts, but
one body." He paused. "I think that applies
not only to our jobs and families but also to
our relationships to one another. For if we're
weaker, we find strength in the body as a
whole."

He might have been speaking directly to
her. For all her qualms with the Church, this
was what brought her to mass every Sunday: to be reminded that she wasn't alone.
She glanced at Anna, quietly attempting to

subdue her mother, who'd grown restless. Compared to Anna's problems—caring for a senile parent in addition to working long hours catering to her sister's every whim—hers seemed small.

When they rose for the final hymn, "Father, We Thank Thee," she felt at peace for the first time in weeks. Even Andie and Justin seemed more at ease. They joined the line of parishioners making their way out onto the steps, where she stopped to have a word with Father Dan.

"Wonderful sermon," she told him.

"You'd have enjoyed last Sunday's even more." A not-so-subtle reminder that she'd missed last week's mass, though his twinkling blue eyes let her know it was only out of concern that he'd mentioned it. "Everything okay?"

"Fine," she lied. "Other than that I could use a vacation."

"The sisters keeping you on your toes, eh?" He smiled broadly. Her job managing the beekeeping operation at Our Lady of the Wayside seemed to amuse him in some way.

"You know the old saying, No rest for the wicked."

"Ah, so it's not just work."

She smiled at the inference to Aubrey. "I'm surprised you didn't hear it from Marguerite."

He arched a brow. "Is there something I should know?"

"Not a thing, Father." She put on an innocent look.

Her hand, when he took it in both of his, felt like a flower pressed between the pages of a book. "When you feel like talking about it, you know where to find me."

Before she could reply he drifted over to a group of ladies from the Altar Guild, leaving her to head off in search of her children. She spotted Andie with several of her friends from school. A short distance away Justin was getting an earful from garrulous old Mr. Hennessey, the former merchant marine who'd been the church caretaker for as long as she could recall.

She remembered that she'd promised to stop at Lickety Split on the way home. Justin was at that age when he could eat an entire banana split and still be hungry for lunch. Maybe later, if Andie and Justin were in the mood, they'd take a hike up into Wheeler Canyon. It was beautiful this time of year, just a hint of chill in the air. Apple weather, her mother called it, for out near the orchards you could still catch the faint cidery scent of windfall. With luck they wouldn't come across any bears, like the one Waldo Squires claimed to have seen last week up on Chorro Ridge (Waldo's word, however, was suspect, given his long and well-documented battle with the bottle). Though after all they'd been through what was a wild animal or two?

She felt a sudden burst of optimism. Things would work out somehow. Eventually her kids would come to accept Claire . . . and Claire would accept them. One day they might all attend mass together, not to mention weddings and christenings down the line: a family like the body of which Paul had spoken, a body made up of disparate parts that was strong as a whole.

Gerry had no sooner reached the bottom step when the world was plunged into shadow. She glanced up at the sky, where the sun had disappeared behind clouds that had come out of nowhere. More were gathering in billowy heaps over the mountains to the west, and the wind picked up, scudding in over the trees with a low, confiding rustle.

Gerry shivered, pulling at the lapels of her blazer.

"Andie! Justin!" she called.

There'd be no outing today. They'd be lucky if they made it home without getting drenched.

Chapter Four

Andie slung her backpack over her shoulder with a sigh and started up the stairwell. Portola High was all on one level, a series of low buildings connected by breezeways, with the exception of the building she was in now. It housed the principal's and vice principal's offices, with a faculty lounge upstairs and a large room overlooking the quad, where the school newspaper put out its monthly ruminations on everything from the football team's current losing streak to the student petition being circulated right now in favor of installing vending machines for condoms in the boys' and girls' bathrooms, and where on this bright Monday afternoon, a good half hour after he'd promised to meet her out front, she was certain she'd find her boyfriend Simon, editor in chief of the *Scribe.*

She ought to have been totally pissed. This wasn't the first time he'd kept her waiting.

He wasn't the best-looking guy around. Nor was he the coolest (not that Simon gave a damn). While other guys looked up to Derek Jeter and Shaquille O'Neal her boyfriend's idols were Bob Woodward and Carl Bernstein. And while jocks like Pete Underwood and Lonnie Thorsen were butting heads on the field or in the locker room snapping each other with towels, her boyfriend could be found on the trail of a hot tip or tapping furiously on a keyboard.

That was the thing about Simon. He cared about stuff like global warming and gun control and wasn't too busy trying to score some action (or in Dink Rogers's case, some dope) to try making a difference—though the editor in chief of the *Valley Clarion,* to which Simon regularly submitted on spec, had suggested that many of his articles were more suited to the *Berkeley Barb*.

He was sexy, too—in a reverse cool kind

of way. The kind that doesn't advertise itself and is always a little surprised that anyone would think so. The reason they hadn't done It yet wasn't because she didn't want to or was holding out for a better offer but simply because she was afraid of where it would lead. She was already crazy about him. What would happen if they were sleeping together?

Andie was halfway to forgiving him by the time she reached the top of the stairs. She found the door to the *Scribe*'s room propped open with an overflowing trash basket. Inside she looked about at the shelves and cubbyholes jammed with reference books and old bound issues of the *Scribe*; the bulletin board that neatly covered one wall layered with index cards and photos and play-off schedules for every sport; the desks on which computers sat, flying toasters and brightly colored cubes floating across their screens. Only one was in use—the one at which Simon sat hunched, oblivious to the world.

He blinked up at her, the thick lenses of his Buddy Holly glasses giving his wide-set hazel eyes a faintly astonished look. "Andie, hey. What are you doing here?"

"I could ask the same of you," she said sharply, placing her hands on her hips. "You were supposed to meet me out front."

He groaned, his gaze dropping to the battered Swatch draped like Dali's clock over the top of the monitor, where he was no doubt under the mistaken illusion it would be more visible. "Damn. I'm sorry. I lost track." He lurched to his feet, nimbly picking his way over the computer cables that snaked like tree roots over the floor. When he pulled her into his arms, she resisted at first, then relented with a sigh. He smelled woolly, like a comfortable old sweater on a foggy day. "Forgive me?" He drew back to give her his endearingly crooked smile, his glasses askew and a tuft of brown hair sticking up over one ear.

"I'm working on it," she said grudgingly.

"One more minute, okay?" He held up an ink-stained index finger. "I promise I won't be long."

"Okay. But this better be good."

"It is. In fact, it may be the scoop of a lifetime." He returned to his computer and tapped in a URL. "I'm interviewing Monica Vincent in"—he glanced once more at his Swatch— "exactly one hour."

"*The* Monica Vincent?" She gaped at him in astonishment.

"The one and only."

"How on earth did you manage that?" Their resident movie star was famous for turning down interview requests.

He tapped his temple, casting her a mysterious look. "I have my sources."

A home page scrolled up on the screen, and a photo of Monica appeared. It must have been taken some years back because she was striding down a red carpet wearing a shimmery aqua dress, her famous auburn hair cascading down over her shoulders. She looked ravishing.

"Seriously," she said.

"All right, it was pure luck. I must have caught her at the right moment." He punched a key and the printer began spewing out pages. "Bob Heidiger at the *Clarion* is so excited he's practically wetting his pants. And if one of the wire services picks it up . . ." He didn't need to add that it would be in papers all over the country.

Andie peered at the photo on the screen. "It's weird when you think how she used to be on the cover of every magazine. You couldn't stand in line at the supermarket without her jumping out at you."

She recalled the piece in *People,* just after the boating accident that had left Monica paralyzed from the waist down, in which her publicist and friends were quoted as saying how courageously she was carrying on. What they didn't mention was what a raving bitch she was—all the shopkeepers down-town had their stories. Monica's mansion on the hill was appropriately named LoreiLinda, after the Lorelei in the *Odyssey* that lured sailors to their death.

"You couldn't get her to pose for the cover of *Time* magazine these days," he said.

"I don't see what she has to hide. I mean, look at Christopher Reeve."

"Ego, pure and simple," he said with a shrug. "She'd rather be remembered in all her glory."

"I guess that means no photos."

"I'm bringing my camera just in case. It's only the local paper, after all." He winked. "Hey, why don't you come along? I'll tell her we're a team."

"I don't know," she said, though it *was*

tempting—no one she knew had seen the inside of LoreiLinda. "I should get home."

Simon logged off. "Why? What's up?"

Something a lot bigger than Monica Vincent, she thought, but only shrugged and said, "I have a paper on *Of Human Bondage* that's due tomorrow, and I haven't even finished the book."

"I'll tell you all about it on the way." He slung an arm around her shoulders. "Besides, how often do you get a chance to observe a praying mantis in its natural habitat?"

"She couldn't be *that* bad."

"Tell that to Herman Tyzzer." Herman, a bearded ex-marine who fancied himself a film buff, owned their favorite video store, Den of Cyn. "She spent fifteen minutes reaming him out for not having every one of her movies. Even Blockbuster doesn't carry them all."

"I waited on her once at Rusk's," she recalled. "She returned a pair of pantyhose that looked as if it'd been worn. Mr. Kremer told me to take it back anyway."

"Smart man."

"Do you think she'd recognize me?"

"I doubt it. From what I've heard, she's

more concerned about people recognizing *her*." He grabbed his bulging backpack from the floor and slung it over one shoulder.

They were halfway down the stairs before she realized she hadn't exactly told him she was coming. Simon had just assumed it. Oh well. It'd be worth it just for the stories she could tell.

His car, a battered tan VW Squareback with more miles on it than a 747, was one of the few remaining in the lot. She was opening the door to climb in when she spotted a briefcase-toting figure trudging their way. Recognizing him as her math teacher, she quickly ducked into her seat.

Simon grinned. "What's wrong—you flunk an algebra test?"

Andie ignored the gibe. Okay, so math wasn't her strongest subject. "Haven't you heard? Mr. Hillman was spotted in a gay bar on Sunset Strip."

"Really?" Simon sounded nonplussed. He started the engine, which sputtered, then caught with a grinding roar.

"Did you know he was gay?"

Her boyfriend shrugged, casting another glance at the teacher—everything about Mr. Hillman was beige: his thinning hair, his coat, his briefcase, even his skin—the last person you'd expect to see in any kind of bar. "I don't know, and I don't care. I'm just wondering who'd be stupid enough to rat him out. I mean, think about it, why would you be in a gay bar unless you were gay yourself?"

He has a point, she thought. After a moment, she said, "My uncle's gay."

"The one in San Francisco?" They pulled out of the lot and started down the hill.

"Uncle Kevin, yeah."

"I'd like to meet him sometime."

"You two would get along." The last time she'd seen Uncle Kevin was a year ago when he'd flown her and Justin up for a visit. It was the most fun she could remember having since the divorce.

Simon flashed her a grin. "I'd like anyone who cooks." He was famous for his appetite, though he never seemed to gain an ounce.

She hesitated before asking, "When am I going to meet *your* family?" In the four months they'd been dating she'd never once been out to his place. It was always one excuse or another.

"You know my sister." Simon spoke guardedly.

"That's only because she goes to school here." Besides, Ricki was a sophomore, which meant they hardly ever saw each other.

"My mom's hardly ever home. And you wouldn't you wouldn't find my brothers all that interesting, believe me."

"Like mine is such a prize?"

"Justin? He's okay."

Andie remained puzzled. Simon had gone out of his way to be nice to her brother, helping him with his homework and showing him stuff on the computer. It didn't make sense that he'd be so dismissive of his own. Was he hiding something? Or—an even more worrisome thought occurred to her—keeping her at arm's length?

The Squareback belched and rattled its way down the hill, making enough noise to drown out a fleet of Hell's Angels. In the opposite lane a school bus, empty of its passengers, was trundling along like an old horse returning to its stable. The driver, heavyset Mr. Drill, who moonlighted with his wife as a caterer, waved to a group of damphaired girls from the swim team, trudging along the shoulder. Andie felt older than those girls by at least a hundred years.

Simon seemed to sense her mood. "Hey, are you okay? You seem a little down." He reached over and squeezed her hand. "You're not still mad at me, I hope."

She slumped back in her seat with a sigh. "It's not you . . . things have been kind of weird at home." Even after two days it hadn't fully sunk in.

"In what way?" He seemed genuinely interested.

She hesitated. It wasn't that she cared if he knew—hadn't she told Finch?—just that it was hard talking about something that still seemed so surreal. "Here's a news flash for you," she said in a lightly sarcastic voice meant to distance herself from the whole thing, but which twisted in on itself, grabbing her about the throat instead. "I just found out I have a sister."

Simon cast her a startled glance, then seeing she was serious whistled through his teeth. "Jesus. How the hell did that happen?"

"The usual way. My mom got knocked up."

"I'm assuming it was before she met your dad."

"*Way* before."

"And she waited all this time to tell you? Wow." For once even Simon was speechless.

"She says it was for our own good. Can you believe it?" Andie bristled anew at the indignity of it.

Simon shrugged. "Normally intelligent people can have an amazing lack of insight when it comes to their offspring." He ought to know. In last month's issue of the *Scribe* Simon had run a column on the realities of teen sex that had outraged parents descending on Mr. Blanton's office like a flock of screeching crows.

"Now we're supposed to welcome her with open arms—one big happy family." It seemed a cruel joke. For the past year and a half she'd wished for things to go back to the way they were before the divorce, but this wasn't how she'd imagined the empty chair at their table being filled. "I mean, it's not like my mom *lied* exactly, but isn't it the same thing?"

They were cruising past the elementary school, where the flag was still at half mast for old Mr. Geiger, who'd died the week before last following a long illness. On the lawn out front a yellow ribbon, drooping now, was tied to the concrete base of the cast-iron bell from the original one-room schoolhouse across town.

"I remember when my dad walked out on us," he said in an odd, tight voice. "I was nine. All I knew was that he went out for a pack of cigarettes and didn't come back. It was at least six months before my mom got around to telling us he was never coming home."

So that's why he never talked about his dad. She felt a new sympathy for Simon; they had more in common than she'd realized. "The funny thing is, I always wanted a sister," she told him. "I just never thought it would be like this."

"Who knows? You might like her."

"That's not the point." Andie thought for a moment, frowning. What *was* the point? "I used to think I knew my mom, but now . . . I'm not sure. It's not like the guys she sleeps with that she thinks I don't know about. It's like . . . well, like all of a sudden she's this whole other person."

It was the same with her dad. She used to think she was the most important person in his life. Hadn't he called her his Best Girl? He even had a special little wink he'd give her when siding with her behind her mother's back. She remembered the mornings he used to wake her while it was still dark to take her fishing at the lake; they always stopped at Lundquist's for coffee and doughnuts on the way home—something he hadn't even done with Justin. But everything had changed since the divorce. Cindy was his Best Girl now. Andie was lucky if she saw him once a week.

"I probably wouldn't even recognize my dad if I saw him now," Simon said.

"She's flying down on Friday." In just three days. Andie felt panicky all of a sudden. "Mom's bringing her home for dinner. How weird will *that* be? I mean, we'll have everything under the sun to talk about . . . but I won't know what to say."

"She's probably just as nervous about meeting you, so you'll have that in common at least. By the way, does *she* have a name?"

"Claire."

"What does she do?"

"She's a lawyer, I think."

"That should be good for at least fifteen minutes. After that you'll just have to wing it." He reached over to give her hand another squeeze. "Don't worry. It'll be all right."

"Easy for you to say." Simon could have conversed quite comfortably with the Dalai Lama.

They fell silent, both lost in their thoughts. They had turned off Agua Caliente and were climbing the steep winding road to Lorei-Linda. On either side of them rose sheer sandstone bluffs scrawled with manzanita and sage. Andie remembered her sixth grade teacher telling them that in ancient times this whole valley had once been part of the ocean floor. As Simon's plucky little car chugged its way upward she imagined them to be sea creatures drifting toward the surface.

They passed Alice and Wes's house, built in levels that jutted like steel and glass risers from the rocky staircase of the hill. Half a mile or so beyond, on an even steeper bluff, stood the house that one magazine had labeled "Monica's mausoleum." Andie could see it glittering in the distance like a temple atop Mount Olympus. Not until they drew closer was it swallowed up by the dense trees that surrounded it like a fortress. Simon drew to a stop before a pair of tall, scrolled wrought iron gates.

He stuck his head out the window and announced crisply into the intercom, "Simon Winthrop. I have a four-thirty with Miss Vincent." As if it were every day that he dropped in on movie stars.

A buzzer sounded and the gates swung open with a low, ominous squeal. Slowly they made their way up a crushed gravel drive that glittered in the bright afternoon sunlight. A lawn worthy of the greens at Dos Palmas rolled away on either side, bordered in low-growing shrubs and shaded here and there by majestic old trees. She watched a squirrel scamper over the grass like a fugitive on the run. It was the first sign of life she'd seen.

They parked under the trees at the edge of the turnabout and got out. The house loomed before them, imposing and slightly surreal with its stone lions flanking the curving steps and soaring Greek columns. There was a fanlight over the front door like the one at her grandmother's, only more elaborate, its frosted glass panels etched with graceful designs of fruit and flowers. On each side of the door was a large bronze urn.

Simon reached for her hand. "Relax. It'll be a piece of cake."

His knock was answered by a plump, mousy-haired woman in a plain white blouse and denim skirt whom Andie recognized from church as Anna Vincenzi—Monica's sister. Anna looked at her in confusion, then gathered her wits and said graciously, "Andie! What a nice surprise. I wasn't expecting you." She turned to Simon, extending her hand. "Hi. We spoke over the phone. I'm Miss Vincezi's assistant, Anna."

It sounded so strange, Anna referring to her own sister that way, but Monica probably insisted on it. Andie wondered how Anna stood it.

Simon shook her hand. "I hope you don't mind that I brought my—" he glanced at Andie— "colleague."

"No, not at all." Anna flushed, and Andie had the feeling Monica might not be so agreeable. "Please, come in. I'll tell her you're here."

They were ushered into a tiled hallway that opened onto a sun-washed atrium ringed with trees in Chinese porcelain tubs. The living room beyond was even more palatial, with its floor-to-ceiling windows offering a breathtaking view of the valley. Andie padded across a cream-colored carpet that was like soft grass underfoot, lowering herself stiffly into a gilt-legged chair.

"I have a feeling we're not in Kansas any-more." She spoke in a hushed tone.

"You can say that again."

Simon was strolling about as if in a museum, pausing to gaze at a portrait of Monica over the fireplace. She must have been in her early twenties when it was painted, and though in her forties now she hardly seemed to have aged. The same flowing auburn hair and emerald eyes, the same million-dollar smile.

He turned at the faint sound of an elevator whining to a halt. A moment later Anna reappeared, pushing Monica in her wheelchair. In her pale green silk top and matching trousers, a string of pearls draped about her long white neck, she might have been a queen upon her throne. Her scent wafted toward them, light and flowery.

"Hello, hello," she called merrily. "Sorry to have kept you waiting. As you can see," she patted the arms of her wheelchair, "I don't get around as quickly as I used to."

Andie blinked at her in surprise. Was this the same Monica Vincent who'd reduced Dawn Parrish, from the Blue Moon, to tears after Dawn had accidentally splashed coffee on her blouse? *This* Monica was as charming as the heartbreaker-with-a-heart-of-gold roles for which she'd been famous.

Simon stepped forward, putting his hand out. "Simon Winthrop. And this is my, uh, associate, Andrea Bayliss." He gestured toward Andie. "It's an honor to finally meet you, Miss Vincent. I've seen every one of your movies, most of them twice."

"Well, aren't you sweet." She smiled coquettishly, revealing a dimple in one cheek. "I'll admit when you called I didn't know whether to keep you or throw you back. What could a boy your age want with an old lady like me?" She looked as if she knew very well what any red-blooded teenage boy might want with her, crippled or not. "But I confess curiosity got the better of me."

Simon seized the opportunity to jump right in. "Look, I'm sure you're tired of people telling you they love your movies—especially *Northern Lights,* that scene at your mother's grave, which is art, true art—so I won't bore you with all that. What I'm after is you as a person. Your likes and dislikes, what interests you, stuff like that."

"I'm afraid you'll find me rather dull." Monica lowered her head, looking up at him from a seductive sidelong angle. "Please, sit down." She gestured toward the sectional sofa, piled with cushions, that would've seated an entire entourage. "Would you like something to drink—iced tea, soda?"

"Iced tea would be nice," Andie piped.

Simon sank down on the sofa. "I'll take a Coke if you have one."

"The usual for me." Monica barely glanced up at her sister, poised at her elbow. Anna nodded, retreating silently into the next room. "Now, where were we?"

Simon pulled a minirecorder from his backpack. "Mind if I turn this on?"

Monica waved disinterestedly, which seemed odd, considering how paranoid she was said to be. Clearly she didn't view Simon as a threat. "So, you're a fan of *Northern Lights*," she said. "You're also a clever boy. You know very well that we actresses never, ever get tired of hearing about ourselves. It's true what they say, every bit of it. Vanity, vanity." She gave an airy laugh that did nothing to dispel the underlying bitterness in her voice. "Of course I have far less to be vain about these days." She cast a longing look at the portrait over the fireplace.

That was Simon's cue to say, "I don't see why you couldn't still make movies. I mean, with that face . . ."

She brightened. "Thank you, dear boy, but I'm afraid there isn't much demand for crippled actresses these days." Andie sensed a vulnerability that made her almost likable.

Simon asked, "What about TV?"

"I've had a few offers. Nothing too interesting." Anna was back, and Monica snatched her drink from the tray she was carrying. "Anyway, why bother? I have more money than I could spend in two lifetimes. People think I sit around all day feeling sorry for myself?" She leaned forward, her mouth turning up in a smile that didn't reach her eyes. "The truth is I've never been happier. Isn't that right, Anna?"

"Yes . . . of course," Anna replied dutifully. Her gait seemed oddly stiff as she crossed the living room with the tray, handing Simon and Andie their drinks.

"What about volunteer work?" Simon wanted to know.

Monica gave her trilling little laugh. "Can you see me at a bake sale? Or collecting donations door to door? Oh, don't get the wrong idea—" She waved a manicured hand on which gold bangles jingled. "I'm involved in a number of charities. Why, just last month I donated a Russian sable to my dear friend Liz's amfAR auction, which, as you know, raises money for AIDS."

A fur coat she couldn't have had much use for here in sunny Carson Springs, Andie thought. In her mind she could see the Vincenzis' shabby little house down the road from Laura's and wondered what that money would have meant to Anna.

Simon glanced at his notes. "A coat valued at a hundred and forty thousand."

Monica looked impressed. "Well, well, I see you've done your homework. What else do you know about me, young man?" Her speech had grown oddly slurred, and Andie noticed the glass in her hand was empty. Clearly she'd been drinking before they arrived.

Simon didn't miss a beat. "You've had fourteen box office number ones, five Academy Award nominations, and an Oscar for your supporting role in *Wild Lilies.*"

"Which was more like a lead role," she sniffed. "But I suppose that's splitting hairs." She gestured toward the gleaming statuette on the mantel. "Go ahead. Pick it up. Don't be shy."

Simon rose to his feet, and Andie followed suit. The Oscar, standing between a pair of Chinese porcelain dogs, was heavier than it looked, and oddly thrilling to the touch. She pictured Monica onstage with it, beaming into the camera. How sad for her that it was the last acceptance speech she would ever give.

They talked more about her movies, and Monica told the story about her first big break, when she was "discovered" waiting tables in the Universal Studios canteen. All the standard stuff, including the tidbits about her three ex-husbands. Her only reference to the accident was the way she spoke about her life, as if it were divided into two parts, like B.C. and A.D. When she could no longer make movies, she told them, she'd gone home to Carson Springs.

"I was born and raised here," she said. "It makes sense that I be buried here as well." She said it jokingly, but there was something in her eyes that sent a chill up the back of Andie's neck, as if in a way Monica were already dead.

After downing a refill, she grew even more talkative, going on and on in a scathing tone

about various untruths that had been per-
petuated by the press. Like the rumor that
she'd been responsible for the breakup of
Roone Holloway's marriage, which anyone
could have told you was on the rocks long
before she appeared on the scene, she said.
And the even more insidious lie that she'd
neglected her poor old mother.

"Who pays for Mrs. Simmons to look after
her while you're at work?" she demanded of
Anna. "Who covers the bills her insurance
doesn't pick up? My God, do they expect me
to play Florence Nightingale on top of everything else?"

"You've been very generous, " Anna murmured, darting a worried glance at the glass
in Monica's hand.

"Christ. Half the time Mother doesn't even
know who I *am*. But what do those sleaze
mongers know? All they care about is dragging me through the mud." Her lovely face
had turned hard, her mouth twisted in an
ugly sneer. "*Now* it's different. They feel sorry
for me. Poor, crippled Monica. You want to
know why I don't give interviews? *Turn that
fucking thing off!*" she shrieked, stabbing a
finger at the recorder. "I'll tell you why. Be-

cause they don't give a damn about the truth. The blood-sucking bastards—they're only interested in what sells."

"Monica, your five-thirty?" Anna tapped her watch in an attempt to cut the interview short.

Simon took the hint and quickly rose. "Thank you, Miss Vincent. I think I have enough to go on." He cast a meaningful glance at Andie, who shot to her feet as well. "I don't want to take up any more of your time."

"Sweet boy." Monica's tirade had passed like a summer squall. When Simon offered his hand, she patted it before turning to smile blearily at Andie. "I'd keep an eye on him if I were you. Otherwise, some smart girl is going to snatch him up."

"I . . ." Andie didn't know what to say. "Thanks for the . . . everything."

Anna seemed tense and distracted as she showed them to the door. Why did she put up with it? Surely she could have gotten a job elsewhere. Did she know that her sister was referred to around town as the Bitch on Wheels? Any one of a dozen shopkeepers would've hired Anna out of pure sympathy alone.

Andie was halfway down the steps when

Anna called after her, "Oh, I almost forgot. Please thank your mother for the honey."

"Sure, I'll tell her." She found the reminder of her mother's thoughtfulness—Mom was always giving away jars of Blessed Bee honey—vaguely uncomfortable for some reason. "Um, I guess I'll see you at the wedding. You're coming, aren't you?"

Anna looked blank for a moment, then brightened visibly. "The wedding. Yes, of course. I wouldn't miss it for the world." She pushed a hand through her lank brown hair, her eyes inexplicably misting over. "Sorry. I'd better . . ." She gestured weakly toward the back of the house. "It was nice meeting you, Simon. Thank you for . . . for not saying anything. She, uh, gets a little down sometimes."

"Understandably so," Simon replied.

"You won't—?"

"I'm just a kid, remember? What do I know?" He flashed her his innocently boyish grin, poking at the glasses that had slipped partway down his nose.

Anna looked relieved. "Thanks."

They were in the car, heading down the drive, when Andie ventured timidly, "You meant what you said, didn't you? You won't say anything about—"

"Her being drunk?" Simon filled in. "Don't worry. I have something a lot more interesting in mind."

She didn't dare think what Monica might do to him otherwise. "You were wonderful back there," she told him. "I'm not sure I'd have handled it as well."

"Does that mean you'll sleep with me?" He tipped her a devilish wink. It was an ongoing campaign, though to Simon's credit he never cajoled or bullied. Andie almost wished he would—it would make him a lot easier to resist.

A short while later they were pulling up in front of her house. It was one of the oldest in the neighborhood, and looked it. Her mother refused to have it painted; she liked its weathered sepia look and the vines crawling up the sides. She kept the hedge shaggy, too, saying she didn't want it to look like every other one on the block. But what, Andie wanted to know, was so great about sticking out like a sore thumb?

"Want to come in?" she asked. Justin was at Nesto's, no doubt, and Mom not due home for hours.

Simon needed no further encouragement. The house was quiet, there was only the wound of Buster's barking in the backyard. Sunlight slanted in through the blinds, casting a ladder of shadow over the carpet and the vintage apothecary chest with its dozens of little drawers in which matchbooks and takeout menus, old letters and lists, sewing patterns and stray buttons from shirts were stowed.

She turned to Simon. "Hungry?"

He shook his head. He was looking at her in a way that made her stomach feel as if it had dropped out from under her. "Why don't we listen to some music instead?"

Andie's heart quickened. He meant in her room, of course.

She met his gaze and shivered a little, wondering, *Am I ready for this?*

Being a virgin wasn't something she was proud of. It was just a promise she'd made to her mother way back when Mom had sat her down for the little heart-to-heart about where babies came from. If her mom had told her to wait until she was married or she'd go to hell—like the nuns in catechism were always saying—she probably would've done It already. But she'd been so reasonable, saying only that Andie should wait until she was sure, until it meant something.

But Andie hadn't known then that her mother was full of shit.

Now a defiant voice whispered in her head, *It's not like you'd be doing anything* she *hasn't done.*

She led the way down the hall to her room, suddenly conscious of the stuffed animals heaped on the bed, the bookcase lined with childhood favorites like *Winnie-the-Pooh* and *Charlotte's Web,* the Backstreet Boys poster she'd long since outgrown but hadn't gotten around to taking down.

She sank down on the bed, feeling a queer lightness in the pit of her stomach. Simon just stood there, looking down at her uncertainly, his hands stuffed into the front pockets of his jeans. She couldn't help smiling. Any other guy would've been all over her by now.

He slipped a CD into the player—the Sarah Vaughan he'd loaned her in an attempt to interest her in jazz—before sitting down next to her on the bed. He looked nervous, though she couldn't think why—they'd fooled around before. It occurred to Andie that *she* would have to take the initiative.

She flopped onto her back. "Aren't you going to kiss me?"

Simon grinned. "I thought you were never going to ask."

She loved the way he kissed—not too wet, and with just the right amount of pressure. She parted her lips, and felt the tip of his tongue playing over hers. The queer lightness in her belly drifted lower, settling like a warm hand between her legs. With her eyes closed she could have been anywhere—a smoky nightclub, or cheap motel like in *Thelma and Louise*.

His kisses deepened, becoming more urgent. She could feel him pressing into her leg, and thought how uncomfortable it must be, all folded over inside his jeans. She unzipped them and pushed her hand inside. She'd touched him once before, but only tentatively and somewhat surreptitiously—as if brushing up against it by accident. Now she boldly explored. It was soft, like rose petals, and marbled with veins that pulsed beneath her fingertips. Simon moaned, placing a hand over hers and moving it up and down until she got the hang of it. After only a few strokes, he abruptly pulled away.

"Stop. I'll come." He sounded hoarse and short of breath.

They undressed to Sarah's sultry crooning. She'd never been fully naked with him before. They'd always stopped short of taking off their underwear. Now she stared at him.

Divested of jeans and jockey shorts, it looked even bigger, rising emphatically from its dark nest of hair. Finch had given her some idea of what to expect, but Andie had never imagined it to be so . . . well, clearly it meant business. She shuddered, folding her arms over her breasts.

Simon took his time. They kissed some more before he gently inserted a finger between her legs. It felt good, and she closed her eyes, letting the warm sensations wash over her like when she touched herself under the covers at night. After a minute or so, she pushed his hand away, whispering, "I'm ready now."

But Simon just lay there, breathing heavily. At last, he croaked, "I don't have a condom." With his glasses off, his hazel eyes wore an odd, unfocused look.

"Oh." It had never occurred to her that he wouldn't be prepared.

"Would . . . would it be okay if I pulled out in time?"

"We shouldn't." She'd heard all the lectures—pulling out in time was no guarantee.

On the other hand, there was about as much chance of her getting pregnant this way as of her parents getting back together. "But I guess it'd be okay . . . just this once."

Simon looked as if he knew better, too, but for once his brain was overruled. He lowered himself onto her, easing in a little bit at a time. His cheeks were flushed, and his hair stuck to his forehead in damp little whorls. "I'm not hurting you, am I?"

"No."

"If it hurts, tell me and I'll stop."

"Maybe you're not in far en—"

She gasped, feeling a hot burst of pain. Not as bad as she'd expected. Then he was moving inside her with careful strokes. The bed beneath her grew damp—blood?—but such thoughts were quickly swallowed by the warm waves of pleasure coursing through her. So this was what all the talk was about. Yet no one could have prepared her for how good it felt—all warm and silky and sweet, like chocolate melting, not just in your mouth, but throughout your whole body.

Simon groaned and with a sharp jerk withdrew. She felt something warm spill onto her thigh. After a moment he drew away, muttering, "Sorry. Close call."

She touched the wetness on her thigh. Its smell was that of an overly chlorinated swimming pool. "Are you sure you pulled out in time?"

He nodded. "Did you—?"

Andie shook her head, smiling to let him know it was okay. "That was your first time, wasn't it?" He'd been evasive about it in the past, alluding to one or two possible encounters.

Simon's flush deepened. "Would you think any less of me if I said it was?"

"Why would I?"

"I don't know. The whole macho thing."

"Since when do you care about being macho?"

"You're right. It's stupid."

"Was it what you expected?" she asked.

He grinned. "Let's just say it beats a solo act."

For a long while they just lay there, gazing up at the ceiling. In the backyard Buster had begun to bark again, and through the open window drifted the faint smell of meatloaf— Mrs. Corliss next door always made meatloaf on Wednesdays. At last Simon got up to use the bathroom. She heard the tap running, and a moment later he returned carrying a damp washcloth, which he used to gently wipe the blood from between her legs. When they were both dressed, he helped her bundle up the stained bedspread. If her mother found it, she'd say it was her period.

Simon put his arms around her. "In movies this is the part where the guy says, 'I love you.'"

"You need a soundtrack for that."

"Like this?" He hummed a few off-key bars of "Memory."

She smiled. "You better quit while you're ahead."

"Okay, but only if you promise you'll still respect me in the morning."

"Which reminds me . . ." She drew away. "If I don't get started on this paper I'll be up all night."

Anyone else would have taken it as their cue to leave, but not Simon. He sat down on the bed, waiting patiently while she dug around in her backpack until she found her battered copy of *Of Human Bondage.* "Okay," he said, "the thing to remember about Maugham is that he was gay, so a lot of people think that when he wrote about Philip's obsession with Mildred he was really writing about . . ."

The following morning Finch caught up with her at her locker. "You hear what happened? That dufus Freischman almost set the chem lab on fire."

"Really?" Andie twirled her combination lock. She'd been up half the night working on her paper (which she never would have finished on time if it hadn't been for Simon) and was more than a little out of it.

"You should've heard Wonderlich scream at him."

"Mmm," Andie murmured.

Out of the corner of her eye she spotted muscleman Russ Benadetto, an arm looped about his girlfriend, blond school spirit commissioner Shannon Harris, coming their way. It was only a little past ten-thirty in the morning and already he was sporting the onset of five o'clock shadow. Shannon, who sat next to Andie in Spanish, swept past them without a glance.

Finch gave Andie The Look—the one that said weren't they lucky to have their own ex-

clusive club while freaks like Russ and
Shannon only *thought* they were one up.

"Hey, what's with you?" she asked when
Andie didn't react.

"Huh? Uh, nothing." She barely glanced at
Finch before going back to twirling her lock.
This was the second time she'd tried it; she
must have gotten the numbers mixed up.

"Nothing, my ass. You've been acting
weird all morning." Finch leaned close, her
hair swinging away from her shoulders in a
silky dark curtain. "You still pissed at your
mom?"

"I'm not pissed. I was never *pissed*. Anyway, I can't talk about it right now." She
glanced over her shoulder at Russ's and
Shannon's retreating backs. Finch was the
only one besides Simon who knew about
Claire, and she'd just as soon keep it that
way. "Damn. This thing must be broken." She
banged on it with the heel of her hand. If she
didn't get it open, she'd be late for Mr. Hillman's class.

"Okay, we'll talk about it at lunch." Finch
impatiently brushed her hand aside and
gave the lock several expert twists. The door
popped open.

"Thanks." Andie gave her a sheepish look.

Finch waved as she headed off to class, a slender dark-haired girl in jeans and funky red top who bore little resemblance to the girl Andie had met for the first time last summer. She remembered waiting on Finch at Rusk's, how withdrawn she'd been, in a mysterious sort of way, as uncertain about Andie as she was about the boots she was trying on. It wasn't until they'd gotten to know each other that she began to open up. Andie was astonished to learn that Finch had spent twelve of her sixteen years being shunted from one foster home to another before running away last year. She was the only one of Andie's friends, even the ones whose parents were divorced, who'd understood completely about her father. Finch didn't have to ask why Andie and her brother didn't spend Sunday afternoons eating Happy Meals at McDonald's with their dad.

An hour and a half later they were seated on the lawn, which skirted the administration building on one side and math and sciences on the other, rolling in a gentle slope to the parking lot and bus stop below. The flagpole stood dead center, and served as the compass by which various factions were grouped. The freshmen, lowest in the pecking order, sat closest to the parking lot, with the sophomores occupying the meridian just above. The area north of the flagpole was informally reserved for upperclassmen like Andie and Finch, with the more popular kids lining the benches along the quad.

"Have you picked out a dress yet?" Andie asked, biting into her tuna fish sandwich. Laura's wedding was less than a month away and Finch still had no idea what she was going to wear.

Finch rolled her eyes. "Don't remind me."

"At least you don't have to wear an ugly one that someone else picked out." Finch was the maid of honor, but since the wedding was so casual she'd been given free rein to choose her own dress.

"That's one way of looking at it," she said. "On the other hand, nobody will care what I'm wearing. The only thing those people will see"—her expression darkened—"is the loser who crashed Alice's wedding."

Andie hadn't gone to Laura's sister's wedding last summer—that was the weekend her dad, in a misguided attempt to get her and Justin to bond with Cindy, had taken them to Tahoe—but she'd heard all about it.

Who hadn't? Finch had shown up halfway through the reception, filthy and starved—she'd been on the road for days with little to eat—and was caught stealing food off the buffet table. Lucky for her Laura had taken pity and brought her back to the ranch. Finch had been there ever since.

"Who cares what anyone thinks?" Andie said. "You've got me—and Laura and Hector and Maude. What else matters?"

Finch shrugged. "Yeah, I know, it's just that I worry sometimes. About not fitting in."

Andie felt privileged that Finch would confide such a thing to her, knowing her friend would sooner cut off her big toe than admit that to anyone else. "You're a million times better than those bozos." She gestured toward Russ and Shannon, seated on one of the benches surrounded by their equally snobby friends, all of them laughing uproariously at some joke—probably one that was at someone else's expense.

"I just hope I don't trip coming down the aisle," Finch said darkly. The permanent crease between her heavy dark brows, which grew more marked when she was worried or upset, was deeply indented and her olive-skinned cheeks stamped with color.

"Lucky for you there isn't going to be one." The ceremony was taking place on a hilltop.

"You know what I mean. The only one looking forward to this wedding less than me is Hector." A corner of her mouth hooked up. "I think he'd just as soon get married with just the four of us and a justice of the peace."

"Well, it'll be over soon. Then everything will be back to normal." She thought about Claire, and her stomach did a little flip-flop. Life in her house would never again be normal.

Finch's brow smoothed, and she leaned back with her elbows planted in the grass. "Yeah, well, what's normal? I'd have to look it up in the dictionary. My definition was being at the same address for more than a few months."

"I know what you mean. Nothing's been the same since my parents got divorced," Andie said, careful to add, "Not that I ever had it as bad as you."

Finch turned to her, squinting against the sunlight. "Does your dad know about your sister?"

Andie felt a familiar hollow open up in the

pit of her stomach. "He was in the middle of something when I called so we didn't get much of a chance to talk." The truth was he hadn't seemed to think it was such a big deal, only commenting mildly that it might be nice for her to have a big sister. "Anyway, it's not like he can *do* anything. I mean, I'm sort of stuck with her, aren't I?"

Finch tossed a crust from her sandwich to a sparrow pecking in the grass at their feet. "It might not be as bad as you think. She might be okay."

"On the other hand, she might not."

"Either way, it's only one person." Finch sat up and tucked the rest of her sandwich into her bag. Andie had noticed that she seldom finished a meal, as if to remind herself that she always knew where her next one was coming from. "Me? Every time I'd go to a new family I'd have a whole boatload of relatives to get to know."

"It must've been rough."

A cloud seemed to pass over Finch's face, with its high Indian cheekbones and dusky skin that made Andie think of the fabled Princess Matilija, buried on Mount Matilija beside her lover. She looked at Andie with her dark eyes that had seen so much and revealed so little. "You get used to it."

Andie felt small and selfish all of a sudden. Was she making too big a deal of this?

She glanced over at the flagpole, where one of the sophomore girls was giggling with her friends, all of them looking straight at Mr. Hillman, scurrying past with his head tucked low. Earlier in the day she'd heard that some anonymous joker had scrawled "X + Y = QUEER" on his blackboard. She wondered if it was what Russ and his friends had thought so hilarious.

"I suppose she couldn't be as bad as Monica," she conceded.

Finch's eyes widened with interest. Andie had only given her the highlights, and she was eager to know more. "I still can't believe you actually *went* to her house."

"We were there almost an hour. She was pretty drunk by the time we left."

"Other than that, what was she like?"

Andie thought for a moment. What was the one thing that summed up Monica? "She seemed sad."

Finch snorted. "Yeah, right. With all her money?"

"I think she'd trade it all for someone who truly loved her."

"She's been married a few times, hasn't she? Never mind, I take it back." They exchanged a look. They both knew that love and marriage didn't always go hand in hand. "I've heard she's slept with half the men in town. Do you think it's true?"

Andie remembered the way Monica had batted her eyelashes at Simon. "I think she likes the attention. Aside from that, don't believe everything you hear." She thought about what had happened afterward, at the house, and the sun beating down overhead grew that much warmer all of a sudden.

Andie looked up to find Finch's dark gaze fixed on her. "Yeah, even if she was sleeping around, what's the big deal? I mean, it's not like she's hurting anyone, right?"

"Why the sudden interest in Monica's love life?"

"I didn't mean just Monica. I meant in general. If someone happened to get it on with her boyfriend, say."

"What are you implying?" Andie narrowed her eyes at Finch.

"Nothing." Finch plucked at the grass, wearing an innocent expression. "It's just that I ran into Simon after first period, and when I mentioned you he turned beet red. Is something going on with you guys that I don't know about?" Andie hesitated just long enough for Finch to get the message. She let out a little squeal. "You *did* it. God, I can't believe you didn't tell me!"

"And spoil the fun of letting you figure it out yourself?" Andie's cheeks felt as if they were on fire, and she glanced about to see if anyone had noticed.

"Okay, give it up." Finch made a beckoning motion.

Andie shrugged. It was no use—Finch would get it out of her one way or another. "Yesterday after we got back from Monica's we kind of hung out in my room . . . and, well, you know . . ." She let the sentence trail off.

Finch, her dark eyes gleaming, leaned close to ask in a hushed voice, "How was it?"

"Okay, I guess." It had been better than okay, but she didn't want to rub it in. Finch was no virgin herself—far from it—but that period in her life, before she moved here, wasn't something she looked back on fondly.

"I hope he was wearing something."

"Not exactly."

"What do you mean? Either he was or he wasn't."

"He pulled out in time."

Finch groaned. "That old line. God, I can't believe you fell for it."

"I didn't really think it through at the time."

"Let's hope you don't get pregnant."

It occurred to Andie then that it wasn't a case of *getting* pregnant—if Simon hadn't pulled out in time she would already *be* pregnant. A shiver went through her, and she was suddenly conscious of the damp ground beneath her, filled with all sorts of live, squirming things.

The bell shrilled just then and they crumpled up their paper bags, brushing crumbs from their laps. They were making their way to third-period gym, the only class they shared, when Andie turned to her and asked, "Am I making too big a deal of this?"

"What—Simon?"

"No, *her.*" The two were suddenly tied up together in her mind, for if she were pregnant wouldn't it be history repeating itself? She'd be in the same boat her mom had been in.

"You won't know until you meet her," Finch

said with the air of someone well versed in such matters.

Andie felt a hole open up inside her chest. She used to believe in wishes coming true, but now knew that was as silly as believing in the Easter bunny. But suppose she could have one wish right now—what would it be? A year or so ago it would have been for her dad to come home, which, as much as she hated to admit it, would have been a disaster. Now it was more of a feeling than a wish . . . of being part of a jagged half that she'd give anything to have whole again. A feeling, she thought darkly, that would only get worse when her mother's bastard arrived on the scene.

Chapter Five

Friday, the day of Claire's visit, dawned cool and cloudy. At breakfast the children were more subdued than usual, especially Andie, who bolted her cereal and dashed off to catch the bus without a word. Gerry scarcely noticed; she was far too preoccupied. Though anyone watching her go about her business would have mistaken it for an air of supreme tranquillity. At work she floated through the morning. From her office in the chapter house, down the hall from the mother superior's, she answered e-mail, tracked orders, and fielded inquiries from several stores interested in carrying Blessed Bee's wares, her mind racing all the while.

What if she doesn't like me? What if the kids don't like her?

She glanced at the digital clock on her desk. Ten to eleven. In a little more than an hour she'd be face-to-face with Claire. Her stomach did a slow cartwheel. No one here knew; she hadn't even told Mother Ignatius. It was enough that a few of the older nuns, the reverend mother included (a number of the others had since passed away), remembered why she'd left the convent all those years ago. They didn't need their noses rubbed in the fact that she had an illegitimate daughter.

When the phone rang, she jumped a little, then snatched it up. "Blessed Bee. Gerry Fitzgerald speaking."

"Will you hold for Marian Abrams?" a female voice inquired.

Gerry searched her mental database. Marian Abrams, yes—the editor from *West* magazine looking to do a feature on Blessed Bee. Gerry had told her she'd get back to her.

Another voice came on the line, deeper

and more assured. "Gerry, I'm glad I caught you. Listen, I was wondering if you've had a chance to look over that stuff I faxed you?"

Gerry racked her brain as she pawed through the reams of faxes on her desk. "We're still a little backed up from the holidays," she said. "Why don't you refresh my memory?"

"The samples from the freelance writer I'd like to use for the piece," Marian said. "She's done quite a bit of work for us in the past, and I think she'd be sensitive in handling, ah, certain issues."

"Such as?" Gerry smiled. Most people assumed that nuns were either one card shy of a deck—or once removed from celestial beings.

"Well, for one thing, how this whole moneymaking operation fits with a life of prayer and contemplation."

Gerry gave a throaty laugh. "Nobody's getting rich, believe me. Most of the income from Blessed Bee goes to the upkeep of the convent. As for the contemplative life, you'd be surprised how much praying you can do with your sleeves rolled up. If you find one of the sisters on her knees, it's likely she'll be scrubbing floors."

And wouldn't Marian Abrams be surprised to learn that nuns weren't above a practical joke? Like Sister John putting sugar in the salt shaker, or the little joke Sister Agnes had played on one of the postulants last spring, instructing her to plant the seeds pointy end down so the zucchini wouldn't grow underground like turnips. The poor girl had yet to live it down.

"I see we have our work cut out for us as well—starting with debunking a few myths," Marian replied with a chuckle. "Why don't we schedule a date to meet in person?"

Gerry glanced longingly at her calendar. "I'll speak to the reverend mother." Mother Ignatius—torn between pride in Blessed Bee and fear that they were becoming a tourist attraction, especially after what had happened following the article in *People,* when curiosity seekers began showing up, snapping photos and peering through the gates—was famous for turning down interview requests. "If she gives it the green light, we'll set something up."

"Fair enough. I'll wait to hear from you, then." There was a polite beat, then Marian added firmly, "Don't take too long, though. I was hoping to slate this for our July issue."

"I'll get back to you on Monday."

Gerry hung up with a sigh. It wasn't just the article in *People.* Earlier this year the newspaper and TV coverage generated by Sister Beatrice's arrest had sent them back into the dark ages as far as public opinion was concerned. One tabloid even had the gall to suggest she'd killed those people out of sexual frustration gone awry. Our Lady *needed* more pieces like the one Marian Abrams was proposing so people could see that, in many ways, its nuns were no different than anyone else. But try telling Mother Ignatius. Paul had had an easier time converting the Romans.

Never mind. She'd deal with it on Monday. There was only enough time now for a quick word with Sister Carmela. Earlier in the week the hive mistress had spoken to Gerry about an infestation in one of the colonies, and though they had enough bottled honey to last until spring, when the wintering hives would be back in production, the poor woman was beside herself. Gerry needed to find out just how bad it was.

She stepped out into the corridor, leaving the door to her office unlocked. At Our Lady, trust was never an issue; it would have been unthinkable for one of the sisters to help herself to a paperclip without asking. And if someone had a problem with something you'd done, she'd tell you to your face. In that way, Gerry was about as far from the corporate world as she could get. Which was why she couldn't imagine working anywhere else. After twenty-eight years this was her second home.

Gerry remembered when old Mother Jerome had approached her about becoming lay manager of Blessed Bee. It was only a few months after she'd given birth to Claire, and she'd been so heartsick she could scarcely get out of bed each morning, much less face another grueling day searching for a job. Word of her predicament must have reached the mother superior, for she phoned Gerry, inviting her to tea.

The old woman had cut right to the chase. "I hear you're having trouble finding work. Not surprising, considering your rather unique qualifications." She smiled, a tiny woman hunched with age holding her teacup in both gnarled hands to keep it from spilling. "Now, now, there's no need for tears—I didn't invite you up for that. The fact is, we could use you here."

Gerry couldn't stop the tears from flowing. "I don't see how I could be of any help." She'd stared down at her plate, on which a scone lay split and glistening with honey. Falling back on the gallows humor that had served her well through the years, she'd lifted her head to add with a small, tremulous smile, "Unless you want me around as a reminder of the perils of falling from grace."

"Horse apples." Mother Jerome was not above the occasional mild expletive. "I'm not looking to make an example of you—goodness, child, I have better things to do. We need someone to see to the business end of Blessed Bee, someone well versed in convent life who can interface with the outside world, and I can't think of anyone more qualified than you."

The reverend mother smiled. "Don't you want to know what your salary will be?"

"I don't have to know," she said. "Whatever it is, I'll take it."

She'd gone to work the very next day, and had been there ever since.

Now she glanced down the corridor to find it empty; even the reception area was deserted. But she was used to that by now. As she stepped outside, a sweet chorus of voices drifted from the direction of the chapel: the chanting of the midmorning office. She paused on the steps, closing her eyes to take in the ancient rhythms of worship. The sun had come out, casting a dappled greenish light over the cloister garden, where tools lay abandoned willy-nilly and a half-drunk glass of soda was attracting flies. Seven times a day, at precise intervals, the sisters dropped everything and headed for the chapel to chant the liturgy of the hours. Needless to say, no one was without a watch.

She stepped down onto the path where she would be sure to catch Sister Carmela on her way out of chapel. The garden lay furled, awaiting spring. As Gerry strolled along, she looked about at the mulched flower beds and bare rosebushes, the skeletal arbor that in a few months would be dripping with wisteria blossoms. By then Sister Agnes and her crew would be going full tilt: their sleeves rolled over their elbows and the hems of their habits tucked up into their belts, declaring war on the weeds and insects. Even the stone statue of Saint John presiding over the medieval knot garden would be given a good scrubbing.

"Since when do you pass an old friend without saying hello?"

Startled, she looked about to find Father Reardon seated on the bench under the weeping willow half hidden by its branches. She smiled apologetically. "Sorry, Dan. I guess my mind was elsewhere."

"You *do* need a vacation." His blue eyes crinkled.

"Vacation? I'll have to look that one up in the dictionary." She cocked her head, looking down at him with mock sternness. "Might I ask what you're doing here, spying on innocent people going about their business?"

He sighed, pushing a hand through his unruly black hair streaked with silver at the temples. "I wish I could say I was up to no good—it's Sister Seraphina."

"Is she—?"

Dan shook his head. "False alarm." This was the third time he'd been called out to say last rites, yet old Sister Seraphina, one of the order's founding members, who was well into her nineties, somehow managed to hang on—if only by a thread. "As you can see, I'm taking a little breather." He inhaled deeply, looking about in appreciation. As if,

in the face of death, it was good to be reminded of what made life worth living.

Gerry didn't know whether to be sorry or
relieved. Clinging to life like Sister Seraphina
was no way to go. "When it's my time," she
told him, "I'd like a huge wave to wash me
out to sea."

"Knowing you, that won't be for quite
some time." He patted the bench beside him.
"Have a seat."

Gerry glanced at her watch. She supposed Sister Carmela could wait. "All right,"
she said, sinking down on the bench, "but
only for a minute. I have to be somewhere."

Dan leaned back, stretching his legs out
in front of him: every Irish mother's dream in
his black suit and white collar—and every
unmarried woman's with his sparkling blue
eyes and broad shoulders straining at his
seams. "And where is it you're rushing off to
this fine day?"

She thought of Claire, and her stomach
executed another cartwheel. "I'm meeting
someone for lunch."

He glanced at his watch. "It's still early."

"You know me—always jumping the gun,"
she said, not wanting to get into it. "My

mother is forever saying that one day I'll get there ahead of myself."

"How is your mother? I didn't see her in church last Sunday."

"Fine—at least that's what she always says. With her dying breath she'll be telling you to put the kettle on and don't bother with a tray, she'll be down in just a bit." Gerry shook her head, though Dan was probably thinking the apple didn't fall far from the tree. "The truth is her health isn't what it used to be. I've been trying to get her to sell that old white elephant of hers, but she won't hear of it."

"She's better off than Sister Seraphina, at least." He eyed a robin perched on the mossy lip of the birdbath. "Why don't I stop by sometime next week? Sounds as if she could use a bit of cheering up."

"She'd love it. Just be sure to bring an empty stomach."

He laughed heartily. "I haven't forgotten the pineapple upside-down cake she made the last time—I had three slices. Don't think I don't have an ulterior motive here."

"Well, she'll be glad to see you either way."

Gerry watched as the robin, with a flurry

of feathers, sent out a spray of droplets that caught the sunlight, sparkling like diamonds.

"What about you? You haven't stopped by the rectory in ages," the priest scolded, studying her intently. "And don't tell me it's because you're too busy. That excuse is worn out."

Gerry felt herself grow warm. From the chapel, wafting like a gentle breeze, came the final chorus of the office: *Glory to the Father, and to the Son, and to the Holy Spirit. As it was in the beginning, is now and will be forever. Amen.*

"I should have told you before," she said.

He lifted a brow, waiting for her to go on.

Gerry drew in a breath smelling of damp earth. "The person I'm meeting? It's my daughter."

He looked confused. "Andie? Isn't she in school?"

"Not Andie. My *other* daughter."

His confusion turned to happy astonishment. "You've found her, then?"

"A few weeks ago."

"Well, then, this calls for a celebration!" He spread his hands—huge, rough hands more suited to the plow than the good book, some might say. "If I were a drinking man, I'd propose a good scotch."

"It would calm my nerves, at least," she said.

"You? Fearless Gerry?"

He knew her too well. This was the man who'd seen her face down an angry mob of Green Earth protesters getting ready to torch the newly built condominiums out by Horse Creek (she'd gotten them to sue instead).

"My kids weren't too happy when I told them."

He shrugged. "There's bound to be a rough patch or two."

"There's her father, too—she'll want to know about *him*."

Dan's ruddy face darkened and the light went out of his eyes. "So you'll tell her the truth—that he's a cold-hearted *shite* who brings shame to the collar he wears."Years ago, when she'd told him the whole ugly tale, she'd never seen Dan so angry. Time had done nothing to blunt his contempt.

For her part, she'd kept silent all these years, and if Father Gallagher's abrupt reassignment had aroused suspicion at the time, she'd done nothing to fan the flames. Nor had she tried to contact him. These days all she knew was what she heard through the grapevine: that he was a favorite to replace Bishop Cardiff when he retired. If word of this got out, it would destroy any possible chance he had.

But why should she care? Was he thinking of *her* when she got pregnant? There'd been no talk of birth control, which they both knew was a sin (as if what they were doing *wasn't*). But Jim hadn't had to live with the consequences. And if it weighed on his conscience at all, which she doubted, he didn't have to face a young woman full of questions for which there were no good answers, or wonder how this new person would fit into a family limping along on three legs.

But if she'd once been full of anger, only the bitter rind remained. "There were nights I used to lie awake thinking of all the ways I'd like to rearrange him. But," she sighed, "I don't know that I have the right to ruin a man's life."

"He didn't care whether or not he ruined yours."

She shot him a look of mild rebuke. "Aren't priests supposed to counsel forgiveness?"

"We're also supposed to keep our pants zipped," he countered without missing a beat. If she could name one fault in Father Dan, she thought, it was his Irish temper.

She smiled. "Well, when you put it that way . . ."

"Sorry. I didn't mean to get carried away." Dan's fists unfurled and he leaned over, propping his elbows on his knees and smiling sheepishly up at her. "Have you thought about contacting him? There has to be a civilized way of handling this."

She felt some of the old bitterness well up in her. "The last time I saw Jim Gallagher it was to tell him I was pregnant. He refused to take even the slightest responsibility. He kept saying I'd tricked him, that it was all my fault." Her mouth stretched in a cheerless smile. "The worst of it was that, at the time, I believed him."

"You don't feel that way now, I hope."

"No, but it was a long time ago. Do we really need to rake all that up?"

"You might not have a choice."

"I'll leave it up to Claire."

"A pretty name, Claire." He smiled.

"I would have chosen something different. Something with a little more flair."

"Such as?"

"Aileen, after my Irish grandmother."

"I had an aunt named Aileen. She was a big believer in spare the rod and spoil the child."

Gerry saw what he was up to here—he was trying to calm her fears—and felt a rush of affection. "All I want is a chance to get to know her. That's not too much to hope, is it?"

He was gazing out over the garden, with its stone paths winding in and out of view and ancient trees bowed with age. "Hope," he said, turning to her with a smile, "is but the poor cousin to faith. And that, my dear, you are blessed with in abundance."He rose with a sigh. "On that note, why don't I walk you to your car? After all this talk, I wouldn't want you to be late."

They'd scarcely started down the path when the sisters began emerging from the chapel, gliding silently onto the covered walkway that linked it to the chapter house. No one raised an eyebrow at the sight of Gerry strolling side by side with the handsome Father Reardon, (all the gossip about Jim had died down years ago), which was exactly how she intended to keep it.

The wrought iron gate creaked as he pushed it open and they stepped out onto the rose-lined drive. She waved good-bye as he climbed into his ancient Pontiac that looked as if it ran on a wing and a prayer. Moments later she was following the cloud of dust billowing in his wake—the sisters purposely kept the road unpaved to cut down on unwanted visitors—bumping over ruts and swerving to avoid potholes.

A troubling new thought occurred to her. What if Claire had changed her mind and decided not to come?

Her heart lurched. *No, she'd have called.*

Gerry was unaware that she was pressing too hard on the gas until her car hit a pothole and for a heart-stopping moment became airborne. Then the wheels hit ground with a jarring *thunk*, hard enough to bring her back teeth together with an audible click. She felt the car start to skid out of control and wrenched hard on the wheel, bringing it back into line. Relief sluiced through her and she began to laugh, a low breathless laugh that held a tiny note of hysteria. It hadn't occurred to her until now that she might be the one who, through no fault of her own, would stand up Claire.

A dozen miles away, Claire negotiated the steep, twisting grade overlooking the valley with the caution of someone who'd been taught from a very early age that most everything in life was an accident waiting to happen. She'd been driving for the better part of two hours and had made it without incident to the outskirts of Ventura, where the road hooked northeast onto Highway 33 and began to climb. Now there was nothing but steep sandstone bluffs on one side and only the narrowest of shoulders separating her from the precipitous dropoff on the other.

It seemed a metaphor for what lay ahead.

Why had she insisted on making this trip? She, of all people, should have known better. She was a lawyer, for God's sake. And wasn't it the first rule of strategy that you were always at an advantage on your home turf? It was why she saw a good number of clients in their homes, where they were more comfortable discussing life and death matters, and mapping out their estates.

Just then she rounded a curve and a graveled overlook swung into view. Scarcely realizing it, she found herself pulling over. As if in a trance she unbuckled her seat belt and got out. A gentle breeze was blowing, and she caught the faint scent of dry grass and sage. Spread out below was a vast tureen of a valley. At the eastern end a wooded lake gazed serenely up at the sky, and to the west a tumble of brown hills, dusky with chaparral, climbed to meet the snow-capped mountains in the distance. Orange groves, crisscrossed like neat rows of stitching, lay in green patches over the valley floor interspersed with clusters of buildings.

She drew closer to the edge, the wind catching her hair and blowing it about her face. She *knew* this place. Déjà vu was too strong a word; it was more a feeling that she belonged somehow. But that was crazy, wasn't it? She couldn't have been more than a few days old when she was taken from here.

She felt a sudden charged lightness, as if she were a spark the wind could snatch up and send spinning out over the scrub-dotted gully below. It didn't matter that after this she might never again see Gerry. The thing she'd wished for all her life was coming true: She was finally going to meet her birth mother.

Millie's words came back to haunt her: *She gave you away as if you were no more than a kitten.* But could Gerry have been so heartless? She hadn't seemed so over the phone. Only one thing was for sure: It had been easier when Gerry was a blank page.

Reluctantly, Claire turned away, her gaze falling on a bronze plaque mounted on a concrete base a few feet away, partially obscured by a tall silver-leafed bush. She peered at its age-blackened lettering. Something about the movie *Stranger in Paradise* having been shot on location here sometime in the fifties. Maybe that's why the terrain looked so familiar.

As she headed back to her car, she wondered what kind of movie *this* would end up being—a weepy melodrama, or one of those artsy-fartsy films in which everyone talks in circles and nothing ever happens? Either way, life was never going to be the same.

She pulled back onto the road to find herself on the downward slope. Nevertheless, it was several more miles before service stations and convenience marts began taking the place of boulders and scrub. Soon she was cruising along the main street of town, with its Spanish-style storefronts trimmed in bright mosaic tiles and its curbs dotted with citrus trees in clay tubs. Little things jumped out at her: a bright blue door festooned with a garland of dried chilies, an old merry-go-round horse sporting a new leather saddle, a pushcart stacked with boxes of fruits and vegetables as lovingly displayed as a jeweler's wares. On the corner, by the stoplight, stood the Depression-era post office pictured on the cover of the guidebook she'd bought. She gazed up at its gilded bell tower glittering in the late morning sun. It seemed a good omen somehow.

Following Gerry's directions, she made a left at the light. On the corner to her right was a tall oak rising above a funky, screened enclosure—what could only be the Tree House Café. She found a parking space and got out. Her hands were trembling as she fed money into the meter, and she dropped a quarter that rolled off into the bushes. She started to go after it, then, straightened with a low, tremulous laugh. How would it look if Gerry was to see her rooting in the bushes?

By the entrance to the enclosure was a rough-hewn bookcase lined with used paperbacks, with a slotted box for paying on the honor system. She pushed her way in through the screen door, stepping onto a patio roughly the size of a baseball diamond over which several dozen tables were scattered. There was a small clapboard building in back, and at the center stood the enormous live oak visible from the street. A tree house accessed by a stout ladder had been built into its lower branches, where several children scampered about, shrieking to one another. In the shade below people sat contentedly nibbling from their plates, some reading books no doubt culled from the crammed shelves in back.

She was greeted by a tanned, athletic-looking man in an open-necked shirt. She unstuck her tongue from the dry roof of her mouth long enough to tell him, "I'm meeting someone. Gerry Fitzgerald."

His smile broadened. He looked to be in his thirties—thick, wavy brown hair, brown eyes, Colgate teeth. "You must be Claire. She asked me to look out for you. Follow me."

She fell in behind him, glancing about in panic.

What if it was like *The Monkey's Paw*? A case of being careful what you wish for. Her gaze fell on a Naugahyde-skinned woman in tennis whites frowning at her menu. Two tables away sat a fat lady in a straw hat and garish muumuu asking in a loud voice about the day's specials. In the sunlight that fell in dappled pools at her feet Claire felt suddenly chilled.

This was a mistake. I shouldn't have come.

Why, oh why, hadn't she left well enough alone?

Gerry had arrived a few minutes before noon, just before the lunch-hour rush. She'd chatted briefly with David Ryback at the door. Little Davey was in the hospital again, and though David must have been under a tremendous strain shuttling back and forth, he seemed his usual laid-back self. She didn't know how he managed it. His days as a high school and college athlete, coupled with the years of working here under his dad, had trained him well.

David showed her to a shady table in back, pulling out a chair into which she sank like a lioness on its haunches, every muscle tensed. Mistaking her obvious nervousness for something else, he said with a wink, "I'll keep an eye out for him. What does he look like?"

"Actually, it's a she." Gerry realized she didn't know what her daughter looked like; she'd assumed she would recognize her.

Now she felt foolish. "About your age. Her name is Claire."

She ordered an iced tea and sipped it slowly. The minutes felt more like hours. Oh, God. Wasn't that Marguerite Moore over there with the ladies from her bridge club? *Please don't look this way,* Gerry prayed. She didn't mind people gossiping about her love life, but this was something else altogether.

Marguerite didn't turn around. For once, she was minding her own business. The same couldn't be said of Dean Cribbs. Gerry noticed that the obnoxious car dealer—he owned the largest Chevy dealership this side of Ventura—had Melodie Wycoff cornered by the wait station. Poor Melodie. Who would come rushing to her defense dressed the way she was? Today's outfit was a short denim skirt and white blouse through which Gerry could see the outline of her bra. She, too, might have assumed Melodie had been flirting with Dean, as she had a tendency to do with male customers, if not for the pained smile she wore.

Dean wasn't letting up. If he'd been standing any closer, his belt buckle would've left an impression. Gerry couldn't hear what he was saying, but from the expression on the blond waitress's face—one of desperate good humor stretched to the breaking point—it was obvious he wasn't soliciting donations for the Red Cross. God, would the man ever learn? He'd been this way ever since high school, when the fat, pimple-faced Dean, who couldn't get a date to save his life, had metamorphosed overnight into a slick-haired salesman with a year-round tan. Gerry watched him place a meaty hand on Melodie's waist, causing her to step back, butting up against the utensils bin with a faint, tinny rattle. From where she sat Gerry could see what was hidden from Dean's view: Melodie's hand snaking around behind her to grab hold of a fork.

Gerry leaped from her chair and darted over. Placing a hand on his shoulder, she said in a firm, pleasant voice, "Why don't you go back to your seat, Dean? Your food's getting cold."

He spun about, his startled look instantly replaced by a grin as bright and cold as a neon sign. "Gerry, always a pleasure." He spoke with an oily, salesman's drawl. "Melodie and I were having ourselves a little chat. Maybe you'd like to join us?" He leered in a way that let her know he'd been privy to the rumors about her as well.

Gerry smiled back, answering agreeably, "Great idea. Why don't I give your wife a call? I'm sure she'd love to come." She glanced pointedly at her cell phone on the table.

Dean's tanned face went the shade of liverwurst. He backed away, still grinning. "Good one, Gerry. You must have them in stitches up on the hill. Nothing like a good nun joke, I always say." He brushed invisible lint from his lapel. "Well, nice seeing you." He winked at Melodie. "Oh, and honey? I'll have that piece of pie after all. I always like a little something sweet after a meal."

Melodie gave a little growl and lunged at him, but Gerry was even quicker. She snatched the fork from Melodie's hand, brandishing it at Dean. "You sure about that pie?"

He blanched, his grin sliding away. "On second thought, I'll take the check."

Claire stared in disbelief at the scene taking place before her: a handsome, stylishly dressed woman holding a heavyset man at

bay with a fork while a frazzled blond waitress looked on. After a tense exchange—
she couldn't hear what they were
saying—the man turned on his heel with a
disgusted look and sauntered off.

"Gerry . . ." The owner rushed over to see
what the fuss was about.

Claire stared in horror. So *this* was her
mother. Dear God. *What am I getting into
here?*

But it was too late to turn back. The
woman was walking toward her—tall and
buxom, wearing tan slacks and a soft camel
sweater, a pair of large gold hoops glinting
amid the tousled dark hair that curled about
her ears. Claire felt a shock of recognition
seeing the same eyes that looked back at
her every morning in the mirror—large and
green and thickly lashed. Eyes now filling
with tears.

"Claire?" Gerry took Claire's hand in both
of hers. Claire could feel her trembling, those
startling green eyes searching hers with an
intensity—a hunger almost—that made her
want to pull back. "You're so pretty. I had no
idea you'd be so pretty." Her voice was low
and strangely lulling.

"It's . . . nice to finally meet you," Claire managed to croak.

"I hope my directions were okay."

"Fine. I left plenty of time just in case."

Gerry flashed her a small, rueful smile. "Sorry about that little incident just now, but I'm afraid Dean had it coming."

"What did he do?"

She glanced at the blond waitress, now deep in conversation with the owner. "Let's just say he wanted more than sugar in his coffee."

"Oh." Claire offered her a feeble smile. How did she know Gerry wasn't some nutcase?

At the table she sank down in the chair opposite Gerry's. The waitress broke away from the owner and hurried over.

"Anything you want, it's on the house," she said, looking down at Gerry with something close to worship. A hank of platinum hair showing more than an inch of dark root had slipped free of the bobby pins holding it loosely anchored atop her head. She tucked it behind her ear. "Hell, if it weren't for you, I'd be keeping Jimmy company down at the station."

"I'll take another iced tea." Gerry smiled

up at her. "And if being locked up by that handsome husband of yours is any kind of punishment, believe me, I didn't do you any favors." She turned to Claire. "What would you like to drink?"

"Same for me," she said.

Gerry waited until the waitress was out of earshot, then leaned forward. "Would you rather we went somewhere more private?"

Claire shook her head. "This is fine."

"The food is good at least. And you can't beat the setting."

Food was the last thing on Claire's mind. The shape her stomach was in right now, she'd be lucky to keep down a crouton. "It's lovely. The whole valley—it's as beautiful as you said."

Gerry sat back, her brow smoothing. "I thought I'd show you around after lunch."

Claire hesitated, then said, "Sure. I mean . . . yes, I'd like that. I'll have to check in at the motel first."

"Where are you staying?"

"The Horse Creek Inn."

"Good. We can stop on the way."

On the way to what? Claire wondered, once more getting the feeling that she'd bitten off more than she could chew. Gerry didn't look the type to take no for an answer.

But she must have sensed Claire's hesitation, for she was quick to say, "On the other hand, you must be tired. Maybe you'd like to rest."

"As a matter of fact—"

"I mean, there's no rush, is there? You're here until Sunday."

"Right."Claire felt drained all of a sudden, but managed to say with the proper amount of enthusiasm, "I'm looking foward to meeting your kids."

Their iced tea came, and she sipped hers gratefully.

"They're more than a little curious about you, too." Gerry took her time removing the wrapper from her straw.

"I guess it's not every day they meet a sister they didn't know they had." Claire had meant it to break the ice, but it came out sounding sarcastic instead. She blushed.

Gerry's expression clouded over briefly. "Speaking of which, you didn't mention any brothers or sisters when we spoke on the phone."

"I'm an only child."

"It must have been lonely growing up."

"My parents made up for it," Claire said stiffly.

"I didn't mean—" Gerry's face crumpled. "Oh, God. I was afraid of this—putting my foot in my mouth. I have a bad habit of it, you see."

Claire softened. "I think we're both a little nervous."

Gerry reached up as if to touch her cheek, her outstretched hand hovering in midair before falling to her side. "I can't tell you how many times I've imagined this. The two of us . . ." A tear spilled down her cheek, and she brushed it away with a self-conscious little laugh. "Oh, God. I promised myself I wouldn't do this—embarrass you with a lot of waterworks. It's just . . ."—her voice cracked "it's been so long."

Claire felt her own eyes fill. "I guess we have a lot of catching up to do."

"You must have a thousand questions."

Claire felt the air around her grow thick. She took a deep breath that filled her lungs like water. "Just one, really—why?"

Gerry searched her daughter's face. Claire wore an expression of mild reproach, coupled with something deeper and more forlorn. She felt a surge of panic, and thought: *I've gotten off on the wrong foot.*

Somehow she had to get back on track.

"I was young," she began haltingly, looking down at the table where her straw wrapper lay pleated in a neat square. "Oh, I knew what I was getting into when I . . . that there might be consequences. I just never thought I'd wind up pregnant."

She glanced up at Claire, who sat silent and watchful, a doe amid the dappled shade. She looked familiar, and at the same time so different from what Gerry had expected, it brought a little jolt each time their eyes met. She'd imagined Claire to be pretty, but not this pretty. She was long and lean like Jim with his mouth and porcelain skin, lightly dusted with freckles. Only her eyes were Gerry's.

"Were you in love with him?" she asked.

Gerry smiled. "It wasn't exactly what you'd call a normal courtship. I was a nun, you see."

Claire looked stunned.

Gerry smiled. "Yes, I know. It's hard to believe looking at me now."

"I had no idea."

"How could you?"

"What happened when you found out you were pregnant?"

"I left the convent and moved back in with my mother. It was tough on both of us. My father had passed away some years before, and she was just making ends meet. As for me, I couldn't find a job to save my life. Who was going to hire a former nun?"

"So you never considered keeping the—me?" Claire's expression was flat.

Gerry choked back an ironic laugh. "I thought of nothing else. In the end, though, I did what I thought was right. For you. For both of us." She paused. "I didn't know I'd spend the rest of my life regretting it."

Something dark flitted across Claire's face. But when she spoke, her tone was light, even upbeat. "There's nothing to be sorry about. I couldn't have asked for better parents."

Gerry forced a smile that felt glued on. "Tell me about them."

Claire's expression softened. "My father's retired. He used to manage a supermarket. My mom worked in the accounting department upstairs—for twenty years—but she quit her job to stay home and take care of me."

"They sound like nice people."

"They are."

"I'd like to meet them sometime."

Claire tensed. "I don't think that would be a very good idea."

Gerry felt stung. What did they have against her? If anything, they ought to be grateful. "It was just a thought," she said with a shrug.

"What sort of work do you do?" Claire seemed eager to change the subject.

"I guess you could say I've come full circle. I'm lay manager of the convent's bee-keeping operation." Gerry gestured toward the register up front, where along with a variety of jams and preserves the shelves behind the counter displayed several dozen jars of Blessed Bee honey. "The only difference is I no longer wear a veil."

"It sounds interesting."

"It is, most days." Gerry's gaze dropped to Claire's hand, on which a small sapphire sparkled. "You didn't tell me you were engaged."

"I'm not, well, not exactly—more like engaged to be engaged." Claire gave a little self-conscious laugh, lowering her hand to her lap. "Byron's in his second year of residency at Stanford."

"Have you two known each other long?"

"You could say that—we practically grew up together. His parents live next door to mine." She blushed a little, and Gerry got the feeling there was more to it than that. "What about you? You mentioned that you were divorced."

"Almost two years."

"He's not—"

"No." Gerry drew in a breath. "That was a long time before I met Mike. Your father was—*is*—a priest."

There was a moment of silence, then Claire broke into a smile. "It's not what I was expecting."

"What *were* you expecting?"

"I don't know—James Dean in *Rebel Without a Cause.*" She shook her head, still smiling. A ray of sunlight found its way through the branches just then, setting her hair ablaze, hair that was a dozen shades of brown ranging from dark honey to ginger. "Does he live around here?"

Gerry shook her head. "He's with the archdiocese in San Francisco."

"Does he want to meet me?"

"You'd have to ask *him.* But my guess is no."

"What makes you think that?"

"First, he'd have to admit you existed."

Claire looked at her in confusion. "Doesn't he know?"

"Oh, he knows all right. But knowing and accepting are often two very different things."

"Maybe if I went to see him . . ."

"You could." Gerry chose her words carefully. "But I wouldn't recommend it."

Claire fell silent, staring thoughtfully into the distance. At last Gerry said, "You must be hungry. Why don't we order?"

Claire's gaze returned to her. "Actually, I don't seem to have much of an appetite." She looked faintly abashed, as if fearful of seeming rude.

Gerry's appetite seemed to have vanished as well. "I have an even better idea— let's skip lunch. We'll make up for it with a big dinner. Do you like Chinese?"

"Sure. Anything."

"I'm sorry I can't offer you a home-cooked meal. I'm not exactly Martha Stewart." A corner of Claire's mouth hooked up, prompting Gerry to ask, "What? Did I say something funny?"

Claire shook her head, holding her lips together to keep from smiling. "It's nothing. I was just thinking that you and my mom have something in common after all."

"We're both lousy cooks?" It was something, at least.

"Let's just say I did most of the cooking in our house."

"A talent you obviously didn't inherit from me." Gerry laughed. "Wait until you meet your—my mother. She makes the best corned beef this side of the Atlantic, and her soda bread is out of this world. You two can talk recipes until the cows come home."

She signaled to Melodie, who appeared to have forgotten the incident with Dean and was busy flirting up a storm with Bobby Treadwell. Melodie came hurrying over. Gerry noticed that her cheeks were more flushed than usual and the top two buttons of her blouse undone.

"We changed our minds about lunch," Gerry told her.

"Is there a problem?" Melodie looked anxious.

"Not at all."

For an instant Gerry almost believed it. They'd made it over the hump, hadn't they? Surely the worst was behind them.

They were outside strolling along the

sidewalk when the absurdity of that notion was brought home. Claire turned to her and asked, "Just how old *were* you?"

"I was twenty," Gerry told her.

Claire's face fell. "I thought . . ."

She didn't have to say it: she'd have found it easier to forgive the actions of a teenager. But twenty—well, that was different. Gerry had been a fully grown adult.

She opened her mouth to explain, but something in Claire's expression made her think better of it. "Right now I feel old as the hills," she said with forced cheer. "In fact, I could do with a little rest myself."

Aubrey gazed out the window at the woman making her way up the front walk. Tall, with a purposeful long-legged stride, her sweater hugging her generous curves. The sunlight was on her face, and even from his study on the second floor he could see that it was mature . . . yet lovelier than that of any of the younger women constantly slipping him their cards. He was glad she hadn't made the mistake of so many closing in on fifty, that she hadn't had a face lift or even colored her hair.

Isabelle would have approved.

The thought, as always, brought a familiar tug—an undertow that could snatch him out to sea if he didn't navigate very, very carefully. His wife would have been forty-six this year. Isabelle, whose hair had been the color of the sunlight on the hills he looked out on every day, and whose eyes and mouth had been etched with feathery lines. Isabelle, who could make a violin sing with joy or weep with despair.

He pushed the thought from his mind. There'd been a time he'd hovered on the brink of madness, and that particular darkness was out there still—crouched like a tiger waiting to pounce. Sometimes bigger, sometimes smaller. But always there. Dr. Drier had said it would get easier with time, but Aubrey had found that, if so, it wasn't a gradual, linear process, like treads wearing down, but a strange and circuitous route that at times seemed to go nowhere. That was the part the good doctor had failed to communicate.

What business are you in, Aubrey?
I'm a conductor; you know that.
I wasn't referring to what you do for a living.
I see where this is leading.
Where is it leading?

Some moronic pap about the business of living, I suppose.

Why do you refer to it as pap?

Because all that crap about life going on is just that—crap. Life isn't just about living . . . it's about dying, too. People you love dying. People who had no business taking the car out at night in the pouring rain.

You sound angry.

I AM angry, goddammit! She didn't think, *she didn't stop for one minute to think what could happen . . . what it would do to us if—*

What? Say it, Aubrey.

But he hadn't been able to. Because then he'd have had to let go and she'd have been gone—really and truly gone. He closed his eyes, and saw her casket covered in flowers. Red and blue and purple cascading to the floor. Isabelle had loved bright colors—their rooms on the rue des Saints-Pères had been all bold stripes and floral prints. The small white casket alongside hers had seemed antithetical almost, a slap in the face of everything she'd loved. But babies' caskets didn't come in dark colors. *You didn't know that, did you, Dr. Drier? No, of course not, you bastard.*

Aubrey moved away from the window. On

the stereo, Franck's Sonata for Violin and Piano in A Major was playing, and he paused to let it sweep through him like a strong breeze blowing away debris. He'd been unsure about this recording at first, with its dreamy, almost Gallic quality and rigid attention to detail, but it was growing on him. Of course none compared to Isabelle's, but her CDs were tucked away in a drawer. He hadn't been able to listen to them since she died.

What most people didn't understand about music, he thought, was that it wasn't fixed. A recording you'd listened to a hundred times could sound different on the hundred and first. A Bach concerto as precise as a mathematical equation could, in the blink of an eye, move you to tears. Music was merely the framework, he thought, on which hopes and dreams, dashed and otherwise, were hung.

As he descended the stairs Aubrey thought how much simpler everything would be if life were broken into movements. An *adagio* followed by an *allegretto,* the restful quiet of a *pianissimo* after the thunder of a *fortissimo*. Gerry, he thought, would be *con brio*—with spirit. After seeing her he always felt refreshed, like after an invigorating walk. And the sex . . .

That hadn't deserted him, at least. Only in the darkest hours of his darkest days had the urge gone. Gerry Fitzgerald had merely opened the door and let in fresh air and sunlight. Better yet, she gave freely of herself, asking nothing in return. What he wanted was what she wanted too: friendship and intimacy without ties. There would be no demands, subtle or otherwise; no tears when it was time to part. Gerry was the only woman he'd known who'd have run for the hills even faster than he at the sound of wedding bells.

He could hear her in the foyer as he descended the stairs, speaking in a soft voice to Angelita. When she saw him, a look of profound relief washed over her face. Her Spanish, he knew, was as spotty as his housekeeper's English.

Angelita turned to him. "Señor Roellinger. I bring drink?"

"There's iced tea in the fridge." He smiled at Gerry, who looked windblown, her cheeks pink and eyes overbright. "Unless you'd like something stronger?"

"Iced tea would be fine," she said.

Angelita hurried off toward the kitchen, a

skinny little thing with big brown eyes who made him think of Bambi. Watching her go, he realized that he hadn't so much replaced Lupe as provided the doughty old retainer with a compromise: Angelita was allowed to do the heavier housework in exchange for Lupe monitoring her every move. It was a tribute to the girl that her great-aunt's demands hadn't put a dent in her cheerful nature.

"You're sure this isn't a bad time?" Gerry kissed him on the cheek. She smelled of the outdoors and something faintly citrusy, like fresh-picked lemons still warm from the sun.

"I can't think of a nicer interruption." When she'd called a few minutes ago, he'd been in the midst of notating a score. But the sound of her voice brought such welcome associations, he'd immediately seized on the excuse to invite her over.

"I promise I won't stay long," she told him.

He remembered that today was the day she was to have met her daughter. Had it not gone well? She looked faintly troubled, and it occurred to him that no one could have lived up to her expectations. Perhaps her daughter felt the same way. That was the trouble with people who were missing—a subject he was all too familiar with—they had a tendency to grow larger than life in the mind's eye. He harbored a tiny seed of suspicion, deep down, that even Isabelle, if she was alive today, couldn't live up to his glorified memories of her.

"Stay as long as you like," he said, smiling. "I want to hear all about it." He took her arm, tucking it through his. "Shall we sit out on the patio? It's warm enough."

They strolled past the sun-washed living room with its dark Mission furniture upholstered in bold southwestern fabrics—all of it Sam's (her taste was exactly his, so he'd seen no reason to change it)—Aubrey recalling his first visit to Isla Verde, not five months ago. Unlike real estate agents who pointed out every virtue until you wanted to toss them out a window, Sam Kiley had let the house speak for itself.

"Take your time. I'm here if you have any questions," she'd said, pausing in the midst of her packing to gesture vaguely in the direction of the stairs. So he'd done just that, strolling from room to room, absorbing it the way he would a particularly harmonious piece of music: its square solidity softened by Mediterranean curves, its stark whiteness bordered here and there with decorative tiles. The view from each exposure was different, but equally pleasing in its own way. The downstairs windows looked out on the garden, the ones upstairs on the distant hills. It was a house that had been built to withstand fire and earthquakes, and now would hopefully guard against memories of Isabelle.

They stepped out onto the patio, where the swimming pool glimmered an unearthly blue and the citrus trees were hung with the green globes of ripening fruit. The high stone walls draped in bougainvillea seemed to cup the sunlight like a bowl. As they settled onto deck chairs, Aubrey could feel the warm tiles through the soles of his loafers.

Angelita appeared just then bearing a tray with a pitcher of tea and a plate of freshly baked *dulces*. She placed it on the glass table between them and scurried off with her eyes downcast.

"Why do I always get the feeling she half expects to find us romping about naked?" Gerry observed with a laugh.

"Maybe because we usually are."

"Behind closed doors."

"If you'd rather we went upstairs—"

"You're incorrigible." A teasing smile flitted

about her mouth—the mouth he couldn't get enough of.

"I enjoy your company either way. With or without clothes."

"That's the nicest thing you've ever said to me."

He poured her a glass of tea before helping himself. "Now, about your daughter. What's she like?"

Gerry's face lit up. "Oh, Aubrey, she's everything I'd hoped—pretty, smart, poised."

"*Oui.* She's your daughter."

"I'm still pinching myself."

He felt a pang and held very still, as if caught on barbed wire. After more than ten years of trying, he and his wife had been overjoyed to learn that a baby was on the way. Now he would never know his child, a son.

He thought of his own childhood. Nine months of the year in the chilly, wet U.K., and June through August with his grandparents in Brittany. He remembered gathering oysters by the bay in Trinité-sur-Mer, his *grandpère* teaching him how to pry open the horny shells. And his *grandmère* with her old-world remedies, like using pulverized cabbage to bring a boil to a head and groundsel to cure stomachache. Their provincial dialect bore little resemblance to the proper schoolbook French he spoke with his father, and amenities were scarce: a well forever threatening to go dry, the only telephone a ten-minute bike ride away. Yet at the end of each summer, when it was time for him to go—to the interminable season at Eton and even more interminable school holidays with his parents in their townhouse on Cheney Walk—he'd stand on the dock with a lump the size of an oyster in his throat, fighting back tears. To this day, on nights when he couldn't sleep, he could close his eyes and summon his grandmother's scent: that of baking bread and sheets drying on the line.

"I'm happy for you," he told Gerry.

Her expression clouded over at once. "The trouble is, I'm not sure if she likes *me.*"

"Give her time."

No one could fail to like Gerry. But, of course, he was prejudiced. Aubrey thought of how she'd brightened his life, how in all the months they'd been seeing each other he had yet to grow tired of her. Looking at her now it was hard to believe that only a year ago he hadn't had the slightest interest in dating.

He recalled their first meeting at the music festival last summer. How vibrant she'd seemed, and how struck he'd been by her utterly refreshing lack of awe. To Gerry he wasn't the great Aubrey Roellinger, merely a man she found interesting.

"I'm bringing her home tonight to meet the kids," she told him.

"That should be interesting," he said.

"That's putting it mildly." She groaned.

He wanted to reassure her, but what could he say that wouldn't be a platitude? Instead, he passed her the plate of Mexican wedding cakes Lupe had baked just this morning.

She took one, nibbling on it halfheartedly. "I still feel like I'm dreaming. And these years wondering how big she was, if she was doing well in school, if she—" She stopped, bringing a stricken gaze up to meet his.

Aubrey's vision blurred, and he became aware of a salty taste on the back of his tongue. Tears, he realized with a small jolt. It had been so long since he'd cried.

"My son would have been four this year," he said quietly.

"Oh, Aubrey . . . I'm sorry." She brought a

loosely fisted hand to her mouth. "I wasn't thinking."

"It's all right," he said.

It was the first time he'd spoken of it to her and he felt something tightly knotted inside him loosen a bit. There was no need to elaborate; it was enough that he could speak of the unspeakable without the earth dissolving beneath his feet.

They moved on to other subjects. He told her of his impending trip to Budapest, where he would be guest conductor at an all-Liszt festival featuring soloists from around the world. She, in turn, told him about the article *West* magazine wanted to do on Blessed Bee, and about the difficulty she was having getting the mother superior to agree to it.

When it was time for her to go, they strolled along the covered walkway that led around the side of the house to the small, gated courtyard in front, deeply shaded this time of day, its koi pond glimmering darkly. He took her in his arms and kissed her lightly on the mouth. "Are you free next Friday? I have tickets to a concert."

"I'll check my calendar."

It was what she always said, and he smiled because it was the same line he'd used—less sincerely—with other women. There'd been so many after Isabelle, all eager to console him, both in bed and out. He hadn't had the heart to tell them he wasn't the least bit interested.

Looking at Gerry now, poised by the pond in the dappled light, he wanted nothing more than to spirit her off to his bedroom. He took her hand instead. Oddly, it was the one thing he missed most about being married: a woman's soft hand in his.

"We should make a habit of this," he said.

She drew away with a laugh. "You say that now."

"I'm serious."

"Famous last words—you'd be sick of me in a week." She dug into her shoulder bag, rooting for her keys. How she could find anything in all that clutter, he would never know. "By the way, Sam wants to know if you're coming with me to Laura's wedding. For some reason she seems to expect it." She paused to smile at him, as if at some quaint old tradition.

He shrugged. "I'm game if you are."

"Great. I'll let her know."

He waved to her as she stepped through the gates. The heaviness he wore like a sodden jacket had lifted. He felt lighter than he had in days. If Dr. Drier had been right, if *this* was his true business—to live life to the fullest—Gerry Fitzgerald had given him a substantial lease.

Chapter Six

"It's beautiful," Claire said.

On either side of her were gently rolling pastures in various shades of brown and green, dotted with giant oaks and sycamores and inhabited only by the occasional horse. They'd been driving for nearly an hour and she had yet to see a strip mall or even a neon sign.

"You should see it in the spring. A few months from now all this will be covered in poppies." Gerry drove with purposeful slowness, like someone accustomed to going faster who was ferrying an elderly relative to the doctor. "When we were little, Dad used to say they were the ghosts of the forty-niners coming back to haunt us."

"When did he pass away?"

"When I was thirteen." Claire detected a note of not quite sorrow—what the French called *tristesse*—underneath her matter-of-fact tone.

"Your mom never remarried?" Claire thought of Lou and Millie, together so long they were like salt and pepper. At times it almost seemed as if they could read each other's minds.

Gerry shook her head. "She was young enough, God knows—only forty. But she always said there was only one man for her, and Dad was it." She slowed to keep from hitting a squirrel that had scampered into the road. "They met during the war, when Dad was on leave in Dublin. He and his buddies were out one night, and Mom happened to be working in one of the pubs they stopped at. When he told her his name was Fitzgerald, she said she knew then—it was like an omen." She smiled. "That was my mother's maiden name, you see."

My grandparents, Claire thought, rolling it about in her mind the way she would savor some new and unusual taste on her tongue.

"It wasn't perfect, mind you," Gerry went on. "They had their share of problems. My dad . . . well, let's just say she had enough backbone for the two of them. Mom kept things going when—" She broke off with a cryptic smile. "You'll see when you meet her."

"I can't wait." They were on their way there now.

At the same time, Claire felt tense and keyed up, not because Gerry wasn't bending over backward to please her, but *because* she was trying so hard. How much easier it would be if Claire could go back to Miramonte safe in the knowledge that her parents had been right all along—that Gerry was a shallow, heartless creature with no more feeling for her child than a mother cat for its grown kitten. Instead, with each kind word and hopeful smile, Claire was left feeling as if the knives in their backs were being given a sharp twist.

"I have a younger brother, Kevin," Gerry went on. "He was a little kid when Dad died."

"Does he live around here?"

They rounded a bend and a red farmhouse by Grandma Moses swung into view. A hand-painted sign out front read lewellyn's antiques. "He's in San Francisco," Gerry told her. "I wish we saw more of him but when he can't get away, he'll fly the kids up for a visit."

Claire could tell from her tone that they were close. "I'm only an hour or so from there," she said.

"I'll give you his address. He's dying to meet you." Gerry brushed back a dark curl plastered to her cheek. "In fact, you two have something in common: You both love to cook. Kevin's the executive chef at Ragout. Have you heard of it? It was just awarded three stars."

"I don't eat out much." Claire's mouth stretched in a humorless smile. Filling in the blanks for Gerry—a brief history of the life and times of Claire Brewster—she realized something: Her life was pretty boring.

"Kevin's just the opposite—he almost never eats at home. Darryl's always com-plaining that he hardly ever sees him." Claire must have looked puzzled for Gerry was quick to add, "Darryl's his significant other."

So her uncle was gay. Claire wondered what her parents would have had to say about *that*. Lou referred to gay men as "queers," and Millie was certain they were all out to corrupt young boys. "Does your mother know?"

Gerry sighed. "Yes, and no. She knows, but she pretends not to. As far as Mom's concerned, Darryl is sort of an extended version of Kevin's college roommate."

"My parents would die."

Claire instantly regretted her words. Suppose Gerry got the wrong idea? Whatever their faults, they were her parents. Gerry was just a nice lady she happened to be related to.

Claire was relieved when Gerry answered breezily, "God knows it's tough enough being a parent even under the best of circumstances. I remember last summer when Andie wanted to get her eyebrow pierced." She chuckled. "You'd have thought she wanted to join the circus the way I carried on."

"Who won?"

"We settled on two more holes in each ear instead."

Claire smiled. "I had a client who wanted it stipulated in his will that if his grandson showed up at the funeral with a ring in his nose, he'd be instantly disinherited," she recalled.

Gerry tossed her head back in an airy laugh, reflections skating over the lenses of her sunglasses like moving images on a darkened screen. "I'll bet you could write a book."

"Not really. In fact," she gave in to a rueful smile, "most of the time my job is pretty boring."

"If you could do it all over again, would you still choose to be a lawyer?"

Claire thought of Kitty. "When I was in school, I worked part-time in a tearoom—Tea & Sympathy—how's that for a name? It's in an old house and my friend, the owner, does all the baking. If I could, that's what I'd do—trade places with Kitty." She shook her head. "But that's like wishing I could go to the moon."

"Why couldn't you?" Gerry spoke as if it were as easy as switching seats on a bus.

"Well, for starters, I don't know the first thing about running a business."

"You could learn. And you already know how to cook."

"As a hobby, not a profession."

Gerry was silent, as if mulling it over. "If you had a partner . . ." she said at last, turning onto a one-lane road riddled with potholes. "This friend of yours, for instance. And you know about things like write-offs and tax benefits and such. It *could* work."

"If either of us had any money, which we don't."

"Couldn't you get a loan?"

"I'm already up to my eyeballs in student loans."

Gerry smiled. "Well . . . it was just a thought."

"More like a pipe dream," Claire said with a laugh.

"Empires have been built from less."

How can you know what's best for me? Claire thought. Gerry might not think twice about chasing after every whim, but in her world every move had to be painstakingly choreographed. The riskiest thing she'd ever done was come here.

Fortunately, Gerry said no more on the subject. A short while later they pulled into the driveway of a shabby, undistinguished Victorian surrounded by tall shrubs and trees. A bird feeder—St. Francis with his arms outstretched—presided over what was left of the balding lawn. On the porch, wind chimes made from abalone shells stirred in the breeze with a faint cackling sound.

The front door was unlocked. As she stepped inside, Claire caught a movement out of the corner of her eye, but it was only her reflection in the mirrored oak hall stand. She froze in the dimly lit entry. The house smelled of cookies just out of the oven, and felt familiar somehow.

"Mom! It's me!" Gerry yelled at the top of her lungs. When several moments passed without a response, she explained, "She's a little hard of hearing."

"You don't have to shout, dear. I can hear perfectly well."

Claire turned to find an old woman walking toward them. She was tall and big boned, with hair the color of rusty wires springing every which way and eyes like chinks of blue sky glimpsed through weathered boards. Claire could see that she'd once been quite beautiful, and as she drew near it was obvious from the way she carried herself that she'd been used to heads turning in her wake.

"You must be Claire." Fingers like burled wood sanded to a smooth finish closed over hers. "I'm glad you're here."

No flowery speech, no embarrassing overtures, just those few simple words.

Claire was instantly disarmed. "Me, too," she said.

"I didn't know when to expect you, or I'd have dressed up." She glanced ruefully down at her apron tied over dungarees and a turtleneck sweater in a shade of blue that matched her eyes. On her feet were a pair of sneakers.

"You look fine, Mom," Gerry told her.

"Well, I'm sure you didn't come all this way just to see what I look like." Her piercing gaze fell once more on Claire. "In fact, right now I'll bet you could use a cup of tea."

Claire smiled. "You read my mind."

Mavis smoothed a hand over her rusty hair, tucking a stray wisp behind her ear. "Make yourselves comfortable while I put the kettle on." She gestured toward the living room beyond. "I'll only be but a minute."

Mavis disappeared into the back of the house, and Gerry led the way into a sunny parlor furnished with overstuffed chairs and bric-a-brac. On the floor was an oriental rug worn threadbare in spots. Claire sank down on the worn plush sofa. On the table at her elbow stood a gallery of framed photos— Gerry and her brother at various ages, and more recent ones of grandchildren. Her eye was drawn to one in particular, its handmade frame studded with cowry shells: a little boy and girl building sand castles on the beach.

Gerry followed her gaze. "That was the year Andie started kindergarten. We'd rented a house in Santa Monica the summer before. I thought those two would never come out of the water."

Memories Claire had no part in. She felt a sudden keen sense of loss. "I grew up a block from the ocean. The best part was falling asleep every night to the sound of the surf."

"It sounds like heaven."

It was on the tip of Claire's tongue to say she hadn't spent much time on the beach as a child—Millie had lived in perpetual fear that she'd drown, or at the very least be burned to a crisp—but thought better of it.

Mavis reappeared minutes later carrying a laden tray that rattled precariously as she lowered it onto the coffee table. It held a flowered teapot with a chipped spout and matching sugar bowl and creamer, cups and saucers from another set, and a plate of home-baked cookies. Her arthritic hand trembled a bit as she poured. "Sugar?"

"Just a touch," Claire said.

"I hope you like gingersnaps," she said, passing her the plate. "They were my children's favorite."

"Mine, too." Claire bit into the cookie, savoring the delicate medley of spices and molasses. "Mmm. Delicious."

Mavis leaned forward and in a hushed voice confided, "The secret is fresh ginger."

Claire smiled. "Really? I'll have to try that next time."

Mavis broke into the wide smile of someone stumbling across a fellow countryman in an out-of-the-way place. "I can see we'll get along just fine."

Then they were off and running, Mavis regaling her with tales of her mother's famous light touch, and of her own equally famous culinary disasters—told with a jollity conveying that such misfires were well in the past. She offered Claire the recipe for her prized soda bread, and Claire in turn promised to send her a few of her own favorites in turn. After several minutes Claire glanced over at Gerry. She wore the strained smile of someone who felt thoroughly left out but was trying hard not to show it.

At last she stood up, brushing crumbs from her lap. "We should be going, Mom. Listen, why don't you give Claire a quick tour while I clean up?"

"Nonsense," Mavis said. "*I'll* clean up."

Claire rose to her feet. "Thanks for the tea, Mrs.—uh, Mavis."

She tagged after Gerry, taking in the big, old-fashioned kitchen that reminded her of Kitty's, with its walk-in pantry and screened porch. Upstairs were bedrooms papered in faded floral designs and furnished in heavy, dark Grand Rapids suites.

"This was mine," Gerry told her as they stepped into a small room that overlooked the garden in back. The bed had been removed, in its place a sewing machine and table piled with old patterns and fabric remnants. It didn't look as if it had been used in a while. Cardboard cartons were stacked against the wall, along with back issues of *National Geographic* and *Saturday Evening Post* bundled with string. Gerry fished inside one of the boxes, pulling out a crumpled manila envelope. She pried open the clasp, spilling its contents—old black-and-white photos—onto the table.

"That's Mom and Dad on their wedding day." She pointed to a tinted portrait of a much younger Mavis, radiant in her bridal gown, posed alongside a stocky, light-haired man in uniform. There were photos of newborns, too—Gerry and her brother—wearing the same lacy christening gown. A heavyset older woman in sensible shoes and hat squinting at the camera was identified as Mavis's mother—the Irish Grandmother Fitzgerald.

"That's me with Ginger," Gerry pointed to a snapshot of a gap-toothed little girl holding a puppy in her lap. "Oh, that was some Christmas. They'd left him under the tree in a crate, only Ginger got out and chewed up everything in sight. It was supposed to have been a surprise for us, but the surprise was on Mom and Dad instead."

There was another photo of a teenaged Gerry in a wedding dress, a crown of rosebuds on her head. "That was the day I took my vows." She spoke matter-of-factly, though Claire couldn't help noticing the haste with which she tucked it out of sight.

"But I thought—"

"You're not a professed nun until your final vows, Gerry explained.

"How long does that take?"

"I was there almost three years."

"Would you have stayed if you hadn't gotten pregnant?"

"I don't think I was cut out to be a nun. Of course, it took getting hit over the head to realize it."

"I suppose an abortion would've been out of the question."

Gerry cast her a shocked glance. "I didn't even consider it. Not for one second."

But you had no trouble discarding me like an old shoe once I was born, Claire thought. "Lucky for me." She didn't bother to disguise the scorn in her voice.

Gerry ducked her head, stuffing the photos back into the envelope . . . but not before Claire caught the gleam of tears in her eyes.

When it was time to go, Claire was left with more questions than answers. Why hadn't Mavis insisted Gerry keep her? Was it because she'd been on overload herself, or were there other reasons?

Mavis followed them out onto the front porch. "I feel as if you just got here. But I mustn't be selfish—I'm sure Andie and Justin are dying to meet you." She gave Claire a brisk hug smelling of strong soap and ginger. When she stepped back, her eyes—those remarkable eyes like chinks of blue sky—were fixed on Claire with shining intensity. "You'll come again, won't you?"

Claire murmured something polite, emotions tumbling inside her like water over rocks. She hadn't been able to think past this weekend. But now looking into the magnificent wreck of her grandmother's once-beautiful face, she had the feeling she *would* be back.

Andie eyed the young woman seated at the end of the table. *My sister.* However hard she tried, she couldn't quite wrap her brain around it. It was like the fairy tales her mother used to read to her when she was little, about peasant girls who were really princesses under an evil spell. When the spell was broken, the princess went back to her real family and everyone lived happily ever after. But that was only in stories. What would it have been like in real life?

And just look how Mom was fawning over her. Justin, too. Right now he was hanging on every word of the story Claire was telling—something about the Miss America state pageant in her hometown.

"The feminists picket it every year," she

was saying. "At last year's one of them wore a dress made out of bologna slices. It was fine until the dogs got wind of it. She was practically naked by the time they were called off."

Justin let out a bray of laughter. "Was she wearing underwear?"

"She must have been. It made the front page of our local paper—ahead of the winner. They put her on page three." Claire smiled, dabbing at her mouth with her napkin. "This is delicious, by the way."

"I'm sorry it's only takeout," Gerry apologized. "Like I said, I'm not much of a cook."

"That's not true, Mom," Andie piped. "You make a great meat loaf."

Gerry rolled her eyes. "Anyone can make meat loaf."

"She makes good waffles, too," Justin told Claire. "Not just the freezer kind."

Gerry beamed at Justin, looking relieved that they were all getting along so well—like she had a clue. "More dumplings, anyone?" She held out the carton.

Andie eyed it longingly, then shook her head. "Better not."

"She's afraid of getting fat." Justin helped himself to two. "As if Simon would notice."

Andie shot him a dirty look. "What's that supposed to mean?"

"Nothing." Justin shrugged, pushing a dumpling around his plate with chopsticks before giving up and stabbing it with his fork. "I haven't seen him around lately, that's all."

"We didn't break up, if that's what you're implying."

The main reason Simon hadn't been over was because she hadn't asked him. It would have felt too awkward. The whole time she'd be imagining it was stamped in red ink on her forehead: We Had Sex. Not that her mom was in a position to judge.

"Simon's your boyfriend?" Claire asked, looking interested.

"Sort of." Andie didn't see what business it was of hers.

"I'll bet he likes Monica Vincent better." Justin smirked.

Andie shot him a dirty look. "Simon's doing an article on her for the local paper," she told Claire. "In fact, I was with him when he interviewed her."

Claire looked impressed. "Really? What's she like in person?"

"Around here she's known as the Bitch on Wheels."

Gerry shot her an admonishing look. "Andie! It's not nice to make fun of people in wheelchairs."

Andie burned as if she'd been slapped. "*I* didn't say it."

"I *have* heard she's impossible." Claire cast her a sympathetic look.

Andie didn't respond.

There was a brief silence filled with the clinking of forks and clatter of Buster licking a plate under the table. As if it were just an ordinary dinner on any old night, as if this *complete stranger* hadn't dropped out of the blue, her mother expecting them to welcome her with open arms. Just add hot water and mix.

On the other hand, was it fair to blame Claire? It wasn't like she'd asked to be a part of this family. *If she could have chosen someone to be her sister, it wouldn't have been me.*

Andie choked down a bite of Hunan chicken. "Mom said you were a lawyer."

"Guilty as charged." Claire's smile didn't quite reach her eyes.

"Like on TV?" Justin asked.

"Not exactly," she told him. "In real life lawyers don't spend nearly as much time in court. Especially not the kind of law I practice. I handle wills and estates."

"Rich people's?" Justin looked hopeful.

Claire laughed, and shook her head. "Sorry to disappoint you, but most of my clients are ordinary people like you and me. Though, believe me, in the end it's all the same. I've seen relatives fight over sets of dishes as if they were the crown jewels."

"I'm gonna be a pilot when I grow up," Justin announced.

"Military or civilian?" Claire, to her credit, wasn't being condescending. She seemed genuinely interested.

"A navy fighter pilot." He straightened, looking as if he'd grown an inch.

"*Top Gun* is his all-time favorite movie," Andie told her. "He knows every line by heart."

"Have you seen *The Spirit of St. Louis*?" Claire asked. When Justin shook his head, she added, "It's about the first solo flight across the Atlantic by a man named Charles Lindbergh. I have the video—I'll send it to you. Which reminds me . . ." She got up from the table and went out into the hall, returning moments later with a couple of wrapped gifts. She handed the smallest to Andie, saying, "I hope you like it."

It was a silver barrette with mother-of-pearl inlay, delicate and beautiful. Cupped in her palm it seemed to glow. Andie felt as if she were going to cry. "Thanks," she said, darting a glance at Claire. "That was nice of you."

Justin's face lit up when he opened his gift—a Game Boy program. "Awesome. Hey, how'd you know? It's practically the only one I didn't have." He looked at Claire as if she walked on water. "Wait till I tell Nesto!" He pushed away from the table.

"Aren't you forgetting something, young man?" Gerry prompted.

"Huh?" He glanced sheepishly at Claire. "Oh yeah. Thanks."

"All right, you're excused." His mother's nod sent him bolting as if he'd been shot from a cannon.

Claire got up. "I'll help with the dishes."

"No." Andie jumped to her feet. "You're company." She placed the faintest emphasis on company. "I'll do them."

The doorbell rang just then and her mother darted out of the room, leaving her alone with Claire. An uncomfortable silence stretched between them. Finally, Claire cleared her throat. "Look, I'm sure this is as weird for you as it is for me." She looked straight at Andie. "I just want you to know I'm not looking for a mother. I have one already."

Andie felt the food in her belly congeal into a heavy stone. Wasn't that what Cindy had said? *I know you have a mother. I'm not trying to take her place.* But it wasn't her mother's place Cindy had taken; it was Andie's. Suppose that happened here? Only with her man instead.

Her mother breezed back into the kitchen before she could reply. "Just the UPS guy—the new cushions I ordered for the patio chairs." She reached for the apron on the hook by the stove, casting Andie a distracted look. "Don't you have homework?"

"Mom, it's *Friday.*" Andie felt absurdly close to tears.

Gerry didn't answer. The tap was on and she was rinsing plates, handing them to Claire to stack in the dishwasher. They looked nothing alike—Gerry was tall and dark and big busted and Claire willowy, with brown hair that fell in soft waves about her shoulders—yet they seemed oddly compatible, moving together like dancers. Andie watched for a moment—she had the oddest feeling she was standing outside looking in through the window—then turned and slipped soundlessly from the room.

"I should be going. I don't want to miss my flight."

Claire folded her napkin and tucked it beside her plate. Sunday breakfast at Lundquist's Bakery Café—famous for their apple pancakes, of which she'd eaten far too many—had been the perfect end to the weekend, and she was eager to be on her way.

"I'll walk you to your car." Gerry gave her kids a look that let them know they were to stay put.

Justin pushed his plate aside, looking up at Claire. "Remember, just download it like I showed you. The rest is easy." He was referring to AOL Instant Messenger. Yesterday, after lunch, he'd given her a brief tutorial.

Claire shook his hand solemnly. "See you in the chat room."

"It was nice meeting you." Andie spoke with formal politeness. She'd ordered French toast, but had hardly touched it. Now she sat perfectly upright in her chair. The barrette holding her dark curls anchored over one temple wasn't the one Claire had given her.

Claire wished there were some way to make Andie see that she wasn't a threat. But this wasn't about her, not really. Andie had clearly been troubled long before she'd arrived on the scene.

She smiled warmly at her half sister. "I like that color on you. You should wear red more often."

Andie blushed, and looked down at her sweater. "Thanks. It was a present from my dad." It was the first genuine response Claire had gotten out of her all weekend.

"Well . . . good-bye." Claire touched her shoulder.

"Bye," Andie said, her eyes downcast.

The weekend, for the most part, had gone well. Which, by Claire's standard, meant there had been no unpleasant scenes and only a minimum of awkward silences. On Saturday, Gerry had shown her more of the sights—including the abandoned school-house where a key scene in *Stranger in Paradise* had been filmed—before stopping in for a visit with Gerry's friend Sam and her live-in boyfriend, Ian.

Claire had hit it off with them right away. Both were down to earth and easy to talk to, and it was impossible to be around them for more than a few minutes without seeing how crazy they were about each other, and how excited about the baby due in a few months. Though they looked nothing alike, Sam reminded her a little of Kitty, and the little house she shared with Ian was so snug and cozy, Claire could have moved right in.

The deep affection between Sam and Gerry was evident as well. At times, Claire had found herself wishing that Gerry weren't her mother, that she could know her simply as a friend. How much easier it would be if everything Gerry did and said didn't feel like a case of too little, too late.

Now, as she wound her way through the thicket of tables draped with coats and armed with elbows, Claire felt a sharp tug of longing. She was somewhere in the middle: neither friend, nor child. Gerry might regret having given her up all those years ago, but was she ready for more than this? A long-distance relationship that wouldn't rock her comfortable boat.

She watched Gerry stop and chat with several people along the way. She seemed to know everyone and was obviously well liked. One of the waitresses, a stout flaxen-haired woman in an apron as pink as her face, waved to her as she passed. Then they were sidling past the bakery case, blooming with fragrant steam, and squeezing through the line that stretched out onto the sidewalk.

Outside, the sun was shining and church bells tolling. Claire glanced up at the steeple rising above a sea of green across from the park. When she brought her gaze back to Gerry, she found Gerry studying her intently, almost as if to memorize her.

"I hope you know what you're getting into," she said. "A chat room full of twelve- and thirteen-year-olds can be quite an education."

"Oh, I think I can handle it."

"Justin really took to you," Gerry said.

"He's a great kid."

"Andie will come around, too. She just needs a little more time."

"I don't take it personally."

"She hasn't been the same since the divorce." A bitter note crept into Gerry's voice. "Mike doesn't make it any easier, either. Half the time it's like he's forgotten he even *has* children."

You're a fine one to talk, Claire thought.

They were strolling in the direction of her car. She waited for Gerry to say how sorry she was that Claire was leaving, or how much it had meant that she'd come—half hoping she would and at the same time that she wouldn't.

She spotted her rented blue Taurus. Turning to Gerry, she said, "Listen, I—" She broke off suddenly.

A cluster of women was hurrying toward them—two sets of identical twins, one elderly and the other teenaged. The older twins were dressed exactly alike, in flowered dresses and matching straw hats, while the younger ones, who had to be granddaughters, seemed to have gone out of their way to set themselves apart. One wore a demure blouse and long skirt; the other, jeans and a funky denim vest.

"Gerry! What a coincidence. Olive was just saying that she hadn't seen you in church," chirped one of the older twins. She and her sister might have been a pair of birds with their inquisitive brown eyes and gray hair pulled back into buns. "Father Reardon's sermon was—"

"—most rousing," her twin finished for her.

"Olive, Rose. Dawn, Eve. I'd like you to

meet . . ." Gerry hesitated. She wanted desperately to introduce Claire as her daughter, but something about the stiff set of Claire's shoulders warned her not to. She might think it pushy or, worse, presumptuous. And the weekend had gone so well she didn't dare rock the boat. Next time—and oh, how she hoped there'd be a next time—when Claire was more comfortable with the whole thing, she'd climb the post office tower and shout it for all to hear. She finished weakly. "Claire Brewster. She's, ah, visiting from out of town."

Claire felt her breath gather into a little knot in her chest. She'd been so expecting to hear the words *my daughter* that at first that's what she thought Gerry had said. A split second later the jarring realization hit: *She's ashamed of me.* It was one thing for Sam and Ian to know—Sam was her oldest friend—and quite another for it to be common knowledge.

"So nice to meet you." One of the elderly twins extended a child-size gloved hand. Rose, or was it Olive? "I hope you're enjoying your stay. We don't get many visitors this time of year."

"I . . . I was just leaving, actually," Claire

stammered. For an awful moment she felt as if she were going to burst into tears.

"Well, then, we won't keep you," her twin said pleasantly. "It was nice meeting you, dear."

"Same here," Claire managed to mutter.

The younger twins eyed her as if they sensed something amiss, but one piped cheerfully, "Next time you should try our café. It's just down the street—the Blue Moon." She pointed the way. "Granny makes a great burger."

Claire watched the two sprightly old ladies head off down the sidewalk, granddaughters bringing up the rear. She could sense Gerry wanting to say something, but whatever it was she'd want to hear it. Right now she couldn't even bring herself to look Gerry in the eye.

At her car, she put out her hand and in the same formally polite tone Andie had used, said, "Thank you. For everything."

Gerry looked as if she were going to cry. "I hope you had a good time."

A corner of Claire's mouth hooked up. "It was an education."

"I was wondering if—"

Claire glanced at her watch. "I've got to run. I don't want to miss my flight."

Moments later she was turning right at the intersection. She drove slowly, half blinded by tears. She hadn't gone more than a few blocks when she abruptly pulled over to the curb and with a small, choked cry dropped her head onto the wheel, which she held clutched, as tightly as if negotiating a sharp curve. She didn't know how long she'd sat like that, struggling to regain her composure. Long enough, apparently, to draw attention.

"Hey . . . are you okay?"

The voice, accompanied by a rapping on her window, sent her head jerking up. A burly man in work clothes, with shaggy blond hair and a thick reddish mustache that drooped over his upper lip, was bent over, peering in at her with concerned brown eyes.

Claire, her face on fire, rolled her window down. "I'm fine . . . thank you."

"You sure?" He eyed her curiously.

A hand fluttered up to her temple. "Really. I'm okay."

"I don't mean to sound rude, but you don't look okay."

"I will be . . . in a minute." She'd never been so embarrassed in her life.

But the man wasn't leaving. "Would you like to come inside? It's none of my business, but I don't think you should be driving in that condition."

Claire looked past him at a small red-roofed house festooned in vines. A for sale sign tilted drunkenly on the scrap of lawn. Crisscrossing it was a banner that read OPEN HOUSE 12–3 P.M.

"I'm—" She opened her mouth to repeat that she was fine.

He smiled and straightened. "Don't worry. I'm harmless."

Before she realized it, she was climbing out of the car, even while a voice in her head cried, *What do you think you're doing? You'll miss your flight!*

The man, who was around her age and taller by at least a head and a half, stuck out a large calloused hand. "Matt Woodruff." The tool belt slung about his hips gave the fleeting impression of a Wild West gunslinger. "Open house isn't for another hour," he said, nodding in the direction of the house, "but there's no law says I can't let you in before then."

"Are you the owner?" she asked, rummaging in her purse for a Kleenex. She probably looked like hell, but what did it matter?

He grinned, showing a mouthful of very large, very white teeth. "Hell, no. I have enough headaches as it is. Mrs. Dalrymple asked me to give the place a once-over, make it presentable." His grin widened. "It's what the real-estate agents call a honeymoon cottage, which is fancy lingo for fixer-upper."

"It looks to be in decent shape from here."

Matt Woodruff regarded her with interest. Little sprinkles of sawdust were caught in the folds of his chambray shirt, and its sleeves were rolled up over his elbows, showing arms as thick and hard as railroad ties. A line from a Longfellow poem, memorized back in grade school, popped into her head: *Under a spreading chestnut tree, the village smithy stands . . .*

"Come on in, I'll give you the fifty cent tour."

"I should be going," she said, glancing at her watch. "I have a plane to catch."

"It won't take long—there's not much to see."

Claire hesitated. She was used to men coming on to her. Was that what was happening here? No, she didn't think so. Matt's face was open and friendly, his eyes, the color of strong brewed tea, sparkling with nothing more than friendly interest . . . .and perhaps sympathy.

"I guess I can spare a few minutes," she said. There was something about this man's sunny demeanor that was catching. Either that, or the weekend with her mother had left her completely unhinged.

Besides, what could be the harm in it?

Chapter Seven

Lamaze classes were held in the VFW social hall—the perfect place for it, according to Sam, who said that childbirth deserved a purple heart, especially at *her* advanced age—where at the moment Sam and Gerry sat cross-legged on their mats. There were nine women, of all ages and walks of life, forming a rough circle around the perimeter of the large utilitarian room with metal folding chairs stacked at one end, a trophy case and a table holding a coffee urn and plates of cookies at the other. The instructor, a trim, sandy-haired woman named Jane, who had to have been a baby herself when Sam was pregnant with Laura, had taken them through the various breathing exercises—all of which were a distant memory to Gerry, who was glad that that part of her life was over. Sam, on the other hand, was loving every minute. And though easily the oldest expectant mom in the class, she was as slim as ever, even at six and a half months. In her baggy sweatshirt—one of Ian's, judging from the paint on the cuffs—she hardly seemed pregnant.

"What will we be packing in our overnight bags, ladies?" Jane, an obstetrical nurse and mother of two, patrolled the circle of mats with her hands clasped behind her back. They were taking a break from breathing exercises to review more practical matters.

"My husband!" cracked heavyset Emma Pettigrew, married to a fireman and the mother of two preschoolers, both of whom had been born when their dad was off putting out fires.

The women shared a laugh.

"My mama says to pack a horse tranquilizer," piped one of the first-time moms—Yvonne Ramsey, a slender, light-skinned black woman with braided extensions arranged in an artful fall. Gerry recognized her as one of the managers at Rusk's.

"Save it for your old man," barked gravel-voiced Kit Greggins, a henna-haired woman with tattoos, six months along with her fifth. "That is, if he don't pass out on his own first."

"Okay, ladies." The instructor smiled as she shook her head. "I think we've heard enough war stories. I'm sure most of you are anxious enough as it is."

"Damn straight," put in Katrina Brill, a forty-something executive who'd gotten tired of waiting for Mr. Right and taken matters into her own hands. She was accompanied by her equally capable-looking sister. "If I come out of this with stretch marks, I'm *never* going to find a husband."

The lighthearted mood was broken by Faye Bontempi, who was acting as coach for her sixteen-year-old daughter Christina. "I have Chris's bag all packed," she announced grimly. "Toothbrush, nightie, lip balm, Walkman—none of that crazy music she listens to, either, something nice and soothing—oh yes, and lollipops. She'll need them to keep her blood sugar up."

There was no mention of a layette.

Christina, a lumpish girl seated docilely alongside her mother, wouldn't be needing one for her baby. Gerry felt a pang, wishing there was something she could say to the girl . . . but what? *Think twice, you might regret it.*

Her thoughts turned to Claire. It had been two weeks, and all Gerry had to show for her visit was a polite note thanking her for her hospitality. She'd phoned several times, leaving messages on Claire's answering machine. None had been returned. The only one who'd heard from her was Justin, with whom she chatted online.

Gerry would've jumped on a plane if she'd thought it would make a difference, but she suspected it would only make things worse. Claire clearly needed time to absorb all this. Gerry could only sit back and wait, and hope she would eventually come around.

In your patience possess ye your souls. Words from Luke that would be sorely put to the test in the days to come.

"I don't have the heart to tell them this is the easy part," Sam muttered under her breath. "Wait till their kids are grown."

She ought to know. Last summer, when she'd taken up with Ian, her daughters had raised a huge stink. Sam, who'd always put her family first and who would have given her life for those girls when they were little, had fortunately come around to Gerry's way of thinking: that it was her turn now. In time, Laura and Alice had seen it that way, too.

"Don't I know it." Gerry groaned. "These days Andie doesn't say anything unless it's to bite my head off."

"She's a teenager." Sam shrugged.

"I wish that were all."

"What makes you think there's more?"

The class was over and they were rolling up their mats. Gerry tucked hers into Sam's voluminous straw tote that also held Sam's cell phone, bottles of Evian, cough drops, and hand cream (Gerry had no doubt her overnight bag was already packed and sitting by her door). The other women had drifted to the refreshment table, where they stood chatting as they sipped cups of decaf and nibbled on cookies. Jane was deep in conversation with Faye Bontempi, whose expression remained grim. Faye, who was forty but looked fifty, stood with her scrawny arms folded over her chest, nodding every so often at something the instructor had said.

Gerry sighed. "It's been worse lately—ever since Claire's visit."

Sam, who knew Gerry better than anyone, including her own mother, winced in commiseration. "Have you tried talking to her?"

"More than once. It's like talking to a brick wall."

"Then wait for her to come to you."

"Remember when she was little?" Gerry grew wistful. "She was such a little chatterbox—you couldn't get her to shut up. My mother used to say it was God's little joke on me after those years in the convent."

Sam was giving her that apple-doesn't-fall-far-from-the-tree look. "They always say it's the ones that are most like you that are the hardest." She heaved herself to her feet. "Nobody could ever get you to shut up, either. Remember in high school, the debate with Kingswood? The bell went off and you kept right on talking."

"I don't think I even heard it," Gerry recalled with a laugh.

"I rest my case."

Sam looked so youthful at that moment, with her cheeks blooming and her auburn hair swinging loosely about her shoulders,

Gerry was immediately transported back to their senior year, when her best friend had been breaking every heart and she'd had one foot in the convent.

Some things never change, she thought. Sam was with the best-looking guy around, and she was still praying—these days to the Patron Saint of Divorced Moms.

Gerry felt a twinge of envy. No, not envy. She wouldn't go so far as to call it that, for she wouldn't have traded places with Sam for all the tea in China. But now and then wouldn't it be nice to have someone other than her children to come home to? Someone with whom she could curl up on the couch and watch old movies. Like the way it had been with Mike when they were first married, back when they'd both been so blinded by love that neither had had the slightest clue what the other was *really* like.

She thought of Aubrey. Of the men she'd dated since her divorce, he was the only one she thought about out of bed as much as in. But lately he'd been on her mind a bit *too* much, which she found disturbing. For even if she were looking to get married again, which she most definitely was not, (Mike had cured her of that), she'd be barking up the wrong tree. There was no room in Aubrey's heart for anyone but Isabelle.

Yes, and what will it be like in years to come, growing old with the nuns on the hill, with only your little romps on the side. Maybe Sam had the right idea after all.

She glanced up to find her friend regarding her curiously, as if Sam sensed something amiss. She tucked her arm through Gerry's. "Buy a pregnant lady a drink?"

"I could use one myself." Gerry didn't normally drink, but tonight she'd make an exception. "What about Sylvester's?" It was a little on the divey side, but just down the street.

Five minutes later they were pushing their way through the saloon-style door. Sylvester's, in one incarnation or another, had been around since the gold rush, first as a stage stop, then as a bordello, and these days as pool hall and tavern. Besides being conveniently located practically next door to the VFW building—which provided a steady trickle of old soldiers looking to relive their glories or drown their sorrows, or both—it was where you went when everything else was closed, which in Carson Springs, where they rolled up the sidewalks at nine, meant a brisk after-hours trade.

"Isn't that Melodie Wycoff?" murmured Sam as they settled in at a table near the bar. On the jukebox Garth Brooks was wailing about a broken heart and in its faint, lurid glow everybody's favorite waitress was slow-dancing with a man definitely not her husband.

"I see nothing, I hear nothing." Gerry had enough problems of her own without adding Melodie's to the list. And from the looks of it, she was too drunk to care if her husband, a cop known for his long arm and quick temper, got wind of this.

Sam ordered a root beer and Gerry a scotch, straight up.

"To saints and sinners." Sam lifted her foaming mug.

"I'll drink to that," Gerry said.

"Listen, thanks for coming with me tonight. I really appreciate it."

"Are you kidding? I wouldn't have had it any other way. In the unlikely event I wind up being your coach, I ought to know what I'm doing."

Sam smiled. "Not much chance of that. I

can't go to the end of the driveway for the mail without Ian's insisting that I take my cell phone. Yesterday I had to virtually boot him out the door. You'd think San Bernardino was a trip to the moon."

Ian wouldn't have left if it hadn't been an emergency, Gerry knew. A ceiling had collapsed on one of his murals, and he'd gone off to salvage what he could.

She shook her head in amazement even so. "Who'd have thunk it?" Even Gerry, who'd championed them from the beginning, hadn't pegged him as father material. For one thing, Ian was fifteen years Sam's junior . . . and for another, he was an artist—a roving one, at that. But he'd proved himself to Gerry's satisfaction. As far as she knew, this was the first Lamaze class he'd missed.

"The day we bought the crib, he was up half the night assembling it."

"A far cry from before." Gerry was thinking of Sam's late husband, who could charm the birds from the trees but had scarcely lifted a finger around the house.

The delicate lines around Sam's eyes and mouth were creased in irony. "Lately I've been thinking a lot about what my mother used to say: There's a lid for every pot. If that's true, I spent a lot of years rattling around with one that didn't fit."

Gerry sighed. "I can relate to that."

"Oh, don't get me wrong—I loved Martin. You know that. But . . ." Sam's voice trailed off, and she gazed sightlessly toward the bar, where a football game was in progress on the TV and a man in overalls sat propped on a stool nursing a beer. "I guess we only get what we think we're owed, and I didn't put a very high value on myself in those days."

What am I owed? Gerry wondered.

She sipped her scotch. At the pool table in back, Jimmy DeSoto was having words with Luis Martinez, while a short distance away Melodie and her friend had gone from slow-dancing to barely swaying to the music. They were so closely entwined you couldn't have fit a playing card between them.

Gerry's mind drifted once more to Aubrey, and she felt warmth spread through her that wasn't entirely due to the scotch. She thought of last night, how he'd undressed her inch by inch, taking it so slowly that by the time she was down to her panties, she'd been begging for it. Even then, he'd taken his time, holding back until she was nearly ready to come. Oh, what that man could do to her! If she didn't get a grip—

She became aware of Sam eyeing her intently. Did it show? But her friend only asked, "Any word from Claire?"

Gerry shook her head, feeling the warmth recede. "I think I might have scared her off for good."

"How so?" Sam smiled, clearly not believing it.

"There're her parents, too." Gerry remembered how defensive she'd gotten whenever the subject came up. "I get the feeling they aren't too happy about the whole thing."

"I can't imagine why."

If her friend had one fault, Gerry thought, it was that she had a hard time finding fault in others. "I suppose they see me as threat." She sipped her drink, frowning.

"It's not like you're out to steal her away. She's a grown woman, for heaven's sake."

"My point exactly."

Sam pondered this for a moment. "People usually see in others what they don't want to look at in themselves. If her parents feel threatened, it's probably because deep down they're afraid they didn't do the best job raising her."

"A comforting thought," Gerry said darkly.

"Oh, don't get me wrong—they loved her, that much is obvious."

Gerry looked down at her glass, which she was surprised to see was nearly empty. She felt only a mild buzz. "I can see that. I just don't know how happy she is."

Sam sighed. "She seems . . . I think unhappy is too strong a word. More like lost."

"God, what I wouldn't give to turn the clock back!" Gerry gripped her glass with such force, it was a wonder it didn't shatter. "Tonight it was all I could do not to march over to poor Christina and tell her what a huge mistake she's making."

"It might not be for her," Sam said softly, her eyes large with sympathy.

"She should know, that's all," Gerry went on in the same low, clenched voice, "what it's like waking up night after night to a baby you heard crying that isn't there. And all the time, wondering how she's doing and if she's happy. If only—" Her throat closed.

"You're raising two beautiful children." Sam spoke firmly, her face seeming to shimmer amid the haze of cigarette smoke that hung in the air. "You have nothing to beat yourself up about."

Gerry drained her glass and set it down with a hard clunk. "Can we talk about something else? This is in danger of turning into a country-western song."

She glanced over at Melodie. On the jukebox Shania Twain was crooning about a broken heart as Melodie and her friend stood entwined in the shallow amber glow cast by the lights over the pool table. Her head was tipped back and he was kissing her. Gerry felt a tingle of remembered pleasure, imagining it was Aubrey's lips on hers.

"I didn't tell you the latest." Sam tactfully changed the subject. "It turns out Hector's family is coming to the wedding after all. Aunts, uncles, nieces, nephews, cousins—not one of whom speaks a word of English. Laura has no idea where she's going to put them all."

"I could take one or two," Gerry offered.

"Thanks, I'm sure she'll appreciate it." Sam's gaze strayed to Melodie, then she quickly looked away—as if remembering when she'd been fodder for wagging tongues.

"By the way, did I mention Aubrey was coming?" Gerry had told Laura, but hadn't gotten around to letting Sam know. Probably because she'd feared the response she was getting now.

Sam wore a knowing smile as she tipped her mug back. "Well, it's about time."

"Don't get any ideas," Gerry warned. Just because he was going to be her date at the wedding, it didn't mean they were closing in on the altar themselves. "Things are perfect as they are."

Sam arched a brow. "For now, maybe."

Gerry didn't like where this was heading. "Even if I wanted more—which I assure you I *don't*—Aubrey Roellinger is the last man on earth I'd marry."

Sam sat back with a puzzled look. "I don't get it. You seem so perfect for each other."

Gerry gave her a sage wink, realizing that perhaps she *was* a little drunk. "I make it a habit never to share my bed with more than one person at a time."

"I take it you're referring to his wife." Sam could be naive at times, but she wasn't blind.

"To say he's not over her is putting it mildly. He can't even talk about her."

She thought about the way his eyes would go dark at times, as profoundly and completely as lights being switched off in a shuttered room. The few times he'd spoken of

Isabelle, Gerry had gotten the impression he was only pretending, for the sake of those who wouldn't have left him alone otherwise, to be getting on with his life. Unlike Sam, who deep down must have been relieved when Martin died, Aubrey guarded his grief like buried treasure.

"It takes time." The sorrowful note in Sam's voice reminded her that, despite everything, she *had* loved Martin.

"Believe me, a lifetime wouldn't be enough." She felt envious. Not of Isabelle herself, but of his devotion. To have been loved so deeply . . .

Sam's hands were folded primly on the table in front of her. Her expression made it plain she wasn't buying it. "It wouldn't kill you, you know."

"What?"

"If you *were* in love."

"Love? What's that?" Gerry gave a cynical laugh.

"Funny. You did such a good job of selling *me* on the idea." Sam was reminding her of how relentlessly she'd campaigned on Ian's behalf. "Now that the shoe's on the other foot . . ."

"It's different with me. I'm only sleeping

with the guy." Gerry spoke lightly, but she knew it wasn't that simple—she *could* fall in love with Aubrey given half a push. "Besides, if what happened to you is anything to go by, I should be running for the hills. Face it, Sam, as much as you're going to love this baby, your days of peace and quiet are over. Me? I plan on fading gracefully into middle age."

"What are you talking about? We're middle-aged now."

Gerry tossed her head. "Speak for yourself."

The two women shared a laugh.

Across the room, Melodie and her current beau were sitting quietly at their table sipping drinks and smoking cigarettes. Jimmy and Luis had quit arguing and gone back to playing pool, and the man at the bar was on his second beer. The jukebox clicked and another song was loaded: an oldie but goodie, Herb Alpert's "A Taste of Honey."

Gerry signaled for the check.

The morning of the wedding was cool and overcast. Gerry had had her doubts about an outdoor ceremony this time of year, but by the time she and the other guests had been ferried by four-wheel drive up the dusty track behind Laura's ranch to the hilltop where the ceremony was to take place, the skies had magically cleared.

She looked about, marveling at the unobstructed view. Nothing but grass and trees rising and falling in gentle waves, and the green heart of the valley stretched out below. Several miles away, atop the neighboring hill, stood the convent, which from this distance resembled nothing so much as a medieval walled fortress. She watched an acorn-size cloud of dust inching its way up the narrow ribbon of road—Sister Josepha, no doubt, back from her weekly expedition into town for groceries.

The mountains beyond seemed almost close enough to touch: Sleeping Indian Chief and Toyon Ridge, sugared with snow, and to the south and west Two Sisters Peaks and the anvil-shaped Moon's Nest. The shadows of the few remaining clouds glided like silent gray barges over the sun-drenched foothills below.

She turned to Aubrey, who stood at her side, his hand resting lightly against the small of her back. "I can't think of a nicer spot to get married."

"My sentiments exactly." In jeans and a navy sport jacket—Laura had specifically requested casual attire—he was the picture of casual elegance. Even his hair fell with just the right touch of louche over the jacket's hand-stitched collar. He pointed to the mountain at the northernmost end of the valley. "What's that one over there?"

"Sespe—Chumash for kneecaps," she told him. "See how it looks like someone squatting?"

"Not very romantic."

"Oh, I don't know. He could be getting down on his knee to propose." She could joke like this with Aubrey, knowing he wouldn't get the wrong idea.

"In that case, we'll never know what her answer was." In the sunlight his eyes, creased with amusement, were the clear golden brown of the creek meandering in and out of the willows below.

It occurred to Gerry that they were suspended in the same way. Two people who'd found temporary shelter in each other's arms and would never progress past that point. The thought made her sad. Maybe it was the occasion—or the image of those eternally frozen lovers. Either way, she found herself wishing for something more; maybe not what Laura and Hector had, but enough to bring comfort on nights when the joy of a bed all to herself paled in comparison to someone snuggled beside her.

"Don't look now," she leaned close to whisper, "but we're being watched."

Alice Carpenter was coolly observing them from the shade of a nearby live oak where she stood with her husband Wes—Ian's father. A few feet from Alice and Wes, Anna Vincenzi sneaked surreptitious looks at them as well.

Aubrey didn't appear the least bit ruffled. "You'd better get used to it. I have a feeling this is only the beginning."

"It's not like they've never seen me with a man," she said.

He arched a brow. "Should I be jealous?"

"Wildly." She never knew when Aubrey was kidding. He certainly wasn't the jealous type.

"At least your private life isn't grist for the tabloids."

"I wonder what they'd say about *us*?" She smiled.

"Oh, they'd probably have us secretly

married by now." His brown eyes sparkled with humor. "Or at the very least engaged."

Gerry allowed herself to imagine it: Aubrey and her. Then the image faded, and with it any silly romantic notions today's occasion might have dredged up. She felt vaguely irritated. She hadn't minded his teasing in the past, but suddenly wished he wouldn't say such things.

She looked over at her children. Andie, in a blue knit dress with rows of sparkly studs in each ear, curving in moonlike crescents, appeared to be giving some kind of pep talk to Finch, who looked darkly exotic in a long-sleeved cotton dress that in the breeze billowed about her ankles. Justin stood kicking at a dirt clod a few yards away, looking uncomfortable in his new jacket and chinos and more than a little bent out of shape that there was no one his age.

What did they make of Aubrey? She'd had him over for dinner last week, they'd both been so well behaved—almost to a fault— she but couldn't tell if they'd liked him or not.

She wondered for the dozenth time if bringing him had been such a good idea. Wasn't it making a statement of some kind?

And come to think of it, what *about* the tabloids? Sooner or later they were sure to get wind of her.

Alice and Wes wandered over. In her pleated cream trousers and chocolate blazer, a scarf artfully knotted about her neck, Sam's younger daughter might have stepped from a Ralph Lauren ad. She glanced from Gerry to Aubrey with a knowing look. No doubt she'd drawn her share of such looks with Wes, who was a good deal older.

Alice kissed her on the cheek before extending a hand to Aubrey. "Hi. I'm Alice Carpenter."

"I recognize you from the photo." Aubrey was quick to explain, "I came across one from your wedding that your mother had forgotten to take with her."

Alice smiled up at Wes. "We were married last summer."

"Now *that* was one hell of an occasion." Wes chuckled, and Gerry knew he was referring to Finch, who'd crashed the reception and nearly ruined it.

"And here we all are again." Alice sighed. "Frankly, I never thought I'd see the day." She turned to Gerry. "Remember when we were kids, how my sister used to follow Hector around like a puppy? He always pretended not to notice, but he'd have to have been blind not to. Wonder what took him so long to pop the question."

Gerry remembered years ago when Hector, a skinny eighteen-year-old speaking no English and without even a green card, had shown up on Sam's doorstep. Sam had taken him on as a hired hand, and he'd been with the family ever since.

"It could have had something to do with Peter," Gerry said dryly, reminding them that this wasn't Laura's first trip to the altar.

"Peter? He was just the warm-up act." Alice dismissed him with an airy wave, saying to Wes, "You see, darling? If you don't watch out, you could end up with second billing."

Wes gave a hearty laugh. "I have two mottoes: Never own a car you can't handle, and never marry a woman you can." Big and handsome in a swashbuckling sort of way, with a head of iron hair and beard to match, he'd always struck Gerry as a man who'd encountered little in life he couldn't handle. He kissed Gerry on the cheek before extending a hand to Aubrey. "I've heard a lot about you." The look Wes gave him was that of a kindred spirit. The founder and CEO of a multibillion-dollar cable network, he, too, had drawn his share of unwanted attention from the press. "Sam tells us she couldn't ask for a better tenant."

"Probably because I'm hardly ever there," Aubrey told him.

"Is Lupe driving you crazy yet?" Of the two girls, Alice looked the most like her mother—she had Sam's delicate bone structure and heart-shaped face, but her hair was blond and her blue eyes carbon copies of Martin's.

Aubrey laughed. "She can be a bit domineering at times."

"Mom's tried for years to get her to retire. I guess she thought renting the house out would do the trick. I guess it hasn't."

"I don't mind—in fact, I'm not sure how much would get done without her."

Alice looked as if she were wondering where Gerry fit in. "Well, I'm glad we finally had a chance to meet. In fact, we'd love to have you two up for dinner sometime."

There was a moment of awkward silence. It wasn't anything against Alice and Wes, just that contrary to Aubrey's public person—or maybe in reaction to it—he almost never socialized outside of family and old friends. Luckily, he was saved from having to reply by the roar of Laura's Explorer making its way up the dusty track, brightly colored streamers rippling gaily from its bumper. As it topped the rise, Gerry watched Finch break away from Andie to attend to her duties as maid of honor.

Hector, in jeans and a pressed white shirt—a silver bolo tie his only concession to the occasion—climbed from the front seat and walked around to Laura's side. As she stepped down, dressed in a plain organdy gown that might indeed have passed for a slip, but which suited her perfectly, Gerry couldn't help thinking of a cactus flower blooming after a long dry spell in the desert. Laura had lost the ten or so extra pounds she'd put on after the divorce and, though Alice had always been the prettier of the two, at this moment she was by far the most beautiful woman on the hill. Her brown eyes sparkled and her olive skin glowed. A crown of baby roses sat atop her shining brown head.

Hector, bandy-legged from a lifetime on horseback, with a broad chest hammered to iron hardness from hoisting bales and heavy machinery, hooked an arm through Laura's, his dark eyes fixed on her as if they were the only two people for miles around.

Gerry glanced about at the other guests—roughly fifty in all, with Hector's contingent far outweighing Laura's. A whole passel of his relatives were talking animatedly among themselves while Sam made the rounds, putting her spotty high school Spanish to use. Luckily, Gerry hadn't had to find room for them in her house. Alice and Wes, as their wedding gift, had put them all up at the Horse Creek Inn.

Gerry's gaze fell on Ian, chatting with Anna Vincenzi by the makeshift altar—fittingly enough, a saddle tree decked in flowers. Anna looked less drab than usual in a flowered dress and lipstick, her plump cheeks pink from the unaccustomed attention—usually she was overshadowed by Monica.

A few feet away, elderly Maude Wickersham, one of Laura's strays who'd stuck around long enough to become a fixture, peeked out from under a cartwheel hat almost big enough to topple her tiny frame. She wore a shantung suit from another era, one of her thrift shop purchases, no doubt. Gerry watched her totter over to greet Mavis, who looked equally festive in a circle-cut denim skirt and fancy cowgirl shirt like the ones Dale Evans used to wear.

The crowd parted as Laura and Hector began making their way to the altar, stopping to greet people along the way. Laura was holding her hem up to keep it from trailing on the ground, revealing a pair of brand-new cream suede cowboy boots that made Gerry smile, they were so . . . well, Laura. Hector had on cowboy boots of his own, black with fancy stitching, and a belt with a conch buckle that would have felled a bull.

Gerry blinked back sudden tears. Dammit, she'd promised herself she wouldn't cry. What was it with her? For someone so dead set against another wedding of her own, how could she be such a sucker for other people's?

She caught sight of Father Dan getting his ear chewed off by Sam's sallow-faced sister Audrey—as different from Sam as night from day. Since Laura was divorced he hadn't been able to officiate, and now it seemed he was fair game for every soul in need of unburdening. Poor Dan. Gerry would be forced to rescue him if she kept it up.

The Episcopal minister was an old friend

of Laura's from college: a tall, plain-faced woman with cropped brown hair. She looked stately standing opposite Laura and Hector, her robe and surplice fluttering in the breeze, yet managed to conduct the ceremony in a down-home manner, more like a big sister handing out advice. Gerry smiled, half expecting her to remind Hector to always put the toilet seat down.

In keeping with the relaxed tone, Laura read aloud a short fairy tale about an elderly couple granted a single wish, which was to die together when the time came, and who were subsequently transformed into trees forever entwined. Hector, his voice hoarse with emotion, followed with a Pablo Neruda poem that he read both in English and in Spanish. It was followed by Finch shyly stepping forward to give a speech about Laura taking her in when no one else would, and how she hoped Hector would be as happy with her mother as *she* was. By the time vows were exchanged, there wasn't a dry eye in the crowd.

Gerry glanced over at Sam, who was smiling through her tears. Both daughters married off, and now she was about to start all over again. Living proof, Gerry thought wryly, that good things didn't necessarily come in neatly labeled packages by registered mail.

"They look happy, don't they?" Aubrey murmured. Gerry thought she caught a note of wistfulness in his voice, and wondered if he was thinking of Isabelle.

"They've earned it." She didn't trust herself to say more—she was too choked up.

When she dared look at him, she saw that he was gazing not at Laura and Hector but at the mountains rising in the distance. Suddenly she wanted to snatch him back from wherever he'd gone in his mind. She could do what Isabelle couldn't—warm his bed—but in every other way he'd remained faithful to his wife.

Then Aubrey took her hand, squeezing it gently and making her wonder if she was only imagining things.

Back at the ranch, decked in balloons and crepe paper streamers—Maude's doing, no doubt—even the animals joined in celebrating: Rocky, the terrier, tagged after everyone holding a plate, hoping for a scrap; dear old Pearl, too old and dignified to beg, padded about with her big yellow head offered up for stroking; while the cats, Napoleon and

Josephine, darted anxiously amid the thicket of legs crowding the living room. Even Punch and Judy, and Finch's new chestnut mare Cheyenne, nickering in the barn, were making themselves known.

Sam darted over to plant a kiss on Gerry's cheek. "I hope you're hungry, because there's enough food for a small army." She didn't have to say it: Lupe was in charge.

The smell of barbecued chicken drifted from the backyard, and Gerry could see past Sam into the kitchen, where Lupe, her thick black braids wrapped about her head—the only thing about her that hadn't aged—bustled about like the world's oldest general. The makeshift table at one end of the cozy living room, an old door propped on sawhorses and covered with an embroidered cloth, was laden with serving bowls and platters and baskets heaped with Lupe's famous jalapeño cornbread. What a difference from Alice's elegant reception on the lawn at Isla Verde!

Sam must have been thinking of Isla Verde, too. She turned to Aubrey with a smile. "By the way, Mr. Hathaway wanted me to tell you the roofers will be finishing up some time next week. I hope all the noise hasn't been disturbing you too much."

Gerry recalled that Mr. Hathaway was the property manager Sam had hired, which in turn reminded her of why Sam had rented Isla Verde out in the first place: All the up-keep had been more than she could handle on her own.

"Not in the least." Aubrey *had* mentioned the noise, but was too much of a gentleman to let Sam know.

"Well, if you need to get away, there's always Gerry's."

Gerry shot her a warning look. "One day at my house and he'd be running home to his leaky roof."

"Not to mention Lupe." Aubrey, thankfully, wasn't taking it too seriously.

"As far as Lupe goes, you're on your own. I gave up on her years ago." Sam said with a laugh. "Excuse me . . ."

She darted off to rescue Anna, who'd been cornered by one of Hector's uncles, a grizzled older man who clearly had an eye for the ladies. From Anna's panicked expression it was obvious she didn't understand a word he was saying.

"So far, so good," Gerry muttered, glancing about. For the moment at least, they were being officially ignored.

Aubrey cast a faintly ironic glance at Andie and Justin, standing in line at the table, plates in hand. "I get the distinct impression your children haven't missed a thing."

Gerry sighed. "Knowing them, I don't doubt it."

Aubrey sipped his wine, regarding her thoughtfully over the rim of his glass. People pressed in around them, laughing and talking, everyone having a good time—even the old Miller twins, Olive and Rose, who'd had a bit too much to drink and were giggling like schoolgirls as Sam's brother Ray attempted to teach them the Texas two-step.

"I'm not sure they know what to make of me," he said.

Tipsy from the champagne, Gerry leaned close to confide, "They're a little intimidated, I think."

"Am I such an ogre?"

"Worse—you're famous."

He smiled. "I hope the two aren't synonymous."

"You're also the second bomb I've

dropped on them in less than a month." The thought of Claire brought a dull ache.

"Your daughter, yes." He sipped his wine, his long fingers curled about the stem of his glass. "Still no word?"

"Not yet." Gerry forced a smile, determined not to cast a pall over the occasion. "Look, forget I mentioned it. I shouldn't be boring you with all this stuff."

His fingertips brushed lightly over her arm. "You could never bore me."

The small hairs on her forearm prickled. Oh, God, she shouldn't have had so much to drink. How much easier to keep everything tidily in a box when you're sober.

"That's why we get along so well—I'm never around long enough to test it," she said tipsily.

Gerry expected him to laugh, but he didn't. She caught a flicker of something in his eyes, and felt a cool rush of unease. So often with him she sensed he was walking in two worlds: the past, with its memories no flesh-and-blood woman could measure up against, and the present, in which each step had to be carefully negotiated. Then the look was gone, and he was once more smiling at her as if she were the only woman in the room.

He took her arm. "Shall we get something to eat before it's all gone?"

By the time they reached the head of the line, serious inroads had been made into the platters. They helped themselves to barbecued chicken, black bean salad, and tamale pie before wandering out onto the porch, where a number of the other guests were enjoying the unusually mild weather. The food was as delicious as it looked and Gerry ate more than she should have. She was about to head back inside for a drink of water to quench the fire from Lupe's jalapeño cornbread when Aubrey said, "Will you excuse me a moment? I see someone I'd like to talk to."

She glanced in the direction he was looking and saw a beautiful young Hispanic woman in hip-hugger jeans and a sleek top that left little to the imagination—one of Hector's young cousins, no doubt. She felt a quick, hot little stab, then saw that it was Hector's brother Eddie he was heading toward. She remembered that Eddie was a minor celebrity in his own right—on the rodeo circuit. Annoyed at herself for jumping to conclusions, and even more for being jealous, she frowned as she pushed open the screen door.

Inside, she caught sight of Father Dan in line at the table. She couldn't help noticing that it was time for a haircut—any longer and Althea Wormley would accuse him of being one of those hippie priests who, according to Althea and her ilk, had taken all the sanctity out of the Church with their guitar masses and freewheeling discussion groups and other such tomfoolery.

She sidled up to him. "Having fun?"

He turned to her with a smile. "To be honest, I feel a little out of place. I don't usually come to weddings as a guest."

"Think of all the future business you'll be drumming up." She glanced in the direction of Sam's nephews—Audrey's boys—both angular and dark-haired like their mother, doing their best to impress Rose Miller's twin granddaughters, Dawn and Eve.

"Oh, there's never a shortage of people wanting me to marry them," he said, blue eyes twinkling in his broad Irish face. "It's when they come to me after the bloom is off the rose that I wish I'd counseled them to wait."

She felt a deep affection for her old friend. How many times had she gone to him for advice? Dan didn't have all the answers, and that's what she loved about him. If he didn't have advice to give, he listened instead. He was the only priest she knew who didn't feel the need to quote chapter and verse for every ill under the sun.

"I don't think the bloom will ever be off *that* rose."

She nodded in the direction of Laura and Hector, surrounded by family and friends. They already wore the look of old marrieds—hands loosely linked, their gazes straying to each other before reluctantly pulling away to focus on whoever was speaking.

"Unlikely," Dan agreed.

"As for me," she felt compelled to add, "once was enough."

"Never say never." He cocked his head, smiling, the only man in this room tall enough to look down on her.

Gerry felt herself blush—had that been in reference to Aubrey? "That's fine and dandy," she said, "coming from a man who's never been to bed with a woman."

"Don't be too sure of that." He winked.
"Remember, I wasn't always a priest."

Aubrey wasn't thinking about Gerry as he
pushed open the screen door. He was thinking about Eddie Navarro, a man who rode
bulls the way Itzhak Perlman played the violin. Surprisingly, it turned out Eddie was a
fan of his as well. He listened to classical
music before each rodeo, not giving a hoot
that the other cowboys thought he'd landed
on his head one time too many. They'd had a
most interesting chat, but after a few minutes he'd found himself, to his surprise,
missing Gerry.

He paused in the doorway to scan the
crowded room, spotting her deep in conversation with the priest. What was his name?
Reardon, yes. A hail-fellow-well-met, broad
as a yardarm across the shoulders and
chest, who without his dog collar would
never have been taken for a priest. But what
struck Aubrey most was the way Gerry was
looking at him, her face tipped up, glowing
like that of a young girl . . .

. . . in love.

The thought startled him. Christ, where

had *that* come from? He had no earthly reason to think such a thing, and what if it were
so? It wasn't as if he had any claim on her.
He nonetheless felt a certain unease, which
took a moment to identify it had been so
long: *I'm jealous.* He stood there, too
stunned to move, the roomful of happily
chatting people fading from consciousness.
What business did he have being jealous?
He wasn't in love with Gerry. He liked her,
yes, quite a bit more than he'd originally
bargained on, but that wasn't the same, was
it? The only reason he'd gone on seeing
her was because . . . well, because . . . he
couldn't *not* see her.

He frowned, the sense of disquiet deepening. After months, years, of merely keeping his head above water, he'd at last
achieved a measure of contentment, which
wasn't the same as happiness, he knew—
that had been buried along with his wife—
but just as precious in its own way. He
hoarded it the way a man stripped of his
wealth might hoard his last remaining coins.
Now his heart was going off in a direction he
hadn't counted on. And he didn't like it; he
didn't like it one bit.

He suspected that Gerry would be equally

appalled. She'd made it plain she wanted nothing more than she herself was prepared to give: sex and affection, in that order.

He took a step back, easing the screen door shut. As he turned, his gaze fell on Gerry's son, seated on the porch steps tossing an old tennis ball to one of the dogs—a little black terrier that growled with mock ferociousness as the boy pried the ball away and sent it hurtling back out over the dusty yard. Aubrey strolled over.

"Mind if I join you?"

Justin only shrugged, but he didn't move when Aubrey sank down beside him.

"I've always liked terriers. They're like big dogs, only smaller." He nodded in the direction of Rocky. "My grandparents had one—his name was Mignon. He'd swim out to get the sticks I threw him and the waves would keep tossing him back onto the shore. He never gave up."

"Dogs don't know any better," Justin said.

Aubrey cast a sidelong look at him. Justin sat slumped over his knees, his shoulders tense. "You're not having a very good time, are you?"

The boy shrugged again. "There's no one my age."

"Yes, I can see that." Aubrey remembered all too well what it had been like for him with his grandparents living several kilometers from the nearest village.

Now the boy did look at him, his green-eyed gaze, so like his mother's, sliding over Aubrey like cool water. "Mom wouldn't let me bring Nesto."

"I suppose because he wasn't invited."

Justin was staring at him openly now. "You weren't either and you're here."

"A valid point." Aubrey smiled. No one was going to get anything past this kid.

"I would've gone to my dad's, but she wouldn't let me do that either." Justin's glum face took on a harder cast—showing a glimpse of the teenager just around the bend.

Aubrey gazed out at the hydrangeas lapping the front walk. It made him think of the cottage he and Isabelle had rented that summer in Aix-en-Provence. It had been smothered in hydrangeas. Pink and blue, with blossoms the size of cabbages. He felt his heart retreat back into the safety of its cave.

When he looked back, Justin was eyeing him narrowly. "Do you know my dad?"

"I'm afraid I haven't had the pleasure."

"He's about the same age as you, only taller."

"Is that so?" If Justin was looking to get a rise out of him, he was going to be disappointed.

"He's practically head of his whole company, too."

"What sort of business is he in?" Aubrey already knew; he was only asking to be polite.

"He loans people money to buy houses and stuff." A hard lob sent the tennis ball bouncing up high and landing it in the bushes. The little dog went charging off in pursuit.

"I see—he works at a savings and loan."

"Yeah, that's it."

"My father was a barrister—that's the British word for lawyer. I didn't see much of him growing up."

"Your parents were divorced?"

"No. I was away at school."

"Like in *Harry Potter?*" Justin looked intrigued.

"Minus the wizardry." Aubrey smiled, watching the dog root around in the bushes in search of the ball.

"Didn't you get homesick?"

"At first, but you get used to it." In his mind Aubrey heard his father saying almost the exact same words, telling him it would make a man out of him—he'd been eight—and realized it wasn't entirely true: There was a difference between getting used to something and merely learning to tolerate it.

Justin took a moment to ponder this, elbows propped on his knees as he gazed out over the yard. At last he swung around, squinting at Aubrey like Clint Eastwood in *Fistful of Dollars*—another cowboy he admired.

"Are you and my mom getting married?"

So that's what was worrying him. Aubrey considered his answer carefully. "Any man would be lucky to have her," he said. "But I don't plan on getting married—to anyone."

Justin looked relieved. "Mom said the same thing when I asked her."

"What else did she say?"

"That you liked living alone."

Aubrey felt a sudden sharp hitch like a lungful of air pressing against a bruised rib. "I was married once before," he said, "to someone I loved very much. She died."

"Oh." Justin dropped his gaze.

Just then the little terrier came bounding

up the steps with the ball, now coated with dirt as well as slobber. Aubrey pried it from his jaws and wiped it on a napkin someone had dropped. On impulse, he said, "What do you say we throw a few?"

The boy brightened, then with a shrug quickly looked away.

Aubrey rose, stepping down off the porch. A moment passed before he heard the scuffle of footsteps behind him. He gave in to a small smile he was careful to erase before the boy caught up with him.

Gerry watched them from the doorway, the skinny kid whose clothes would have to go straight into the wash as soon as they got home and the elegant, silver-haired man mindless of his expensive jacket. Something floated up in her chest. How had he known what Justin needed? The same boy who'd been moping about all day was now grinning from ear to ear.

"It looks like he's made a new friend."

She turned to find that Sam had slipped up alongside her.

Gerry shrugged. "You know Justin—he gets along with everyone."

"He needs a man in his life."

"He has his father."

"When Mike can find the time." Sam had an even more jaundiced view of her ex-husband than she did, if that was possible.

Gerry shot her a stern look. "Look, whatever it is you're selling, I'm not interested."

She watched Justin leap up to snag the ball and lob it back to Aubrey, who caught it easily. Aubrey spotted her and waved. Gerry waved back, motioning to let him know it was almost time for the cake to be cut. When she turned, bracing herself for another earful, she saw that Sam had drifted off. Gerry spotted her at the other end of the porch, chatting with Tom Kemp. From the glowing tips of his ears—the curse of redheads—it was obvious he still had feelings for her. Gerry wondered if love was always that transparent, even when those afflicted were blind to it.

Aubrey and Justin tramped back up the steps, and they all headed back inside. In the living room the platters had been cleared away, replaced by plates of cookies and a large bowl of fruit salad. The triple-tiered cake stood in the center of the table—a towering tribute, if one that listed slightly, to Maude's baking. Gerry filled two cups from the coffee urn and handed one to Aubrey. Wandering over to the fireplace, they found room on the cat-scratched sofa to sit down.

"That was nice, what you did," she told him.

He shrugged. "I enjoyed it."

"Well, it was nice anyway."

"He's a good kid."

"After the divorce I tried doing all that stuff—one time I fell into the lake trying to reel in a fish that turned out to be a water-logged T-shirt." She smiled ruefully at the memory. "But if there's one thing I've learned it's that you can't be both a mother and a father to your kids."

He shot her an odd look, and she felt a little chill crawl up from the pit of her stomach. Was he warning her not to make too big a deal of his being nice to Justin? Lumping her in with single moms who used their kids to sweeten the deal?

Gerry was heading back to the table for a refill when she caught sight of Andie with a handful of CDs. Laura must have asked her to reload the player. Gerry smiled at her and for once Andie didn't give her the evil eye. She looked as if she was having a good time.

The room fell silent just then as Maude

rose to make a toast, teetering a little from too much champagne. The bundle of white hair atop her head was coming undone and snowy wisps floated about her apple-doll face. "To two people I love dearly," she said, lifting her glass high overhead. "May they live long and be happy . . . and never get tired of taking in strays."

There was a chorus of hoots and cheers and barks, then the cake was cut. Laura fed a bite to Hector while everyone snapped photos with the disposable cameras that had been left about. She looked a little embarrassed by all the attention, and at the same time pleased that everything was going so well. Hector, for his part, wore the somewhat dazed look of a man who'd been thrown from a horse.

The music started up again—not soft rock like before, but a lovely violin concerto. It wasn't until she glanced over at Aubrey that Gerry knew something was wrong. He wore a stricken look, his mouth frozen in a ghastly parody of a smile. That's when it hit her: The music was Isabelle's.

Andie. It was Andie who did this.

Gerry, stunned by the casual cruelty of it, stood rooted to the spot as people swirled about, clapping and making toasts—some ribald, like curmudgeonly Doc Henry joking that Laura and Hector were sure to give new meaning to the term animal husbandry. Glasses clinked and more champagne was poured. All the while the heartbreaking beauty of Isabelle's music, coupled with the sorrow on Aubrey's face, was almost more than she could bear.

Chapter Eight

Claire eased into the right lane. Just ahead, a tractor-trailer was pulled over, and though she didn't see any flares, she slowed as she passed it. *No sense buying trouble,* warned a voice in her head—Millie's. She smiled at the irony. For on this chilly February day, as she made her way north on Highway 101 to San Francisco, wasn't trouble the very thing waiting for her at the other end?

When she reached San Mateo, she fished her cell phone from her purse and punched in Byron's number. He was off today, and it was early still—just after ten. She might catch him.

He picked up on the fourth ring.

"Hi," she said.

"Hey, babe." His voice was groggy with sleep.

"I thought you might be out. I was going to leave a sexy message."

He yawned. "I was on call until four. I just got up."

"Sorry. I didn't mean to wake you."

"Hey, no problem. Can I still get the sexy message?"

"Not now—I'm driving."

"Where to?"

"You know."

"Oh yeah. I forgot."

"He's there. I called before I left to make sure."

"What did you say to him?"

"Nothing. I hung up."

"He might be gone by the time you get there."

She felt a tiny prick of irritation. Didn't he think she knew that?

"I'll try him later, then." She could always look up Gerry's brother in the meantime. She'd planned on doing so anyway.

"Yeah, but there's still no guarantee he'll see you."

For an instant she thought he was referring to Kevin, before realizing he meant Father Gallagher, of course. "I guess that's the chance I'll have to take." Her pulse quickened at the thought.

She heard the pad of footsteps at the other end, then the sound of Byron peeing into the toilet. God, they weren't even living together and already they were like old marrieds. Then she remembered that in Byron's house no one was shy about such things; his parents even sunbathed in the nude. She'd spied them once over the backyard fence.

"Listen, I'm all for it," he said, "as long as it's going to help you get some closure." He'd fallen into the habit of using such lingo since starting his current rotation in psychiatry.

Personally, she distrusted such words. Twenty years ago no one had heard of "closure" and wouldn't have known what you were talking about. "I'm not doing this to heal my wounded psyche," she said a bit testily. "I just want to know what he's like. He's my father, after all." It felt strange saying it; the only image that came to mind was of Lou.

"Hey, I'm on your side, remember?" She heard the toilet flush.

"I know," she said with a sigh.

"I miss you, babe."

"Me, too."

"I wish I could be there."

She wished it, too. At the same time she cringed at the thought of Byron looking on, however sympathetically, as she struggled to make sense of this family that had been dumped in her lap.

"I'll give you a full report on the way back," she promised.

"Good luck."

"Thanks, I'll need it."

"Love you."

"Love you, too."

She thumbed the end button, wishing the words so often whispered in her ear were accompanied by a living, breathing Byron. It was hard seeing so little of him. And what worried her most was that their long-distance relationship had begun to seem normal.

That thought led to ones of Gerry. At least a dozen times over the past few weeks she'd gone to pick up the phone, but something always stopped her. What would be the point? One thing would lead to another, and before she knew it she'd feel pressured into inviting Gerry here. And how would she explain *that* to Lou and Millie? She'd been able to justify the first meeting, in her own mind at least, but her parents would see another as nothing short of a major betrayal.

Then she remembered Justin's sweet, funny e-mails. And the recipes Mavis had sent, painstakingly copied onto index cards in her crabbed, arthritic hand. Even the memory of Gerry's ambivalence and Andie's pushing her away weren't enough to blot out the warm feelings that crept in.

But first she needed to solve the puzzle of her father. Using the little bit of information Gerry had given her, she'd gotten his home number from the offices of the archdiocese in San Francisco. Luckily his housekeeper had answered when she called. With her fingers crossed behind her back, Claire had told her she worked for the *Marian Reader* and would like to send Father Gallagher a copy of the article in which he'd been mentioned.

Now, armed with his address, she was going to confront him face-to-face.

She saw that she was nearing the Civic Center turnoff, and her stomach did another free-fall. Was it fair to ambush him like this? Maybe she should have told him who she was over the phone. If Gerry was right, it would have saved her a trip.

And what about her parents? She hadn't told them about this little jaunt. They could hardly stand to hear about Gerry. After Claire's weekend in Carson Springs they'd asked only the bare minimum—what was she like, how were her kids? She knew they felt bad about the stink they'd made. Millie had been going out of her way to be nice, and Lou had volunteered to fix a leak under her sink. So Claire had stuck to the facts, not elaborating. It was easier to let them think her curiosity had been satisfied, that she'd gotten . . . closure.

Father Gallagher lived on Turk Street in a narrow, two-story clapboard house tucked back from the sidewalk. She circled the block several times before she found a parking space. Fog had crept in, and the dampness clung like wet flannel as she walked back to the house.

She let herself in the gate and made her way up the front path. In the yard, dwarf trees and shrubs were bowed with moisture, and the house seemed to loom like a ship in the fog. Her heart was pounding as she mounted the steps to the porch.

She knocked on the door and a long minute passed before a pair of washed-out blue eyes below a fringe of gray bangs appeared in its beveled glass oval. Claire must not have looked threatening, for the door swung open. A heavyset older woman in a nubby brown sweater that bagged down around her hips stood before her, a lime-green duster in hand.

"Can I help you?"

"I'm looking for Father Gallagher," Claire said.

"Oh yes, he's expecting you." Claire's heart lurched. How had he known? Then the woman said, "Father said they were sending over some papers for him to sign." She stepped back to let Claire in.

She was ushered into a shabby but scrupulously neat living room with a small dining ell off to one side. She caught the faint odor of cooked fish from the night before. Apparently the easing of restrictions brought by Vatican II hadn't penetrated this corner of the ecclesiastical universe.

What am I doing here? This is crazy. She ought to be looking ahead to the future, not mucking around in the past. Didn't she have enough with just Gerry? What could this man offer her that would be worth the grief?

She heard the creak of someone descending the stairs, and a moment later a man stepped through the archway into the living room, walking with a slight limp—a priest from central casting with piercing blue eyes and wavy silver hair brushed into wings over his temples. His face was smooth and serene except for the deep line, like a chevron, between his brows.

He stuck out a large dry hand smelling faintly of soap. His grip was firm. "I'm sorry the archbishop had to send you all this way." He smiled and tapped his leg. "Touch of rheumatism. I'll be back at my desk in a day or two."

Her cheeks grew warm. "I'm afraid you have me confused with someone else."

He cocked his head, wearing a faintly puzzled look, as if trying to remember if he knew her from somewhere. "Well, my mistake, then. What can I do for you?"

"My name is Claire—Claire Brewster." She waited to see if her name would ring a bell and when it didn't grew lightheaded. "Would it be all right if I sat down?"

"Of course." He gestured toward the sofa.

Claire had the strangest sensation of its cushion falling away from her even as she sank into it. She waited for Father Gallagher to sit down as well, but he remained standing, favoring his good leg as he leaned up against a wing chair.

She cleared her throat. "Gerry told me where to find you."

"Gerry?"

"Fitzgerald."

He only frowned slightly, then tapped his temple and said, "Ah yes—Our Lady of the Wayside. She was one of the sisters there. She taught catechism, didn't she?"

"But weren't you—?" She stopped, feeling suddenly unsure of herself.

"Friends? Yes, I suppose you could call it that. As much as any spiritual adviser can be." Father Gallagher regarded her mildly. "I don't mean to be rude, Miss Brewster, but I'm rather busy at the moment. Perhaps you can tell me why you're here."

Claire drew in a deep breath. "I thought— she told me you were my father."

The chevron on his forehead deepened, and now he did sit down, sinking heavily into the wing chair. "What would make her say—or even think—such a thing?"

"The truth is, I don't know her that well. I was adopted, you see. " Claire plowed on. "I didn't know much of anything until she called me out of the blue."

His expression didn't change, but what she'd taken for priestly serenity suddenly seemed far less benign—a kind of eerie detachment. Even as Claire searched for a resemblance, she was glad when she didn't see one.

"Whatever she told you," he said in a voice as eerily detached as his expression, "I'm afraid you've been led astray."

It couldn't have been more than seventy degrees in the room but sweat was oozing from her armpits. It was just as Gerry had said—he wanted no part of her. Oh, God, why had she come?

"I don't see why she would make up a thing like that," Claire said.

"Oh, I don't doubt that she's sincere in her belief." His expression shifted subtly, like that of an actor slipping into a role. He leaned toward her with a look of concern. "It happens more often than you'd think—young nuns becoming infatuated with priests to the point of hysteria . . . and sometimes even delusion." He shook his head. "There's a whole body of literature on the subject, if you'd care to read it."

"She . . . she's not like that."

If anyone was lying, it was Father Gallagher. She'd *swear* to it. At the same time, she couldn't be 100 percent sure.

"You said yourself that you hardly know her." He brought his fingertips together in a steeple under his chin, and she caught the glint of a gold signet ring. "May I make a suggestion, Miss Brewster? Let it sit for now. In time, perhaps the truth—the *real* truth—will come out." He sounded so sincere—as if she were nothing more than a parishioner who'd come to him for spiritual guidance— that for a moment she almost believed him.

"But—"

He glanced at his watch and rose. "I'm afraid I'm going to have to cut this short. I'm sorry you had to come all this way for nothing."

Claire dragged herself to her feet, cheeks burning as if with fever. "Thank you for seeing me, Father." The irony of addressing him as "Father" wasn't lost on her.

"Not at all, my child." He spoke as if she

were just another member of his flock, and
when she put her hand out, he took it between both of his, patting it gently.

Then she was out the door, stumbling
down the steps in a daze. What had happened back there? Claire scarcely knew
what to make of it. She *had* heard of cases
where religious fervor crossed the line into
sexual hysteria. Was it possible the affair existed only in Gerry's mind? In which case, if
that man wasn't her father, who *was*?

Father Jim Gallagher couldn't remember a
time when he hadn't wanted to be a priest.
While the other boys were sneaking cigarettes in the parking lot of All Saints and
bragging about their sexual exploits with the
girls from Holy Cross (most of it wishful
thinking), he'd found solace in Father
Czerny's cool book-lined study, where they'd
spend hours discussing biblical text and the
radical changes wrought by Vatican II.

Father Czerny, a large shaggy-browed
man with a habit of blinking rapidly when ag-
itated (as he generally was when discussing
such things as the Vatican's mandate that
mass be said in English instead of Latin),
had been more than parish priest and men-

tor. He'd been a true savior. It was from him
that Jim had learned to cope with his father's
drinking and his mother's neglect. The old
priest, who was no saint himself—he
smoked too much and enjoyed the occasional card game—had done more than
show him the light, he'd shown him the way
out: from the neighborhood, and from the
bottom of the heap where nothing ever
changed, where every day looked like the
one before, with your mother screaming at
your father for running up a tab at O'Malley's
and him screaming back at her to show him
some respect and Mrs. Malatesta downstairs thumping on the ceiling with her
broom, yelling, *Shaddup, ya goddamn
micks, shut up or I'll call the cops, I mean it
this time.*

Over the years little Jimmy Gallagher,
whose sleeves were always too short and
whose nose was always running, had gradually given way to Father Jim Gallagher. The
seminary some viewed as restrictive had
been a haven of quiet and sanity. Even
celibacy, with which he'd struggled at first,
had grown easier with time and with the
knowledge that a life without sacrifice was a
life much like the one he'd abandoned: un-

structured, undisciplined—and generally un-
fit. It wasn't until he was assigned to St.
Xavier's and a pretty young novice named
Gerry Fitzgerald came into his life that
everything changed, that he began to wake
in the middle of the night to find his sheets
damp and stained.

Oh yes, he remembered her all right.
Gerry, with her sloe eyes and bewitching
smile, her hips that swayed enticingly beneath her habit. Gerry, whose very inno-
cence inflamed him. It was as if an exotic
bird had flown over the wall, its bright
plumage visible only to him, its silver-
throated song for an audience of one: a
creature of God's creation who flew in the
face of everything godly, who through no
fault of her own was wreaking havoc with his
carefully ordered existence. All this before
they'd scarcely exchanged more than a word
in passing.

When did it cross the line? He couldn't recall the precise moment, only the small
breaches along the way. A hand lingering on
hers a beat too long. Pleasantries that
evolved into lengthy conversations. Visits to
the convent that became more frequent and
were not so coincidentally timed to when he

was most likely to run into her. Even when she knelt before him in the confessional, where her very nearness was like a drug making his head swim and his heart race, he took more time with her than with the others. Now, in retrospect, he saw those confessions, in the shadowy cubicle steeped in her scent, their murmuring voices intimate as lovers', as the precursor of what was to come. The absolution he gave felt like dirty coins passing hands. For wasn't he guilty of sins far worse than hers? Even the exquisite release in the privacy of his room afterward did little to alleviate his torment.

He remembered as though it were yesterday the night he'd tumbled over the edge into the abyss. Gerry had been assigned by Mother Jerome to take over a catechism class taught by a teacher who'd become ill. Soon she fell into the habit of stopping by the rectory afterward for a cup of tea and a spirited debate—Gerry was in favor of Vatican II; in fact, she argued passionately that even more changes were needed. Over the weeks his chair began to creep closer to hers. Their tea would be long cold by the time one or the other remembered to glance at the clock and remark on how late it was getting. They both knew that what they were doing was wrong—it was forbidden for a nun to be alone with any man, even a priest—but neither made mention of it.

Then one evening as Gerry was getting ready to leave, the heavens opened with a crack of thunder. She stood in the doorway looking out at the rain sheeting down.

"You can't go out in this," he told her.

"I can't stay, either."

They eyed each other like guilty schoolchildren.

He went off in search of an umbrella, but just then the rectory was plunged into darkness. He bumped about, hands outstretched, groping for familiar outlines with which to orient himself. He located a drawer, sorting through its indecipherable jumble until he found a book of matches. Only then did it occur to him that if his housekeeper had stocked any candles, he hadn't the faintest clue where they'd be.

He struck a match and Gerry's face, framed by its white wimple and veil, flared into view: flushed and wide-eyed. He didn't realize he'd been staring fixedly until he felt the flame singe his fingertips. He dropped the match with a cry.

"Are you all right?" Her voice floated from the darkness.

She must have moved toward him, for they collided. He grabbed hold of her to steady himself, catching her scent: that of starched linen and milky-sweet tea and flowers.

It seemed only natural when they kissed.

She drew away with a gasp, whispering in a low, trembling voice, "No . . . we can't."

"I'm sorry . . . my fault . . . I shouldn't have." He felt an almost crushing despair coupled with a sweet, uplifting relief: He'd stumbled but hadn't fallen.

"No, it was my—"

"It won't happen again."

"Oh, Jim." She exhaled deeply, pressing up against him: warm and soft and yielding.

He kissed her again, both of them shivering as if the door had been flung open to let in the cold and sheeting rain.

Then somehow they were in the bedroom with their clothes off, Gerry's pale skin glowing with a pearly luminescence except where a dark triangle disappeared between her thighs, her full breasts—the thought of them all these years later brought a faint stirring in his loins—spilling onto the worn chenille spread, soft and inviting.

He'd never been with a woman until then. Sex had been divided into two distinct categories: the sacred unions alluded to in the Bible and the animal grunts he'd heard through the thin wall of his parents' bedroom. Gerry was somewhere in the middle: shy and virginal, with more than a touch of wantonness. As thunder boomed and lightning strobed—bringing the crucifix on the wall over the bed to life in brief, stark flashes like exclamation points—she grew bolder, stroking and teasing him to a frenzy. He could hardly believe it was her first time. Not until he entered her and she cried out did he know for sure. Then every conscious thought was obliterated by the fearsome heat in his loins, mounting to a point that seemed to verge on madness itself. Gerry cried out again, not in pain this time, her legs tightening about his, her fingers digging into his flesh. Then he was lost as well, tumbling over and over down the slippery slope he'd spent his entire adult life painstakingly climbing.

In the days and weeks that followed he couldn't walk into his bedroom without thinking of her: her soft breasts and beckoning thighs, her lips crushed against his like bruised petals. He would see the crucifix gazing down on him with blank detachment and wonder, Was God testing him in some way? Would he emerge from this a better priest? Or was it the devil's work? Either way, it had to end.

Then she would appear and he'd be no more able to prevent what happened next than his father had been able to keep from drinking. Except for a few fleeting moments here and there, like the lightning flashes that had simultaneously lit his way into heaven and hell that first night, he hadn't stopped to consider the consequences. Incredible as it seemed to him now, he hadn't thought of the child that might—*had*—come of it.

Now, all these years later, Jim Gallagher lowered his head into his hands. He was trembling all over as if chilled to the bone, though his skin was feverish to the touch. The years he'd spent convincing himself it was all a wonderful, terrible dream—a spell that'd been cast over him—had been in vain. All at once he was back in the rectory at St. Xavier's, reliving the awful moment when Gerry had told him she was pregnant.

And now she'd turned up again, like the

proverbial bad penny. Except that it was her child—*their* child—she'd sent in her place, a young woman who bore so striking a resemblance to him it was all he'd been able to do to maintain his composure.

He had to find a way to stop the infection from spreading. All these years he'd known where Gerry was, that she was still within the community, close enough to do him harm. For a long while he'd feared she *would* seek revenge, but with the passage of time he'd worried less and less. For whatever reasons—reasons that probably had more to do with her than with him—she'd chosen to keep their secret. Only a select few, that he knew of, had been entrusted with it, and of those only two were still living—Sister Agnes and the current superior, Mother Ignatius.

But now that their child was here there would be no sweeping her under the rug. The rumors would begin again—rumors he'd been able to squelch once but might not be able to again. His only hope was to sever any connection Gerry had with the Church. The less contact, the less likely this was to reach the ears of the archbishop. A long shot to be sure, or perhaps only the desperate measure of a desperate man, but what other choice did he have?

He thought of Brian Corcoran, his old friend from the seminary. He'd had lunch with Brian just last week—he saw a lot of old friends these days, friends that might not have looked him up had he not had the ear of the archbishop—and hadn't Brian mentioned in passing that his sister Caitlin was assistant superior at the mother house in San Diego?

The chevron in Father Jim's forehead deepened into something that, had he glanced in the mirror just then, would have profoundly disturbed him. It might have been the mark of Cain. At last he rose on unsteady legs, the ache in his bones so deep it made him think of those underground fires that burn for decades, and hobbled over to his rolltop desk, where he thumbed through his address book, then picked up the phone.

"Is this a bad time?" she asked.

The man in stained chef whites who'd emerged from the kitchen to greet her was angular and loose limbed, with cropped carrot hair and a boyish quality to his finely lined face that instantly put her at ease.

"To hell with it." He ignored her outstretched hand to scoop her into a bear hug. "I can't think of a nicer interruption." He drew back to smile at her, tiny creases like sun rays radiating from the corners of his bright blue eyes. "My sister made me promise not to bug you, or I'd have come to see you myself. She said you'd met the entire Fifth Division and needed time to sort it all out."

Claire smiled back, disarmed. "Something along those lines."

"Have a seat while I scare up some coffee."

He gestured about at the dining area, deserted but for a lone waiter putting the finishing touches to the table settings. Ragout occupied the top floor of a gingerbread Victorian, and had a bay window with a view of the Golden Gate rising from the fog like some fabled city of yore. Its formality was offset by the vintage circus posters on the walls and whimsical arrangements—like the one of artichokes and oat grass on the harvest table in the center of the room—taking the place of more traditional floral displays. She'd looked it up in *Zagat*'s, which had given it a rating of twenty-six with special mention of the decor, but hadn't expected it to be quite so charming. After her morning with Father Gallagher, it was as welcome as a warm jacket on a freezing day.

Gerry's brother reappeared a few minutes later with steaming mugs and a plate of crostini, which he pushed toward her. "I'm experimenting. I'd like your opinion."

She helped herself to one, and her mouth was flooded with a range of subtle flavors. "Amazing. What's in it?" She reached for another, suddenly aware that she'd skipped breakfast.

"A mixture of red pepper, shallots, and salmon roe." He sat back, regarding her with open curiosity that somehow didn't seem intrusive. "My sister tells me you like to cook."

She felt herself flush. "I'm not in the same class as you."

"Hey, we're related, aren't we?" His smile broadened, showing the slight gap between his front teeth. "She told me some other stuff, too. But it would only embarrass you, so I won't repeat it." His expression let her know it was complimentary.

"I've heard a lot about you, too."

"Don't believe a word of it." He winked.

"I'm sorry I didn't get in touch sooner."

"I wouldn't have been surprised if you'd decided to chuck the whole lot of us."

Claire gave a guilty start. Hadn't she considered doing just that?

"It *is* a little overwhelming," she admitted.

"I can't imagine waking up one day to a whole new set of relatives. It's hard enough dealing with the ones I have."

"How so?"

Kevin sipped his coffee. "Except for Gerry and me, the term 'dysfunctional family,' as far as I'm concerned, is an oxymoron. They're *all* Looney Tunes."

"The trouble is, they never see it that way."

He chuckled. "Don't I know it. Here, have the rest." He nudged the plate in her direction. "Try growing up gay in a small town. I was outed by my gym teacher, who yelled at me in front of the whole class to get my faggoty little ass off the field."

Claire was appalled. "What did you do?"

"Got my faggoty little ass off the field—and kept right on going. Straight home to my mother, who had a fit when I told her why I wasn't in school. You'd have thought Jesus died all over for my sins alone." If he'd been traumatized at the time, he seemed to be over it now. "What about you? Any skeletons in the closet? Any Dutch elm disease in the family tree?"

"Not that I know of." She told him about Lou and Millie and what it was like growing up in the house on Seacrest, skimming over the part about how lonely she'd been.

"How'd the visit with my sister go?" he asked at last.

"Good." Claire grew guarded.

Kevin wasn't fooled. "It couldn't have been easy."

"Compared to where I just came from, it was a Sunday stroll in the park." She told him about the visit with Father Gallagher. "I just wish I knew what to believe. He was so . . . well, like I meant nothing to him."

Kevin fell silent, toying with a sugar packet. From the kitchen came the sounds of hissing steam and clanging pots, and several languages being spoken—no, shouted—at once. After a moment he said quietly, "I was only thirteen, but I'll never forget the look on my sister's face when she came home from the hospital. It was as if she'd had her heart torn out. For two whole days she just sat there, staring into space, not eating or even sleeping as far as I could tell. It scared the hell out of me." His blue eyes hardened. "There's something you should know about my sister: She's made her share of mistakes, but there isn't a dishonest bone in her body."

"What if she only believes he's my father?"

"If she does, it's because he is." His fingers tightened about the handle of his mug. "And believe me, she's paid the price."

"I wish she'd told me what you just did." Kevin's memory was far more revealing than anything Gerry had said. "I had no idea. If I'd known—" She broke off abruptly. Why should she feel sorry for Gerry? Had Gerry stopped to consider what it would do to *her*?

"She doesn't want your pity," Kevin said gently. "She wants you to like her."

"I hardly know her." It came out sounding harsher than Claire intended.

"Give it time." He sounded sad for some reason.

She turned her head to gaze out the window. The fog was lifting and she could see out over the bay, where seagulls circled like pale riders on an invisible carousel and toy sailboats raced along whitecaps. Time? She could spend the whole rest of her life getting to know Gerry and it wouldn't make up for the years that were lost.

Claire finished her coffee and the rest of the crostini. Kevin talked about other things—the almost dizzying success of Ragout and the branch he and his partners were opening in Sonoma, hopefully by the end of the year; Kevin's boyfriend Darryl; and their three cats named Ducasse, Boulud, and Gerard—after legendary chefs. She in turn told him about wanting to quit her job and asked his advice about going into a food-related business—like, say, catering. Kevin said that unless she planned on starving the first year or two, she'd better think twice about giving up a steady paycheck.

When she finally glanced at her watch, she was surprised to see that nearly an hour had elapsed. "I should be going," she said.

He saw her to the door, where he hugged her again. He smelled of oregano and something faintly smoky. "Don't be a stranger, hear?"

"I won't." Oddly, she felt as if she'd known Kevin all her life.

"And if you go broke starting a business,

you always know where to come for a free meal."

"Oh, I couldn't—"

He drew back with a grin. "Hey, what are family for?"

Kitty slid the tray of buns from the oven, looking more flushed than usual. Today was Josie Hendrick's ninetieth birthday, and a group of former students was throwing her a party. Out front every table was filled and the tea kettles steaming. In addition to Willa and her part-time girl Suzette, Kitty had hired a pair of high school girls for the afternoon. Even so, she could hardly keep up. Only four-year-old Maddie, delighted by the fuss being made over her by Aunt Zee-Zee (as Josie was known to her) and all her friends, would have been content for it to go on forever.

"Thank God you're here. I don't know what I'd do without you," Kitty told Claire.

She set the tray on the counter and pushed wisps of flyaway hair from her forehead with the back of a floury wrist. It was four o'clock and there was no sign of a letup. Through the swinging kitchen door came the din of chattering voices; children squealing

with laughter; and in the thick of it all, old
Josie thumping her cane.

Claire couldn't help but smile. *She thinks
I'm doing her a favor?* It was the other way
around: If she hadn't volunteered to lend a
hand, she'd have spent the afternoon cleaning closets or, worse, at her desk.

She grabbed the tray with a pot holder
and carried it into the front room, where the
sticky buns were snatched up almost as fast
as she could slide them onto a platter. The
birthday girl was ensconced in a wicker chair
by the window, her smudged red lipstick
making her look like a very old child who'd
gotten into the jam. A party hat was perched
crookedly atop her snowy head and one of
the guests had wound a red crepe paper
streamer about her cane, making it look like
a large peppermint stick.

One of the kettles behind the counter was
whistling. While Suzette and her helpers
cleared away cups and saucers and plates,
Claire made tea the way Kitty had taught
her, pouring an inch or so of boiling water
into one of the teapots, no two alike, then
swirling until the leaves at the bottom were
thoroughly soaked before filling it to the top.
She let it steep for a minute before placing it

on a tray along with a silver tea strainer, creamer and sugar bowl, and small plate of lemon wedges.

Over the next hour she didn't stop moving. There was more tea to be made, creamers to be refilled, cookies and scones and tarts to be brought in from the kitchen. Yet she never felt tired or harried. Someone had once told her—it might have been Byron— that only things you didn't like doing were tiring, which would explain why an hour at her desk was more exhausting than five on her feet.

At a few minutes past five Josie hauled herself to her feet and everyone gathered around to sing happy birthday. When she blew out the candles on the cake—coconut with lemon filling, her favorite—the clapping was as enthusiastic as if there had been ninety instead of nine, one for each decade. Then the cake was cut and passed around. Claire noticed that Maddie had fallen asleep on the lap of a plump blond woman, the mother of two young boys who hadn't been able to get enough of the darling little girl in her frilly pink dress. She gently scooped Maddie up and carried her upstairs to her room.

When she came back, the crowd had begun to thin out. Kitty emerged from the kitchen with a gift for Josie: a tool box containing a hammer, nails, several screwdrivers, a bottle of glue, and a can of WD-40. The old woman, diligent to the point of obsessive about pointing out every rusty hinge, wobbly table leg, and peeling section of wallpaper, enjoyed a good laugh at her own expense.

"Which reminds me . . ." she said as she was being half carried out the door, supported at each elbow by a pair of middle-aged men who'd probably looked nothing alike as students but who now sported matching paunches and bald crowns, ". . . I noticed a crack in one of your plates."

After everyone had gone, Claire enjoyed a quiet moment alone with Kitty while Willa and the girls washed up. She looked about the airy front room with its mismatched tables and chairs and its eyelet lace curtains through which the last of the sunlight sifted, casting hazy patterns over the floor below.

"I can't remember when my feet ached this much," she complained good-naturedly. Kitty opened her mouth, no doubt to thank her yet again, but Claire preempted her, saying, "It's good to be back. I've missed this."

"What's to miss?" Kitty said with a laugh. "You're over here practically every other day."

"The only difference is I'm not getting paid for it," Claire joked.

"Only because you won't *let* me."

"Consider it a labor of love."

"You're crazy, you know that?" Kitty shook her head, nibbling on a leftover cookie. "You make more money in an hour than I do in a day. Why on earth would you rather be *here*?"

"Look who's talking."

"All right. You've got me there." Kitty hiked her feet onto a chair. For a moment she appeared lost in thought, perhaps remembering when she'd been a teacher like Josie. "I don't know what it is—maybe I like feeling needed."

Claire couldn't have said it better. Tea & Sympathy, she thought, was as much food for the soul. People came to exchange ideas along with the latest gossip, to kick around business propositions and play chess—but mostly just to be where someone was always glad to see them and where they were welcome to stay as long as they liked.

"Maybe you need this place as much as it

needs you." Claire realized as soon as the words were out that they said as much about her as they did about Kitty.

"Oh, I don't doubt it." Kitty's eyes crinkled. "Plates aren't the only thing cracked around here."

"I mean what I said before—I'd trade places with you in a heartbeat."

Kitty looked as if she'd given it some thought since then. "In that case, what about our going into business together?"

"What about it?"

"I was just thinking . . ." One of the cats leaped onto Kitty's lap, and she stroked it idly. "What if I were to open a branch of Tea & Sympathy? We'd be partners, only you'd be in charge of the day-to-day operation."

It was as if Kitty had read her mind. Claire's pulse quickened. "It would have to be somewhere outside of Miramonte, where you wouldn't be in competition with yourself."

The little house in Carson Springs with "loads of potential," in the words of Matt Woodruff, popped into her head. She hadn't dared dwell on it at the time—what would have been the point?—but now her mind raced ahead, filled with possibilities.

Then reality stepped in, bringing her to a rude halt. "There's just one little thing."

"What?"

"Money."

"True." Every extra cent Kitty made went into Maddie's college fund. "But there has to be a bank that'd give us a loan."

"I don't mean to be a party pooper, but your only collateral is this house, which is mortgaged to the hilt." She'd drawn up Kitty's will, so she knew exactly where her friend stood. "As for me, I'd have better luck robbing a bank than borrowing from one."

"What about tapping some of your wealthy clients? It'd be a great investment opportunity."

"Sure, and maybe while I'm at it I could show them a nice swamp in Florida." A familiar heaviness was settling in—the sense of hopelessness that always followed such flights of fancy.

"I just thought of something." Kitty brought her feet to the floor with a thump, causing the cat to leap from her lap with a look of reproach. "My sister Alex. I loaned her some money a few years back. I wasn't expecting to be repaid any time soon, but she just landed a big commission on a house she sold. She's giving me half, so that's twenty grand right there. If we could scare up another twenty or so—"

"This is insane, you know that, don't you?" Claire broke in.

"Not half as insane as *not* doing it." Kitty's blue eyes sparked with challenge.

For a delicious stolen moment Claire allowed herself to imagine it: her very own Tea & Sympathy. Her heart soared—then just as quickly plummeted. It was nothing short of madness. For one thing, she'd never hear the end of it from Lou and Millie. And what about Byron? They'd been counting on her income for when they were married.

Sean clomped in from outside just then. He was several weeks into a big job for the city trimming the elms along Cypress, and looked it: deeply tanned, his T-shirt and jeans smudged with tar, and a sprinkling of sawdust in his spiky black hair.

"Hold it right there." Kitty put out a hand, stopping him at the threshold. "Boots and socks," she ordered, waiting while he pried off his tar-stained Redwings. A small pile of sawdust appeared on the mat as he peeled off his socks. "Okay, now the rest." She was grinning as she spoke.

Sean pretended to take her seriously, going so far as to unbuckle his belt before Kitty dashed over to throw her arms around him, mindless of the tar on his jeans. Claire couldn't help envying them a little. But why? She had Byron, didn't she?

But it wasn't Byron she was thinking of now. Maybe it was the smell of sawdust, but she found herself remembering Matt Woodruff. She pictured him walking from room to room, his boots leaving faint waffled treads on the hardwood floor, the muscles in his broad back straining the faded fabric of his shirt. When it occurred to her that the house might already be sold, she felt a sudden and entirely unreasonable pang of loss.

It would be perfect, she thought. Smaller than this one and all on one level, but with a large kitchen and a garage that could be converted. And Matt had mentioned that it was zoned for commercial use.

All at once her excitement was doused by a cold dash of reason. What would it do to her parents if she moved to Carson Springs? And what would Gerry think?

They'd all assume the reason she was taking such a drastic step was to get to know her family—and they'd be partly right. For over the past few weeks she'd felt something gathering in the back of her mind, nothing as definite as a decision, only the growing certainty that a change was coming, a change like warm winds blowing from the south that, if she positioned herself just right, would send her sailing off into exciting new territory. If she didn't grab hold of this opportunity, even at the risk of hurting her parents, she knew she'd spend the rest of her life regretting it.

Chapter Nine

The rutted dirt lane dipped like the grooved handle of a spoon to the meadow below. Walking down it, all you saw at first was an unbroken sweep of grass bordered by wild blackberries and eucalyptus at one end and a long corrugated shed at the other. It wasn't until you drew nearer that you saw the rows of evenly spaced hives, like a subdivision of miniature ticky-tacky white houses, tucked in among the trees.

It all looked so pastoral, but as Gerry strolled among the hives with Sister Carmela at her side, she reflected, as she often did, on the delicate thread by which

their little cottage industry hung. A tiny para-
site, an invasion of wild bees, even the pre-
mature death of a queen could decimate an
entire colony. If enough were affected, production slowed and the honey yield dropped:
like the year an infestation of foulbrood had
nearly wiped out the entire apiary.

"It's not every colony, not yet, at least."
Sister Carmela, as short and thick as Gerry
was tall and shapely, stumped along the
path, hands horned with calluses clasped
behind her back. "We're dosing them with fu-
magillin and it seems to be doing the trick,
but we'll have a better idea in a week or two.
I'm hopeful." Her flat tone and the deep lines
creasing the worn leather of her face suggested otherwise.

Gerry didn't have to be told how serious
an infestation of *Nosema* was. If it wasn't
eradicated in time, the annual cleansing
flight would be marked by bees crawling
over the ground instead of making their
springtime forays into the field.

"How many do we stand to lose?" she
asked.

They paused in front of a partially dismantled hive. Its lid and shallow super had been
removed, leaving only the two deep brood

chambers. The ground around the hive entrance was scattered with what at first glance appeared to be blossoms from the trees overhead, but which on closer inspection Gerry recognized as dozens of dead bees.

Sister Carmela shook her head mournfully. "Nothing worth saving here." It would be burned along with the other badly infested hives. She continued along the path, stopping to pry the lid off another hive, lifting the heavy super as easily as if it had been the lid of a Styrofoam cooler. Mindless of the bees—her skin was so tough from the years of working outdoors she no longer needed the cumbersome protective gear—she reached inside to extract a frame from the brood chamber. The bees were sluggish from winter, but looked healthy enough. Satisfied, she replaced it. "If we're lucky, we won't lose more than a few."

"Let's keep our fingers crossed."

"I've done more than that. I've asked Father Reardon to say a special mass."

Gerry looked for a sign that she was being facetious, but the older nun's creased brown face was solemn. As far as Sister Carmela was concerned, it was no different than offering up prayers for a sick parishioner or family member who'd fallen ill.

"It couldn't hurt," she said.

Something flared in the nun's gentle brown eyes. "Oh, I know what they say about me: All Sister Carmela cares about is those bees. But they're God's creatures the same as you and me."

Gerry happened to agree, though Sister Carmela took it to extremes at times, extolling their virtues to anyone who would listen, about how bees were a model society, every member of the colony with a job to do and everything in its proper place. Rather like the convent, she thought. She slipped a comforting arm about her old friend's shoulders. "If people were as well behaved the world would be in a lot better shape."

She looked out over the meadow, where a few of the bees from hives with sunnier exposures were already making forays, bobbing drunkenly amid the goldenrod and timothy grass. She loved the whole concept of the cleansing flight, like spring-cleaning in a way: the bees removing those that had died over the winter, along with bits of wax and debris.

In a way, hadn't she done the same?

Decades of old regrets and wishful thinking had been swept away. Her daughter had a name and a face. She knew the color of her eyes and the sound of her laughter. She could close her eyes and see Claire at the kitchen table, in the extra chair at the end. If that memory was all God saw fit to bless her with, well, she'd just have to find a way to live with it.

Her heart ached nonetheless. Here it was March—six weeks since Claire had visited— with only the one stilted thank-you note. Her hopes had been raised when she heard from Kevin that Claire had been to see him. But he'd advised her to keep a low profile for now, saying that while Claire had seemed genuinely interested in getting to know them, her first loyalty was to her parents.

"Those people did a real number on her." She could hear the disgust in his voice.

"What did she tell you about them?"

"Nothing much—just the impression I got. You know that expression about loving someone to death? Well, with her folks it's literal."

"I got the same impression."

"The last thing she needs is another guilt trip."

Gerry could certainly relate to that. Hadn't she gotten a good dose from her own mother growing up? Not to mention the Church, which had had thousands of years of practice at it. "Do you think I'll ever hear from her again?"

"Hard to say, but my guess is yes."

Gerry's heart had leapt. "You don't sound too sure."

"She's been to see Gallagher." Kevin's voice hardened. "Apparently he denied the whole thing. Now she's more confused than ever."

She'd known this was coming, of course, but it caught her by surprise even so, nearly knocking the wind from her. She felt the old anger surface. "Oh, God, poor Claire."

"It's not Claire I'm worried about—it's *him.*"

"What do you mean?"

"Just be on your guard, that's all," Kevin warned.

"Against what?"

"I don't know, but something tells me we haven't seen the last of him."

Now, as she wandered along the shady path, Gerry wondered if her brother was right. She didn't expect to hear from Jim—

hadn't he made it plain he wanted nothing to do with either her or Claire?—but that didn't mean the ripple effect from Claire's visit wouldn't be felt. She'd best keep an eye out for trouble just in case.

When they'd finished inspecting the hives, she and Sister Carmela headed back to the honey house, where another kind of spring cleaning was under way. Decapping tanks, extractors, strainers, and centrifuges were being scrubbed down in preparation for the combs that would soon be ready to harvest. Even Sister Paul, their resident biochemist, had gotten into the act, giving her cluttered laboratory in back—the birthplace of Blessed Bee's brand-new line of hand creams and moisturizers—a thorough cleaning.

By the time Gerry returned to the chapter house for her interview with Marian Abrams from *West,* to which Mother Ignatius had reluctantly given her approval, it was almost noon. As she made her way through the cloister garden, her thoughts turned to the reverend mother, who'd seemed unusually subdued these past few days. Was she finally slowing down? The woman was in her late eighties, after all, though the thought of her succumbing to age was as unimaginable as the mountains crumbling.

I ought to have a word with her just in case . . .

Gerry was the only person Mother Ignatius would consult—not in spiritual matters, of course, but about concerns that ranged from which shade of white to paint the chapel to whether or not they ought to invest in a new car—perhaps because Gerry was the only one who didn't tremble in her presence. If she was ailing in some way, the reverend mother would tell her.

She was nearing the chapel when she spied Sister Agnes, her old friend and one-time novice mistress, kneeling with her trowel in the garden that had been her lifelong project—one that contained every plant and tree and bush mentioned in the Bible.

Gerry stopped to peer at a laminated plaque:

OLIVE
(Olea europaea)
And the dove came in . . . and lo, in
her mouth was an *olive* leaf
Genesis 8:11

"Come to help me with the spring planting, are you?"

Sister Agnes peered up at her from under the brim of a floppy straw hat, shading her eyes against the sunlight: a little cupcake of a woman without a square edge or angle. Though nearly as old as Mother Ignatius, she wore her years well.

"Believe me, there's nothing I'd like better," Gerry answered with a sigh.

"Even God rested on the seventh day." Sister Agnes's apple cheeks shone as if polished, and a silvery wisp had escaped from under her wimple. "What is it you're so busy rushing off to you can't spare a moment to enjoy a bit of fresh air and sunshine?"

Gerry told her about Marian Abrams. "Heaven knows we could use some good publicity for a change." She held back from adding, *After the ordeal with Sister Beatrice.*

But Sister Agnes must have read her mind, for she settled back on her heels, making the sign of the cross. "The poor woman—I hope she's found some comfort."

Only Sister Agnes would be so forgiving of someone who'd taken two innocent lives and nearly a third—Sam's. "I'm sure she has," Gerry said, thinking that in the psychiatric hospital to which she'd been confined, Sister Beatrice had to be heavily medicated at least.

"I pray for her every day."

Gerry knew what her former novice mistress was thinking—that no one was without sin. What would the other sisters think if they knew that Sister Agnes had been caught shoplifting in Delarosa's a few months back? If it hadn't been for Sam's discretion in handling it, she might have spent some time behind bars as well. Though Gerry could hardly compare a weakness for pretty things to the homicidal acts of a madwoman.

"I'm just glad it's behind us," she said.

"Yes, though it's certainly taken its toll. Our reverend mother doesn't look at all well these days."

So Sister Agnes had noticed it, too. "Has she said anything to you?"

The little nun shook her head. Crouched on her haunches, she looked like one of the wild hares Gerry often spotted early in the morning on her way to work, frozen amid the tall grass. "Do you think—?" Sister Agnes broke off, not daring to voice her fears. The threat of illness, especially Alzheimer's, hung over the community's mostly aged population like a pall.

Gerry saw the concern in her eyes, and knew she was thinking of poor old Sister Seraphina, clinging to life by a thread. "I'll see what I can find out."

Sister Agnes rose to her full height—the top of her head barely reached past Gerry's shoulder—and laid a hand on her arm. It was the size of a child's but roughened from years of outdoor work. "You'd tell me, wouldn't you? If something *were* wrong."

"You'd be the first to know," Gerry assured her.

Sister Agnes caught up with her as she started down the path. She was carrying a basket from which a bunch of lavender poked, tied together with a piece of rough string. She caught Gerry's glance and said, "It's for Sister Seraphina. They're saying she can't hold on much longer, that she wouldn't know her own mother from a hole in the wall, but I'm thinking she can't be too far gone for a little breath of the outdoors."

Gerry smiled. "I'm sure she'll appreciate it."

" 'Tis an awful pity."

"Her being so sick?"

"No, not that—we all have to die sometime. It just seems a shame, that's all, her being robbed of her thunder." A reference, no doubt, to the numerous false alarms that would make Sister Seraphina's death, when it came, seem anticlimactic.

They strolled past the chapel along the covered walkway lined with bas-reliefs—fourteen of them, one for every Station of the Cross. When they reached the path that led to the infirmary, Gerry paused to help herself to a sprig of lavender, holding it to her nose and breathing in its fragrant scent. She was about to put it back when Sister Agnes took it from her, tucking it in a buttonhole in Gerry's sweater instead. "For luck." Her eyes were the violet-blue of the lavender.

"Thanks." A small gesture, but Gerry felt moved; it was as if Sister Agnes had read her mind. She glanced about before bending down to give Sister Agnes a quick peck on the cheek. Displays of affection were frowned on here and as the lone lay member of the community she had to be more careful than most.

Minutes later she was seated in the reverend mother's office two doors down from hers. The window was open, letting in a mild breeze scented with jasmine—a reminder that spring was just around the corner. It was also the only indication that any time had passed since she'd last sat here. For as long as she'd been at Our Lady, the sturdy oak desk across from her had held the same ink-stained blotter and vintage metal fan propped on a volume of the *Encyclopaedia Britannica,* and the bookcase had been home to the same cracked leather spines. The plain wooden crucifix and faded tapestry—Mary kneeling before the Angel Gabriel—had hung on the walls since Mother Hortense's time, the only things saving them from being utterly bare.

Mother Ignatius was seated in the chair behind her desk regarding Gerry somberly. "I hadn't planned on saying anything until I knew for sure," she said, her hands folded on the blotter in front of her. "Someone from the motherhouse alerted me last week—I'm not saying who—but it wasn't until a few hours ago that it was confirmed. Mother Edward called to let me know they're sending someone—a Sister Clement—to do an evaluation. Based on her report, they may make some changes."

"What kind of changes?" A stitch formed in Gerry's belly.

"I can't be sure . . . ," she paused, ". . . but I had the distinct feeling it has something to do with you."

"Me?"

"Mother Edward seemed quite curious about you. She wanted to know what, if any, involvement you had with the community outside of Blessed Bee and what effect your, shall I say, secular, influence might have had on us." She lifted a hand, holding it out as if to caution Gerry not to jump to any conclusions. "Maybe I'm reading too much into it. After what happened with Sister Beatrice we're all a bit skittish."

The stitch in Gerry's belly tightened. "Are you saying I could be fired?"

"I've always been honest with you, Gerry, so I won't mince words now: Yes, your job could be on the line." She sighed. "If it's any consolation, I have a feeling I may be next in line." Her pale blue eyes shone with indignation—and perhaps a touch of resignation—in the alpine crag of her face.

Gerry felt her own indignation flare. "You?"

"Well, I'm not getting any younger."

"Says who?"

"I'll remember that next time I have trouble getting up off my knees in chapel." The old woman's mouth flattened into the faintest of smiles. "As for you, if I'd thought she wouldn't misinterpret it, I'd have told Mother Edward the truth—that you're a breath of fresh air around here."

"It sounds as if they think of me more as poison." Gerry appreciated the reverend mother's words of support, but she'd need more than that to keep from getting fired.

"We won't know anything until Sister Clement does her report. Until then, I suggest you go about your business as usual."

Business as usual—with this hanging over her head? "What should I tell Marian Abrams when she gets here—that the bees aren't the only things to watch out for around here?"

"I wouldn't advise it." The reverend mother's voice was stern.

"It's not fair," Gerry pushed on regardless. "They're looking for a scapegoat, and who better than me?" She cast a rueful glance at her skirt, which ended demurely at her knees but nevertheless stuck out like a sore thumb around here.

Mother Ignatius sighed. "I wish it were as simple at that, but the truth is they have a point. Not about you in particular, but I don't have to remind you that a spiritual community is like . . . well, like a chorus line." She smiled at the analogy, one she would have used only with Gerry. "What happens to one affects us all."

" 'Friendship of the world is enmity with God' ?" Gerry quoted from James. "I'm not sure it's as high-minded as that."

She remembered her brother's warning. Could this have something to do with Jim? What if he were secretly plotting to get rid of her? It was far-fetched, sure, but she wouldn't put it past him. And with the influence he must yield in the archdiocese . . .

The thought was interrupted by Mother Ignatius saying forcefully, "If anyone's motives are less than pure, we'll get to the bottom of it, I can assure you."

The brief silence that followed was disturbed only by the ticking of insects against the screen and the swish of a scrub brush down the hall. Gerry stood. "When is Sister Clement coming?"

"Monday. I trust you'll make her feel welcome." Mother Ignatius rose and stepped out from behind her desk, tall and spare in the dark serge habit that fell about her in folds, reminiscent of the flinty-eyed pioneer women in the sepia photos hanging in the museum downtown.

Gerry mustered a smile. "I'll do my best."

She floated to her feet and started for the door. All at once it sank in: She'd spent her entire adult life behind these walls. What would it be like without this place to come to every day? Without the garden to stroll through, and the sweet sound of voices joined in song? Without the hives and the honey house and Sister Agnes? They might as well pack her off to be with Sister Beatrice.

Marian Abrams turned out to be a stylish middle-aged woman with dark shingled hair and an artfully made-up face. It was only a preliminary interview, but she'd come prepared: a briefcase containing a notepad and minirecorder, and a camera case holding a fancy Nikon. Gerry gave her a tour of the grounds, followed by tea in the visitors' room, where she told the story of the origins of Blessed Bee.

"It all started back in the early thirties with Sister Benedicta," she began. "She was sent here to recover from tuberculosis—it was felt she'd benefit from our dry climate. And at first she *did* get better." Gerry smiled, relishing the tale as much as she had the storybooks she'd read to her children when they were little. "She was full of joy, always singing, always a kind word—but the most amazing thing about her was her way with animals. It was said that sparrows would alight on her shoulders and deer would eat from her hand. She could walk among bees and not be stung, even reach barehanded into a hollow tree trunk and pull out a honeycomb.

"Soon the nuns had all the honey they could use—honey that was rumored to have curative powers. Before long they were inundated with requests from the outside, and Sister Benedicta was put in charge of constructing an apiary. Within a few years Blessed Bee was being sold throughout the valley and beyond." She paused, taking a sip of her honey-sweetened tea. "Then Sister Benedicta fell ill again."

"Hold it!" Marian scrambled to pop another cassette into the recorder.

When the tape was whirring, Gerry went on. "She died shortly thereafter and was buried in the graveyard on the hill. I'll have one of the sisters take you up there, if you'd like. It's a bit of a hike."

"Okay if I take pictures?"

"I'm sure that won't be a problem." She took another sip of tea. "Where were we? Yes, the burial. It was winter, the time when bees normally hibernate, but the most incredible thing happened: A swarm gathered on Sister Benedicta's headstone. Efforts to brush them off were useless. When the weather grew colder, they began to die off, dropping onto the grave. The following spring, wildflowers grew up out of the husks of all those dead bees. Some of the nuns say that if you listen closely, you can still hear a faint hum in the air."

"That's quite a tale." Marian smiled, clearly not believing a word of it. Her eyes shone with excitement nonetheless. She knew a story her readers would gobble up when she heard one. "I'll give this to our writer, if that's all right with you." She tapped the cassette with a long red fingernail. "She'll be giving you a call sometime next week."

"Good. We'll set something up." Anything to take her mind off Sister Clement's impending stay.

They finished their tea, and she passed Marian on to Sister Carmela for a tour of the honey house and apiary. An hour later Marian was back in her office. "I can't thank you enough," she said, gripping Gerry's hand. "This is terrific stuff—just what I was hoping for."

Gerry ushered her to the door. "Call if you have any questions."

Later that afternoon, on her way home, it occurred to her that she might not be around to answer them. Depending on Sister Clement's findings, she could be out on her ass long before the *West* article appeared in print. She grew cold at the thought. Never mind her own needs, how would she feed her kids?

She thought about phoning Aubrey; it would be good just to hear his voice. She hadn't seen him since the wedding—he'd left for Budapest the following day. It had been two weeks since then and she'd missed him more than she would have thought possible. It was for that very reason she hadn't rushed to his side the day before yesterday when he returned. She needed to prove to herself she could get along fine without him.

Then there was that awful incident at the wedding. Aubrey hadn't mentioned it—he was far too nice. Gerry, on the other hand, had given her daughter an earful when they got home. She still hadn't quite forgiven Andie, who claimed she hadn't done it on purpose and that it was only a coincidence Isabelle's CD had been among the ones she'd pulled from the rack—an excuse Gerry found hard to swallow.

No, she'd wait a day or two longer. Last night they'd talked briefly on the phone and Aubrey had seemed eager to see her, but she was certain that was only because he'd missed the sex. A month ago it might have been the same for her, but a subtle shift had taken place over the past few weeks. She'd realized she wanted more, and the thought terrified her. If she kept her distance the feeling would pass, she told herself.

She was driving past the Dalrymple house when she noticed that the FOR SALE sign out front was gone. She wondered who'd bought it. Had Fran O'Brien changed her mind? Or had some smart doctor or lawyer snapped it up? She'd noticed a number of the houses along this street had discreet signs advertising the services of attorneys, medical professionals, accountants, even a psychic reader. Business must be good.

She arrived home minutes later to find

Justin's bike blocking the driveway. Again. She honked the horn. When he didn't come running, she climbed from the car with an exasperated sigh.

It wasn't until she was dragging his bike into the garage that he came charging out the door with his friend Nesto at his heels. "Sorry, Mom." He darted over to help while Nesto, as dark as Justin was fair, hung back timidly. As soon as the bike was safely stowed alongside the washer and dryer, Justin blurted, "Mom, can Nesto stay for dinner?"

Gerry felt her irritation rise. How many times had she told him not to ask in front of his friends?

"Sure," she said sweetly. "What's on the menu?"

Justin gave her a slack-jawed look. "Huh?"

"I figured you must be doing the cooking if you're inviting your friends for supper." She winked at Nesto.

"Uh, well, I sort of thought . . ." Justin glanced toward the house. "Since we were having company anyway."

She felt a jolt of alarm. No, Mike wouldn't do that to her, not after all this time. She winced at the memory even so. Shortly after they were separated, she'd dragged home from work late one evening to find her estranged husband ensconced on the sofa, a kid under each arm, watching TV.

"Andie was scared," he'd said, as if she were the kind of mother who left her children unattended for hours, even days, on end.

It was all Gerry could do to keep from exploding. Hadn't she phoned to let the kids know she'd be late? Andie had used the oldest ploy in the world to bring her daddy running. And the worst of it was, Gerry had had no choice but to let him stay. It was that or risk causing a scene.

Now she eyed Justin warily, asking, "What company would that be?"

He looked up at her agape. Clearly, he hadn't expected it to be a surprise. "Claire," he said. "Claire's here. I thought you knew." His face, she saw, was lit up like Christmas and Easter rolled into one. "She's moving here, to Carson Springs. She bought a house and everything. Isn't that *awesome*?"

Gerry didn't stop long enough to answer. Anyone who happened to glance out their front window just then would've seen her flying up the walk, her overstuffed shoulder bag bumping against her hip and a grin as wide as back and beyond spread across her astonished face.

"I didn't want to tell anyone until I was sure it would go through." Claire was seated on the sofa, a glass of wine on the coffee table in front of her. "I came straight over from the Realtor's office. The closing is tomorrow."

Gerry could hardly believe what she was hearing. Her daughter was moving here! Claire had explained that she was opening a tearoom with her former boss, Kitty, but Gerry knew that couldn't be the only reason. Joy welled in her until she thought she would burst with it.

"Well, you'll have no shortage of helping hands." She glanced at Justin, who nodded enthusiastically. He seemed to have forgotten all about Nesto, who'd had the good sense to head home. "We're a full-service crew—everything from unpacking to hanging curtains. We're especially good at ordering pizza," she added with a smile.

Claire looked dubious. "I wouldn't want to put you to any trouble."

"Oh, it's no trouble at all." She grinned and nodded, feeling like one of those silly dogs stuck to a dashboard that waggled its head every time the car moved.

Cool it, a voice warned. *You don't want to scare her off.*

"We'll see how it goes." Claire looked happy but Gerry sensed a slight reservation nonetheless.

"I'm sure you have your work cut out for you," she said.

Claire laughed knowingly, taking a sip of her wine. "I haven't even started packing. I gave notice a couple of weeks ago, but my bosses wanted me to stay until everything was tied up. I didn't get here until yesterday."

"Yesterday? You should have called." She tried not to sound hurt that Claire hadn't. "We have plenty of room." A bit of a stretch, she knew, but Andie could have bunked in with Justin. "In fact, why don't you stay here tonight?"

She was glad Andie wasn't here to object—she must be off with Simon or Finch. Even knowing she'd be less than thrilled by Claire's news didn't dim Gerry's joy.

"Thanks, but I'm paid up in advance at the inn." Claire was making it clear she had no intention of allowing herself to be swallowed up. "Besides, I have to be up at the crack of dawn. Big meeting with my contractor."

"Well, if you change your mind . . ." Gerry was torn between disappointment and relief, for asking Andie to bunk with Justin would be a sure recipe for mutiny. And she couldn't very well expect Claire to sleep on the couch.

Claire heard the relief in Gerry's voice and thought, *I should have given her some warning.* Springing it on her had been a mistake. Gerry was probably wondering how she was going to bill it to her friends and neighbors. *Oh, by the way, have you met my daughter? You didn't know I had more than one? Well, you see . . .*

If Gerry was enthusiastic at all it was only because she had mixed feelings. But what had Claire expected—to be greeted with open arms? That was a child's fantasy. As foolish as hoping her parents would understand.

Lou and Millie hadn't gone ballistic when she'd told them. It had been more of an implosion, like a condemned building being brought down—a crumpling inward that was painful to see. Millie had cried, and Claire had cried too, while Lou just looked on, shaking his head in bewilderment. No amount of explaining could dissuade them of the notion that her sole reason for buying a house in Carson Springs was to be near Gerry.

But if that had been true, she'd be sorely disappointed. Gerry didn't want her, not really. Oh, she was happy they'd found each other . . . but not that she was here to stay. It was a little like someone saying they're not racist, she thought, then having it put to the test when a black family moves in next door. One thing was for sure: Gerry would have a whole lot of explaining to do.

The front door swung open just then and Andie came tramping in. At the sight of Claire, she froze.

Before Claire could greet her, Justin jumped up to announce, "Hey, Andie, guess what? Claire's moving here. Isn't that awesome?"

Chapter Ten

If this was a TV movie, Andie thought, they'd all be crying and hugging each other, with Claire making some corny speech, saying how thrilled she was that she finally had the brother and sister she'd always dreamed of. Instead she was quietly explaining over a glass of wine that she was doing this for *herself,* for the opportunity to go into business.

"It's a lot to take on, I know." Claire sat on the sofa, sipping her wine. She looked nervous but excited, too. "The place needs work and we're on a pretty tight budget."

"It doesn't look too bad, from the outside," Gerry said.

"It's more than you think. But the good news is that Matt—my contractor—isn't going to cost an arm and a leg."

"That *is* good news." Gerry was looking at Claire as if she'd hung the moon.

Andie thought, *I'm going to puke.*

"As for the financing, it turned out Kitty had some money coming in, enough to get us started."

"If you need any help . . ." Gerry started to say, but didn't finish, as if thinking better of it.

"We'll be okay." Claire looked a little embarrassed.

"Well, you can count on us to help with the heavy lifting."

Andie felt her heart sink.

"Yeah, I could mow your lawn. You wouldn't have to pay me or anything," Justin put in.

Claire turned to him. When she smiled at Justin, it was with her whole face, not just her mouth. "For now would you settle for all the cookies you can eat?"

Justin's eyes lit up. "Maybe Grandma could help out, too. She's always talking about how much she misses her job."

"Grandma's too old," Andie said.

But her mother said thoughtfully, "You

know, that's not such a bad idea. I'll talk to her about it, see what she thinks."

If this were *Little House on the Prairie*, Andie thought, they'd all be pitching in to raise a barn. She became uncomfortably aware that her mother was eyeing her, as if waiting for her to say something.

"Um . . . I could probably get Simon to do a write-up for the paper," she said.

It didn't pay to make waves. She'd been in the doghouse since the wedding, never mind that it had been an innocent mistake. How was she supposed to have known it was Aubrey's wife?

"That'd be great—though I won't need it for a while," Claire told her. "Even if everything goes smoothly, we're looking at at least two months."

"A tearoom . . ." Gerry gazed dreamily off into the distance. "You know, it's just what this town needs. A real getaway, like something out of my mother's era."

"With profits to match," Claire answered with a laugh. "I just hope it's not too far off the main drag." She bent down to pet Buster. His tail was thumping against the table leg and there was an ecstatic look on his face.

Even their dog had defected to the other side, thought Andie.

"It might work to your advantage," Gerry said. "You could even put tables out back. I'll have Sam take a look at the garden—she knows more than most landscape architects. It could be a real oasis."

Claire sat back, folding her arms over her chest. Her look of bright anticipation had dimmed ever so slightly. "I wouldn't want this to take up too much of your time. I know how busy you are."

Andie wanted to shake her. Couldn't she see how hard her mother was trying? She wanted it to be about *her,* not some stupid tearoom. Was Claire really that clueless?

Gerry had apparently gotten the message. Her cheer seemed forced as she asked, "When's the big move?"

"Next week. Matt says he can have the place livable by then. But I suppose that depends on your definition of livable. I just hope it doesn't mean a cot and a Coleman lantern."

Andie prayed that her mother wouldn't invite Claire to stay with them. A wave of relief swept over her when Gerry said, "Those rooms at my mother's are just sitting empty. I'm sure she'd love to have you."

Claire shook her head. "I'll be better off where I can keep an eye on things."

"I have an extra bed in my room," Justin piped.

Andie should have been angry at him, but all at once she felt proprietary toward her little brother: Justin, flapping about in his jeans and T-shirt three sizes too big, who had to be reminded to bathe and who right now smelled more like dog than Buster. He was a pain in the ass, sure, but he was the only brother she had.

Claire's expression softened. "Thanks, Justin. If I get tired of sleeping on a cot, I just might take you up on it."

"Here's to Tea and Sympathy South." Gerry lifted her wineglass. Her cheeks were flushed and her hand a little unsteady. "I'm sure it'll be a huge success."

"With all the cookies I can eat," Justin crowed.

"Oh God, that reminds me—dinner. All we have are leftovers." Gerry looked chagrined.

"Never mind. I should be going." Claire abruptly rose.

"Don't be silly." Gerry jumped to her feet as well. "I'm sure there's enough."

"Mom, when was the last time you checked the fridge?" Andie's voice was tinged with exasperation.

But her mother wasn't going to let go of Claire that easily. "Okay, then, what do you say we order Chinese?"

"We had it the last time," Andie reminded her.

Claire surprised her by saying, "I have an idea—why don't *I* cook?"

"I'll help." Justin catapulted off the sofa.

Andie rose heavily. "I'll set the table."

In the kitchen her mother peered dubiously into the refrigerator. "We have eggs," she said. "I think there's some cheese, too—oh yes, here it is." She turned with an apologetic look, holding out a chunk of moldy cheese wrapped in Saran. "I'm afraid it's pretty slim pickings."

Claire didn't seem to mind. "I've worked with less."

Suddenly she was all business, peering into cupboards and poking through the spice rack. She unearthed some potatoes, an onion, a can of artichoke hearts. Before long butter was sizzling in the skillet, and the kitchen was filled with tantalizing smells. While she peeled potatoes and chopped the onion, Gerry made a salad with what was left of the greens. When the contents of the skillet were nicely browned, Claire carried it to the table and plunked it down.

"What is it?" Justin asked.

"A frittata," she told him. "Which is just a fancy word for eggs and potatoes and any-thing else you want to throw in. I'll show you how to make it sometime, if you like."

"It smells delicious." Gerry settled into her chair.

Andie's mouth watered. It *did* smell won-derful. She sampled a bite. It tasted even better.

Before long, every scrap was eaten and the skillet picked clean. Justin gave a loud burp, then clapped a hand over his mouth, giggling. For once, his mother didn't scold him.

"Better than any restaurant." Gerry beamed at Claire. "They'll be lining up at your door."

Look at me, Andie wanted to cry. *I'm here. I'm your daughter, too.*

She jumped to her feet instead. "I'll wash up." She could win a few points doing that, at least.

"Thanks, honey," her mother said distract-

edly as she rose from the table. "I was thinking Claire and I could pop over to your
grandma's. I can't wait to give her the good
news." She turned to Claire. "If you're not in a
rush."

Claire smiled. "Sure, why not?"

"Can I come, too?" Justin wanted to know.

Claire ruffled his hair. "If it's okay with your
mom."

"Don't you have homework?" Gerry was
already reaching for her coat, on a peg by
the door.

"I did it already." Justin ducked his head,
but not before Andie caught the guilty gleam
in his eyes: He was lying.

Claire turned to Andie. "Want us to wait for
you?"

"No, it's okay." She tried not to sound hurt
that she'd been an afterthought. "Tell
Grandma I said hi."

Then they were trooping out the door,
leaving her with a sink full of dirty dishes, a
pile of homework, and something she'd
done her best not to think about until now—
a period that was overdue.

Andie was reaching into the cupboard under the sink for the detergent when she
abruptly burst into tears. Claire might not

turn out to be her worst problem. What if she was pregnant? What then? Her life would be ruined.

Before she knew it, she was picking up the phone and punching in her father's number. Luckily, he was home.

"Daddy?"

"Honey, what's wrong?" The concern in his voice was almost more than she could bear, reminding her of when she was little and would come to him with a scraped elbow or skinned knee.

"I'm fine," she sniffed.

"You don't sound so fine."

"Oh, Daddy." A sob broke loose, and she quickly muffled it with her hand. "I miss you so much."

"Me, too, sweetheart." It wasn't like the other times she'd called when he'd been too busy or distracted to talk. This was how it had been before the divorce—and before Cindy.

"Are you busy?" she asked even so.

"Not especially. Cindy's up at the club—it's her bridge night. I'm just clearing some stuff off my desk." There was a pause, and she listened for the familiar background noise of her father in his den—the shuffle of paper and faint clatter of his keyboard—but there was only the sound of his breathing. "What's up?"

"Claire's moving here."

He was silent a moment, then said, "Well, that *is* something."

"It's not that I hate her or anything." It occurred to Andie then that her mother wasn't the only one who'd kept Claire a secret all these years. Now she was shocked to hear the five-year-old Andie's voice coming out of her mouth. "Oh Daddy, why didn't you tell us? If I'd known all along, it wouldn't have been so bad."

Her dad sighed heavily into the phone. "I would have, sweetheart, but it wasn't my place. I had to respect your mother's wishes." He paused, and she could hear the sound of a drawer closing. "What's she like? You haven't told me much. All I know is that your brother thinks she walks on water."

"Nice. She's nice."

"Well, that's a start at least."

"Daddy," Andie drew in a watery breath, leaning her head against the wall. "Would it be okay if came to live with you?" She hadn't meant to ask; the words were out before she realized it. Now she felt a stab of guilt. Her mother would be furious. And her father . . .

God, please don't let him say no. I don't think I could stand it.

But for once there wasn't another call he had to take, or somewhere else he had to be. He didn't reach into his grab bag of excuses, either. Instead, in the Daddy-voice she remembered from when she was little, he said the words that were like sweet music to her ears.

"Of course you can, sweetheart. Any time you like."

MONICA'S MANSION ON THE HILL
by
Simon Winthrop

The wrought iron gates guarding the entrance to Lorei-Linda open with the magic words *Monica Vincent is expecting us.* As we pull up in front, we're unprepared for the sheer sprawl of it: more Greek temple than mansion, with grounds that might have been a botanical garden closed to the public year round. We're struck, too, by how quiet it is; even the birds seem to know better than to make a peep.

We are greeted at the door by Monica's assistant, Anna Vincenzi. If there's a resemblance, it's because Anna is her sister. Monica shortened her name to Vincent when she moved to Hollywood more than a dozen years ago, her ticket to stardom a face mere mortals would kill for. Though her first movie, *Holy Smoke,* was a self-described "unholy mess," she fared better with her second feature film. For her starring role in *Tender* she was nominated for an Academy Award as Best Actress. The rest is history. She went on to make more than thirty films before her star crashed to earth, in 1996, with a boating accident that left her paralyzed from the waist down.

The auburn-tressed Monica is as lovely as ever. As she's wheeled into the luxuriously appointed living room where we've been kept waiting, it's like Cleopatra being borne in on her pallet. There is nothing about her that evokes pity. When asked about her famous reclusiveness, she dismisses it with a wave of her hand. "If it's Garbo you want," she says, "you're barking up the wrong tree." Miss Vincent, as she insists on being called, even by her sister, is still in the game and ready to fight another day. It's a feistiness that becomes increasingly clear as we sit with our drinks—soda for us, something stronger for her—in the pink light of the setting sun, looking out over the valley she once called home and now jokingly refers to as her prison . . .

"So, what do you think?"

Andie looked up from the newspaper to find Simon eyeing her eagerly. They'd stopped at the bookstore on their way home from school, where she'd snagged the last remaining copy of the morning's *Clarion.* Apparently word had gotten out, and there'd been a run on it the likes of which hadn't been seen since the scandal involving Sister Beatrice.

"I love it," she said. "But I'm not so sure Monica will."

She'd be none too pleased with the veiled references to her drinking and quotes on everything from ex-husbands and old flames to the sad state of today's movie industry.

"She can sue me if she likes. I have it all on tape." He spoke blithely, but she knew it was only a cover. He was anxious, not so much about Monica, but about whether or not the piece would be picked up by one of the wire services.

"Uh-oh, speaking of the devil." She nudged

Simon, who glanced over his shoulder, his eyes widening at the sight of Monica wheeling in through the door. "Look where she's headed."

Monica, dressed in a black turtleneck and slim black trousers that made her look like a spider in its web, was going straight for the newspapers and magazines by the register.

"She's obviously gotten the four-one-one," he observed dryly.

"What are our chances of sneaking out before she spots us?" Andie muttered under her breath.

"About a million to one." He didn't look too concerned. Then she remembered: Simon thrived on controversy.

Andie glanced around. The store was mostly deserted except for a few browsers in back. She watched Monica roll to a stop in front of the register, nearly blocking the entrance. If they tried to slip out now, she'd have to be blind as well as crippled not to see them. Andie shrank out of sight behind the bookcase, pulling Simon with her.

"I see you're out of the *Clarion*," she said sweetly to Myrna.

Andie peeked out to see Myrna McBride pause in the midst of ringing up a purchase.

In her bulky hand-knit sweater and tweed skirt, her tufted swirls of strawberry blond hair bringing to mind a guinea pig, Myrna was as frumpy as Monica was fashionable.

"Sorry," she said. "I just sold the last one."

"Will you be getting any more?" Monica asked.

"That's it for today. You could try the library."

"I've *seen* it, thank you. I wanted my own copy." She was losing patience. "Do you know where I could *buy* one?"

"The drugstore sells them, but they're out, too."

Myrna had clearly dealt with Monica in the past, and, besides which, she wasn't the type to be pushed around. When she and her husband, with whom she'd co-owned the town's only other bookstore, had gotten divorced, Myrna had opened her own rival bookstore just across the street—appropriately named The Last Word.

Simon stepped out from behind the bookcase. "You can have this one."

He plucked the newspaper from Andie's hand and strode over to Monica, handing it to her with a flourish. God, where did he get the nerve? If Andie had written that piece she wouldn't have been able to look Monica in the eye.

But if Monica was angry at him, it didn't show. "How gallant." Her mouth curved in a sultry smile. "I suppose they paid you in copies." A not-so-subtle reminder that the *Clarion* was small-town, not to be confused with the publications she was used to being featured in.

Simon shrugged, his hands stuffed in the pockets of his chinos. "I'm not in it for the money."

"Don't tell me. It's the hunt—the *kill*—that excites you." A disdainful note crept into Monica's voice. At the same time she sounded faintly amused, as if toying with Simon.

He didn't bat an eye. "Whatever. I just didn't see the point in recycling all the usual crap—you know, Monica Vincent the Legend. People are tired of it. I'll bet you are, too. I wanted to show you as a real person." He looked so sincere, with his brown hair flopping over his forehead and his glasses slipping down his nose, Andie almost bought it herself. She wasn't surprised when a slow smile spread across Monica's face.

"Local girl made good?" But there was no

malice to it this time. "You certainly have balls, I'll give you that much. How old did you say you were?"

"Sixteen." A pink flush crept into his cheeks.

"I suppose you have your eye on the Ivy Leagues, a smart young man like you."

Simon averted his gaze, his blush deepening. There was no question he had the grades and board scores—straight As and fifteen hundred on his PSATs—but without a full scholarship he'd be out of luck. A state college was all his mother could afford.

"Columbia and Stanford are my top choices," he told her.

Monica eyed him speculatively. A look of true interest had replaced her tailored-to-the-public face. "It just so happens the admissions director at Stanford is an old friend of mine," she said.

Simon perked up. "Really?"

"I could put in a good word. Why don't you stop by the house tomorrow around this time and we'll discuss it?"

For once, Simon was speechless. Then he gathered his wits and stammered, "Tomorrow? Sure, that'd be great."

"Good. I'll have Anna put it on the calendar."

Before he could say another word, she was propelling herself out the door, the afternoon sunlight catching the chrome hubs of her wheels in little pinwheels of reflected light.

Andie stepped out from behind the bookcase. She looked at Simon. He looked at her. For a full thirty seconds neither of them spoke. At last she drew in a breath and said, "I can't believe it."

"What?" Simon was putting on his innocent act.

"That you fell for it."

"Didn't you hear her? This could be my lucky break."

"Yeah, right."

"I'd have been insane to say no."

"If you think it's your *mind* she's interested in, you're not as smart as I thought."

Simon gave a nervous little laugh, as if he knew he'd been busted. "Get real. She's got to be my mom's age."

"Except she doesn't look anything like your mother, I'll bet." She wouldn't know. She had yet to meet his mom—another sore point.

"Come on, Andie, don't be this way." It wasn't until she'd stalked past him on her way out the door that he seemed to realize she was serious. He caught up with her outside. "Look, this is crazy. She's in a *wheelchair,* for God's sake."

"It hasn't stopped her so far."

"You're being paranoid."

"Am I? Did you see the look on her face?"

"What look?"

"Like a cat who ate the canary." She hurried along the arcade, stepping around a heavyset woman juggling several shopping bags and a Pekinese whose leash had gotten tangled around a bench leg.

He quickened his pace to keep up with her. "Okay, just for argument's sake, let's say she *does* have the hots for me. What makes you think I'd do anything about it?"

"So you admit she has the hots for you."

"You're twisting my words."

"You just said—"

Simon grabbed her by the elbow and spun her around. "What *is* it with you? If it's because of your sister, I'm here for you, you know. All you have to do is—"

Andie glared at him, tears springing to her eyes. "It has nothing to do with *that.*"

"Look, I understand."

"You don't understand a *thing.*" She had a sudden image of him scooping Monica into his arms and carrying her off into her bedroom, whispering, *Don't worry, I'll pull out in time.*

She jerked from his grasp, scurrying off down the arcade. Shoppers swirled past in a blur while little things jumped out at her like freeze frames: ice cream drying to a rubbery puddle on the sidewalk outside of Lickety Split, a mother tugging on the arm of her whining toddler. At the corner, as she waited for the light to turn, she spotted a stout, middle-aged woman with hair that curled in crisp iron waves about her ears. Andie recognized her as Dr. Rosario, her mother's OB who'd delivered both her and Justin.

The fear crouched in the back of her mind once more sprang into full consciousness. What if *she* were pregnant? Her period was only a little late, less than a week, which wasn't unusual, but still . . .

A baby would screw up everything. It'd be like her mother and Claire—history repeating itself. But suppose she kept it? That'd be worse in a way. She could kiss college goodbye. While her classmates, including Simon, were off at school, she'd be stuck home changing diapers. Just another statistic.

When Dr. Rosario caught her eye and smiled, Andie turned with a choked cry and fled.

Chapter Eleven

"Mom?" Claire sat cross-legged on the floor with the phone to her ear. The living room was bare except for the cartons stacked against the wall, Matt's toolbox, and an old carpet remnant by the door.

"Claire, honey. Is everything okay?" Millie's anxious voice at the other end sounded faint and far away. Claire might have been calling from Tasmania.

"Everything's fine. I was just calling to see how—"

"Do you have everything you need?"

"I haven't finished unpacking. Most of it's in storage until the work is done." She spoke with forced cheer. "My contractor's already made some inroads." She could hear ominous creaks and thuds as Matt crawled around on the roof overhead.

Claire felt her gut clench. This was such a huge risk. What if it didn't pan out? Though quitting her job and moving here had been easy compared to trying to make her parents understand. It was useless to explain; they refused to look beyond their own fears, leaving her to stew in her guilt—guilt that washed in and out like the tide, strewn with the flotsam of doubt and self-recrimination.

"I didn't know you had a phone." Millie's tone was faintly accusatory.

"I just got it hooked up—about an hour ago."

"Oh, I thought . . . never mind."

You thought I was at Gerry's. Typical of Millie to imagine the worst. "Let me give you the number. Do you have a pen?"

"Somewhere in here . . ." Claire heard a rattling sound as her mother pawed through a drawer. There was a time she'd have had six pens on hand, but lately she'd become forgetful.

She waited what seemed an eternity while her mother found a pen and copied the number down. "As soon as I'm all set up, I'd like you and Dad to visit," she said.

"Oh, honey, I don't know." Millie's vague, drifting voice was worse somehow than recriminations. "Dr. Farland says I should take it easy."

A tiny alarm bell went off. "Any particular reason?"

"Oh, you know him—such a stickler. It's nothing to worry about, I'm sure, just some chest pains."

Chest pains? The alarms were clamoring now. "Why didn't you say something?"

"Like I said, it's probably nothing. Besides, I didn't want to bother you. You being so busy and all."

"I'm never too busy for something as important as that, Mom."

Silence at the other end.

The tide rose a little higher, nudging past the high-water mark.

Claire could feel the muscles in her jaw knotting. Her dentist had told her she ground her teeth in her sleep and had recommended a bite guard. *What I need even more is to stop feeling like the bad guy,* she thought. "Mom, look, I know you're upset with me right now," she said gently. "But nothing's changed. I still love you and Dad. This isn't an either-or thing. I just felt I owed it to myself to give this a try."

Millie sighed. "Yes, dear, you told us already."

"I just wish there were some way to convince you."

Another, longer silence. There was only one thing she could have said that would have satisfied her mother: *This was all a terrible mistake. I'm coming home.*

Then Millie said wearily, "I'd better go. I hear Dad in the kitchen. You know how hopeless he is. Whatever he's looking for is probably right under his nose."

"Remember the time he hunted all over the house for his keys and it turned out they were in his pocket?" Claire clung to the slender thread connecting them over the miles.

"Which time was that? I've lost count." Millie gave a weak chuckle, and for a moment they were joined by their shared history: all those memories like odds and ends in the cupboard her father was probably rummaging through right now, seemingly random and not terribly valuable until you needed something. "He always remembered what mattered, though." There was no irony in her voice; Millie wasn't capable of irony.

Claire closed her eyes. "Bye, Mom. Give my love to Dad."

"I will, honey. You know we're thinking of you."

She hung up feeling guiltier than ever. If her mother hadn't sounded so defeated just then, Claire could have gotten angry. Instead, she felt like a criminal.

What made it worse were her own doubts. She could have prepared a brief on all the valid reasons for moving here, but that wasn't the same as *knowing* it was right. What she'd done, for the first time in her life, was simply follow her heart—a heart as unused to taking risks as a fledgling flying from its nest.

Even Byron, who'd always been so supportive, was having a hard time with it. Which she'd anticipated—and which was why she'd driven all the way to Palo Alto to break it to him as soon as her offer on the house had been accepted.

"I can't believe I'm only just now hearing of this," he'd said, incredulous.

"It wasn't definite until today."

"But you were *thinking* about it."

"Well, yes . . ."

They'd been in bed. She'd waited until after they'd made love, which had seemed like a good idea at the time, but had turned out to be a mistake. Byron felt tricked.

He sat up, running a hand through his hair. "Jesus, Claire, do you have any idea what this means?"

"It wasn't a snap decision," she'd said, swinging her legs out from under the covers and bending down in search of her clothes.

"There's no way we'll be able to manage on just my salary, not with this bitch of a loan I'll be paying off."

"That's two years away," she'd reminded him.

"What's going to be different in two years?"

"A lot could happen."

"Yeah, we could be even deeper in debt."

She straightened, regarding him coolly. "All I'm saying is that I want to stop feeling like my life is on hold."

"Who says it's on hold?"

"I do, Byron. *Me.*" It was the closest she'd ever come to shouting at him. "I hate being a lawyer. And I'm sick of living down the street from my parents."

"We'll move, then. My uncle wants me to go in with him."

"Is that what *you* want?" She remembered the days when Byron used to make fun of the fact that his Uncle Andrew, an orthopedic surgeon with a fancy practice in Hillsborough, lived in a minimansion and drove a Jaguar, claiming he'd rather work at an inner city clinic tending to poor people. "I thought you wanted your own practice."

"I did . . . I do. But he says I should get a few years under my belt first. And . . . well, I'm thinking maybe he's right."

She was pulling her T-shirt on, and when her head emerged she found him sitting on the edge of the bed, his speckled green eyes fixed on her with an odd mixture of chagrin and defiance.

"Why am I just hearing about this?" she asked, echoing his earlier words to her.

"I was getting ready to tell you when you dropped *your* bomb."

"Let me get this straight." She took a deep, leveling breath. "It's not okay for me to go after what *I* want, but I shouldn't hesitate to rearrange my entire life for *you*."

"I thought it's what you wanted, too."

He'd looked so mournful, she'd relented

at once, plopping back down on the bed and winding her arms around him. "I'm sorry. I guess I'm a little touchy." She didn't have to explain; he knew how it was with her parents. "You're right—I should have told you sooner."

"If this is really what you want," he said, stroking her hair, "we'll make it work somehow."

Byron's dear face flashed through her mind now in a series of timed-release sequences: the little boy next door tossing pebbles up at her window to catch her attention, the gangly sixteen-year-old she'd danced with at his prom (and who later held her hair while she threw up from drinking too much of the spiked punch), the young medical student who'd watched proudly from his seat in the auditorium as she'd received her law school diploma. Byron had always been there, and would be in the days and years to come.

Claire looked about the room where she sat contemplating her future as if seeing it for the first time—its hardwood floors and beams, its solid oak doors and lintels. Kitty had once told her that the scariest thing for a woman was to take a chance on herself.

"We'll marry a man with a prison record and sixteen tattoos before taking out a small business loan," she'd said, only half joking. But look how well it had worked out for her— a thriving business, a child she adored, *and* the man of her dreams.

She heard the clump of boots on the porch and looked up to find a huge figure silhouetted in the doorway, edged in a molten glow. Matt, back from his expedition onto the roof.

"It better be good news," she said. "At the rate I'm going, I'll be broke before I open for business."

He stepped inside, thoughtfully remembering to wipe his boots on the carpet remnant. "You'll need to replace the gutters, but the roof looks solid enough. It should last a few more years at least."

She breathed a sigh of relief. "You made my day."

"Don't thank me, thank the climate," he said. "It only rains a couple of months out of the year."

She glanced out the window. "How does it stay so green?"

He pointed toward the frosted peaks of the mountains only just visible in the distance. "All that snow has to go somewhere. Been out to the lake yet?"

"Just to drive past."

"It's more than half a mile deep," he told her. "Colder than a witch's tit, too, even in summer. Something to keep in mind next time you feel like going for a dip."

"I'm afraid I won't have much time for that."

"Too busy baking cakes?" He stroked his mustache, tugging at its ends as if to keep from smiling. For some reason he seemed to find the idea of a tearoom amusing.

"Don't knock it. You haven't lived until you've tried my chocolate cake."

"That how you stay so skinny, by making the rest of us fat?"

Matt wasn't fat, just big. He reminded her of the friendly giant on the old *Captain Kangaroo* show. Not her type, though. His hair was too bushy and his mustache needed trimming. And look at those hands—like shovels.

He must have picked up on her thoughts because all at once she became aware of his gaze. Her cheeks warmed and she dropped her eyes. There was a tiny hole in a pocket of his jeans where she caught the glint of a key poking through.

She could hardly believe she'd known him only a matter of weeks. It felt longer. Probably because he'd been here every day pulling up rotten boards, ripping out old wiring, crawling about underneath the house in search of dry rot and termites (apparently he didn't trust engineers' reports). Yesterday he'd met with an inspector from the health department. Everything had to be up to code if she was to be licensed for food service.

"I used to get paid to fatten people's wallets," she told him.

"That so?"

"I was a lawyer. Technically, I still am. Tax and estate, intergenerational trusts, that kind of thing."

"Intergenerational trusts, that's what they're calling it these days?"

"Don't look at me—I didn't make it up. One of the reasons I left was because I got sick of all the pretension."

"A lawyer, huh?" He gazed at her with new respect, not for her profession—she suspected he held a pretty dim view of lawyers—but for her courage in chucking it all. "How come you never mentioned it before?"

Claire shrugged. "It never came up."

She started to get up off the floor, but Matt

was already bending down with his hand extended. She grasped hold of it, feeling its dry heat and the calluses ridged along his palm. For a split second she was a little girl again, her child's hand engulfed by her father's, feeling the same sense of safety, the absolute assuredness that all was right with the world.

"I'll bet you could use a cold beer," she said, remembering that it was hot up on the roof. Almost in the same instant she recalled that the elderly Frigidaire that'd come with the house had been hauled off to the dump this morning. The new one wouldn't be delivered until later in the day.

Matt shrugged. "I'll take whatever you've got."

She retrieved two bottles of Evian from the grocery sack on the floor.

He cracked his open and took a gulp. The creases on his throat were penciled in with the dirt from crawling around on the roof, from which his Adam's apple stuck out like a polished knob. He lowered the bottle, wiping his mouth with the back of his hand.

"Thanks. That hit the spot."

She asked, "Anything besides the gutters?"

"Hornet's nest. I took care of it."

"Without getting stung?" She was amazed.

He patted his shirt pocket, from which a cigarette pack bulged. "I smoked 'em out."

"I didn't know you smoked."

"I don't. Gave it up last year." Which didn't explain the cigarettes. But she was learning that with Matt it was best not to ask too many questions; if you were patient, he'd eventually get around to telling you whatever it was you wanted to know.

"I'll remember that next time I run into any hornet's nests." She took a sip of her water and smiled. "I wonder if it would work as well on the proverbial kind."

"Your family giving you a hard time?"

He must have gotten the picture when she'd introduced Gerry as her birth mother that hers wasn't exactly conventional. "Let's just say my parents aren't too happy with me right now." She didn't know why she was telling him. Maybe because she had no one else to talk to. And Matt was a good listener.

"Why is that?" he asked.

"They didn't want me to move."

"We all have to go sometime."

She watched him stroll over to the window, where he leaned into the sill. The sunlight at his back sent his shadow angling over the scuffed oak floorboards.

"How would you feel if it were *your* kids?" she asked a bit testily.

Matt had two, a boy and a girl. That first day, after the tour of the house, he'd pulled out his wallet, worn to the thinness of a wood chip and curved to the shape of his rear end, producing photos of a little boy around eight, with his father's brown eyes and reddish hair, and a girl with dark brown pigtails who couldn't have been more than five. Since then he'd brought them by a few times, usually when he was dropping something off. They always stayed in the truck. Matt didn't like their being around sharp tools unless he was supervising.

"Probably no different from the way I do now." His eyes grew remote all of a sudden, and she remembered that he was divorced.

"I'm sorry. It must be hard."

"Hey, it could be worse. I have them two nights a week and on Sundays, plus six weeks in the summer." It sounded like a lawyer's words he was parroting. "My ex-wife and I fought over just about everything else, but the one thing we agreed on was that the kids come first." He paused, clearly uncomfortable with the subject. "What about you? Any ex-husbands in the closet?"

She shook her head. "Just the longest running engagement in history."

"Have you set a date?"

"Not yet." She felt a tiny pang of misgiving at the ease with which she said it. She used to count the days, and now it seemed she wasn't in any rush.

"Well, he's a lucky guy, whoever he is."

Claire looked away, her cheeks warming. Was Matt flirting? If he was, she had only herself to blame. What was she doing, anyway, dumping all this stuff on him?

She glanced at her watch. "I should be going. Heavy date with a guy selling used restaurant equipment."

"Me, too. I have to pick my kids up from school." He straightened, placing his empty bottle on the sill and scooting a hand into his pocket to retrieve his keys.

"Will I see you tomorrow?"

"Bright and early." He tipped an invisible cap.

She watched him stroll outside, a shaggy bear of a man in jeans and paint-spattered Timberland boots. She wondered if his kids knew how lucky they were.

She and Byron had discussed having children, but always in the abstract. "We'll have the requisite two point two kids. A dog will round it out to an even three," he liked to say. She'd always gone along with the joke, but for the first time she felt a small tug, wondering what it would be like to be a mother.

Two years suddenly seemed like a long time.

The next few weeks Matt and his crew worked every day from sunup to sundown, replacing windows and doors, tearing out old bathroom tiles and fixtures, installing a new kitchen sink and hooking up appliances—she'd splurged on a Sub-Zero and a secondhand Viking stove, plus a second dishwasher to handle the extra load. Claire grew accustomed to seeing trucks and vans in the driveway, and hearing the whine of saws and pounding of hammers. She had never felt more exhausted, and at the same time more exhilarated. When doubts and worries crept in, she had a ready cure: staying one step ahead of them at all times.

As soon as the kitchen was minimally operational she began experimenting with recipes: Gran Brewster's maple doughnuts, a tangerine tart that would take advantage of the valley's abundance of citrus, an updated version of *Fannie Farmer's* black-bottom pie. With Matt and his crew, she had no shortage of willing guinea pigs; the trouble was keeping up with the demand. Matt had confided with a twinkle in his eye that his plumber, Billy Bremerton, had said he'd work for free provided she kept the baked goods coming.

Justin was equally happy to sample her wares. True to his word, he'd been bicycling over after school and on weekends. When he occasionally got in the way—pestering Matt or the workmen with questions—she sent him outside to sweep the front walk or mow the lawn. Most of the time she enjoyed his company. It was nice having a little brother, though she couldn't say the same about Andie. With her, Claire felt like she did with her parents: as if she were walking on eggshells.

Mavis had been the most welcome surprise of all. The old woman who'd moved about with such difficulty when they'd first met had been replaced by one with seemingly boundless energy. Maybe because Mavis, too, was finally doing something she enjoyed. Either way, she'd been a godsend:

lining cupboards and organizing kitchen shelves, even tackling the daunting task of organizing Claire's recipe file. She was full of suggestions, too, for how to promote Tea & Sympathy.

"You'll need a flyer," she said one morning, seated at the old Singer sewing machine from her house that she'd had installed in Claire's kitchen (no reason to buy curtains when fabric was so much cheaper). "Something really catchy that'll get people to sit up and take notice."

Claire thought of her dwindling reserves with something close to panic. "I'm not sure it's in my budget."

"Who said anything about money?" Mavis straightened, brushing away a loose thread. She was wearing her hair knotted in back, and fine wisps the color of the copper wire in snippets all over the house drifted about her head. "My friend Lillian will design it for free. She used to work in advertising, so she knows what she's doing. In fact, I've already spoken to her about it. She said she'd love to help."

"I'd feel bad not paying her."

"Nonsense. What else does she have to do all day?" Her direct blue eyes fixed on

Claire. "One thing you've got to understand if you're to make a go of it here: People *like* being asked, especially old people." She jabbed a finger, knotted like a piece of old rope, in the direction of the hutch Claire was painting, a vintage flea-market find. "You missed a spot."

Claire couldn't help comparing Mavis to her mother's mother, Nana Schilling, a dour woman best remembered for the sweater that dutifully arrived each Christmas and birthday, and that was invariably a size too small. Once a year Nana would take the train from Albuquerque. She always stayed exactly two weeks—not a day more or less. During that time she would go through Claire's drawers, making sure everything was neatly folded. If she noticed the absence of all those sweaters she never said anything.

She'd felt more of an affinity with her father's mother, Gran Brewster, who'd provided her earliest inspiration in the culinary arts. Claire remembered her as always in the kitchen, stirring something on the stove or pulling a pan from the oven. If she was making a cake, Gran always let her lick the bowl. It was Claire's only good memory of Gran—

that, and her sublime maple doughnuts—
who'd tended to be bossy and sharp-tongued.

Mavis wasn't a bit like either of them. Nor
was she a sweet little old lady form central
casting. She spoke her mind and had opin-
ions on everything from the Catholic Church
to the present state of affairs on Capitol Hill.
She also firmly believed in living in the present. In Mavis's view, too many trips down
memory lane kept you from enjoying the
here and now.

Claire dipped her paintbrush in the can
and dabbed the spot while Mavis returned to
her sewing. A neat stack of cloth squares
waiting to be hemmed sat on the card table
at her elbow: the napkins made from the
same fabric as the curtains.

"As for getting those flyers out," she said,
raising her voice to be heard over the
whirring of the Singer, "we have a secret
weapon—Justin. Who'd be the wiser if he
tucked them into the papers on his route?"

Claire eyed her in admiration. She never
would have thought of that herself. Never
mind Mavis having all her marbles; she
seemed to possess more than most.

Just then Gerry walked in with Sam, who
presented Claire with a bunch of daffodils

wrapped in newspaper. "The first of the season," she said, heading for the cupboards in search of a vase.

Claire was touched. She set aside her paintbrush, and rose to her feet with a crackling of joints. "Thanks. It was sweet of you."

"Don't mention it. I went a little overboard with the planting last fall and now everything's growing like topsy. In a few months, when the zucchini is coming in, you're not going to want to know me." She found a pitcher and carried it to the sink. The old pipes groaned as she cranked on the tap: another thing on Matt's to-do list.

"Don't worry. I have a great recipe for zucchini bread," Claire told her.

Sam smiled. "You'll need it."

Claire secretly thought that if Sam had been her mother instead of Gerry, it would have been a closer match in some ways. Sam, who looked as if she'd stepped from a Lands' End catalog, came across as ladylike, even a bit prim, until Gerry made some off-color remark that made her laugh—a laugh as unbridled as Gerry's.

Gerry fingered the pile of napkins Mavis was hemming—bright yellow patterned with strawberries. "It looks as if you've got enough here to cover every lap in town."

"Let's hope they're put to good use." Claire felt the familiar niggling of money worries—a more or less constant drumbeat these days.

"It won't be for lack of trying." Mavis pressed her foot down on the Singer's pedal, its furious whirring seeming to underscore her words.

"That reminds me." Gerry turned to Claire. She was wearing a variation of her usual weekend attire—jeans, stretchy top, cork-soled mules—in which no one would ever take her for a former nun. "I spoke to Kevin. He said to tell you that he and Darryl will be here for the opening. His exact words were that he'll be here with bells"—she darted a glance at Mavis—"that he wouldn't miss it for the world. He wanted to know if you'll need a hand with anything."

"And have him show me up as the rank amateur I am? No way." Claire appreciated the offer nonetheless. "Tell him not to worry—Kitty'll be here."

"Your friend Kitty who walks on water?" Mavis seemed eager for them to get off the subject of Kevin and his lover. "What will she think of us mere mortals, I wonder?"

"She'll want to whisk you off to Miramonte to sew napkins for *her,*" Claire answered with a laugh.

Sam was arranging the daffodils in the pitcher when she paused suddenly, bringing a hand to her pregnant belly with a smile. "Junior's frisky today."

"What makes you think it's a boy?" Gerry reached for the fruit bowl on the table, helping herself to a banana. From the front room came the banging of Matt's hammer.

"Just a hunch," Sam said. "Though I'd be just as happy with a girl."

"Too bad you didn't hang onto all those little dresses of Alice's," Gerry said.

"If I had, they'd be musty with age." Sam sank into a chair at the old pine table from the attic at Isla Verde—her housewarming gift to Claire. "Imagine having sisters as old as Laura and Alice. It'll be like having *three* mothers."

"Make that four," Gerry said.

Silence fell, and Claire had the sudden sense of every eye on her, though they were all going out of their way not to look in her direction. It wasn't that she hadn't forgiven Gerry—she had, for the most part—but there was still a gap that would never be bridged, and thoughtless remarks such as the one she'd just tossed off only made it wider. If Gerry wanted to be a mother to Sam's baby, she should try remembering she had more than one daughter of her own.

Claire walked over to the refrigerator. "Who wants something to drink? There's iced tea and lemonade."

Gerry rushed to the cupboard where the glasses were kept as if eager to make herself useful.

She filled them with ice while Claire set out pitchers of iced tea and lemonade and sliced the loaf of banana bread cooling on the counter. Matt was herded into the kitchen, looking like the proverbial bull in the china shop. Watching him, Claire had to struggle not to smile. He was clearly out of his depth amid all these women with their talk of layettes and breast-feeding and natural childbirth versus epidural. She didn't blame him when he escaped as soon as he could without seeming rude.

Claire lingered at the table while Gerry and Sam washed up. It had been a long day and it wasn't over yet. There was still so much to do: boxes to be unpacked, their contents organized, and in the garden years' worth of weeds to be pulled. When Matt was a little further along, she'd start ordering bulk supplies. Kitty had given her a list of wholesalers for dry goods, but she'd need local outlets for produce. Last week she'd driven around visiting various orchards and citrus groves, and had talked to a chicken farmer who'd promised all the eggs she could use.

"It looks as if your garden could use a little therapy." Sam, gazing out the window, seemed to have picked up on her thoughts. "I'd take it on myself, but my doctor would read me the riot act." She turned away from the window with a wistful smile. "No reason I can't help sketch out a plan, though. We'll hire some strapping young man to do the dirty work."

Tears came to Claire's eyes. "That would be . . ." She didn't know what to say. Everyone was being so kind, including Gerry. "I can't thank you enough."

"Don't be silly. You'd be doing *me* a favor. To tell the truth, I'm going a little stir crazy." Sam stroked her belly absently, smiling her secret little smile, before moving on to a story about her last doctor's appointment. Her chart, it seemed, had gotten mixed up with that of a patient having twins. She'd nearly fainted when the nurse at the desk glanced at it and joked, "Double the pleasure, double the fun."

When the plates and glasses were dried and put away, Sam went outside, accompanied by Mavis, to have a look around. Alone with Gerry, Claire felt some of the old awkwardness return. If only Gerry had been someone other than her mother; if they'd met under different circumstances, she'd be able to shake loose this feeling, like a bone in her throat, that despite all her bending over backward to prove otherwise, Gerry would just as soon she'd stayed in Miramonte.

"Sam's got the greenest thumb of anyone I know. Even in kindergarten her avocado seeds had more leaves than any of the other kids'." Gerry folded the dish towel over the drainer, smiling at the memory. "One of these days I'll take you up to Isla Verde and show you the garden there. The only one that's a patch on it is Our Lady's."

Which Claire had yet to tour. She'd hinted a few times to Gerry that she'd like to see the convent, but Gerry always put her off. No doubt she didn't want the awkwardness of having to introduce her around. Some of the nuns had to have been around back when Gerry was a novice and would be reminded of why she'd left. Why should she risk her safe little world for the sake of someone she'd only just met?

Never mind I'm her daughter.

She watched Gerry's gaze drift to the window. She appeared lost in thought. No, more than that, troubled in some way.

Claire was prompted to ask, "Is something the matter?"

Gerry turned away from the window with a sigh. "I haven't told anyone yet, but it looks like I might be out of a job." She went on to explain—something about the motherhouse thinking she was a bad influence—which didn't make much sense considering how long she'd worked there. Then she said something that jumped out at Claire: "Someone's behind this, and I have a feeling it's your father."

In that first startled instant she thought of Lou, before she realized Gerry meant Father Gallagher. "What makes you think that?" she asked. She hadn't said anything to Gerry about her visit. There was still a little part of her that wasn't quite sure who to believe.

"Kevin told me you'd been to see him," Gerry said.

Claire slumped back in her chair, the memory rushing up at her. "It was awful. He denied everything—just like you said."

Gerry didn't look surprised, only disgusted. "I suppose he told you I imagined the whole thing."

"Something along those lines." Claire ducked her head so Gerry wouldn't see that she'd had her doubts, doubts that now seemed foolish.

"Well, he knows the truth as well as I do."

"I still don't get it," she said. "What would getting you fired accomplish?"

"I know the way he operates—hide your head in the sand and it'll go away. It's worked so far—until you came along. Now he has to cover more than his head. Which means erasing me—*us*—from the picture."

"Haven't you been in the picture all along?"

"Sure, and it was fine as long as I kept our little secret. But now all bets are off. You must have shaken him up pretty badly. If this was to get out, the archdiocese would reassign him to its equivalent of Siberia."

It still made no sense to Claire. "Even if he can get you fired, it's not like you'd be dead."

"As far as he's concerned, I would be. For him nothing exists outside the Church."

"What would stop you from going public?"

Gerry's mouth thinned in a humorless smile. "He knows me too well. I might be inclined, but not if it meant dragging the Church through the mud. For all its faults, I owe it too much."

Claire sat there, mulling it over. None of this was her fault; she'd only been the catalyst. But she saw now that Gerry's reluctance to publicly acknowledge her had been rooted in more than a wish to avoid embarrassment to herself.

The hammering in the next room dwindled to a sporadic thud, and the voices in the yard faded as Sam and Mavis made their way around to the front.

"I guess I'll just have to see how this plays out," Gerry said, though God knows patience isn't my long suit."

Claire felt guilty all of a sudden. "If it makes any difference, I'm sorry. I should have taken your advice."

Gerry shook her head. "You did what you

had to do." She quickly turned away, reaching for her purse on the table by the sewing machine, but not before Claire saw the shine of tears in her eyes. "I'd better go round up Sam. If she starts going at those vines, I'll catch hell from her doctor, not to mention Ian."

Claire trailed after her into the living room, where Matt was measuring for the wainscoting—his suggestion for making it seem more like a tearoom and less like a house. He was crouched down with his back to her, and she couldn't help noticing the sweaty patches on his T-shirt that made it cling, outlining the muscles underneath.

She caught herself staring, and looked away. What was the matter with her?

You miss Byron, that's all.

They were stepping out onto the porch when a car pulled up—a silver Jaguar so stunningly out of place in the neighborhood that Claire's jaw dropped. A man climbed out, athletic-looking but slightly built, with an elegance about him that matched the Jaguar's. His wavy hair, she noted, was the same silver as his cars.

"Aubrey!" Gerry called out, her face lighting up. "What on earth are you doing here?"

"I called the house. Justin told me where to find you." He paused on the path, looking up at them: a man in jeans and a navy cashmere blazer, with dark brown eyes in a narrow, beveled face that shouldn't have been handsome but somehow was. A man who could be none other than Gerry's boyfriend, though she stubbornly referred to him as her *friend.* "I thought this was as good an excuse as any to meet Claire." He stepped lightly up onto the porch, holding out the shopping bag in his hand—bright red, embossed with a discreet gold logo. "This is for you. Redundant, I know—but I couldn't think what else to get you."

Inside was an assortment of teas in glossy tins. Claire had only to glance at them to know he'd paid a small fortune. "My cup runneth over—no pun intended." She smiled and extended her hand. "You must be Aubrey. I've heard a lot about you." She saw him arch an eyebrow at Gerry and was quick to add, "Justin thinks you're awesome."

"High praise coming from him. The boy is nothing if not discerning." He spoke with a slight accent she couldn't quite place. British . . . or was it French? More like a mixture of both.

Claire could see why Justin had taken a shine to him: For someone so famous, Aubrey wasn't the least bit stuck up. "Would you like to come in?" She gestured toward the house.

"I'm afraid I'll have to take a rain check." He glanced at his watch, slim and expensive. "I'm due at the airport in a couple of hours."

"Aubrey has more frequent-flier miles than he could use in ten lifetimes," Gerry said with a laugh. Underneath it, though, Claire detected a tiny grain that chafed.

"It's only overnight this time. I'm dedicating a new concert hall in Marin." He leaned in to kiss Gerry lightly on both cheeks, continental style. When he turned to Claire, she saw the light in his eyes. He was clearly as crazy about Gerry as she was about him. "I'm glad we had a chance to meet. You're every bit as lovely as Gerry said." He touched her elbow, smiling.

Sam and Mavis wandered over, and he waved to them as he started back down the path, calling, "Another time, ladies."

Claire's gaze fell on the clippers in Sam's hand.

"I tried to stop her. She wouldn't listen."

Mavis waved toward the small pile of clippings by the garage.

"If you don't watch out, *we'll* be delivering your baby instead of Inez," Gerry scolded. She marched down the steps and held out her hand, forcing Sam to relinquish the contraband clippers, which she must have found in the garage.

Claire heard an engine gun, and looked up to see the Jag streaking off down the street.

"Well, at least you got to meet him." Gerry spoke cheerfully, as if it meant no more than a neighbor dropping by.

She was obviously crazy about the guy. What had made her so gun-shy? Was it because of her divorce or . . . Another thought occurred to Claire: that it might have something to do with *her*. Giving her up had to have affected Gerry as much as it had her. While she was growing up, blissfully ignorant, Gerry had been left to battle her demons. Demons that might have led her to marry unwisely—and to distrust a good thing when it came along.

Claire became aware of the phone ringing in the house. She was turning to go back inside when Matt stuck his head out the door. "It's your dad. He sounds kind of upset."

Claire raced into the house and snatched up the phone. "Dad? What is it? Is everything—"

Her father didn't let her finish. "I'm at the hospital. It's your mom. Her heart—" He let out an odd, gasping little breath. "I think you'd better come."

Chapter Twelve

Days later, when she'd had a chance to reflect, what struck Gerry most was that she hadn't hesitated. No stopping to consider the potential fallout: Claire's family and her own, even the day of work she'd be missing at such a crucial time. One look at her daughter's pale, stricken face, and she did what she should have years ago: She took a stand.

"I'm coming with you," she said.

But Claire wasn't hearing. She sat on the floor with the receiver in her lap, staring vacantly ahead. Her face was the color of the Sheetrock stacked against the wall.

"She was fine. I talked to her just this morning. This wouldn't have happened if—" Her mouth snapped shut, her lips pressed together so tightly they quivered.

Gerry crouched down in front of her, gently taking hold of her shoulders. "Listen to me, Claire. People get sick for all kinds of reasons. No one's to blame. And it might not be as serious as you think. There's no sense in even speculating until you've seen her. Now why don't you pack some things while I call and book us a flight?"

Claire blinked, bringing her into focus. "Us?"

"Yes, *us*. You and me."

This time it sank in. Claire gaped at Gerry as if she'd suggested they firebomb the house next door. "What? Are you crazy? You can't go anywhere *near* her."

"I should have done this weeks ago." Gerry stood up, the popping in her joints a reminder that none of them were getting any younger. "Seeing me couldn't be worse than what she's imagined."

She and Claire had grown closer these past few weeks, but no amount of bonding would ever fill the gap of all those lost years. It was something she'd had to make peace with, something that ought to bring comfort to Millie Brewster as well: Even if Gerry wanted to take her place, there was no way she ever could.

"I couldn't do that to her." Claire was shaking her head.

As she struggled to her feet, Gerry noticed the part in her hair was crooked, and remembered when she used to patiently comb and braid Andie's, a section at a time. *If only I'd been able to do that with Claire.* But she wasn't a child; she was a grown daughter in need of more than a mother's touch.

"It might be the best thing for all of us," Gerry said.

The room had grown still, and sunlight slanted over dusty floorboards ghosted with overlapping shoeprints. Matt was nowhere to be seen, though evidence of his handiwork was all around: the partially installed tongue-and-groove wainscoting, the newly stripped lintels and molding, the shelving on the wall where the display case would stand. On the floor at Claire's feet was the red shopping bag from Aubrey—Gerry recognized its embossed logo as that of Celi Cela, a pricey Santa Barbara gourmet shop. Tea for a tearoom, that was Aubrey for you. She smiled inwardly at the reverse subtlety of something so obvious. Like the catcher's mitt that had arrived in the mail the other day for Justin: an ordinary Spalding like every other boy's, remarkable only in the fact that neither she nor Mike had thought to replace the old one of Kevin's he'd been using.

"I used to think I knew what would make her happy," Claire said with a sigh. Some of the color had crept back into her cheeks; now she merely looked tired. "I thought it was my job to . . . fill in the blanks. But I can't anymore. I don't know that I ever could."

"Oh, honey, it doesn't work that way. We have to fill in our own blanks." Gerry's heart ached for her daughter. For it was becoming increasingly clear to her that the Brewsters, however well-meaning, hadn't always had her best interests at heart.

"Easy for you to say. You have so much. My mother—" The urgency of the situation sank in, and Claire glanced about with something close to panic. "I have to go." All at once she was dashing down the hall. She emerged minutes later wearing a clean blouse tucked into her jeans and carrying an overnight bag.

Gerry had used the time to phone her travel agent and was just hanging up when Claire walked in. "I booked us seats on the five-forty to San Francisco," she said, her tone leaving no room for argument. "We'll take my car." Sam could give Mavis a ride home.

Claire hesitated, looking torn. Then she seemed to come to a decision. "All right, but on one condition—you don't go anywhere near my mother unless she okays it."

Gerry nodded. "Fair enough."

Then they were stepping out onto the porch, where Mavis and Sam sat gossiping on the steps, oblivious to the drama unfolding. Gerry drew Sam aside. "Something's come up. I have to fly to San Francisco with Claire. Could you keep Andie and Justin overnight? I'll tell you all about it when I get back."

Sam gave her a curious look, but all she said was, "No problem. I'll swing by your house to pick them up after I drop off your mom."

Gerry silently blessed her for simply knowing what needed to be done—a reminder of why they'd stayed friends all these years: There was never any fuss with Sam.

A short while later, as they were making their way over the hill, Gerry pondered what lay ahead. For close to three decades— nearly half her life—she'd wondered about the people raising her daughter. The only image that had come to mind, those long nights as she'd lain awake in bed, staring up at the ceiling with tears drying to a crust on her temples, was of the mother and father in the old *Dick and Jane* readers: a bland, nondescript couple in fifties attire. The kind who would attend church regularly, serve three balanced meals a day, and engage in conjugal relations as opposed to making love. They would never swear, or lose their tempers, or drive outside the speed limit. In short, they were everything she wasn't.

Not until she'd had Andie did she realize it wasn't about being perfect, that it didn't really matter how often you went to church, or how many men you'd slept with, or if you drove within the speed limit at all times. The only thing that truly mattered was whether you loved your child. Everything else came second.

They arrived at LAX with nearly an hour to spare. After they'd checked in, Claire insisted on writing Gerry a check for her ticket,

and Gerry relented only because it was easier than having to explain that this was
something *she* needed as well. She'd given
these people the gift of her child. The least
they could do was allow her—and Claire—
the chance to get to know each other.

Half an hour after takeoff they were touching down in San Francisco. They made their
way to the Avis desk, where there was a
long line followed by an even longer wait for
the shuttle bus. It wasn't until well after six
that they found themselves inching along the
freeway in rush hour traffic. Gerry tried to remember when she'd last been in the Bay
Area. When Kevin's restaurant had opened?
It seemed that decades had passed since
then.

Her thoughts turned to Aubrey. At the airport she'd found herself keeping an eye out,
her pulse quickening at every silver-haired
man glimpsed from afar, never mind that he
was probably in a different terminal. That
she hadn't spotted him seemed beside the
point; she'd been *hoping* to see him. For
months he'd been tidily tucked away in a
box, and now he was out playing havoc with
her life. Befriending Justin, and now Claire.
Even Laura had taken her aside at the wed-

ding to confide that she thought he was "absolutely perfect" for her.

What made it so unsettling was that Aubrey, unlike some of the men she'd been with since her divorce, had no ulterior motive. He was merely being *nice.* Which worried her more than if he'd been angling to marry her. Dammit, why couldn't he have been a shit? Or, at the very least, a shit with redeeming qualities. *That* she could relate to.

"We'll never get there at this rate," Claire fretted.

"If I go any faster, we'll be eating that guy's exhaust." Gerry glared at the dark blue Subaru creeping along in front of them as if it were the cause of the jam.

"I wish I bit my nails. It'd be something to do."

"Justin cracks his knuckles."

"I've noticed."

"It drives me up a wall."

Claire gave a tiny smile. "I've noticed that, too."

"You'll see when you have children of your own."

"That might not be for a long time."

Gerry caught a note of yearning in her voice. She asked pleasantly, "How does your boyfriend feel about kids?" The traffic had slowed to a near standstill, and she eased her foot off the accelerator just in time to keep from kissing the Subaru's bumper.

"Oh, he wants them ... one of these days," Claire said.

"Well, that's a start at least. By the way, when am I going to meet this guy?"

Claire stared distractedly out the window. "Soon, I hope. It's hard for him to get away."

"He'll be here for the opening, won't he?"

"He said he'd try."

Gerry sensed there was more to it than her boyfriend's busy schedule, but she let it drop. Whatever was going on with them, Claire didn't need her putting her two cents in. She thought, too, of Matt. She couldn't help but notice he and Claire had gotten pretty chummy. Was he giving the boyfriend a run for his money?

She was surprised when Claire volunteered, "The truth is, Byron's not exactly thrilled about all this."

"The tearoom?"

"Let's just say it wouldn't exactly be to his advantage if it's a roaring success."

"How so?"

Claire frowned. "Well, for one thing, Carson Springs isn't exactly where he planned on opening a practice . . . and I wouldn't exactly be in a position to move."

"They're building a new medical center out near Dos Palmas," Gerry told her. "I've heard they're looking for doctors."

"It's a thought." Claire perked up a bit, then went back to staring gloomily out the window. "Either way, we'll be strapped for cash. Let's face it, even if I can pull this off, you're not likely to see Tea & Sympathy in the Fortune 500."

Gerry gave a knowing laugh. "The same is true of Blessed Bee. "I guess neither of us is in it for the money."

Her stomach did a nosedive at the thought of Sister Clement, who'd arrived earlier in the week. What would she say if she knew about Claire?

"Byron and I'll work it out," Claire said. "We always do." It sounded more like bravado than conviction.

"The real test comes when you're married." Gerry thought of her own marriage, which had been a rude shock after the wine and roses of their courtship. "This might sound strange, but I sometimes think that if Mike and I had lived apart, we'd still be together."

Fog was rolling in off the bay in soft gray bales, cocooning them in a heavy, gray mist, and making the cars ahead look as if they'd been sketched in pencil. After a moment Claire said, "Would you have married my father if he'd asked?"

Gerry shrugged. "Let's just say I'm glad he didn't. It would have been a disaster. The one thing I *do* know is that I wouldn't have married Mike if it hadn't been for Jim."

"Why is that?"

"I couldn't see past the fact that he wanted kids. And I was desperate to be a mother."

"Ironic, isn't it?" Claire's voice was flat.

Gerry felt something come loose inside her chest, like a cog holding some vital piece of machinery in place. She asked softly, "Do you think you'll ever forgive me?"

"There's nothing to forgive." Claire shot her a cool glance.

"What is it, then?"

Claire hesitated a moment, then said, "It's not about what happened then. It's just that I can't help wondering if you're ashamed of me *now.*"

Gerry was so startled she nearly plowed into the car in front of her, and had to bring her foot down hard on the brake. "Ashamed? Why on earth would you think that?"

"That first weekend, when you didn't introduce me to your friends, I got the feeling you didn't want me to be the scarlet A on your chest."

Gerry was stung by the unfairness of it. All this time she'd been holding back because she'd thought *Claire* was the one who'd have been embarrassed.

"If you only knew," she said, her voice trembling. "I'd have shouted it to the heavens if I'd thought . . ." She pulled in a deep, steadying breath. "I was afraid that if I came on too strongly you'd run in the opposite direction."

Claire was looking at her in a new way—thoughtful and considering. "I guess we were both wrong." She seemed to be struggling to hold her emotions in check. A moment later she pointed toward a sign up ahead. "It's the next exit."

It was well after dark by the time they turned off Highway 17 onto the Pacific Coast Highway, which became the main road into town. They cruised past tourist shops and boat dealerships and eateries with names like Rusty Anchor and The Crow's Nest. Gerry found Miramonte to be pretty much as she'd remembered it except for the newer-looking houses and condos now interspersed with the older beachfront cottages.

Dominican Hospital lay at the southernmost end of town: a modern concrete-and-glass building with a steel cross above the lighted sign out front. Gerry pulled into the parking lot to find it full, the only spaces available those for staff. She circled it several times before nosing their rented Taurus into the slot labeled CHIEF ADMINISTRATOR.

"If we get towed," she said, "we might as well go out in style."

Claire looked as if she were about to protest, but said nothing.

They walked along the juniper-lined path to the main entrance, where they pushed their way through thick plate glass doors into the lobby. Wall-to-wall glass soared to meet the solar-paned ceiling, which at this hour gave it the look of a cavern. At the far end was a reception desk flanked by rows of chairs. Claire hurried over to it, returning moments later wearing a distraught look.

"She's in the CCU."

"Go on. I'll wait here," Gerry told her.

Claire shot her a grateful look, then made a dash for the elevators, leaving Gerry to wonder if this would turn out to be a wasted trip. *No,* she thought. If nothing else, she'd been given the opportunity to set the record straight with her daughter—a misunderstanding that, if left to fester, would have had consequences far beyond anything the Brewsters could dream up. As she made her way over to the waiting area, she offered up a little prayer of thanks. God did indeed work in mysterious ways.

She found an empty seat and fished her cell phone from her purse, punching in Sam's number.

"'Lo," Sam sounded distracted.

"How's it going?"

"Fine. We just had supper. Listen, Gerry—"

"The kids behaving themselves?"

"Justin's good as gold. But—"

"Andie?"

"She's not here."

From the agitation in her voice, Gerry knew that Andie wasn't out with Simon or over at Finch's. She felt her heart lurch. "What do you mean? Where is she?"

"At her dad's. I just got off the phone with Mike."

"There's nothing wrong, is there?" Gerry struggled to remain calm.

There was a beat of silence, a solitary beat, no more, but enough for Gerry to feel her world start to crumble. "According to Mike, she wants to stay with him. For good."

Gerry gripped the edge of her seat. "Are you sure he wasn't just saying that?"

"I don't think so. She was at the house when I went to pick up her and Justin. She got pretty upset when I told her where you'd gone." Sam's voice was muffled, as if she were holding a hand cupped around the receiver.

"Oh, God, I didn't think." Gerry felt sick. She'd been so busy blaming Andie for what had happened at the wedding that she hadn't seen this coming. Why couldn't she have given Andie the benefit of the doubt?

"It's not too late," Sam said. "If you talked to her . . ."

Gerry's head spun. Since when had it become Andie's decision? Wasn't *she* supposed to be in charge? She tried to remember the last time they'd had anything close to a heart-to-heart talk. Days? Weeks? Months? She couldn't recall.

"Would you put Justin on?" She'd die if she couldn't talk to at least one of her kids.

She spoke briefly with her son, who seemed oblivious to all that was going on with his sister. An equal opportunity hero-worshiper, he was delighted to be able to spend time with Ian. Listening to him babble on excitedly was like warm water rinsing the salt from her wound.

Being a mother was like triage, she thought. You were constantly forced to choose, doling out hugs and kisses and precious private time to whichever child was most in need at any given moment. Which meant that someone was always going to feel left out. And what did you say to *that* child? That life isn't fair, and the sooner they realized it the better?

An hour passed. She flipped through out-dated magazines and glanced up from time to time at the TV, on which captions scrolled across the bottom of the screen in lieu of sound. It was tuned to the news, and she saw just enough to get the drift: police shoot-ings, protests, Middle East terrorist attacks. Just when she was beginning to give up hope of Claire's return, she caught sight of her emerging from an elevator. Gerry scarcely recognized her. She seemed to have aged a dozen years. Her head was down and her shoulders pulled up around her ears, her gait as deliberate and heavy as if she were lugging a heavy bundle on her back.

Gerry walked over to meet her. "How is she?"

Claire seemed almost surprised to find her still there, then quickly recovered, saying, "It's not as serious as they first thought." *You wouldn't know it from your face,* Gerry thought. "The preliminary diagnosis is angina. Her doctor wants to do some more tests, but if everything checks out, she can go home tomorrow."

"You must be relieved."

If she was, it had done nothing to ease whatever was weighing on her. "I told her you were here."

"And?"

"It took some convincing, but she finally agreed to see you."

Gerry's heart went out to Claire. "I won't stay long. I imagine she's pretty tired."

Claire's only reply was to smile grimly, as if to say that Gerry couldn't possibly make things worse.

As they rode up in the elevator, Gerry thought of Millie Brewster steeling herself against her unwanted visitor as she must have the results of her EKG. She smiled at the irony of it. Years ago *she'd* been the one consumed with jealousy. Now it was up to her to put Millie's fears to rest.

The CCU was on the third floor, just around the corner from the nurses' station. It had four beds, each sectioned off by a curtain, and enough glowing monitors to light the room without benefit of fluorescents. Millie Brewster was in the bed nearest the door: a gray-haired woman so small and frail she left barely a dent in the mattress. She lay very still, her eyes closed, the hand hooked up to the IV resting pale and weightless on her bosom.

The line on the monitor overhead undulated in even waves.

Claire's father sat in the chair beside the bed, a large balding man running to fat. He'd been staring vacantly ahead, lost in thought, but started at their approach, a momentary alertness animating his sad, defeated-looking face. He looked from Claire to Gerry, his gaze lingering only a second longer than was polite.

"She just dropped off," he whispered.

Gerry had a sudden urge to flee. What had she hoped to accomplish? "I could come back later if you like." She kept her voice low, not wanting to wake Millie.

But Millie stirred, her eyes fluttering open—small and anxious. She stared at Gerry, waiting for her to make the first move.

Gerry touched her hand. She saw no need for introductions. "Claire tells me you're going to be okay."

"So they say." Millie's voice was a dry croak, her face as pale as chalk. If Gerry hadn't known better, she'd have thought the woman was at death's door.

Lou patted his wife's shoulder. "You'll feel better when you're in your own bed."

"My mother always says hospitals are no place for sick people." Gerry's feeble attempt at leavening fell flat; Millie stared at her blankly. She tried a different tack. "I'm sorry. This must seem like the world's worst timing, but Claire was so upset . . . " She hesitated, panic setting in. But the words came easily. "I'm glad we finally had a chance to meet. I want you to know how grateful I am. You did a fine job raising her."

It clearly wasn't what Millie had been expecting to hear. "I don't need *you* to tell me that."

"Mom—" Claire took a step forward.

Gerry put a hand out. "No, it's all right." She looked back at Millie. "I'm not trying to take your place, Mrs. Brewster. I couldn't if I tried. All I want is to be a part of her life."

Millie's face twisted, a hard, gray knot against the pillow. "Well, you got your way, didn't you?"

"Mom. It was *my* decision." Claire looked stricken.

Millie's gaze fell on her daughter. The angry look faded, replaced by an expression of almost unbearable tenderness. "Oh, honey, I don't blame you. If anything, I blame myself." Her voice was a thin little treble. "I know we leaned on you more than we should have. It's like you . . . completed us."

She melted into the pillow as if spent. Claire stood looking down at her mother, arms hanging lifelessly at her sides and her eyes filling with tears. On the monitor over the bed, the LCD readout showed a slight but noticeable spike.

"I didn't ask for this." Claire's voice was small and choked. Gerry didn't know if she meant her parents' excessive love . . . or Gerry's refusal to take no for an answer.

"I know, honey. I know." Lou slipped an arm about his daughter's shoulders.

Claire gave him a stern look. "I want you and Mom to visit."

"We will," he said wearily. "Soon as Mother's back on her feet."

Gerry cleared her throat, which felt tight all of a sudden. "I hope you can make it for the opening. I'd love for you to meet my family."

Lou turned to her. "Claire tells us you have children of your own." He flushed as if realizing how it had sounded—as if Claire weren't her child, too.

"Two, a boy and a girl," Gerry told him. She felt a pang at the thought of Andie. "My son thinks Claire hung the moon."

Lou managed a weak chuckle. "We feel the same way." He cast an adoring look at his daughter. "Among other things, we miss her cooking."

"I'm not much of a cook myself." Gerry seized the opportunity to change the subject—anything to divert herself from the eyes staring up at her like the unblinking red lights on the monitor. "Potato salad is about all I can manage without a mix."

"I make mine with sour cream. Gives it a nice tang," Millie said.

Gerry suppressed a smile. "My secret is Miracle Whip."

Millie's face relaxed a bit, and Gerry saw how she must have looked when she was younger, how people might have seen a resemblance between her and Claire. Both were delicate-boned and fair, with the same air of thoughtful seriousness. Millie exhaled with a long, sighing breath. "I'm a little tired," she announced to no one in particular.

Gerry took the hint. "I should let you get some rest," she said, stepping away from the bed.

Lou tenderly pulled the blanket up around his wife's shoulders before turning to Claire. "Why don't you get something to eat, honey? I'll still be here when you get back."

"It was nice meeting you, Mr. Brewster." Gerry put her hand out.

"Lou. Call me Lou." He gave her hand a little squeeze, his eyes meeting hers only briefly before sliding away. "It was nice meeting you, too."

"Can I bring you anything?" Claire asked.

"I wouldn't say no to a cup of coffee."

Claire kissed him on the cheek. "Be back in a bit."

Gerry walked with her into the corridor. Lit by the eternal noon of fluorescents, it made her think of a spaceship, the nurses, doctors, and orderlies bustling past like aliens in search of the true meaning of life on earth. She realized how hungry she was—starving, in fact. Even hospital food would taste good right now.

They rode the elevator down to the mezzanine level, where the cafeteria occupied the balcony opposite the gift shop and florist. They carried their trays to a table by the railing, where they had a bird's eye view of the lobby. Nearby, a man with thinning gray hair sat hunched over a bowl of soup, and several tables away a group of nurses were engaged in an animated discussion.

"I'm sorry about my mother," Claire said.

"Don't be." Millie hadn't acted out of meanness, Gerry knew; she was frightened, that's all. And old—Gerry had been unprepared for how old they'd both seemed, more like grandparents. "They seem like nice people."

"They mean well." Claire was looking down at her tray, making no move to pick up her utensils. A pale tendril of steam from a Styrofoam cup of tea caressed the delicate curve of her cheek.

"It's obvious they love you."

Claire lifted her head, her mouth twisting in a pained smile. "Sometimes it feels like too much of a good thing."

Gerry wanted to say, *I love you, too,* but this wasn't the time or place. Instead, she asked, "Will you be staying long?"

"Hopefully not more than a few days. I'll be at Kitty's. She said to tell you you're welcome, too, if you'd like to stay the night."

Gerry shook her head. "I should be getting back."

Claire poked listlessly with her fork at the mashed potatoes on her plate. "Would you keep an eye on things while I'm gone? Tell Matt . . ." She glanced up, her cheeks reddening. "Tell him I'll be back."

"I'll tell him."

Gerry ate half her sandwich, wrapping up the other half to take with her. Claire, she saw, had barely touched her food.

"You shouldn't have any trouble getting a flight," she said. "Not at this hour."

Gerry only nodded. Claire didn't have to know she had other plans. The idea had come to her during the interminable wait downstairs. God had brought her here for a reason, she'd concluded. Not just to give comfort to Claire, or force the Brewsters to acknowledge her, but to take care of some unfinished business of her own. It was time, she thought, to pay a little visit to someone who'd be even less happy to see her than Millie Brewster, someone from the past who held the key to her future.

It was midnight by the time she reached San Francisco. On the drive north she'd booked a room at the Hilton, and by the time she checked in she was long past exhaustion. She was asleep almost as soon as her head touched the pillow.

Gerry awoke to find sunlight streaming in through the nylon sheers. She bolted upright, squinting at the digital clock on the nightstand. Nine-thirty. How had she managed to sleep so late? She scrambled out of bed and hit the shower running. She was dressed, checked out, and in her car by half past ten.

A short while later she was pulling up in front of Father Gallagher's neat frame house on Turk Street. Her knock was answered by

a heavyset gray-haired woman who informed her, "You just missed him."

"Oh dear." Gerry smiled ingratiatingly,
holding her sweater closed so her wrinkled
blouse from the day before wouldn't show. "I
should have called first. I just thought . . .
well, I was passing through. I'm an old
friend, you see."

The woman looked her up and down, but
was apparently satisfied that she was telling
the truth. "He hears confessions Thursdays
and Fridays." She gave Gerry directions to
the church.

As she drove off in search of it, Gerry's
heart was knocking in her chest and she felt
sick to her stomach. What would she say to
him? More important, what would he say to
her? It was one thing for him to lie to Claire,
but Gerry knew better. She wouldn't let him
worm out of it this time.

St. Thomas Aquinas was a square, fea-
tureless concrete building in the middle of a
graffiti-scrawled block, situated between a
Laundromat and an all-night bodega. Its
shabbiness struck her as odd until she recalled that Jim had always chosen humility
as a means to an end. And clearly it had

paid off. Rumor had it that he was one of the archbishop's most trusted aides.

She pushed open the wooden door, pausing just inside the vestibule to let her eyes adjust to the dimness. In the sanctuary, which smelled close and cedary like a trunk in which winter clothes are stored, feeble rays shone from high recessed windows that might once have been made of stained glass but were now reinforced safety glass. Scattered about the pews were half a dozen worshipers, old women mostly, their heads bent low in prayer. She drifted to the bank of votive candles. Only a few flickered wanly in their ruby glass holders. She dropped a coin in the donation box before lighting one.

She caught a movement out of the corner of her eye, and turned. Someone was emerging from the confessional—an old woman bent nearly double with arthritis. Gerry watched her shuffle to the nearest pew, where she sank down slowly, clutching hold of the pew in front of her.

Before she could lose her nerve, Gerry darted over and pushed aside the heavy, velvet drape. Inside, she sank down on the padded kneeler. *Forgive me, Father, for I have sinned . . .* She nearly lapsed into the familiar recitation before realizing how ludicrous it would be under the circumstances.

She could see a darkened silhouette through the grille and heard the faint, even sound of breathing. After a moment a voice prompted, "Yes, my child?"

"It's me," she hissed. "Gerry."

She became aware of a sudden stillness, then in a hoarse whisper, he demanded, "What do you want?" From the fear in his voice, anyone eavesdropping might have thought it was a holdup.

"I think you know."

This was a sin, what she was doing, but she didn't care. Exhilaration rose in her.

"For the love of God—"

"You bastard. She wasn't asking anything of you. All she wanted was the truth."

"This . . . this is an outrage." His voice rose to a shrill whine. "Have you no decency?"

"Decency? How dare you speak to me about decency?" She leaned so close her mouth was almost touching the grille. "Tell me, Jim, while you were sweeping it all under the rug, did you ever stop to think of me? Or of your daughter?"

A memory surfaced: Jim reaching to cup

her bare breast as if bringing his hand to a flame, a look on his face like in the portraits of martyrs—a mixture of fear and rapture that seemed to hover on the very brink of madness.

She closed her eyes, seeing him naked in her mind, his body pale as a statue's. Yet in her arms he'd been liquid heat, not so much making love to her as *consuming* her. Maybe it was because he'd been her first, or because it was forbidden, but she'd sensed then what she now knew to be a certainty: No one would ever make love to her quite the same again. For all its passion, deep down she'd felt afraid, as if not sure she would come out alive.

Now in the closeness of the confessional, she caught his scent, that of a trapped animal. He hissed: *"Get out."*

"I'll go when I'm good and ready." She felt oddly cleansed—more so than if she'd confessed. She ought to have done this years ago. "Oh yes, I'm responsible, too. I'm not denying that. And I've paid the price. I won't be punished anymore."

"What do you want?" he repeated. Only this time he sounded defeated—and old, far older than his years.

"Call off the dogs or I'll—" What? Go to the archbishop? What would that accomplish? It might ruin Jim, but it wouldn't keep her from being fired. "I'll make you sorry you ever knew me," she finished somewhat less spectacularly than she'd intended.

"I don't know what you're talking about," he insisted.

"Am I supposed to believe it's pure coincidence that the motherhouse is nosing around?" She gave a dry little laugh. "If I was that stupid once, I'm not anymore."

"You attribute far too much power to me."

"Just the opposite—I've underestimated you."

His shadowy silhouette loomed, becoming something monstrous. "If I'd wanted to have you fired, I'd have done it years ago!"

"Who said anything about my being fired?"

A tiny beat of hesitation. He realized he'd given himself away. Even so, he continued the charade. "It's a natural assumption."

"Like your assuming this would be our little secret forever?"

"It . . . it . . . was a mistake. I never intended—"

"To fuck me? Or for me to get pregnant?"

Nearly thirty years of keeping her mouth shut hadn't caused it to diminish; just the opposite—it had grown so huge it would no longer fit in its box. "I think the archbishop will have a hard time believing you were taken advantage of by a nineteen-year-old virgin."

"Get thee behind me!" For a moment she feared he'd come completely unhinged, then in that same shrill whisper he went on, "It was *your* doing. You . . . you . . . led me into temptation." He broke off with a choking sound, followed by an incoherent mumbling that she recognized after a moment as the Act of Contrition. *"Oh God, I am heartily sorry for all my sins . . ."*

Gerry gave in to a bleak smile. When she was little, she'd thought it was "hardly sorry," which would have been more fitting in this case. She opened her mouth to tell him he had no business asking God's forgiveness when he had yet to make amends to her, but he was clearly beyond her now. He wouldn't hear anything she had to say.

Silently she rose and pushed open the curtain to see a startled face eyeing her aghast: a doughy middle-aged woman, with the collar of her coat pulled up around her ears, who'd clearly heard enough, if not every word.

Millie was sent home the following day, much to Claire's relief. With the medication her doctor had prescribed, her heart had settled into a steady rhythm, and some of her old color was back. When Millie jokingly asked if she'd live to see her first grandchild, Dr. Farland had chuckled and said, "I think that depends more on Claire."

After the first night at Kitty's, Claire stayed at her parents' house, nursing her mother and seeing that her father, who lived off canned soup and Rice-A-Roni otherwise, was properly fed. She also cleaned the house from top to bottom, noting that Millie in her old age, had grown slipshod. When she ran out of things to clean, she went over the checkbook her father hadn't balanced in months.

The first Sunday in April she was heading out to the grocery store—today was her last day, and she wanted to stock up—when she spotted a familiar car in the driveway next door: Byron's blue Hyundai. Her heart skipped a beat. The next moment she was racing across the lawn, mindless of the dew soaking her shoes.

Byron met her at the door, bare-chested and wearing a pair of his oldest jeans, his hair damp from the shower. She noticed his ribs sticking out a bit—he'd dropped a few pounds—and the thought of Matt flashed through her mind: his big arms and chest, his muscles like a longshoreman's. She immediately felt disloyal.

Her boyfriend stepped out onto the porch, easing the door shut behind him. She remembered that the Allendales slept late on weekends, sometimes into the afternoon—a habit Millie considered to be just this side of pagan.

"I got in late last night. "I was just on my way over to surprise you." He wrapped his arms around her, shivering a little with the cold. He smelled of shampoo and pipe tobacco—his father's—and she had a sudden sense, like a crooked picture frame being straightened, that everything was going to be all right.

"You should have called to let me know you were coming." She couldn't keep the faint note of accusation from her voice.

"I wasn't sure until the very last minute that I could get away." He drew back with a smile, his eyes searching hers. "God, it's good to see you."

"Feel like taking a walk on the beach?" The shopping could wait. She had all morning. "We'll grab some coffee on the way."

"Sure. Wait here while I throw something on." He disappeared into the house, emerging a few minutes later buttoning up an old flannel shirt she recognized from his college days. His hair was in a ponytail. On his sockless feet was a pair of ancient battered Weejuns.

"How's your mom?" he asked as she drove toward town.

"She's fine, but she insists on staying in bed. She's worried she'll have another attack."

"Is she taking anything?"

"Coumadin. And something to help her sleep at night."

He nodded as if concurring, and she remembered when they'd played house as little kids, how he'd strut about holding his father's pipe while she traipsed after him, trying not to trip on her mother's skirt. Even then he'd worn this faintly professorial air.

After a quick stop at Starbucks—it was

the one thing their mothers had in common: they both made lousy coffee—they headed out to the Dunes, steaming cups in hand. It was where they'd hung out as teenagers, and she still preferred it to the more sheltered beaches, which were usually awash in sunbathers. Here the wind blew brisk and cold year round, bringing the sting of spray from the waves churning into the shore.

They strolled along the beach, deserted this time of day, where they'd once made love amid the dunes. The fog had burned off and the sky was a brilliant, scoured blue. Down by the tidemark, a flock of sandpipers mined for insects amid the kelp. When Byron took her hand, she scarcely noticed—as if they'd been old marrieds. There'd been a few other guys in college, sure—like the one she'd slept with after a drunken fraternity bash, whose smelly socks by the side of the bed she remembered more vividly than what he'd been like *in* bed—but no one who'd been a threat to Byron. She'd always known she would come back to him, and in the end she had.

They found a small cove that provided at least some shelter from the wind, and sank down, huddled together under the blanket she'd wisely thought to bring. For a long while they didn't speak, just sat sipping their coffees and watching the waves pound into shore.

Byron was the first to break the companionable silence. "I've thought a lot about what you said. I mean, I knew you hated your job, but I wasn't expecting it, that's all. I'm sorry if I overreacted."

"I'm sorry, too," she said, lacing her fingers through his. She was glad he'd brought it up; how much better than these past few weeks of brief, stilted conversations over the phone. "I did sort of drop it on you like a ton of bricks."

His green eyes seemed brighter than usual, and she realized it was because he was so pale from all his long hours indoors. She felt selfish. Here she was making far-reaching decisions about her future—*their* future—while he'd been nearly killing himself just to keep up.

"If this is really what you want, I'm all for it," he said with more conviction than she sensed he felt.

She looked out at the waves racing into shore, silvery at the crest with smooth green underbellies. She missed the ocean, its rhythms and moods, but she'd missed Byron most of all.

"This could be the worst idea ever," she told him. "I could fall flat on my face." She paused to take in a breath of salty air laced with the scent of smoke from a driftwood fire. "All I know is that for the first time in my life I wake up every morning looking forward to the day." She turned to him, beseeching him with her eyes. It wouldn't work if he was only going along to please her.

"I'll admit, I never pictured you as the proprietress of a tearoom," he said, smiling faintly. "It seems so old-fashioned."

"Maybe I *am* old-fashioned."

"One way or another, I guess I'm not exactly in a position to throw my weight around." He glanced wryly at the braided thong on his wrist that seemed a relic of a more carefree past. "It's not like I can support you in fine style on what I'll be making."

"Poor Byron." She leaned over and kissed the reddened tip of his nose. "Should we take up a collection?"

He laughed. "I'm not that desperate. Not yet at least."

"Only two more years to go." The new medical center would be up and running by then. She hadn't said anything about it to Byron; she'd been waiting for the right moment.

"It seems more like a lifetime," he said, injecting the right note of mournfulness into his voice.

She poked him with her elbow. "Stop it. I feel guilty enough as it is."

"Okay. How's it going with Gerry?"

She thought about what Gerry had done, flying up with her to see her mother. "She's been great. They all have—Justin and Mavis, too. I don't know what I'd do without them." She was careful to make no mention of Matt.

"It sounds as if you have it all worked out." He sounded genuinely happy for her.

"Everyone's looking forward to meeting you."

"Same here."

"When *are* you coming?"

He shrugged. "Who knows? I had to promise my firstborn child just to get away for one day. It might be awhile before I can get a whole weekend off, but I'll try."

She wanted to cry in frustration that she couldn't wait forever, that there were times, more and more lately, when she felt him slipping away. But she said nothing. What would have been the point? It wasn't as if he could help it.

"I'll keep my fingers crossed," she said.

"Before I forget, thanks for the pictures."

She'd e-mailed him photos of the house. "I always imagined us picking out a house together, but I hope it meets with your approval."

"All I saw was a lot of Sheetrock and lumber," he kidded.

The thought of Matt once more tiptoed across her mind. "In that case, you have a surprise in store."

"More than one, I'm sure." He drew her against him so that she was tucked under his arm, her head nestled on his shoulder. "That reminds me, I have something for you." He pulled something clumsily wrapped in tissue paper from his pocket. It was so light that, as she took it from him, the wind nearly snatched it from her hand.

It was a silver heart on a gossamer chain. Claire held it up, the sunlight winking off its filigreed surface in brilliant Morse-like flashes. "It's beautiful. You shouldn't have."

"Don't worry, I didn't break the bank."

That wasn't what she'd meant; she'd been

thinking of the trouble he'd gone to. "Still, you shouldn't have." She held it up to her neck, her chilled fingers fumbling with the clasp.

"Here, let me help."

Byron's fingers were cool against the back of her neck. By contrast, the warmth of his lips, when it came, caused her to jump a little as if goosed. Smiling, she dropped back into his arms, offering herself up to be kissed. *Yes. This is what I need.* Just lately she'd had enough of his telling her how much he missed her, and of their long talks over the phone about a future that had begun to feel like a savings account accruing interest. Life, her recent experiences had taught her, was meant to be *spent,* not hoarded.

She reveled in the familiar pressure of his lips against hers, the darting tip of his tongue. He knew her so well. Hadn't they made love in the shelter of these dunes as teenagers? In daylight and by the light of driftwood fires—shivering partly with cold and partly with delight, her terror of Millie and Lou's finding out making it all the more thrilling.

But now, as they kissed, she had the oddest sense of simultaneously being an onlooker, as if a part of her were in a dark theater watching this take place on screen. Scenes from movies flashed through her mind: Deborah Kerr on the beach with Burt Lancaster in *From Here to Eternity,* Sandra Dee and Troy Donahue in *A Summer Place.* That same part of her, the part watching, was feeling a bit smug as well, as if to say, *See? No problems here, folks.*

Byron pushed a hand under her jacket. "You're shivering."

"Warm me up." She burrowed into his embrace. Her fingers had thawed and she had no trouble unbuttoning his shirt. Lowering her head, she pressed her cheek against his bare rib cage. It was lean and smooth, almost hairless. An image of Matt's thickly muscled chest matted with hair rose unbidden, bringing a rush of guilt.

She abruptly pulled away and wriggled out of her jeans. "Come on. Let's." She laughed, feeling the old thrill from long ago. "We won't get caught. There's no one for miles."

Byron looked less than convinced, and she felt a moment of impatience—in the old days he wouldn't have needed to be talked into it—then with a wicked laugh he was pushing her back onto the sand. When he shucked off his jeans she saw that *that* at least needed no encouraging.

Now he was in her, the heat from his body warming her inside the cocoon of the blanket. Oh God, yes . . . *yes.* It had been too long. This past week alone had seemed an ice age. In a burst of abandon, she rolled over so that she was on top. She caught a flicker of surprise in his eyes; she'd never been the aggressor (not that Byron expected her to be submissive). But now, as she sat astride him, the wind catching her hair and blowing it out around her face, she might have been a Siren luring some poor sailor to his death. She laughed out loud at the image, while beneath her Byron begged for mercy, saying breathlessly that if she kept it up he wouldn't be able to hold out.

"It's okay," she said.

"Are you—?"

"Not yet."

He groaned. "Oh God . . . I'm coming."

She felt him pulsing inside her. Curiously she didn't mind that she hadn't come. In some ways it was better this way. She felt wilder. Freer somehow. She rolled off him onto the sand, the cold, wind-whipped air against her flushed skin intoxicating.

Mindful that someone could come along at any moment, they were quick to throw on their clothes. All the while she could see the question in Byron's eyes: Where had *that* come from? Not that they hadn't made love in some strange places. And not that she wasn't capable of initiating it. But something had been different this time, something a less trusting soul might have imagined to mean she'd learned a few tricks in his absence.

Her thoughts turned once more to Matt. Why did she feel unfaithful when they'd done no more than shake hands?

She scrambled to her feet. "I'm starving. Have you eaten?"

"Does half a bagel count?"

She grabbed his hand. "Come on, if we hurry we can snag a table at Manny's. I have a sudden hankering for *huevos rancheros.*"

Then they were racing down the beach, the wind blowing her jacket out like a sail. Byron pulled ahead, knees pumping, sand spurting from his heels, grinning like a madman. Her heart swelled with love. She didn't want him to be any different, just for him to see *her* differently. Was that too much to ask?

The following day Byron headed back and Kitty drove Claire to the airport. On the way they talked about Tea & Sympathy South, as they'd dubbed it. Kitty was planning to fly down the week of the opening. Until then they'd rely on phone, fax, and e-mail. Already Kitty had made arrangements with her tea distributor in Oregon.

"It's all going to work out just fine, don't worry." She pulled into the terminal, skirting double-parked cars with the ease of someone who scarcely noticed they were there. She was dressed in her usual crazy-quilt assortment of layers, as if a wind had blown through her closet and she just happened to be standing nearby: a beltless red kimono over a tunic and drawstring trousers, a bright green scarf tied about her head.

"What could I possibly have to worry about?" Claire answered dryly. "Only six weeks to go, and we're nowhere near finished. Not to mention I'm a nervous wreck."

Kitty smiled reassuringly. "Par for the course. My first year everything that could go wrong did—the dishwasher died, I kept running out of things, and the girl I'd hired quit. Oh yes, and the chickens stopped laying eggs."

"Chickens?" This was one story she hadn't heard.

"I had the bright idea that with my own coop I'd save money on eggs. It didn't occur to me that playing chicken farmer and running a tearoom were two very different things."

"I feel like a fake," Claire confessed. "As if any minute someone's going to call my bluff."

"Go on thinking that way. It'll keep you on your toes." Kitty pulled to a stop and leaned over to give Claire a quick hug smelling of spices. With her kimono sleeves fluttering, she looked like an exotic bird. "Bye, kiddo. And remember, it's the chicken that comes first, not the egg." Whatever *that* meant.

An hour later Claire was touching down at LAX. Earlier in the week, she'd phoned, and Matt had assured her that everything was under control. No surprises there, at least. What she was unprepared for when she stepped off the plane was the big, shaggy-haired man in jeans and a worn denim jacket who greeted her at the gate.

Matt strode over to her, a toothpick angling out from under his mustache. "I figured you'd need a lift." As if he'd come from around the block, not two hours away.

Claire, too flustered to think straight, said the first thing that came to mind. "You didn't have to. I'd have taken the bus." He reached for her bag, and they wrestled with it a moment before she released her grip with a smile. "I'm sorry, I didn't mean that the way it sounded. It was nice of you to come."

"Don't mention it." He tossed the toothpick aside, flashing her an easy grin. In clean clothes, with his hair neatly combed, hair that usually made her think of an unmade bed, she was suddenly seeing him in a different light—not so much Paul Bunyan as Sundance Kid. And from the looks he was getting from other women, she wasn't alone in her opinion.

It wasn't until they were in his pickup, barreling along the interstate, that she got up the nerve to ask, "Is it the house? Did something happen that you didn't want to tell me about over the phone?" She imagined the roof caved in from a fallen tree, an exploded furnace, a flooded basement—maybe all three.

Matt shot her an amused look. "Do you always think in terms of worst-case scenario?"

She noticed he'd taken the time to shave, and for some reason it touched her. In the bright light bouncing off the hood she could see the little webs of lines around his eyes. He wasn't as handsome or as well educated as Byron, but there was something so . . . well, *solid* about him.

"Force of habit," she said, smiling a little. "When I'm not around, things have a way of falling apart." She was thinking of her parents.

Matt cast her a sidelong glance. "How's your mom?" He seemed to have read her mind.

"Sitting up doing needlepoint when I left." Her gaze dropped. The hole in his pocket was large enough now to wiggle a finger through.

"A heart attack's nothing to fool around with."

"Actually, it was a false alarm." Before Matt could comment she found herself adding, "But guess what, it worked—I came running, didn't I?" Claire immediately felt ashamed. Had she really said that? Oh, God, what must he think.

But if Matt thought she was a terrible person, it didn't show. "People do strange things in the name of love, even when they don't know they're doing them," he said in a soft, considering voice. "Like this girl I knew in high school who got knocked up. When she told her folks, they went ballistic. Talked about disowning her and the kid, and how she might as well be dead. Well, to make a long story short, she lost it, the baby. Started bleeding right there on the spot."

"What an awful story. Are you sure it's true?"

He flipped on the turn signal and edged into the right lane as they approached the turnoff for 33. "I oughta know. I married her—the minute she turned eighteen."

"That was your *wife*?" Claire stared at him. "Then . . ."

"Yep. My kid, too." He shrugged, but she could see from the tightening of his mouth that he wasn't completely over it, even after all these years. "The damnedest thing is they were right: It probably would've ruined our lives, though we did a pretty good job of that on our own. But, hell, I got two great kids out of it."

"I guess that's all that matters."

The sky was beginning to cloud over by the time they made it to the outskirts of town. She said she hoped it wouldn't rain, at least not until the gutters were replaced, and Matt had assured her there was very little likelihood of it this time of year. When he suggested they pick up a pizza on the way, she didn't have the heart to say no. He'd gone out of his way to pick her up; the least she could do was see that he got fed.

The moment she walked in the door, she saw why he'd been so eager to accompany her home. The front room that had been in shambles when she'd left was swept clean, the wainscoting gleaming with a coat of wax and the newly installed shelves varnished. Claire did a slow circuit of the room, running her hand along the woodwork, breathing in the scent of turpentine.

"Oh, Matt, it's beautiful." She turned to him. "How on earth did you manage to get it done in time?"

"Me and Gil, we worked most of last night. I wanted to surprise you."

She watched him place the pizza box gingerly atop the table by the door, and thought of the care that had gone into leveling every surface and hammering every nail. If this were a boat, it would be seaworthy.

Claire had a sudden image of Matt and her adrift on the open sea, and for an instant could almost feel the floor rocking gently beneath her feet—an illusion aided by the fact that she hadn't bothered to switch on the lights. Outside, dusk had faded into twilight, and the ghost of a moon floated on a raft of clouds above the distant hilltops.

When Matt slipped an arm about her waist, she didn't pull away. She dropped her head onto his shoulder instead, as if they'd stood like this on many a night, looking out at the lengthening shadows and listening to the call and response of dogs up and down the street. He smelled of shaving cream and pepperoni.

"Thank you," she said.

Matt drew her around and put a hand under her chin, tipping her head up to meet his gaze. His eyes were dark and unreadable, glimmering with the reflected glow from the porch light. *He's going to kiss me,* she thought with a mild panic that ran through her like a faint electrical current. *He's going*

*to kiss me and I have to stop him before he
does because if I don't—*

His head dipped. His mouth closed over
hers, warm and firm, lips parting just enough
to feel the tip of his tongue. His mustache
tickled her upper lip, sending the current
amping up a notch. Oh, God. She'd only just
come from Byron's arms . . . his bed . . .

Matt made a noise deep in his throat,
holding her so tightly she could scarcely
breathe. She could feel how much he
wanted her, and all the resistance went out
of her then. He could have picked her up
with one arm and slung her over his shoulder like a goose-down pillow.

"Don't you have to be somewhere?" she
murmured.

"The kids are with their mom." He studied
her in the half light, his eyes pooled with
shadow, his mustache drooping at the ends.
"Listen, if you're not sure . . ."

She let out a cracked little laugh. "I've
never been less sure of anything in my life."

He grinned, his teeth white below the
dark line of his mustache. "Should I take that
as a no?"

"Would it matter what I said?"

"No, I don't believe it would."

He kissed her again, more slowly this time, cradling her head in one huge hand as his mouth moved lower, exploring her throat. The prickling of his mustache, coupled with the softness of his lips and barest hint of tongue, shot through her like sparks from a frayed cord. Small muscles and nerves buzzed below her skin. She was melting, her insides flowing downward. *This isn't happening,* she thought in some distant part of her brain. But right now Byron was the furthest thing from her mind.

Matt unbuttoned her blouse and ran his thumb along the soft curve of a breast just above the line of her brassiere. She felt her knees start to buckle, and she might have sagged to the floor if he hadn't been holding her so tightly. His hugeness made her feel small, almost dainty.

Silently she took his hand and led him into the bedroom. She hadn't gotten around to buying a frame for her mattress—the old one, a hand-me-down from her parents, she'd left on the curb when she moved—but from the look on Matt's face, it could have been a haystack for all he cared. She watched with a smile as he tugged off his boots, awkwardly hopping about on one foot.

Moments later they were lying on the mattress, their clothes heaped on the rug. They kissed some more, and she was reminded of when she'd been a kid in an amusement park, dizzy from the rides, not knowing which one to go on next. He guided her hand until she was touching him, but after a minute pulled away.

"I want to be inside you when I come," he murmured.

Then he was touching her. Down there. And oh, how sweet . . . his big fingers that might have looked clumsy moving with expert feather strokes. The heat between her legs built to an exquisite point. She moaned, threading her fingers through his hair.

"Now," she whispered. "Make love to me now."

He groped blindly on the floor in search of his jeans. In the minute or so it took for him to fish out a condom and put it on, her head cleared and she thought, *Do I want this? Am I ready for what it will mean?*

The hell with it, a voice whispered back.

She gasped a little as he entered her—he was so big—then it was okay. He was going slow, taking care not to hurt her. She tilted her hips up, wrapping her legs about him. It ached a little when he drove in, but she was past the point of separating pain from pleasure. Yet Matt wasn't in any hurry. She'd start to slip over the edge and he'd slow his strokes. When she couldn't hold back a moment longer, she gripped hard, pulling him in tight.

She came with a dull white roar, only dimly aware of Matt's coming, too. It was like a dream—mindless, wordless, nothing but this heady rush of sensation.

Matt's face hovering above her in the dark only gradually came into focus, his broad cheekbones polished with sweat, his eyes blackened by shadow.

He rolled over onto his back. They were both drenched with sweat and breathing hard. It felt as if her heart would never stop pounding. "God in heaven, where did you learn to do that?" She hiked herself onto her elbow facing him, placing her fingertips lightly over his mouth. "No, don't tell me. I'm not sure I want to know."

He pulled her hand away, and she saw that he was grinning. "Look who's talking."

"For your information," she informed him, "I've been with exactly four men in my life, counting you."

"Does *he* know?"

But she didn't want to think about Byron. There would be plenty of time for that later on. She laid her head on Matt's shoulder, and he drew her close. She could hear the steady thumping of his heart, like an engine built before the days of planned obsolescence. Everything about Matt was like that: solid, dependable, built to last.

Except the wild streak that ran through him like a vein of gypsum through bedrock.

The second time was slower, like savoring dessert at the end of a meal. Matt touched and licked her all over, even down there. When she'd had her fill, she took him into her. Her climax was less explosive than before, but more satisfying somehow. They were both gasping by the time they came up for air.

After a while they roused themselves and Matt went to fetch the pizza, long since gone cold. They washed it down with beers from the fridge, and she thought she'd never tasted anything quite so good. Tomorrow would be a different story, she knew, but at this moment, seated cross-legged on the mattress across from a naked bear of a man with a slice of pizza drooping over one knee, she thought, *Lord, it doesn't get any better than this.*

Chapter Thirteen

Since her arrival the week before, Sister Clement's presence had been felt like a sudden cold spell after an endless stretch of sunny days. A plain-faced woman whose only distinguishing feature was a port stain that covered half of one cheek, she sat in silently on community meetings and appeared to mentally take note of every confessed failing in Faults. In chapel, her sharp ears took in every rustle and cough, and during the chanting of lauds the sisters who were off-key would suddenly become conscious of the fact, their cheeks warming. She seemed to know who was quick to return from sext and whose lengthy meditations spoke of a fully examined conscience. Now, as she toured the honey house, her apparent lack of interest had the feel of a foregone conclusion: Sister Clement's mind was already made up.

Gerry had taken her through the packing process and showed her how orders were tracked on the computer. As they headed into the next room, she felt a sense of doom settle over her, thick and pervasive as the honey sticking to every surface. It was all she could do to put on a cheerful face.

"This is where the decapping is done." She gestured toward a large stainless tank in the center of the room, where a pink-cheeked novice held a frame from one of the hives propped on the board across the middle and was deftly running a trowellike device over its thickly crusted comb. Beeswax peeled away in long, curly strips, sending honey dribbling into the tank.

"Rather warm in here, isn't it?" Sister Clement fanned herself with her notebook. Her face was flushed, the stain on her cheek darker than usual.

Gerry was so used to it, she hardly noticed. "It makes the honey easier to handle," she explained, leading the way to the corner where a pair of radial extractors stood on cinder blocks. She raised her voice to be heard over their whine. "Each one holds fifty combs. The runoff goes into a straining tank." She pointed toward a large heated tub lined with nylon mesh. "It sits for a day or so, then whatever's floated to the surface is skimmed off. What we're left with is one hundred percent pure Grade-A honey."

Sister Clement gave a perfunctory nod, scribbling something in her notebook. Gerry noted that while the rest of her was plain, even ungainly, her hands were oddly delicate, their pearly nails deeply embedded in the soft pink flesh of her fingertips. Gerry thought of a large cat, its claws sheathed.

Sister Clement looked up, surveying the room where half a dozen sisters in long aprons, their sleeves rolled up and veils neatly safety-pinned in back, worked side by side, each at her designated task: among them wiry Sister Andrew filling a fifty-gallon tin from the tap at the base of an extractor, and portly Sister Pius hefting a full one from the warming cabinet—honey that would go into the rows of sparkling jars fresh from the sterilizer.

"What's the annual output?"

"In a good year, two thousand pounds or more." Gerry couldn't keep from boasting. In the years since she'd taken over as lay manager, production had more than doubled. "Though with bees, it's hard to predict."

"I've never thought of them as anything other than pests."

"They're fairly harmless if you know how to handle them." Gerry had a sudden inspiration. Maybe Sister Clement would understand when she saw them in action. "Come, I'll show you." When they reached the door, where a row of pegs along the wall held half a dozen white canvas suits and netted hoods, she said blithely, "We won't be needing those." They'd be far enough away, and the bees were still a little sluggish from winter.

Outside, the mild spring air felt cool after the overheated confines of the honey house. They struck out along the narrow path, worn to a groove by decades of sandaled feet, that cut in a diagonal across the meadow. The dry brown stalks of winter had been replaced by new grass that swished about Gerry's knees. Everywhere she looked wildflowers were in bloom—bird's foot, blue thistle, alfalfa, sweet clover, wild licorice—the rich potpourri that gave Blessed Bee honey the distinctive flavor for which it was known. As they approached the grove of eucalyptus on the far side, she could hear the faint drone of bees, and caught sight of Sister Carmela waving a tin smoker over one of the hives, puffs of smoke drifting up into the branches overhead.

"It's mating season." Gerry turned to Sister Clement. "Do you know how bees mate?"

"I'm afraid it wasn't among the courses being offered when I was at Notre Dame," Sister Clement answered dryly. It was the closest she'd come to showing that she had a sense of humor.

Gerry knew she should quit while she was ahead, but some inner demon egged her on. "Every spring the queen embarks on her annual flight, chased by lovesick drones. As soon as one impregnates her, he explodes."

"How charming." Sister Clement wore a look of disgust.

Gerry knew she was only making matters worse, but thought, *Damned if I do, damned if I don't.*

"It's really pretty amazing when you think about it," she persisted, maintaining a sweetly innocent tone. "The drone gives her a lifetime supply of sperm when they mate, so in her case, once is enough."

"Fascinating," the nun said coldly.

The sense of futility was stronger than ever. What was the use of trying to win her over? By this time tomorrow Sister Clement would be on her way back to the mother-house. After that, it would only be a matter of days, weeks at the most, before Gerry was asked to resign.

If that were her only problem, she might have been able to put it in perspective. But there was Andie, too. Yesterday, when she'd returned home from the airport, Gerry had phoned her at Mike's. Andie had been tearful but firm—she had no intention of coming home. It had been all Gerry could do to keep from jumping in her car and roaring up the hill to her ex-husband's. The situation had to be handled carefully, she knew. Andie was hurting. *And didn't I ignore all the signals?* Though it killed her to do so, she'd agreed to let Andie stay put for the time being.

A favorite saying of her mother's popped into her head: *You'll catch more flies with honey than with vinegar.* She prayed the same was true of Sister Clement. Maybe it wasn't too late after all. If she could convince the woman she was doing more good than harm, maybe, just maybe . . .

They'd reached the edge of the clearing, with its rows of hives tucked amid the trees. Off in the distance she could hear the faint gurgling of the stream.

Gerry noticed Sister Clement hanging back, clearly nervous.

"Are you sure we won't get stung?" She eyed the bees lazily circling the hives.

"Don't worry, we won't go any closer."

The years of constant exposure had left Gerry fearless, but Sister Clement was eyeing the nearest hive, a good fifteen feet away, as warily as if it had been a rattlesnake coiled to strike. Nearby, one of Sister Carmela's helpers, garbed in protective gear—white canvas jumpsuit, leather gauntlets, netted hood—was bending over a dismantled hive. Bees clung to her back and shoulders like a furry mantle.

"She's cleaning away the propolis," Gerry explained. "It's a kind of resin the bees use like Spackle." She indicated the gluey deposits being gently wiped away with turpentine. "It's also used for embalming."

"Embalming?"

Gerry pointed out a yellowish clump the

size of a small soap bar stuck to the frame. "Probably a mouse that wandered in by accident and was stung to death."

Sister Clement looked distinctly pale. "I . . . I think I've seen enough." She held her notebook tightly clutched to her bosom. "I should be heading back. I'd like a word with the reverend mother before I go."

Gerry's heart sank. "In that case, I don't want to keep you." She turned but noticed Sister Clement wasn't falling into step. She stood rooted to the spot, batting at a bee that buzzed about her head.

"It won't sting if you hold still," Gerry advised.

Too late. It was as if the woman were on fire. She waved her arms wildly, using her notebook to slap at the bee, which only served to attract more. With a jolt of alarm, Gerry realized the cause of all this excitement. The notebook was a dark maroon, a color that had the same effect on bees as the whirl of a matador's cape has on a bull. And Sister Clement's frantic movements weren't helping any. A small swarm had gathered now. A bee landed on her arm, and she let out a shriek. *"Oww, owww, owwwwwww . . ."*

More bees fastened themselves to her arms and back, and one resembling a large mole clung to the port stain on her cheek. "Don't just stand there!" she squealed. *"Do something!"* She slapped at it, letting out a high, injured yelp.

Gerry approached her slowly so as not to excite the bees further. "Listen to me," she said, her voice calm and steady. "Do exactly as I tell you and you won't get hurt. *You've got to hold perfectly still."*

But Sister Clement was beyond all reasoning. Ignoring Gerry, she bolted down the path, shrieking at the top of her lungs. The bees, in a frenzy now, swarmed after her.

With a groan Gerry took off in pursuit. A dozen or so yards ahead, Sister Clement was zigzagging like a crazed buffalo amid the tall grass, arms flapping and veil flying. It might have been comical if Gerry hadn't seen it for what it was: the sealing of her fate.

She'd chased Sister Clement halfway across the meadow before the nun tripped on her hem and went sprawling facedown on the ground. Gerry caught up with her and dropped onto her haunches, ignoring the few bees that hadn't tired of the chase.

"Are you all right?" She seized Sister Clement by the arm, hauling her upright.

The woman was trembling all over, her eyes wide and staring. The port stain on her cheek had begun to swell, resembling a large purple contusion. *"You did this on purpose!"* she cried, flecks of spittle spraying from her contorted mouth.

"I'm sorry. I had no idea—" Gerry stopped, realizing anything she said right now would fall on deaf ears. "Would you like me to take you to the infirmary?"

Sister Clement ignored Gerry's outstretched hand. "Thank you, Mrs. Fitzgerald, but I won't be needing *your* assistance." Her veil was awry and a clump of gray hair poked from under her starched wimple. With what little dignity she had left, she reached up to adjust it before stalking off in the direction of the road.

Gerry stood there, flooded with hopelessness. *This is a joke,* she thought. A cruel joke God was playing on her. She began to laugh hysterically, plunking down amid the sweet clover and timothy grass. She laughed until her stomach hurt and tears were streaming down her cheeks.

"For the love of God, what's gotten into you?"

Gerry looked up to find her old friend Sister Carmela gazing down at her with concern. "I've just screwed myself out of a job, that's what," she said, pulling herself to her feet.

Sister Carmela's expression didn't alter. No doubt she'd heard saltier language growing up in one of L.A.'s worst neighborhoods. "So I see." She glanced at the distant figure trudging up the road, her mouth stretching in a smile as if she believed Sister Clement had gotten exactly what she deserved.

Gerry felt a rush of affection. "Oh, Sister, I'm going to miss you."

"Now, now. I won't be hearing any such talk. You haven't been fired yet." The older woman patted her arm. "Perhaps if I put in a good word with Sister Clement . . ."

Gerry shook her head. "Thanks, but it wouldn't do any good." She gazed out over the meadow, where larks sang and hummingbirds caught the sunlight in flashes of iridescence. "I'll be okay. Don't I always land on my feet?" She smiled bravely, hoping that saying it out loud would make it so.

Making her way across the meadow, she glanced over her shoulder to find Sister Carmela standing motionless amid the tall grass, her creased brown face that of a mother anxiously watching her child cross a busy street. Gerry's gloom lifted. She had friends here, *good* friends. In the months to come those friendships would sustain her.

Minutes later she was back in her office, listlessly sorting through the morning mail, when she heard a knock at the door. Mother Ignatius poked her head in.

"Do you have a moment?"

One look and Gerry knew she'd gotten an earful from Sister Clement. Her heart sank. "You've heard, I see." She gestured toward the chair opposite her desk, but the reverend mother chose to remain standing. A bad sign.

She didn't mince words. "I had someone take her to the infirmary. Let's hope she isn't allergic. But that's not what concerns me. It seems Sister Clement is under the impression you purposely put her in harm's way." Mother Ignatius's eyes were wintry.

"Is that what she told you?" Gerry grew warm with indignation before remembering there was more than her own future at stake here. "I suppose I should have been more careful, but I certainly didn't mean her any harm," she said.

"I told her as much." The stern lines in the mother superior's face relaxed. "Though I don't suppose it made any difference. I believe Sister Clement has—what do they call it nowadays—an agenda?"

"I didn't do anything to help, that's for sure."

"I won't disagree with that."

"Well, she can take her report and—" Gerry stopped, ashamed of what she'd been about to say. "I'm sorry. I know it's not just *my* job on the line."

A weary smile touched the reverend mother's lips, and she suddenly looked every day of her age. Without a scrap of self-pity, she said, "Whatever happens, the needs of our community come first."

"How soon will we know?"

"They'll call a council. After that, it should go fairly swiftly."

Gerry appreciated her directness. Mother Ignatius had never been anything less than honest, if at times brutally so. "I just wish there was something we could do." Clearly her heart-to-heart with Jim Gallagher hadn't helped.

The reverend mother started for the door, then turned with a smile of such illuminating sweetness her austere face was at once transformed. "It wouldn't hurt to pray."

Yes, Gerry thought. *And where would it get me?* These days God's presence was like a distant bell she could no longer hear. All her life, even in her darkest hours, she'd been comforted by the knowledge that He was looking over her. But now all she felt was alone.

She thought of Aubrey, and before she knew it was reaching for the phone. It had been more than a week since she'd seen him. He'd had a recording session in L.A, followed by a concert. Not that she minded his absences—just the opposite, in fact. Wasn't it wonderful they both had their own lives, that neither of them had to sit home pining? Except now . . . well, right now she *needed* him—a need as profound as the relief that swept through her when he answered.

"Hello?" He sounded distracted.

"It's me." Was she interrupting something?

"Gerry." His voice softened. "I was just thinking of you."

She relaxed. "You were?"

"This very moment. You must have read my mind."

"Good. That means I shouldn't have any trouble finding another job."

"What's this? Don't tell me you've been fired!" The concern in his voice was like a soothing balm.

"It's a distinct possibility," she told him. "Look, I don't want to get into it over the phone. Can I see you?"

"I'm free tonight."

"I was thinking more like right now." She was quick to add, "If you're not too busy, that is."

"Aren't you at work?"

"I could always play hooky." God knew she was entitled. Hadn't she given herself heart and soul to Blessed Bee, most days scarcely taking so much as a coffee break?

There was a pause at the other end, and her heart seemed to hover motionless between beats. Then came the answer she'd been hoping for. "Shall I pick you up?" .

"No . . . thanks. I'm on my way." She wasn't so distraught she couldn't drive, but bless Aubrey for wanting to saddle up his white charger.

Fifteen minutes later she was climbing Isla Verde's steep, tree-lined drive in her car. She waved to old Guillermo, taking a break from the gardening, and he brought a finger to his lips to warn her not to say anything to Lupe about the cigarette he was enjoying. She smiled back, turning an invisible little key in the corner of her mouth the way she had with Sam when they were kids: His secret was safe with her.

She was pushing open the courtyard gate when Aubrey emerged from the house to greet her, dressed in a suit and tie as if she'd caught him on his way out the door. At once, she knew she had.

"You shouldn't have canceled your plans for me," she scolded lightly.

He kissed her on the mouth. He smelled faintly and deliciously of Lupe's strong coffee laced with cocoa. "It wasn't important—just lunch with Gregory." His agent, she recalled. "I told him something had come up. He was most understanding."

"Now I feel twice as guilty."

"Don't. I think we're beyond that, don't you?"

He studied her in the dappled green light filtering through the tall ferns, and she had the strangest sense of being stored away for future reference. She felt a sudden chill. Was he growing tired of her? If so, there was nothing to suggest it. More likely he felt as she did, that this wasn't what they'd bargained on. Somewhere along the way it had crossed the line between intimate friendship and . . . something more.

"I'll bet you say that to all the ladies," she teased, but her heart wasn't in it. What if Aubrey decided to end it? Once she might have been all right with it. But now . . .

"Only the pretty ones." He flashed her a mock seductive smile, one eyebrow arched.

"Aren't you going to ask me in?"

"I thought we'd take a drive instead. I had Lupe pack us a picnic lunch."

"Sounds like heaven." If anyone was a mind reader, it was Aubrey. A picnic was just what she felt like.

"Wait here. I won't be a moment."

He reappeared minutes later in khakis and an open-collared shirt, toting a wicker hamper. "It's not exactly Fortnum & Mason," he said. "But it's as good as you'll get on such short notice. Come, we'll take my car."

They strolled out onto the drive, their feet crunching over the drift of dried blossoms from the acacia tree overhead. More were scattered like tiny fallen stars over the hood of the Jaguar parked outside the garage. He escorted her around to the passenger side and held open the door. Gerry sank into the glove-leather seat with a sigh. She could easily get used to this, no doubt about it.

The morning's tension began to drain away as they sped along the winding, tree-lined road. Aubrey drove too fast, hugging the curves, but for some reason it didn't worry her. She sensed that he was in control.

Before long they were turning onto Schoolhouse Road, named after the town's original one-room schoolhouse, now a dilapidated old wreck. In the fifties, it had enjoyed a brief second life in *Stranger in Paradise,* the movie that had put their valley on the map. She recalled how Sam's mother used to enthrall them with the story of the day she'd visited the set as a guest of the director, a legendary ladies' man, which had left Gerry and Sam to speculate endlessly. Sam insisted it was innocent; Gerry hadn't been so sure.

The road grew steeper, and soon they were rattling over the wooden bridge that spanned Horse Creek. They passed several designated picnic areas, then the turnoff for the Horse Creek Inn. Gradually the dense trees began to thin, giving way to rolling hills purled with grapevines. Far off in the distance she could see the turreted Horse Creek Winery, modeled after a French chateau.

Aubrey turned onto a dirt access road herringboned with tire tracks, and soon they were bumping along between rows of vines, dust boiling up around them.

"Aren't we trespassing?" she asked.

"Theo and I are old friends," he replied with a Gallic shrug. "He won't mind."

He was referring to Theodore Carrillo, of course, owner and current patriarch of the winery and a descendant of the *gente de razón.* "Is there anyone you *don't* know?" she asked with a smile.

When she'd belonged to the country club, she'd occasionally seen Theo around. She recalled when Mike, who fancied himself quite the connoisseur, had gone out of his way to butter up the old man at one of the functions, and been politely, but summarily, snubbed.

"Theo throws a big party every year at harvestime," Aubrey told her. "There's an enormous vat of grapes, and all the ladies take turns stomping them."

"Sounds messy." Gerry tried to picture herself, skirts held high, grapes squishing between her toes, but the only thing that came to mind was an episode of *I Love Lucy*.

"It was Theo who convinced me to come here after—" he faltered "—when I decided to leave L.A."

His wife. It always came back to that, didn't it? Gerry realized to her dismay that she was jealous—of a dead woman.

They pulled to a stop before a windbreak and climbed out. The only things moving were the pale scarf of dust floating over the road down which they'd come and the leaves of the laurels overhead, rustling in the breeze. From somewhere off in the distance came the faint drone of a tractor, and closer by the hollow chuckle of water making its way along an irrigation pipe.

Aubrey spread the blanket over the soft grass beneath the trees, and Gerry kicked off her shoes, hesitating only a moment before muttering, "Oh, what the hell," and lifting her skirt to shuck off her pantyhose as well. She sank down, stretching out on her stomach with her chin propped on her hands.

How long since she'd last played hooky? Not since she was in school. The only difference was that back then she hadn't had anyone to gaze appreciatively at her legs.

Aubrey unpacked the hamper: roast chicken, potato salad, Brie, and a loaf of French bread. From a freezer pouch he produced a bottle of Chenin Blanc bearing the distinctive Horse Creek label. "It seemed only fitting," he said, uncorking it and pouring them each a glass. He lifted his in toast, the sunlight catching on its rim and wheeling outward in a brilliant flash. "To a day that was salvaged after all."

Gerry, surprised to find that she had an appetite, ate half the chicken, most of the potato salad, and several slices of bread slathered with cheese before collapsing onto her back with a groan. The sun had passed its zenith, leaving the sky the deep, crystalline blue of a mountain-fed lake. Gazing up at it, tipsy from the wine, she imagined them to be on a raft slowly drifting downstream.

She told him then: about the disastrous morning with Sister Clement, her trip to San Franciso with Claire, and Andie's going to her father's. When she'd run out of breath, he observed lightly, "It sounds as if you've been trying to please everyone and not doing a very good job of pleasing yourself."

"Mothers don't have that luxury."

"Andie strikes me a sensible girl. She'll come around."

"What makes you so sure?"

He smiled. "Call it an educated guess."

"How do I know she won't be better off with her father?"

"You don't really believe that."

"I'm not even sure I'll be employed."

Aubrey brought a hand to her face, his fingertips like soft leaves brushing over her cheek. "I could find you one at double the salary just by picking up the phone."

She sat up, fixing him with a stern look. "It's not your job to fix my life."

He shook his head, chuckling softly. "Believe me, I wouldn't dare. You'd shoot any man who tried."

What am I trying to prove? Gerry wondered. That she didn't need a man in her life? That she wasn't in love with Aubrey? Did she think that if she said it enough times, in enough ways, it would become true?

She looked at his long legs stretched out on the blanket. He still had on the expensive calfskin loafers, now filmed with dust, that he'd worn with his suit. It seemed the perfect metaphor for Aubrey himself: a man living in two worlds who didn't fully belong in either one.

She lifted her glass. "Here's to friendship . . . and great sex. Not necessarily in that order."

"Ah, a woman after my own heart." He touched his glass to hers.

It was the kind of banter she'd once found sexy and at the same time safe—for it kept her from having to do more than skim the surface. But now she found herself hating it, while at the same time feeling helpless to change course.

Maybe it was for that reason, or maybe just the wine, but she blurted, "I'm sure you've known your share of the other kind—women who thought it their Christian duty to jump in and rescue you from the burning pyre." She saw his expression darken, and clapped a hand over her mouth. "Oh, Aubrey, I'm sorry. It just slipped out."

"It's all right. *Not* talking about her doesn't make it any easier." He placed a hand over hers. "I know you felt bad about what happened at the wedding, but the truth is, I rather think Isabelle would have liked her music being played on such a happy occasion."

Gerry felt something flit over her heart. "She sounds like someone I would have liked."

"Oh, she had her faults." Usually, when speaking of his wife he appeared remote, as if in a place she had no way of reaching. But now he seemed to want to tell her about Isabelle.

"Such as?" Gerry was suddenly curious.

"She could be a prima donna at times."

Gerry wondered if he saw her as just the opposite: steady and dependable. Good for a laugh and to service his sexual needs. "I suppose it goes with the territory." Isabelle had been celebrated in her own right, after all.

"She was a bit of a hypochondriac as well. Always running to the doctor for one thing or another." His voice was tender and he smiled at the irony of it—Isabelle couldn't have known that what was in store for her would be far worse than any of the ailments she'd imagined.

She studied his strong Gallic profile. In the light filtering through the branches overhead, she could see darker strands amid the silver hair that fell over his collar. He looked relaxed and happy. As if he'd at last made peace with his wife's death—or perhaps with the fact that such peace was unattainable.

Gerry felt relaxed as well. On this day when it had seemed nothing could go right, suddenly she could find no wrong. When he leaned close and touched his lips to hers, she tasted the wine on his breath, sweet and tantalizing. It had been awhile since they'd made love, and with a teasing laugh, she wound her arms around his neck and rolled onto her back, pulling him with her.

It was crazy, she knew; someone might see them—once with Mike, on a hike, when they'd been fooling around in the woods, a young woman had come bursting into the clearing—but right now she didn't care. The threat of discovery only made it more thrilling.

She took off her blouse. She was glad she was wearing her best lace bra and not one held together with a safety pin. (Not that Aubrey would have minded—he claimed to like her even in her rattiest old underwear.) She shivered as he removed it and traced each nipple with the tip of his tongue. Softly, oh so softly. Setting off an avalanche of sensation. She offered no protest when he reached under her skirt and pulled her panties down over her ankles, sending them sailing out where they snagged on a bush.

Aubrey slipped off his shoes and tossed his socks onto the bush alongside her panties. Moments later he was straddling her. His unbuttoned shirt caught the breeze, blowing out around him. She ran her fingers through the hair on his chest, which was dark and soft, like the pelt of some sleek, exotic animal.

He gazed down at her with a kind of reverence. "Christ, you're beautiful. "You have no idea."

Aubrey bent down to cover her mouth with his. The sun was a molten glow behind her closed eyelids, and she had a sudden sense of falling upward. With a soft moan she lifted her legs, wrapping them about his hips, and felt him slide into her. This was how it had felt making babies, she thought in some distant, still-functioning part of her brain—an added dimension, a sense of something greater than just two people. Only with Aubrey there would be no babies. Perhaps no future, either.

Then she *was* falling. Spinning toward the sun like a planet cut loose from its orbit. She clutched hold of Aubrey, tightening her legs and burying her face in the crook of his neck as she cried out—a sharp cry, like someone in pain. Anyone looking on from afar might have mistaken it for a struggle, a woman fighting for her life, and they wouldn't have been entirely wrong. For in the midst of her pleasure Gerry had the sense of something being wrenched from her against her will.

Then Aubrey was coming, too, teeth gritted and neck arched. She felt the warm pulse of his seed, and tilted her hips to keep it from escaping—not from any vestigial desire to be pregnant, but from some deep need to take as much of him into her as she could.

For the longest time afterward neither of them moved. Aubrey remained inside her, elbows propped on either side of her to keep from crushing her with his weight. They were both breathing hard. Then she became aware of something tickling her leg—an ant. Somehow they'd managed to work themselves off the blanket onto the grass. Aubrey rolled away, and helped her to her feet. She reached for her clothes, glancing about furtively.

"My God, what were we thinking," she said. "*Anyone* could have come along."

"What if they had?" Aubrey sauntered leisurely over to the bush to retrieve her panties and his socks.

She giggled at the sight of him bending over naked. "You look as if you're hanging Christmas ornaments." She giggled even harder at the image of her panties adorning the People's Tree.

He tossed her the panties with a wicked grin. "At least we know who's been naughty or nice."

They dressed quickly, and she was careful to keep her eyes averted lest the sight of him bring on another onslaught of giggles— or another ill-advised tumble in the grass. She felt all of sixteen, though as a teenager she'd felt more certain of her destiny than she did now.

She sneaked a glance at Aubrey. Had his feelings toward her changed? At times she sensed that he was holding back, but maybe it was her own mixed feelings she'd seen reflected in his eyes.

Now she sank back down on the blanket, light-headed, her heart pounding in shallow thuds. This definitely wasn't what she'd signed up for.

Aubrey must have sensed the shift in

mood, for all at once he seemed to withdraw into himself. In silence, they packed up the hamper and shook out the blanket. This time her eyes were averted for a different reason: She didn't want him to see what was written there.

They were in his car, bumping along the road, when he said casually, "I suppose I should have told you before, but I didn't want it to spoil our afternoon—I've been offered a guest conductorship in Brussels."

All at once she couldn't quite catch her breath. "Really? For how long?"

"Six months, maybe a year."

"It sounds as if you've decided to accept it."

"That's why Gregory and I were having lunch. He wanted to fill me in on all the details."

"What about Isla Verde?" She maintained a light, even tone.

"I'll keep it until my lease runs out."

"Justin won't be happy when I tell him."

"You won't have to. I'll tell him myself." Aubrey looked sad.

Gerry was glad for her sunglasses—he wouldn't see the tears in her eyes. She reminded herself that love had never been part of the deal. If Aubrey had the good sense to pull out before they got in over their heads, the least she could do was go along.

She gazed out the window at the neat rows of vines lined up like sentences on a page, a page out of a story she suddenly didn't want to end. *It's good that he's going,* she told herself firmly. For even if she could put aside her own fears, there would always, always be Isabelle tugging him in another direction, filling his head with the sound of her music.

"Don't forget," she said, "you promised to teach him how to throw a curve ball."

"He has his father for that."

She gave a snort of derision. "The only sports Mike knows are golf and fishing. Last year he gave Justin a set of clubs for his birthday. There was just one problem—they were right-handed and Justin's a lefty."

Aubrey grimaced. "Poor kid."

She wondered if he was thinking of the child he'd never know—a longing she was all too familiar with, and one that made her feel close to him even as he pulled away.

"When will you be leaving?" she asked.

"Not until the end of the month."

But from the look on his face she saw that he was gone already—lost to her in a way that was all the sadder because she'd never really had him to begin with. Her heart cracked, and feelings she hadn't even known were there came spilling out. All her big talk of wanting to be on her own felt like just that: talk.

"I'll miss you," she said.

"Me, too." The words came out tight and clipped.

"You'll keep in touch?"

"Of course."

"A year's a long time. I'm sure we'll be seeing other people." She tried not to think about what they'd been doing just minutes before.

He shot her a glance that told her this wasn't a decision that had been made lightly. "Just so you know, there's no one else. That's not why I'm leaving."

She knew the real reason—Isabelle.

"I didn't think that," she said.

"I'll be back and forth. We'll still see each other."

"Yes." But she knew it wouldn't be the same.

"Ever been to Brussels?"

"No." She'd been to Europe exactly once—on her honeymoon. Two days in Paris and another two in London. It had rained the entire time.

"It's lovely. You should come for a visit."

"I doubt I'll be able to afford it."

"I don't suppose you'd let me send you a ticket?"

"Not a chance."

"In that case, you're forcing me to run up an enormous long-distance bill." He laughed, but it had a hollow ring. They were back on the main road now, driving north. As they crested the hill she could make out the winery ahead—a cluster of stone buildings similar to those in pictures she'd seen of the Loire Valley, another place she was unlikely to visit any time soon.

The world had never seemed so vast.

And yet she had no one to blame but herself. She had chosen this as much as Aubrey, so it was no use crying. There would be time for that in the weeks and months ahead; nights of lying awake in bed wondering how she could ever have thought she'd had it all figured out when she didn't know a thing.

Chapter Fourteen

When Andie was eight she'd had her tonsils out. Her mother had sat with her for hours each day until visiting hours were over, reading aloud her favorite books. Her father had been away on a business trip—just like when she was starring in her sixth-grade play, and when she was presented with an award for the best essay on "What World Peace Means to Me" her freshman year in high school. When she looked back, it seemed she'd spent most of her life waiting for her dad: listening for his car, for the thump of his briefcase in the front hall, and more recently for the phone to ring.

She'd been at her dad's a little over a week, and there'd been something going on nearly every evening: friends for dinner, some function at the club, a cocktail party he and Cindy couldn't miss. Tonight was the birthday party Cindy was throwing for her best friend, Melinda. Her stepmother had been running around all day, mostly in circles—bossing poor Consuelo around, pestering the caterer with last-minute changes, chewing out the pool boy for tracking muddy footprints all over the patio. And now, with the house spotless, the flowers arranged, and every last bit of silver polished, she was turning her attention to Andie.

"Can I ask a favor, hon?"

Cindy stood in the doorway of the guest room, which Andie was currently occupying, smiling that sweet smile like hard candy on a cold day. Plus, she was calling her "hon"— never a good sign.

Andie pasted a smile in place. "Sure, whatever."

"If you have to use the bathroom, could you go next door?" It was clear from Cindy's tone that she thought it a perfectly reasonable request. "I phoned Mrs. Chambers and she said it was okay."

God forbid the sink should be wet or a towel awry when the guests arrived. Andie's smile slipped a little. "No problem," she said, thinking there was no way she was going next door to pee. She barely knew Mrs. Chambers, a little old lady with a fat miniature poodle that yapped at everything that moved. She'd hold it in if she had to.

"Thanks. It's a little crazy right now. If people would just *do* their jobs . . ." Cindy raked a hand through hair the color of buttered toast, looking supremely put upon. She'd been to the hairdresser yesterday and her new blond highlights made it look as if she spent loads of time at the beach—an illusion underscored by the fact that, in her long-sleeved striped tee and size-two white slacks, she bore an uncanny resemblance to Malibu Barbie. "Oh, one more thing, would you phone your dad and ask him to stop at the store on his way home? We need film for the camera."

All those Kodak moments you wouldn't want to miss. Never mind there were hardly any photos of her and Justin. But that was Cindy. She didn't have any kids of her own, and hadn't bargained on stepkids, either. It was the only thing they had in common: They were all in the same boat.

"That's it?" Andie got up off the bed, where her homework lay scattered over the quilted spread: her American history textbook, several ink-stained notebooks, a dogeared copy of *Silas Marner,* and a binder covered in stickers.

"We're a little low on dishwasher soap, too." Cindy scanned the room with the eagle eye of an admiral making sure everything was shipshape. Andie had straightened up, but if the smallest thing was out of place, her stepmother would be sure to spot it. "Oh, and hon? Would you mind running the Dustbuster over the carpet in here?"

A crumb didn't fall in the house without Cindy racing for the Dustbuster. After supper the night before, her father had joked that he was going to have a special holster made so she could carry it around on her hip. Cindy had laughed, which showed she had a sense of humor at least. No, Andie thought, she wasn't a bad person. Just anal, which when you got right down to it was just another word for full of shit.

Still, she *was* trying—last weekend treating Andie to lunch at the Tree House, and afterward to a manicure. Now that she had her learner's permit, her stepmother had even offered to take her driving. Andie had politely declined. A scratch on Cindy's brand-new Audi convertible was the last thing either of them needed.

She thought of her mother: How when Andie was practicing parallel parking and had crashed into the garbage cans set up along the curb, Gerry had laughed it off, saying, "You'll get it. Just keep trying." Her throat tightened. She might as well face it: Her mother no longer cared. The last straw had been when she'd dropped everything to go running off to San Francisco with Claire. No warning, no note, just the one lame-ass phone call when she got back. She hadn't phoned since.

She was walking over to the closet—there was a Dustbuster in every room—when she caught her toe on the carpet's thick pile and stumbled. She bumped up against the dressing table—trimmed in a ruffled Laura Ashley skirt that matched the curtains and bedspread—sending her hairbrush skidding onto the carpet. Out of the corner of her eye, as she bent to retrieve it, she saw Cindy frown. Andie knew what she was thinking: What if it had been something breakable?

"Are you okay?" Cindy started toward her,

stopping a few feet away from where Andie stood—like it was a game of Mother-May-I and she hadn't been given the green light.

"I'm fine—just a little klutzy today. I always get this way before my period." Andie bit her lip. Why had she said that?

Her stepmother gave a knowing laugh. "Tell me about it. When it's my time of the month, your dad says I'm not fit to live with. What I hate most is the bloating—I might as well be in a tank at Sea World." Andie could see her reflected in the mirror, patting a belly you could have fried eggs on. "Need any tampons?"

"No. Thanks. I have enough." She'd bought a box in the hope it would bring on her period—a period that was weeks over-due. The only sign of it was sore, swollen breasts, which could just as easily be a symptom of—

"Well, let me know if you run out." Cindy's chirpy voice interrupted the thought.

Yes, Cindy was trying. At times like these she seemed almost lonely. Though in some ways Andie would have preferred a step-mother out of a Grimm's fairy tale. It was easier to hate someone mean than some-one you felt sorry for.

Her stepmother was turning to go when Andie asked, "Uh, Cindy? Would it be okay if I stayed over at Finch's tonight? We're working on this project that's due on Monday."

An outright lie, but a safe one. Neither Cindy nor her dad had a clue about her school work. And Andie couldn't bear the prospect of yet another evening holed up in this room, or worse, being fawned over by Cindy's phony friends. She needed to get away from this house, where you had to remember to take your shoes off before setting foot in the living room, with its carpet the color of Cream of Wheat and its objets d'art (that's what Cindy called them, though at her grandmother's the same stuff was called knickknacks) that looked as if they'd shatter if you breathed too hard. She longed to be home, but since that was out of the question, her friend's house, with its cats and dogs that roamed freely and the faint smell of horses that clung to everything, would be the next best thing. You could clomp around in riding boots, and if you broke a dish, Laura would simply shrug and say she'd been meaning to replace it anyway.

But Cindy was even more clueless than she'd thought. "You'll miss the party," she said, her glossy lower lip pushing out in a mock pout.

Andie tried to look disappointed. "I know. I'm sorry. I . . ." She started to say she'd been looking forward to it, but that was too big a lie. "Wish your friend happy birthday for me, okay?"

Cindy sighed. "Between you and me I don't think she'll notice one less guest. That's what this party is all about—I was hoping it'd cheer her up." She dropped her voice, spelling out, "D-i-v-o-r-c-e."

"Um, that's too bad." It felt weird talking with Cindy about divorce. "Do they have kids?" she asked to be polite.

"Just one—but he's away at school. Poor Mel. She's really broken up about it."

Andie thought of Simon, who'd been calling and leaving messages that she hadn't returned. What would have been the point? He'd only have given her more bullshit about Monica being his mentor when everyone in town knew that, crippled or no, she was a Venus's-flytrap as far as men were concerned. Just the other day Andie had heard she'd had an affair with Andie's history teacher Mrs. Farmer's husband, who owned the music store and tuned pianos on the side. "I heard Monica's baby grand got quite a workout," Herman Tyzzer at the Den of Cin had joked.

Even so, the thought that she and Simon might be broken up for good brought a little ache to her throat, like a pill that hadn't gone down. And what if she were pregnant? What then?

"Maybe they'll get back together," she said without much enthusiasm.

"Fat chance. He's already living with someone." Cindy blushed, as if realizing her words had hit a little too close to home. She cast Andie a vaguely sheepish look. "Listen, I know it's been rough for you, too. I just want you to know that if you ever need someone to talk to . . ." She paused as if not quite sure what to say. "You'd do that, wouldn't you—come to me if you had a problem? I'm not such an ogre, am I?" She gave a nervous little laugh.

Oh, God. Cindy was trying to befriend her. Not just to be nice, but out of some pathetic need of her own. "Sure . . . I mean, yeah, if I was—if I had a problem." Andie put on a bright smile, hoping to convince her stepmother she hadn't a care in the world.

But why feel sorry for Cindy? She had

everything. And her father absolutely worshiped her. As much as he had fought with her mother, he thought Cindy could do no wrong.

A crashing sound in the next room caused Cindy to spin about. An instant later she was racing down the hall, squawking, "Bernard! What on *earth*?"

Andie's need to escape was overwhelming. Right now she'd have traded every CD she owned for her driver's license, but she had no choice but to try to bum a ride from her dad.

She reached for the phone on the nightstand—a cutesy white and gold vintage reproduction—and dialed his number. Luckily, he was still in his office. His secretary, Mrs. Blanton, put her on hold, then her father's deep voice came on the line.

"Hi, cookie. I was just on my way out. What's up?"

"Cindy wants you to pick up film for the camera. And dishwasher soap. Oh, and one other thing—" She crossed her fingers. "Could you give me a ride to Finch's?" Andie would clear it with Finch, with whom she had a standing invitation, as soon as she got off with her dad.

He blew out a breath. "Can't someone else take you?"

"Cindy's getting ready for the party." Andie could hear her in the kitchen yelling at the caterer. "I don't think now would be a very good time for me to ask."

"All right . . . but on one condition: We stop at your mother's on the way."

Andie grew very still, as if the world were suddenly made up of razor-sharp edges that would cut her if she moved so much as an inch. "Why? "We don't have anything to say to each other," she said coldly.

"We'll discuss it on the way." Mike's voice was firm.

Half an hour later they were in his car, the baby-blue Lincoln that Cindy made fun of, saying it was something *her* father would have driven. As they glided along the streets of Hidden Valley Estates, the gated community where Mike and Cindy lived, she thought how different it was from the neighborhood she'd grown up in. As perfectly manicured and maintained as Disneyland, its houses, which her mother called McMansions, set far back from the sidewalk and surrounded by lawns as lush and green as the fairway at Dos Palmas.

"This is stupid," she said.

Her father didn't respond.

"She doesn't even want to see me. If she did, she'd have called."

He flashed her a small smile. "You sound exactly like when you were little."

She remembered when she used to threaten to run away, how her mother would always nicely offer to help her pack. Reverse psychology, she now knew, though at the time it had felt like she didn't care.

She studied her father out of the corner of her eye. He was a handsome man with most of his hair, but he'd put on weight since marrying Cindy. Which was weird because her stepmother was just the opposite: She worked out like a demon and lived off what her father called rabbit food. He was like the paunchy middle-aged guy—wasn't there always at least one?—lagging behind on the jogging path, making all those ahead of him feel that much better about themselves.

"Your mom phoned me today," he said. "She sounded upset."

"She did?" A little shiver went through her. "How come she didn't act that way with me? It was like she could give a shit."

He shot her an admonishing look. "Watch

your language, young lady. Just because
you're not at ho—" He paused, and quickly
switched gears, saying, "Your mom thought
you needed some space."

Andie pictured her mother and Justin in
the kitchen getting dinner, her brother bitch-
ing that it wasn't the right kind of pasta, and
her mother saying agreeably that it all tasted
the same and if he didn't like it he could fix
his own. Suddenly she missed them terribly;
it was all she could do to keep from crying.

But there were no cooking smells when
she walked in. Her mother was sacked out
on the sofa with her eyes closed, looking so
utterly beat, all the anger went out of Andie.
She wanted nothing more than for her
mother to put her arms around her and rock
her like when she was little.

"Mom," she called softly.

Her mother's eyes flew open, and she
looked uncomprehendingly at Andie for an
instant before a tentative smile took hold.
"Hi, honey. I thought you were Justin." She
didn't get up. It was as though she were waiting for Andie to make the first move.

Buster wandered over and licked Andie's
hand. When she crouched down to scrub
behind his ears, he whined deep in his

throat, grinning his doggy grin, his whole body wagging.

"I can't stay," she said. "Dad's waiting out front."

"Would you like to ask him in?"

Andie knew it hadn't been easy for her to offer. "No, it's okay. He said he had some calls to make."

It was getting dark. Her mom got up and switched on the lamp, which briefly lit her face with a Halloweenish glow, making the hollows under her eyes more pronounced.

"How have you been?" she asked.

"Okay."

"Do you have everything you need?"

"Pretty much."

"If you feel like a snack there's some pizza in the fridge. It won't take a minute to heat up."

Andie shook her head, giving her mother a reproachful look. "You shouldn't eat that stuff, you know. It's not good for you." Mom was like a kid that way.

Gerry smiled. "You sound just like your grandmother."

Andie glanced about the room, reassured to find it exactly as she'd left it, everything in place—even that stupid fishing pole that should have found its way into the garage by now. She cleared her throat. "Dad said there was something you wanted to talk to me about?"

Her mother looked tense. This wasn't easy for her, either. "I wanted you to know . . . well, that this wasn't what I had in mind when Claire moved here. I saw us as one big family. I didn't stop to think that you might not feel the same way."

Andie sighed. "It's not just Claire."

"I know, honey."

"You should've believed me about that CD."

"I know that, too." Andie caught the flash of tears in her eyes.

She felt her resolve waver. "Even if it wasn't on purpose, I'm sorry Aubrey was upset."

Her mother looked sad at the mention of Aubrey, and Andie wondered if they'd split up. She hoped not. With him, her mom had seemed happy for the first time since the divorce.

"Is it too late to say I'm sorry?" her mother asked plaintively.

Andie couldn't bear seeing that look on her face. At the same time it filled her with hope, hope that things would get better. She risked a tentative smile. "Aren't you the one who's always telling me it's never too late to apologize?"

"I promise things will be different."

"How?" Andie hadn't meant to sound rude. She honestly wanted to know.

"For one thing, we'll be together more."

Andie was prompted to ask, "Did you and Aubrey break up?"

Her mother glanced down. "What I meant was it looks like I'm about to be fired."

"No way." Andie shook her head in disbelief. "They can't do that to you, can they?"

Her mother's mouth flattened in a humorless smile. "You've heard that saying, Let sleeping dogs lie? Well, apparently it's true. Claire met her father, who was none too pleased and decided it was time to put an end to this once and for all. Either that, or he's doing it to get back at me."

Claire. So she was the reason. A short while ago Andie might have held it against her, but she saw now that Claire hadn't asked for this any more than she had.

"Can he really get you fired?"

"Apparently so."

"That sucks."

"I couldn't have put it better myself. Yes, it sucks."

They looked at each other and began to laugh. That was the thing about her mother: She could always make Andie laugh. Even when what they were laughing about wasn't the least bit funny.

It broke the ice, though, and when Andie spoke the words came more easily. "I'm sorry, Mom. I wish there was something I could do."

"There is. Come home." The laughter went out of her mom's face, and she looked expectantly at Andie.

Andie wanted nothing more than to fly into her arms, but something kept her from moving. "I'm staying over at Finch's tonight," she said. "Dad's giving me a ride."

"I gather he and Cindy are having a party."

"It's for Cindy's friend."

It must have shown on her face, for her mom smiled knowingly. "Not your scene, huh?"

"Not exactly."

"Do you like it at your dad's?"

"It's okay." Andie shrugged. "I have my own room and everything."

"Which reminds me, I was thinking we could redecorate your room here. New wallpaper, the works. I remember you had your eye on that wicker headboard at Pier One."

Before Andie could reply, her father tapped on his horn out front.

"I should go," she said.

Her mother walked her to the door, where she hugged Andie tightly. She was wearing the Calyx cologne Andie had given her for Christmas the year before. Andie found herself remembering that after those times she'd threatened to run away from home, her mom would always do something fun with her—like bake cookies, or help make a playhouse out of blankets.

Suddenly Andie was in no hurry to leave.

Her mother stepped back, wearing a crooked little smile. "If you don't come home soon, I'll have to break down and buy myself a decent hair dryer." It was a family joke that her mother was the only one on the planet who borrowed her daughter's.

Andie was halfway down the front path when she glanced over her shoulder. Her mother looked so forlorn, standing in the doorway, Andie thought of a flood victim stranded on the roof while her house was being swept downriver. It was all she could do not to turn around and run back. But just then her father honked the horn again, more urgently this time.

He shot her a funny look as she climbed in, but didn't say anything until they were rounding the corner onto the next block. "How did it go?" he asked.

"All right," she said.

"You didn't give her a hard time, I hope."

Andie sighed, and shook her head. "It wasn't like that. We talked."

"So it's all settled then?"

"What?"

"You and Mom."

She studied the profile that in a year or two would sport a double chin. She knew then that he wanted this as much as her mother did—for reasons entirely his own. It wasn't anything specific, just a feeling she had—that life would be a lot easier without her around.

"I'll pack my stuff tomorrow," she told him.

He reached over to pat her knee. "That's my girl."

She could see the relief in his face, but surprisingly it didn't hurt as it once might have. She only felt sad. In his own way he loved her, she knew. Just not as much as she needed.

It was nearly dark by the time she got to Finch's. Andie found her in the barn with Hector, mucking out a stall. She grabbed a rake and pitched in, spreading clean straw over the floor while Punch stood hooked to the crossties by the tack room. Judy, the Appaloosa, and Finch's chestnut mare, Cheyenne, peered over the tops of their stalls, patiently waiting their turn. When all the stalls had been seen to, the horses were each given a scoop of bran mash with molasses as a treat. Hector went outside to hose off, and Andie and Finch took turns washing up at the tack room sink.

Supper, courtesy of Maude, was baked beans with frankfurters and homemade buttermilk biscuits. They sat around the kitchen table, all talking at once—Andie and Finch, Laura and Hector and Maude—eating off mismatched plates and using knives and forks from at least three different sets. Andie had never seen Laura so happy, except maybe at her wedding. She chattered on about her day—after a slow spell, it seemed business at Delarosa's was really picking up—but every so often she'd dart a look at Hector, who'd glance back with a little smile as if they shared a secret of some kind.

"More beans?" Maude, who reminded Andie of a snow-white canary she'd once had, waved in the direction of the stoneware casserole dish that had been Finch's present to the newlyweds, then went chattering on about the vegetable garden she'd planted, the cats' needing to be wormed, and the falling star she'd wished on last night.

No wonder Finch fit right into this family of odds and ends. Andie could remember a time, not so long ago, when she'd seemed instead like a square peg in the round hole that was the world. But now, watching her butter a biscuit while talking animatedly about the Japanese exchange student in her geometry class who'd invited her over for sushi, Andie was struck by how happy she seemed—as if nothing bad had ever happened to her, as if she hadn't been as foreign as Mariko when she'd first come to Carson Springs.

Halfway through the meal Laura remarked to Andie, "I hear you've been staying at your dad's." She'd changed out of her work clothes into jeans and a sweatshirt—her usual at-home attire.

"I'm going home tomorrow," Andie told her.

"Your mom must be happy about that."

The words came easily. "She is."

Laura smiled. "By the way, I finally met Claire."

"Oh?" Andie waited for the little inner downbeat that always came when Claire was mentioned, but found that she felt only mildly curious to know what Laura had thought of her.

"That tearoom of hers is the talk of the town."

"I, for one, can't wait." Maude was all but clapping her hands with glee.

"I stopped by the other day to see if she needed a hand." Hector reached for another biscuit. "That contractor of hers does nice work. Place is really shaping up."

Andie felt guilty that she hadn't been by to see it, and was relieved when talk turned to other things: the new roof that was going on the barn, the pickled string beans Maude was entering in the county fair, and Hector's class in literature at the community college that'd had him up half the night plowing through *War and Peace.*

Dessert was cobbler made from apricots Maude had put up last summer. After which, Finch sat back and announced, "I'm stuffed. I couldn't eat another bite if you paid me."

"In that case, you can help with the dishes," Laura told her.

"You ladies take it easy. *I'll* wash up." Hector's chair scraped back from the table, and he gave Laura's shoulder an affectionate little squeeze as he rose. "That goes for you, too," he called to Maude, who was already tying her apron on.

"We'll walk the dogs." Finch cast a meaningful glance at Andie, then whistled for Pearl and Rocky.

As she stepped out through the back door, Andie saw that it was a clear night—the moon out, and the stars like bright light shining through velvet. Cold, too. She could see her breath and was glad she'd thought to bring her warm jacket.

They picked their way up the path that led up the grassy slope behind the barn. It had rained the night before and the air smelled of damp earth and sage. In the distance, the mountains were like construction paper cutouts against the starry horizon.

They paused every so often to let old,

half-blind Pearl and Rocky, who found it necessary to pee on every bush, catch up. At
one point, Finch crouched down to pry
something from his jaws. "What's that you've
got there, boy?" She peered at it in the darkness, then flung it into the bushes with a grimace. "Uck, whatever it is, it's dead."

Andie would've puked, but she supposed
a rotting mouse carcass was nothing compared to the things Finch had seen. Like her
foster father getting shot by drug dealers
and bleeding to death before her eyes. It was
amazing how normal she was, considering.

They continued on, their shadows stretching like elongated scissors over the moonlit
path. After a while, Finch said, "I'm glad you
and your mom made up."

"Yeah, me too." Andie kicked at a rock.

"Is your dad cool with it?"

"Actually, I think he's sort of relieved that
I'm going back." Finch was the one person
she could confide in.

"Because of Cindy?"

"In a way."

"What a real bitch."

Andie shrugged. "She's not so bad."

"I thought you hated her."

"I used to . . . but not anymore."

They'd reached the top of the hill, where they sank down on a large flat rock while the dogs went charging off to explore. The Big Dipper looked almost close enough to touch. After a moment, Andie asked, "Do you ever wonder about your mother?"

"I don't really remember her." As far as Finch was concerned, Laura was the only mother she had. "I was two—at least that's what it says in my file. They found me all alone at a McDonald's." She smiled faintly. "Sometimes I have this dream—well, not really a dream, more like a memory—of a blond lady in a blue dress bending over me. She must be my mother."

"Is it a good memory?"

Finch tugged at a weed growing up through a crackin the rock. "I guess so. It'd be nice, though, if I could remember more."

Andie's own troubles all at once seemed small in comparison. "Claire must have wondered, too."

"Lucky she doesn't have to anymore."

"Yeah."

"I've been thinking." Finch turned to her. "Maybe we could drive over to her place after school on Monday and, you know, check it out."

"I suppose it wouldn't hurt." Andie didn't tell her the same thought had occurred to her as well.

"I'd like to meet her."

"Why didn't you go with Laura and Hector?"

"Like I'd do that to you." Finch gave her a stern look, letting her know that she wouldn't even have considered it without Andie's knowing.

Andie ducked her head, not wanting Finch to see the tears in her eyes.

Rocky came rustling out of the bushes just then, carrying a stick that Finch pried loose and tossed down the slope for him to retrieve. On the opposite hill a line of trees stood starkly outlined against the sky, and farther off in the distance the open scrub gave way to houses that glinted like scattered dice against the dark landscape.

When it grew too cold, they started back, the dogs trotting at their heels. It wasn't until they were halfway down the hill that Finch turned to ask casually, *too* casually, "Heard from Simon lately?"

"You mean have I returned any of his calls?" Finch knew perfectly well that she hadn't. "I doubt he's holding his breath."

Finch cast her a faintly injured look. "Hey, I was just asking."

"Sorry. I guess I'm a little touchy."

"Still no sign of your period?" Finch dropped her voice though there was no one around to hear.

Andie shook her head, suddenly filled with dread.

"What about the test? Did you take it?"

"Yesterday." She'd picked up one of those home pregnancy kits when she stopped to buy tampons.

"And?"

"It was negative."

Finch came to an abrupt halt. "Why didn't you *tell* me? I've been worried sick."

"Tests can be wrong."

"Just how late *are* you?"

"This is the second period I've missed."

Finch frowned. "You should see a doctor."

"The only one I know is my mom's."

"We'll find someone, don't worry."

Andie was instantly reassured by her use of "we." The thought of having to go through this alone was almost more than she could bear. "I still haven't told Simon."

"Don't you think you should?"

"He won't take it seriously. He'll say the test can't be wrong." Simon was, first and foremost, a reporter. He dealt in facts, not speculation.

"Okay, then why don't you wait until you're sure? One way or the other," Finch was quick to add. "In the meantime, you should at least *see* him. You don't know for sure that there's anything going on with him and Monica."

An owl hooted somewhere in the darkness; it seemed like the loneliest sound in the world. Andie thought for a moment, then said, "You're right. This is stupid."

The truth was, she missed Simon almost as much as she'd missed her mother. She missed his backpack bumping companionably against hers, and the look on his face when she'd sneak up on him in the library, the way he'd blink up at her in happy surprise. She even missed his dumb little gifts: the Skittles he knew she loved; a box of colored paper clips; the key ring he'd given her to celebrate her getting her learner's permit.

"Why don't you call him when we get back to the house?" Finch quickened her step.

Andie shot her a narrow look. "Did Simon put you up to this?"

"Who me? I don't know what you're talking about."

But from the suddenness with which
Finch darted ahead, Andie had a pretty
good idea he *had*. For some reason, it didn't
make her mad. She smiled at her friend's retreating back in the darkness.

But Simon wasn't home when she called.
The only thing his little brother (Andie didn't
know which one; they all sounded alike)
would tell her was that he was out. With
Monica? She didn't dare ask. Nor did she
leave a message, since she knew from experience that there was less than a 50 percent chance he'd get it.

The following morning she and Finch rose
just after dawn. With the sun a fat peach in a
watermelon sky, they saddled the horses—
Andie on Punch, and Finch on Cheyenne—
and set off. They rode all the way to the
creek, where they stopped to let the horses
rest. By the time they returned, sunlight was
warming the barn's weathered boards and
they were both starving. As they rubbed the
horses down, Andie thought of toast
slathered in butter and Maude's peach jam.

Fortunately, Maude was up and about,
coffee brewing and a pot of oatmeal steam-

ing on the stove. Andie helped herself to a heaping bowl, and two slices of toast with jam. Halfway through breakfast, Hector ambled in yawning and asked Andie if she'd like a lift in to town. She was quick to take him up on his offer, asking if he'd drop her off at Simon's.

A short while later she was getting out at the entrance to a rundown trailer park. She looked around in dismay. She'd imagined Mariposa Gardens to be like the mobile home park her dad's sister, Aunt Teresa, had lived in at one time—nice, double-wide trailers with well-tended yards. Here there were only patches of dried brown grass where the yards weren't scuffed completely bare. As she walked along the sparsely graveled drive, she saw that the cars in the tiny carports were mostly older models marred with dents and patches of primer. The only signs of life were the clotheslines from which laundry flapped dispiritedly, and the toys scattered about—Hot Wheels, an inflatable swimming pool half filled with scummy water, a rusty Tonka truck overturned in the dirt.

No wonder Simon hadn't been in a rush to have her visit.

The few people out and about—a man

trying to start his car, the sound of its engine like the moan of a dying beast; an old woman in flip-flops and a faded housecoat taking out the trash; and a towheaded boy of around ten perched on the tailgate of a battered yellow pickup sporting a bumper sticker that read if you can read this, eat my shit—glanced at her without interest as she passed. It was obvious Simon's neighbors were used to seeing strangers wandering about at odd hours.

Near the end of the drive, she spotted Simon's beat-up squareback parked in a carport that was little more than a sheet of corrugated plastic propped on aluminum poles and felt a wave of relief wash over her. If he'd been at Monica's the night before, he wasn't there now. She climbed the steps of the trailer, distinguished from the ones on either side by the window box from which tendrils of ivy straggled forlornly, and knocked on the door. Inside, a dog began to yap.

The door cracked open and something small and white and furry came hurtling out—Bartlesby, the mutt Simon had adopted from Lost Paws, where she volunteered. She bent to scoop him up.

"Andie! What are you doing here?"

She straightened, holding the wriggling dog in her arms, to find Simon gaping at her. "I was in the neighborhood," she told him.

He looked flustered as he stepped back to let her in. He was wearing a faded Monterey Jazz T-shirt over rumpled pajama bottoms, and, with his hair flopping down over his brows, looked all of about twelve. He offered her a tentative smile. "I'm just surprised, that's all. You didn't return any of my calls."

"I called last night. You weren't home."

Andie glanced about. A pair of dark-haired boys who bore a striking resemblance to Simon lay sprawled on the carpet in front of the loudly squawking TV. A third, younger than the other two, sat at the table a few feet away, slurping cereal from a bowl while a little girl alongside him drank milk from the carton.

"Junie!" Simon stalked over and snatched the carton from her hands. "How many times have I told you to use a glass?"

"I couldn't reach!" she whined.

He fetched a glass from the cupboard. Ricki, whom Andie recognized from school, wandered in just then, barely glancing at her as she plopped down on the couch.

"Guys, this is Andie," Simon announced.

"Hi," she said, lowering the dog onto the carpet.

The boys mumbled something without tearing their eyes from the TV. Ricki, a lanky dark-haired girl in leggings and a baggy black sweatshirt, lifted a hand in greeting while Junie flashed her a milk-mustachioed grin, crowing, "It's Simon's *girl*friend."

Color rushed up into Simon's cheeks, and he shot Andie an apologetic look. "They're not very big on manners."

Andie glanced down the narrow hallway. "Your mom asleep?"

He nodded. "She works the night shift. Don't worry, a bomb could go off and it wouldn't wake her."

Andie watched Bartlesby race over to the table, where the milk Junie had spilled was dripping onto the floor. "About last night," she said. "I would have left a message, only I wasn't sure you'd want to hear from me."

"That's funny, considering all the messages *I've* been leaving." Simon's tone was dry, and his hazel eyes large with reproach. He poked at his glasses, which had slipped down his nose.

"Maybe I should have called you at Monica's."

Simon's face flushed an even deeper red, and he cast a nervous glance at his brothers and sisters, who'd gone from watching the Power Rangers to eyeballing them. He grabbed Andie's arm and steered her to the door. "Come on, we can talk outside."

"Watch out for Mrs. Malcolm," Ricki warned with a laugh. "Her TV's on the fritz again."

"Do we look like fugitives from *The Young and the Restless*?" Simon shot back.

The screen door slapped shut behind them with a tinny rattle. He led the way to a pair of aluminum folding chairs tilting to starboard on the scrap of lawn under a huge old chestnut. He gallantly chose the one with the most broken straps.

"Sorry about that. We don't get much company," he said.

"I didn't come for coffee and cake."

"Why *did* you come?" He sounded hurt, and she wondered if she'd been too quick to judge him—like when her mother had jumped to conclusions about that stupid CD.

"I thought we should talk."

"About Monica?" She caught an edge of sarcasm in his voice.

She looked down at her shadow stretching over the stunted brown grass. "I'm sorry. It was a stupid crack."

"I hate to break it to you, but you had to find out sometime: Monica and I are eloping to Vegas. We figured, why wait until I graduate? There's no time like the present. Who gives a shit about college when I can live like a king, lounging around the pool all day sipping piña coladas?"

She looked up to find Simon regarding her with a deadpan expression.

"Piña coladas?" She giggled.

He cracked a smile. "It sounded good."

Andie felt foolish all of a sudden. "Come to think of it, you and Monica would make a cute couple."

"Yeah, I could visit her behind bars when she gets arrested for having sex with a minor."

She laughed at the idea, at the same time seeing his knee-jerk wisecracking for what it was: a front. The truth was, Simon was ashamed—of *this*, which made it all the more understandable that he'd jumped at Monica's offer.

"I really *am* sorry," she said. "I should have trusted you."

"Okay, I'll let you off easy this time—considering it's your first offense." His smile widened into a grin. "By the way, I thought you'd be interested to know that Monica wasn't bullshitting when she said she knew the dean of admissions at Stanford. It's all set. I'm meeting him in a few weeks."

"That's amazing! You must be psyched." Andie was happy for him—even though it would mean their being separated. No way was she getting into Stanford with her grades.

"Just for the record, she never laid a hand on me."

"Not even make a pass?"

He smiled mysteriously.

"Should I be jealous?"

He put on an innocent expression. "Do I look like the kind of guy who'd cheat on his girlfriend?"

Andie drew in a deep breath. She might as well get it over with. "There's something *you* should know—I think I might be pregnant."

He didn't say anything at first, just sat there staring at her in disbelief. Not Clark Kent or even Carl Bernstein, just a lanky kid in a faded red T-shirt and pajama bottoms that bagged down around his ankles. Someone who looked after his brothers and sisters and took in stray dogs.

"You *think*, or you *know*?" His voice was surprisingly calm.

"I took the test—it was negative."

He sagged with relief. "Well, then."

"I won't know for sure until I see a doctor." It hit her full force. "Oh, Simon, what if I am?"

He regarded her gravely for a long moment, then rose with a creak of nylon webbing and sank down on one knee, taking her hands in his. "We're too young to get married. It would only make things worse. How do you think my mom ended up in this shithole with six kids? But I *can* promise you one thing: Whatever happens, I won't let you down."

Her heart swelled until she felt as if she could be lifted up and carried over the treetops like a balloon. "I don't want us to get married," she said in a small cracked voice. "But thanks for not asking."

He flashed her his familiar lopsided grin. "You're welcome."

She caught a movement out of the corner of her eye, and glanced up to find an old woman with her hair in curlers peering out the window of the trailer next door.

Andie smiled, asking in a low voice, "Do you think we're giving your neighbor her money's worth?"

"Are you kidding? The show hasn't even started." Simon rose to his full height, pulling Andie into his arms. He smelled muzzily of sleep and T-shirts from the bottom of the drawer. When he kissed her, she grew weak-kneed, forgetting the old lady until he pulled back to whisper in her ear, "We're doing her a favor, you know. Why spend money on a new TV when she has *this*?"

Andie knew then that it was going to be okay. Whatever happened. For at this particular moment, with the sun climbing over the treetops and Mrs. Malcolm settling in for the rest of the show, there was no doubt in her mind that Simon loved her.

Chapter Fifteen

The first strawberries of the season were small and as sweetly tart as candied rind. Claire had bought several flats from a small farm off Route 128 owned by an old man and his middle-aged son, Chester and Chuck Dunlop, with whom she'd arranged to get regular deliveries when Tea & Sympathy opened in a month. That's how such business was conducted around here, she'd discovered, in the barns and farm stands scattered over the fields and groves that stretched in a broad green band across the valley floor and produced an embarrassment of riches: cherries, peaches, apricots, plums, grapes, and berries in summer; apples, pears, persimmons, and pomegranates in the fall, with citrus fruits being in abundance nearly year round. The opening-day menu had been planned in accordance and would include strawberry tarts, blueberry scones, apple-lemon turnovers, and Kitty's famous orange cake drizzled in orange syrup, which Gladys Honeick, a Tea & Sympathy regular, had once described as a trip to heaven and back for seconds.

Kitty had been on Claire's mind a lot these days. She always made it seem so effortless, as if the people who flocked to Tea & Sympathy were neighbors who'd happened to drop in just as she was taking something from the oven. Even her past failures seemed amusing in the retelling, because Kitty was, well, Kitty, and it wasn't just her baked goods that drew people in. What remained to be seen was whether they'd feel the same about *her*.

Claire pondered this as she stood in her kitchen slicing strawberries. Her fingers were stained a deep crimson and her apron polka-dotted with red. Boiled jars filled every inch of available countertop, and a kettle on the stove emitted a fragrant steam.

Even so, she felt a kind of panic at the thought of what lay ahead. Tomorrow would be the test run. She'd invited her new friends and family for tea: Gerry and the kids; Aubrey, who'd said he'd be delighted, but would have to duck out early; and Mavis, who'd be here in any event. Not to mention Sam and Ian, Alice and Wes, Laura, Hector, Maude, and Finch. And Matt, of course.

Matt. She warmed at the thought of him— his large calloused hands, his mustache tickling her. In her mind she saw his clothes at the foot of the bed: jeans and shirt and boots and socks and underwear in a heap that seemed to give off a heat all its own.

They'd fallen into a sort of routine. On days when he didn't have to pick up his kids he'd hang around after work, and they'd sip beers at the kitchen table until the light had faded and the sun was a rusty streak across the horizon. Matt would pry off his boots, and she would slip out of her shoes to prop her aching feet on his lap. Invariably, they'd wind up in the bedroom.

She grew even warmer remembering the night before. Even her trick of mentally sum- moning Byron failed to bring the usual cold dash of guilt. It was as though this thing with

Matt were happening to someone entirely separate from herself. As if the person she'd been in Miramonte had been discarded like a pair of shoes that pinched or a dress that no longer fit. At the same time, she didn't want Byron to be cast aside as well. She still wanted the life they'd planned together those summer evenings out on the porch—the house, the kids, the two careers. The question was, where did Matt fit in? If this was nothing more than a case of spring fever, why did she feel so torn?

It wasn't just Matt—there were his kids. He'd brought them by a few times, letting them play in the yard while he finished up. Yesterday Tara had hung around the kitchen watching her bake while her brother, Casey, helped his dad with the garbage-can enclosure Matt was building alongside the garage. Claire had been making cookie dough for the deep freezer, and the little girl had been so fascinated with the whole process she'd tied an apron around her and let her cut some of the dough into shapes, which they'd frosted with colored icing and decorated with sprinkles once they were baked.

That night after he'd dropped them off at

their mother's, as he and Claire lay snuggled in bed, he'd said softly, "They like you."

"They're sweet kids. I'll bet they like everyone." She wasn't going to let him make a big deal of it.

"Tell that to Casey's teacher. Last week he called Miss Hibberd a butthead."

Claire smiled. "How do you know she isn't?"

"You're missing the point."

"Which is?"

"That they *don't* take to everyone." Matt nuzzled her neck. "The other day Casey wanted to know if I was going to marry you."

Claire's heart began to pound. "What did you tell him?"

"That I couldn't because I was marrying Miss Hibberd."

He grinned, his teeth a flash of white in the darkness, and she'd felt herself relax. Talk of marriage, even in jest, made her nervous.

Now, in the broad light of day, marriage—to anyone—was the furthest thing from her mind. She glanced over at Mavis, cracking walnuts at the table. Thank God for Mavis—for her crabbed hands in perpetual motion, her cheerful if somewhat off-key warbling, and her steady stream of household tips, like using salt to scrub stubborn pans and milk to remove red wine stains. With Mavis everything had to be done the old-fashioned way.

Claire tuned in to hear her snort in contempt: "Ever see an expiration date on one of those bags?" She tossed another shell onto the growing pile. "Milk, you know what you're getting. Fruit, you can see when it's spoiled. But for all you know those supermarket nuts could be as old as the shelf they're sitting on." She shook her head. "It never ceases to amaze me what people will put in their mouths."

"Most don't know any better." Claire recalled her revelation, early on in life, that food was more than just three basic groups.

She'd been in the eighth grade. One day she'd been home sick with a cold and, bored out of her mind, had happened to tune in to a cooking show: Julia Child demonstrating the perfect way to roast a chicken. For Claire it had been a turning point of sorts. She'd fooled around in the kitchen before, using the Betty Crocker kids' cookbook (with recipes like pigs in a blanket) from Gran Brewster, but after that began experimenting in earnest. She'd snipped recipes from magazines and pored over cookbooks. She'd discovered James Beard, Maida Heatter, and Craig Claiborne, along with old standards like *Joy of Cooking* and *Fannie Farmer.* She'd learned the proper way to mash potatoes and to tenderize a roast. She discovered that curry wasn't a single spice but a number of them ground together, and that parboiling string beans with a teaspoon of sugar will keep them looking fresh picked. Along the way, she found her true love: baking. It was what eventually led her to Tea & Sympathy, which had gained a devout following with such retro desserts as devil's food cake, icebox cookies, and black bottom pie.

"Nonsense," Mavis huffed. "If I've told Gerry once, I've told her a thousand times: It's as easy to make macaroni and cheese from scratch as from a box." She shook her head in despair, her rusty hair floating about her head. "How my daughter, who grew up on home-baked bread, could eat the way she does is a mystery to me."

"If everyone turned out like their parents, it'd be pretty boring." Claire thought of Lou and Millie.

Mavis cocked her head, smiling up at her

thoughtfully. "Maybe it skips a generation. Heaven knows you're more like me than either of my children."

"I guess there's something to be said for nature versus nuture," Claire replied, more than a little uncomfortable with the subject.

"Though I'm sure your folks can take their share of credit for the way *you* turned out," Mavis was quick to put in.

Her parents, who still didn't know if they were coming. Millie kept insisting she wasn't well enough to travel, but the other day Lou had let drop that they'd visited Aunt Lucille and Uncle Henry in Monterey. Claire hadn't pressed the issue, but it hurt even so.

Lifting the lid off the kettle, she said with a wistful smile, "I used to think of families as being made of whole cloth, but they're not, are they? They're more like—" she looked up from the simmering contents of the kettle, her gaze falling on the basket of remnants by the sewing machine "—scraps stitched together."

"Like a quilt. Yes." Mavis smiled, setting aside her nutcracker to survey the mound of cracked nuts on the table. "Well, now. That should be enough to supply the entire western hemisphere." She rose to her feet, wincing only a little. The new prescription her doctor had given her must be working, though Claire suspected it had as much to do with her indefatigable spirit—Mavis was not one to go gently into that good night. "While you're finishing up with that, why don't I get started on the dough?"

They had three dozen tart shells ready for the freezer by the time Mavis's friend Olive Miller arrived to pick her up. Claire glanced out the window as they were pulling out of the driveway in Olive's big blue Plymouth— two old ladies perched on the front seats like a pair of nuthatches on a fence, so busy chattering Olive narrowly missed backing into the mailbox. Claire smiled. These past weeks she'd grown closer to Mavis than she'd been to either Gran Brewster or Nana Schilling. Even with Gerry, she felt more at ease. The only one she wasn't sure about was Andie. She and her friend Finch had dropped by earlier in the week but hadn't stayed long—an encouraging sign, though Andie had hung back, letting Finch do most of the talking.

The following afternoon, hours before the guests were due to arrive, Claire was in the kitchen making spreads for sandwiches when she heard the tinkle of the bell over the front door. Thinking it was Mavis, she didn't stop what she was doing until she heard a polite cough and turned to find Andie poised hesitantly in the doorway.

"Hi. I was wondering if you needed any help." She was dressed in jeans and a cropped T-shirt that showed her navel—an outie like Claire's."

Noting how self-conscious she looked, Claire felt a tug of sympathy. She could re-member when she'd been that age, feeling like she'd been turned inside out, her every thought and emotion on display.

"Right now, I could use six hands." She gestured with a laugh toward the loaves of banana bread cooling on the counter, the strawberry tarts just out of the oven, and brownie batter in a bowl. "Check the broom closet—I think there's an extra apron. Oh, and the good plates and teacups are in the hutch. You can set them on the table out front while I—" She paused, smiling. "Hey, thanks. I appreciate it."

"No problem." Andie ducked her head, fiddling with one of the dozen earrings in her ears. She was cutting the crusts from sandwiches and arranging them on the lovely old Meissen platter Sam had given Claire when she looked up and said, "Your kitchen smells like my grandma's. I used to love spending the night at her house when I was little. We always made sugar cookies. She had all these cookie cutters in the shapes of animals."

Claire wordlessly walked over to the long cupboard by the fridge, rummaging inside until she found what she was looking for: a battered shoebox that made a faint, tinny rattling as she carried it over to the table. "My housewarming gift from your grandmother," she said.

Andie pried off the lid, reaching inside to finger a cookie cutter in the shape of bear. She smiled at the memories it evoked. "They'd be perfect for kids' parties."

"Kids' parties? Now *there's* an idea." Claire could envision it: birthday teas for pre-teen girls, like grown-up versions of the pretend tea parties they played at when they were little. "How would you like to be in charge? We could split the profits down the middle, fifty-fifty."

Andie's gaze met hers, still a bit wary.

"Sure, why not? It might be fun." A small smile surfaced. "I'll talk to Finch. I'll bet she'd like to go in with us."

"Your friend seems nice."

"Finch? Yeah."

"She's not from around here, is she?"

Andie stiffened a bit, as if Claire were suggesting she was a misfit. "She's from New York."

"That must be it. She seems so . . ." Claire searched for the word, ". . . sophisticated."

Andie's face relaxed. "She's adopted, you know."

"So I've heard."

"It'll be final in a few weeks."

"How nice for her."

"Yeah, she's pretty happy about it." They went back to work cutting up sandwiches, and after a minute or so Andie ventured, "It must be weird for you—having two mothers."

"I don't think of Gerry as a mother." Claire paused in the midst of chopping parsley. "She's more like a friend."

Andie looked relieved.

A little while later, when Gerry appeared with Justin and Mavis in tow, the tables out front were covered in the flowered tablecloths Mavis had stitched and the good china laid out. There were platters of sandwiches, banana bread, gingersnaps, brownies, and strawberry tarts with a bowl of fresh strawberries on the side. Noting Gerry's look of admiration as she surveyed the room, which Sam had brightened with flowers from her garden, Claire couldn't help feeling proud. For the first time, she allowed herself to feel the tiniest bit optimistic that Tea & Sympathy would be a success.

"Not so fast, young man." Gerry lightly slapped Justin's hand as he was reaching for a brownie. "I want to take a picture first." She reached into her voluminous shoulder bag for her camera, and after snapping off several shots, herded everyone together for a group photo. Andie hesitated at first, then stepped up alongside her brother, wedged in so tightly against Claire she could easily have given him a black eye with her elbow. "Okay, smile everybody!" Out of the corner of her eye, Claire saw Mavis blink and recoil as the flash went off.

Gerry used the rest of the roll on the room itself. "I can't believe what you've done with this place," she said when she finally lowered her camera. "I hardly recognize it."

"Matt deserves most of the credit." Claire

felt her cheeks warm, thinking of how handy he was in other areas as well. "Some of it he's not even charging me for. I think he's afraid I can't afford it."

She glanced about at the wainscoting, and the rows of shelves behind the display case, which she'd picked up for a song from a deli going out of business, on which her collection of vintage teapots was displayed. Another of Matt's ideas had been the built-in cabinet alongside the counter with its miniature drawers in which different kinds of loose tea were stored: Lapsang Souchong, China Oolong, Blue Flower Earl Grey, and Blood Orange Sencha, to name a few.

Mavis gave a knowing chuckle as she hobbled over to the kettle hissing on one of the cast-iron burners. "From the way that man looks at you, I'd say it's an even trade."

Claire felt her blush deepen. Mavis's eyesight might not be what what it used to be, but she saw well enough. Claire was grateful when Andie, seeming to take pity on her, changed the subject.

"Simon might drop by. I hope that's okay."

Claire smiled. "The more, the merrier."

"I'm warning you, he eats like a horse."

"Which is what we're all going to look like

when we're through with this," Gerry joked, eyeing the platters.

Andie looked distracted, as if she were reminded of something. Then everyone was bustling about all at once, trying not to bump into each other as they carried things in from the kitchen.

Sam and Ian were the first to arrive. Watching them stroll in through the door, Claire couldn't help thinking again what an unlikely couple they made—Sam, so ladylike and perfectly put together even in maternity clothes, and Ian, with his ponytail and stud in one ear.

"Something smells good," he said.

"I'll have two of everything," Sam joked, patting her belly.

"Remember what the doctor said," Gerry warned.

Sam sank with a sigh into the nearest chair. "One Lamaze class and she's my self-appointed watchdog." She turned to Claire, adding, "Based entirely, and may I say unfairly, on my age, it seems I'm high risk. Never mind I'm healthier than I was with the last ones." She didn't add that it'd been more than a quarter of a century since then.

"Let's keep it that way," Gerry growled.

Sam cast Ian a beseeching look, but he only shrugged. "Sorry, I'm with Gerry."

Alice and Wes were next, Alice looking as if she'd stepped from *Vogue* in slim camel slacks and fitted black tunic, her honey-blond hair swept back in a sleek bun. Wes, more sportily dressed in jeans and an old tweed blazer, followed her with his eyes as she crossed the room to give her mother and Ian pecks on the cheek.

"Hey, Mom, looking good." Ian flashed Alice a grin.

She swatted him lightly on the arm. "Watch it. You're older than I am."

Ian turned to Claire with a wink, "Gets her every time."

"My son's taking good care of you, I hope." Wes slipped an arm about Sam's shoulders.

"The best." She smiled the smile of a supremely satisfied woman.

Laura and her entourage trooped in minutes later. In their jeans and snap-button Western shirts, she and Hector were a matched set. Finch, on the other hand, wore a clingy top and sarong skirt that made her look utterly unique. Claire thought how stunning she'd be in a few years, when she grew into those long legs and eyes too big for her face. Finch's hand was lightly cupped about Maude's elbow, as if to keep her from tipping over in her high heels and ankle-length skirt. Their affection for each other was obvious; they might have been related.

Maude paused on the threshold to bring her hands together in a soundless little clap. "Wake me if I'm dreaming. I think I've tumbled down Alice's rabbit hole."

"Did you do all of this yourself?" Laura eyed the spread in amazement.

"I had help." Claire glanced at Mavis and Andie.

"Who else is coming?" Alice wanted to know.

Before she could answer, Gerry put in, "Aubrey, for one." She glanced at her watch. "He said he might be a little late."

"I invited Matt, but I doubt he'll be able to make it," Claire said, knowing how he felt about large gatherings.

She heard the clomp of footsteps on the porch just then and, out of habit, her heart skipped a beat, but it was only Andie's boyfriend, looking exactly as described: tall and loose-limbed, like a junior Clark Kent complete with glasses perched halfway down his nose.

"Hi. I'm Simon." He flashed her an affable grin, shaking her hand with the firmness of an executive. "I've heard a lot about you."

Claire hoped some of it had been good. "Same here. Andie tells me you like to eat. As you can see, you came to the right place."

Everyone was seated and the tea ready to be poured when Aubrey finally strolled in, looking as elegantly European as usual in a three-button jacket and black T-shirt, a pair of slim calfskin loafers peeking from under the cuffs of his trousers.

"I hope I'm not too late," he said.

"You're right on time." Gerry got up and kissed him lightly on the cheek, and Claire thought she caught a hint of something bruised in the look that passed between them.

"I'm afraid I can't stay long. I'm on my way to the airport," he apologized in advance, sinking into the empty chair next to Gerry's.

"Where to this time?" Mavis inquired brightly.

"Brussels."

"Oh? For how long?"

"Indefinitely, I'm afraid." He seemed to be studiously avoiding Gerry's gaze.

Sam was the only one besides Gerry and her kids who didn't look surprised; then Claire remembered Isla Verde—he couldn't very well have left without informing her.

"Too bad you'll miss Justin's game," Andie said.

Justin cast him a reproachful look from under the bill of his baseball cap. Aubrey was clearly just one more father figure to bail out on him. "It doesn't matter. I probably won't get to play anyway," he said glumly.

"Just because you were benched the last time—" Gerry stopped, as if realizing that this had nothing to do with Justin's record.

The minor cloud was swept aside by the torrent of raves that followed. And judging from the quickness with which the food was gobbled up, it wasn't just talk. Claire felt happy and proud. It was only a small hurdle compared to what she'd be up against on opening day, but it was a good omen. Watching Maude tuck into her second tart, pausing to dab at a spot of strawberry filling on her chin, it occurred to Claire that her biggest problem might not be a shortage of customers but keeping up with demand.

"These are the best brownies I've ever had," Sam declared.

"I use Kahlúa in place of vanilla," Claire told her.

"And these cookies—my God." Laura rolled her eyes in ecstasy.

"Mavis's recipe." Claire glanced over to find the old woman beaming.

Hector helped himself to another gingersnap. "Whoever made them, they're damn good."

Laura shot him a mock injured look. "I guess my baking doesn't measure up."

Hector patted her arm. "No one can touch your cornbread."

She turned to Claire. "Mom finally got Lupe to divulge the recipe. Would you believe the reason she was so secretive all those years was because she'd never written it down?"

"Now I know where I went wrong. Instead of trying to follow recipes, I should have been making them up as I went along." Gerry gave a self-effacing chuckle.

Her laughter seemed too bright, her smile a tad brittle, yet she ate as heartily as the others and downed several cups of tea. When it was time for Aubrey to go, she showed no visible signs of distress other than the slight tremor in her hand as she rose to smooth his lapel. The gesture seemed oddly proprietary, and Claire wondered if the others had noticed as well. Sam clearly had; she chose that moment to retrieve her napkin from the floor. Alice, no stranger to unorthodox relationships, wore a knowing expression.

Claire's thoughts turned once more to Matt. Lately she'd been aware of a subtle shift in their relationship. Where he used to tease her about Byron, he now seemed uncomfortable when the subject came up. Once, when Byron called, the pounding of Matt's hammer in the next room became almost deafening.

Gerry walked Aubrey to the door. "I wish you didn't have to go so soon. It feels as if you just got here," she said, glancing out at the black limousine idling at the curb.

"If I didn't have a plane to catch . . ." He smiled with regret, glancing over at Justin. "I'll send you a souvenir—a cricket bat perhaps." Ignoring the resentful look Justin shot him, he turned to Andie. "I almost forgot. I have something for you, my dear." He pulled a slim, gift-wrapped package from his breast pocket, watching with a faintly ironic expression as Andie opened it. It was a CD. "Schubert's late sonatas. Many consider it my wife's best recording," he said. "I hope it brings you as much pleasure as it has me."

Andie blushed crimson. "Thank you," she said shyly.

Gerry cleared her throat and said, "I'll walk you to your car." She allowed herself to meet his eyes, and for a long moment they stood there on the threshold, gazing at each other as if no one else existed. Then they disappeared out the door.

No one spoke at first, then they were all talking at once. By the time Gerry reappeared, looking flushed and determinedly upbeat, it was as if nothing were amiss.

Before long, everyone was getting up to go.

Sam kissed Claire on the cheek on her way out, advising, "Keep fertilizing those roses the way I showed you and they'll bloom all summer long."

"Wonderful party, my dear." Maude teetered on her high heels as if having enjoyed something stronger than Earl Grey. "I can hardly wait for the official opening."

"I must have gained two pounds," Finch complained good-naturedly.

Laura rolled her eyes. "I'm not even going to step on the scale."

"Let me know when you're ready to go public," Wes teased. "I'll put you together with my broker."

Gerry lingered on the porch as the others trooped down the path. "It *was* a wonderful party," she told Claire. "I'm just sorry Aubrey couldn't stay."

Claire hesitated, then said, "You'll miss him, won't you?"

Gerry looked as if she were about to deny it, then sighed and said, "Yeah, I will." She tucked a stray wisp behind her ear, smiling ruefully. "What about you? Which will it be, the doctor or the carpenter?"

Claire blinked at her in surprise—how had she known?—then let out a self-conscious little laugh. "And here I thought I was being so discreet."

"My mother has a big mouth. Besides, I've been around the block a few times, remember?"

Claire's face was on fire. "The thing with Matt . . . it's not serious."

"Does *he* know that?" Gerry cast a wry glance over her shoulder.

Claire turned to find Matt striding up the

path, a cone of flowers wrapped in newspaper balanced in the crook of one arm. Her heart soared, then plummeted. Oh, God. Had he overheard? No, from the look on his face it was obvious he hadn't.

He bounded up onto the porch. "Sorry I'm late." He nodded in passing to Gerry as she vanished into the twilight. "But at least I didn't come empty-handed." He thrust the flowers at her.

Dahlias and asters, her favorites. "You didn't have to."

"There's a story behind them." He winked, strolling in through the door. "I was doing some work out at the Flowermill this afternoon. The irrigation system in their greenhouse had crapped out. Joanne—she's the owner—was all set to load up the back of my truck, she was so grateful, but I was afraid it'd look as if I were on my way to a funeral."

"Well, I'm glad I didn't have to die to get these," she said with a little laugh, looking around for something to put them in and seeing that every vase she owned was in use.

In the kitchen she fished a plastic bucket from under the sink. It would have to do for the time being. While she was filling it from the tap, Matt carried a stack of dirty plates in. "Looks like the party was a hit. I just wish I could've gotten away sooner. But, well, you know how it is." He shrugged, placing the plates on the counter.

In his Timberland boots and lumberjack shirt, he seemed to fill the room. Below the ragged line of his mustache, the gleaming edges of his teeth showed, and she had a sudden impulse to kiss him and run her tongue along the underside of his lip. God, what kind of person was she? One minute dismissing him, the next wanting to make mad, passionate love. Certainly not someone she recognized . . . or particularly liked.

"Oh, well, there's always next time." She dropped the flowers into the bucket, wondering if there would be a next time with Matt.

They finished loading the dishwasher. She was sweeping up the crumbs in the front room when he pulled the broom from her hands. "That can wait," he said. "Come on, let's go for a drive."

"Now?"

"There's something I want to show you."

Claire shrugged. Why not? Some fresh air would do her good.

Outside, she hopped into his truck. It was a balmy night, the air scented with the lilacs blooming along the drive. They drove in companionable silence, Claire, enjoying the warm air rushing in through her open window. Before long, the downtown area was a distant twinkle in the rearview mirror.

They'd gone several miles into the countryside when Matt pulled into a graveled drive, where they bumped to a stop in front of a dilapidated barn. There was only the trill of crickets and distant barking of a dog. Farther down the drive, the lighted windows of a farmhouse glowed—a Hallmark greeting card.

"Yours?" She'd never been to Matt's place. Whenever he'd suggested it, she'd put him off, feeling—naively, no doubt—that it would signify something she wasn't ready for.

"Nah. It belongs to a friend of mine. I do repairs in exchange for rent." He produced a key for the padlock. The door squealed on rusty hinges as he pushed it open.

As they stepped into the dark interior, the first thing Claire noticed was the absence of any barnlike smells. The only scents were that of new lumber and varnish. When he switched on the overhead lights, she immediately saw why: A nearly completed sailboat, a good fifteen feet in length, sat on wooden supports in the center of the barn, alongside it power tools shrouded in plastic, cans of paint, and, lying on a tarp, a freshly lathed mast.

Claire ran a hand over the keel. "You built this?"

"All except the fittings." Matt looked as proud as if she'd praised one of his children.

"It's unbelievable." She spoke with awe.

He must have read the question in her eyes. "You're probably wondering what a landlubber like me is doing with a boat. Well, I wasn't always a landlubber." He scrambled easily onto the deck, holding out a hand to hoist her up. When she was seated on a bench, he said, "Before I went into business for myself, I was a naval architect."

Claire was so amazed that she was only just now hearing this, she blurted, "What happened?"

"I was married then and living in Oakland. Working days, taking classes at night at Berkeley. A few months after I got my degree, I had an offer from a shipbuilder in New Orleans. That same week Lainie told me she wanted a divorce and that she and the kids were moving back to Carson Springs to be near her folks." He shrugged, fiddling with a pulley on the halyard. "It was a no-brainer. I didn't want my kids growing up without a dad."

"That was . . ." She struggled to think of the word, ". . . noble of you."

He looked at her, his tea-brown eyes crinkled with bemusement. "Noble of me?" He gave a dry little laugh, sweeping a wood shaving into his hand and releasing it over the bow as if it had been an insect he hadn't wanted to kill. "Hell, it wasn't just my kids I was thinking of. It would have killed me to be so far from them."

"Couldn't you have gotten a job nearby?"

"There's only a handful of shipbuilders left in this country. A few more than there are makers of carriages and buggy whips." He smiled ruefully. "Part of it's my fault for picking such an obscure profession—but my dad built boats and his dad before him. I never wanted to do anything else."

Claire understood now why he'd seemed so amused about her opening a tearoom: He hadn't been making fun of her; he'd been indulging in a bit of wishful thinking.

"Why didn't you tell me before?"

"I didn't want you to feel sorry for me." He held her gaze, and she saw in his eyes no pity for himself, either. "Anyway, as you can see, I haven't given it up completely." He glanced about with the look of a man who, if not 100 percent satisfied with his lot in life, had more or less made peace with it.

"Are you going to sell it?"

He nodded, running a hand along the rail, as if any profit would be beside the point. "What would I do with a boat? Unless you'd like to sail off to Tahiti with me." He broke into a wide grin.

He'd only been teasing, but she felt herself stiffen slightly. "Hold that thought," she answered lightly. "If I go bust, I just might take you up on it."

He looked down at his feet, then back up at her, shyly almost. "Would you consider something a little less romantic in the meantime?"

"Like what?"

His expression grew serious. "I was thinking of something along the lines of an exclusive relationship."

Claire's heart began to pound, and she dropped her gaze. "I can't. You know that."

"I guess what it comes down to," he said softly, but firmly, "is that you have to decide which one of us it'll be—him or me."

"What if I *can't*?"

She looked up to find him rubbing his jaw pensively, more like a man considering his options than one about to get hurt. "You've always been straight with me. I appreciate that. And I knew it was serious with this guy Byron, so that's on me. But we can't go on like this—just playing house. I'm running out of things to fix."

Panic seized her. "Please, Matt. Don't do this."

"Do what?" Matt stared at her, his mouth hard. "Hell, woman, I want to *marry* you."

All at once she felt as if she'd been torn from her bearings. "Oh, Matt." She brought her hand to her mouth. "I never thought—"

"To tell the truth, neither did I. It sneaked up on me, too."

She was shaking her head, pressing so hard with her knuckles she could feel her teeth cutting into the underside of her lip. "You don't understand. Byron and I . . . we've been together since we were kids."

His gaze wouldn't let go. "I'll accept that . . . if you tell me you're not in love with me."

Claire couldn't bring herself to say it. If she told him no, it would be a lie. But how could she be in love with two men at once? "I can't." The words emerged in a cracked whisper.

Matt looked down at his hands, at a scrape on his knuckles that hadn't quite healed. When he brought his gaze back to her, she saw that his eyes were bright with unshed tears. His voice, though, was firm with resolve. "The only nice thing my wife ever had to say about me was that I was a one-woman man. I'm not interested in another man's leftovers. I'm not built that way. If you can't choose, I guess this is good-bye."

"Just like that?"

"Just like that."

She thought of Byron. Breaking up with him would be like severing a limb. She couldn't do that to herself . . . or him. But could she be without Matt? It wasn't just the sex. She'd miss his voice in the next room, the sight of him across from her at the table, and the little ways he stuck up for her—like with the buildings inspector who'd insisted on addressing Matt as if *he* were the owner, as if a woman didn't count, until Matt had turned to him and said with a twinkle in his eye, "You'll have to ask the lady of the house. She might not look it, but she understands English."

How could she let him go? How could she bear not seeing him again?

"I'll miss you," she said softly.

Matt's red-rimmed eyes fixed on her with an intensity that seemed to burn into her flesh. Then he was rising heavily to his feet, and swinging one leg over the bow before jumping nimbly to the ground. Looking down at him, at his head tilted back and his arms raised to help her down, she had the oddest feeling that the boat was no longer on solid ground, that it was slipping out to sea.

Chapter Sixteen

"That was fun."

Gerry glanced in surprise at Andie in the rearview mirror—no, she wasn't being sarcastic—and smiled. "It was, wasn't it?"

The ache in her chest eased ever so slightly. She would survive. How much could you miss a man you hadn't even known you were in love with until now? Even so, watching him go had been one of the hardest things she'd ever had to do. Would she see him again . . . or be left with only his music? Lazy afternoons lying on the sofa listening to Beethoven while picturing him on a podium somewhere: dreaming aloud of Isabelle.

Tears blurred her vision, sending brilliant star points shooting from her headlights into the darkness on either side of the steep, winding road. She blinked, and everything sharpened back into focus. She saw that they were heading into a hairpin curve and eased up on the accelerator.

"That girl is a Fitzgerald, no doubt about it," said Mavis, buckled in beside her. "She has my mother's light touch. Your great-grandmother," she turned to address the kids, "was famous all over the county. People used to say you hadn't lived until you'd tasted one of Fiona Fitzgerald's currant scones."

Gerry braced herself. *Uh-oh. Here we go again. Another reminder of how the famous Fitzgerald touch skipped over me, and how I can't boil an egg to save my life.*

But Mavis's mind was clearly elsewhere as she gazed out the window, a small re-membering smile on her lips. This wasn't about her, Gerry realized. It was about Claire and the light touch she'd brought to more than just the kitchen. They'd all felt it. Mavis, who was once more fully engaged in the business of living. Justin, except for his little sulk over Aubrey, happier than she'd ever seen him. Even Andie seemed more at ease, though that probably had to do with her being back home. If she still resented Claire, there'd been no sign of it this evening.

"I wonder what Kevin will think when he sees it," Gerry said.

Justin perked up. "Uncle Kevin's coming?"

"For the opening yes." Kevin had confirmed it the other night. "He told me his pastry chef just walked out. I made him promise not to try to steal Claire."

"She wouldn't leave us, would she?" Justin sounded worried.

"Of course not. I'm only kidding." Gerry glanced at him in the rearview mirror, wondering why she felt so sure. Maybe because it was her heart, not her head, telling her.

"I put flyers in all the papers on my route," he said proudly. "I gave Laura the rest to hand out."

Dear Laura, always the first to volunteer for a worthy cause. And after this evening's feast, she'd be able to tout Tea & Sympathy from personal experience as well. A good thing, because Claire would need all the help she could get. Gerry knew from her friend Myrna McBride that even an event promoted to the high heavens could result in a small turnout. On the other hand, if books were food for the soul, they didn't satisfy a sweet tooth. Tea & Sympathy would have The Last Word beat hands down there. Still . . .

"Claire's going to need a lot of help these next few weeks," she said.

"I can come after school," Justin said excitedly. "Except the days I have Little League."

"You'll eat her out of house and home," Andie teased.

Justin shot her a dirty look. "Mom, if Andie moves back in to Dad's, can I have her room?" It was a running argument between them that Andie's room was the bigger of the two.

"Don't be fresh," Mavis scolded, though her heart clearly wasn't in it.

"Your sister's not going anywhere." Gerry sneaked another glance at her daughter. Andie had her window partway down and with the breeze blowing her dark curls about her face, she might have been Merle Oberon in *Wuthering Heights,* poised atop a crag, pining after Heathcliff. Her little girl. When had she grown up?

Andie's eyes met hers in the rearview mirror, her lips curved in an answering smile. No, she wasn't going anywhere, at least not for the time being, though Gerry knew that her days as Andie's caretaker were numbered. The thought made her sad.

"Aunt Sam is getting big," Andie remarked.

"I was even bigger with you," Gerry told her.

"I hope it's a boy." Justin spoke with the wistfulness of someone one player shy of a team.

"How come you're not throwing her a baby shower?" Andie wanted to know.

"She wouldn't let me."

"Why not?"

"Superstition—she was afraid it'd jinx things."

"I seem to recall her having showers when she was expecting Alice and Laura," Mavis said.

"She said it was okay then because she was younger."

"What in heaven's name does that have to do with it?"

Gerry shrugged. "I asked her the same thing. She said I should try having a baby at this age, then I'd know."

Andie's eyes widened in horror. "You *wouldn't.*"

"Not on your life." Gerry laughed. "I'm holding out for grandchildren."

Andie looked panicked for some reason.

"I still think it's a shame," Mavis clucked as they wound their way up Oak Creek Road. Not their usual route—a detour due to construction. "People are so excited about this baby. It's like . . . well, like a sign of something. Hope, I guess. We're all being reminded that it's never too late to start over."

Not everyone shared that enthusiasm. Gerry recalled Marguerite Moore's attempt to oust Sam as president of the music festival committee last year. She'd been voted down unanimously. It seemed Sam had more friends in the community than Marguerite did.

"We'll throw a party afterward," she said. "Though this baby will need more than ten fingers and ten toes for all the stuff you're knitting it, Mom."

Gerry rounded a sharp curve, her headlights illuminating deep skid marks cutting in diagonal slashes across the graveled turnabout just ahead. The guardrail was badly buckled, and the bushes around it broken. An accident, and from the looks of it, a recent one.

Adrenaline sluiced through her in an icy rush, throwing everything into vivid Technicolor clarity. *Sam,* she thought. She and Ian had left a few minutes ahead of them, and would've taken the same route. *Dear God, don't let it be them . . .*

Gerry braked to a stop and jumped out. She caught the sickening smell of burnt rubber and saw streaks of paint on the guardrail. *Red* paint.

Sam's Honda, she recalled, was red.

Her heart tipped over in her chest.

"Mom, what is it?" Andie and Justin spilled out of the backseat.

Gerry waved them back. "Stay put. I'm going to have a look." It was all she could do to keep the panic from her voice.

She peered over the guardrail into the shadowy darkness of the ravine below. At first, all she could make out were bushes and scrub pines, their needles glinting silver in the glow of her headlights. Then she spied it at the bottom of the steep slope: a car lying on its side. The only thing keeping it from plunging into the creek below was the stout tree against which it was wedged. She didn't have to see its make to know it was Sam's.

Gerry's breath left her and her heart

seemed to hang suspended in her chest. Then in a flash she was vaulting over the guardrail, half scrambling, half sliding down the slope.

"Call 911!" she yelled up to the kids, whose faces peered whitely over the guardrail in the stark wash of her headlights.

The darkness seemed to rush up at her as she skidded several more yards in a hail of loose dirt and gravel. A memory surfaced: the fun house at the county fair. She'd talked Sam into going. They'd been what—ten, eleven? Sam, who even then had liked everything lined up and neatly squared, couldn't get out fast enough, but Gerry had loved every minute of it—the undulating floor and zigzagging corridors, the mirrors that made her look fat then thin. Only now it felt as if *she* were the one thrust against her will into a place where nothing made sense, and where none of the corners met.

She cupped her hands around her mouth, calling, "Sam! Ian!"

No answer.

Please, God, don't let them be dead. She thought of the baby due in just two weeks. It wasn't fair. Not after everything they'd been through. They had to be okay, they *had* to be.

Gerry lost her footing and skidded the rest of the way down, catching hold of a low-hanging branch just in time to keep from tumbling over the creek's steep embankment. She landed on her backside with a jolt a few dozen feet from the overturned car—a Honda.

She lost it then, shrieking, *"Sam!"*

The open door to the driver's side was sticking straight up like a hatch, the bushes around it broken and flattened as if someone had crawled out. She clambered onto the sharply angled running board, getting that creepy fun-house feeling again as, holding herself braced with one hand on the door frame and the other on the steering wheel, she peered into the shadowy recesses of the front seat. A figure was slumped against the passenger door at the far end: Sam.

Gerry's mouth went dry and she uttered a small, choked cry that was more of a whimper. She unstuck her tongue from the roof of her mouth long enough to cry, "Sam! *Sam!*"

She heard a groan, but it was coming from behind. Gerry jerked about so suddenly she lost her balance and went tumbling into the dirt below. That was when she saw Ian, several yards away, his right leg cocked at an angle so unnatural it could only have been broken. She crawled over to him.

"Ian?" She touched his face. "Ian, are you all right?" She placed an ear to his chest, and felt it rise and subside. When she lifted her head, she saw that his lips were moving, and bent close to hear.

"Forget . . . me. Take care . . . of . . . Sam." His voice was so faint it might have been air whistling from his lungs. He tried to pull himself upright, then collapsed back with a moan. His jeans below the knee of his painfully twisted leg glimmered darkly with blood. But he was alive. That was all that mattered.

He tried once more to sit up, but she gently forced him back. "Ian, listen to me. The ambulance is on its way. Just . . . don't move . . . *please.* I'll make sure Sam's okay." Her voice, steady and calm, seemed to be coming from somewhere outside her.

He subsided with a grimace, his face the color of chalk. *"Sam . . ."*

Gerry felt as if she were plowing through water, icy and full of treacherous currents, as she crawled back to the overturned Honda, branches tearing at her clothes. *Dear Father in heaven,* she found herself praying. *I know it's a sin for me to ask, but if You have to take someone, let it be the baby. Not Sam. Please, not Sam.*

The Honda rocked slightly with her weight as she climbed back onto it. She looked up to find that several of the branches against which it was wedged had broken off. The low chuckling of the stream suddenly seemed malevolent. She gritted her teeth, resisting the urge to retreat. *If Sam goes, we both go.*

Holding herself braced against the steering wheel, she reached down, her fingers dancing along a limp arm to grasp hold of Sam's wrist. Its warmth traveled through her like an electrical current, and she went dizzy with relief.

"Sam? It's me . . . Gerry."

Sam stirred and blinked up at her uncomprehendingly. "Whuuu . . . ?"

"You were in an accident."

Sam's hand jerked free to cradle her belly. "The baby," she croaked.

"The baby's fine. You're fine." Gerry's voice was a high, thin warble. She felt as if she'd drunk ten cups of coffee on an empty stomach. If she could just keep it up, keep talking, keep from losing it. "Does it feel like anything's broken?"

"I . . . I don't think so." Sam's ashen face contorted suddenly, and she pressed down on her belly. "The baby . . . oh, God . . . "

The world all at once seemed to recede, as if Gerry were looking through the wrong end of a telescope, seeing only the rearview mirror peering up at her like a darkly glittering eye, Sam's purse caught on the gear shift, and Sam's dear face peering up at her out of shadows—a pale cameo in a tarnished setting.

From somewhere deep inside her, she mustered the necessary calm. "Andie called for help. You'll be at the hospital before you know it," she soothed, groping until she found the buckle on Sam's seat belt. The click of its releasing might have been a gun going off in the stillness.

Sam seized her hand. "Where's Ian? Is he all right?"

Gerry pried her fingers loose. "He's a little beat up, but otherwise fine. Don't you worry. You'll both be seeing this baby into the world—a nice, fat healthy baby. This is just a bump in the road, that's all." She smiled grimly at the unintended pun. "Did you think you were going to go about this like any normal person? After the way this baby was conceived? As if having a baby at your age weren't enough, you had to turn it into an episode of *ER*."

Sam managed a weak smile. "Does this mean I get to meet George Clooney?"

"Meet him? He'll be standing in line for *your* autograph." Gerry gave a small, teary laugh.

Sam's face twisted, and she once again seized hold of Gerry's hand, gripping it tight enough to cut off circulation. "I feel something. I . . . I think I'm bleeding."

"Are you sure it's not your water?" Now she *did* hear the panic in her voice.

"P-pretty sure."

"Hang on, kiddo. It'll be any minute now." Where the hell was that ambulance?

Then, blessedly, she heard it: the faint whine of a siren.

Relief washed over Gerry in a cold, clear wave. *Thank you, Lord.* Through the roaring of blood in her ears, she could hear the siren's pulsing wail grow louder.

"Promise me—" Sam broke off with a moan.

"What?"

"Promise you won't let anything happen to the baby. Please, Gerry. You've got to *swear*." Her fingers bit into Gerry's wrist.

If Sam was willing to risk her life for her baby's, Gerry felt torn, unable to reassure her. If it came down to a choice, there was no question in her mind: The idea of life without Sam was unthinkable. On the other hand, Sam had gone through so much for this child, in defiance of all odds. How could Gerry refuse?

From the depths of her being, she summoned the necessary reassurance. "I won't be hearing any such talk. You've made it this far. And boy or girl, that's one hell of a kid. If it's anything like you, it'll be too stubborn to give up." She felt Sam's fingers loosen, and watched her slump back. "The only bad news is, it looks like I'll be your coach after all. And if you think I'm cutting you any slack, forget it. Just try wimping out on me. I'll come down on you so hard you won't know what hit you."

The sky above, in all its magnificent sprawl, seemed to mock her, the thought of Aubrey swooping down like a falling star: his pregnant wife crushed to death in a car wreck. For the first time she truly understood what it must have been like for him.

The thought was driven from her head by the crunch of tires, and headlights panning in an arc overhead. As if on another plane she heard the slam of car doors, followed by the babble of voices—Andie's among them, high and anxious. Light from the ambulance's pulsing dome washed down the slope, tingeing the foliage around her a lurid red, and now she could make out a pair of jumpsuit-clad figures expertly picking their way down the slope, a travois bobbing between them.

She smiled at Sam. "Relax, kiddo. The marines have landed."

Andie waited anxiously for her mother. She could hear the receding voices of the paramedics as they made their way down the slope, along with the faint crackle of their walkie-talkies. A short distance away, Justin squatted before the guardrail like a faithful dog, peering over the edge into the ravine. In the pale gold shaft from the headlights, flying insects darted and spun like fireflies in a jar. Except for the occasional whisper of cars, they were the only things stirring. Even her grandmother sat stoically in the car, though it had to be killing her. It was one of the things Andie loved best about Grandma: She knew when she'd only be in the way.

"See anything?" she hissed at her brother.

Justin turned to glance at her, his baseball cap casting a wedge of shadow over his face. "I think so. Yeah, someone's on the stretcher."

"Who?"

"I can't tell. Aunt Sam, I think."

Andie prayed she'd be okay. The baby, too.

Her mouth filled with a taste like curdled milk. Tonight she'd planned on telling her mother about her period being late. Now this . . .

She suddenly thought of Aubrey's wife dying in that car wreck—she'd been pregnant, too. *Why wasn't I nicer to him?* Remembering the CD he'd given her made her feel twice as bad. Even though she hadn't meant what happened at the wedding, wasn't it partly *her* fault he was leaving?

Andie looked down, almost surprised to see that she was still holding her mother's cell phone. Before she knew it, she was punching in Aubrey's name. Her mom had all her important numbers on speed dial; one of them had to be his. She heard a series of beeps, followed by a faint ringing.

"Aubrey here."

Her heart began to race, and for a moment she was tongue-tied. "Mr. Roellinger? This is Andie . . . Andie Bayliss. Sorry to bother you, but there's been an accident."

"Is it your mother? Is she all right?" His voice seemed to float up from the bottom of a well, so eerily calm that it was a moment before Andie recognized it for what it was: the flip side of panic.

"She's fine. It's . . . it's Sam and Ian. Their car went off the road. I . . . I don't know how bad it is. The ambulance just got here." She drew in a shuddery breath. "My mom can't come to the phone right now. But I . . . I thought she'd want you to know."

"Thank you, Andie. You did the right thing."

She knew there was nothing he could do. He was on his way to the airport, after all. Her father wouldn't have turned back, he'd have phoned later on to see if everything was okay. But if that was all Aubrey could do, it'd be better than nothing.

Just then the paramedics—one burly and long-haired, the other wiry with a crew cut— loomed into view hoisting the travois. Andie's heart nearly stopped when she saw Aunt Sam. She was white as a sheet, cradling her belly as if the canvas straps holding her in place weren't enough to protect it. Andie wanted to run to her, but found she couldn't move. Then Aunt Sam disappeared into the back of the ambulance.

The paramedics headed back down the slope. Hours seemed to go by—though Andie's watch showed that only minutes had passed—before they reappeared carrying Ian. His face was contorted in agony, and the blanket covering him from the chest down stained with blood. When the travois tipped sideways and he cried out in pain, the burly man squeezed his shoulder and said, "Sorry, buddy. I know it hurts like hell." Minutes later the ambulance was tearing off down the road, dome light flashing and siren wailing.

It wasn't until her mother surfaced at last, pale and disheveled with a scratch on one cheek, that Andie came unglued. She threw herself into her mother's arms, and Gerry clutched her as if she, too, would have drowned otherwise.

"Is Aunt Sam going to be okay?"

"She'll be fine." But her mom didn't sound convinced.

"Ian, too?" Justin wanted to know.

Gerry drew back with a smile that looked carved into her face. "Nothing a little plaster won't fix." Justin trotted over, and she pulled him into a three-way embrace. "Come on, guys, let's get going. We have a long night ahead of us."

A moment later they were in the car, racing toward the hospital.

Aubrey settled back, staring out the window at the gray river of the freeway rushing past while he seemed to sit motionless, a rock amid the swirling eddies of light. He felt a stillness come over him, a kind of clarity he hadn't felt in years. *All this time I've been running,* he thought, *I've only been going in circles.*

Now he collided with the memory full force.

She'd been wearing a yellow dress that day, the one he'd brought her from New York. It had tiny polka dots and a ruffled neckline, which had made Isabelle laugh when she tried it on.

"I look like I belong in a Henry James novel," she'd said, twirling this way and that in front of the mirror.

"You look like you."

He'd caught her and pulled her against him. She smelled faintly of perfume, something light and floral, and even more faintly of the Gauloises she'd been after him to stop smoking, though he indulged only on occasion. It had been only a few days, but he'd missed her. *No more out-of-town dates until the baby comes.* It was the same promise he made every time, then there was always one more he couldn't get out of, and another after that. Tonight's concert, at least, was at the Music Center.

"Does it make me look pregnant?" she'd asked.

"Darling, nothing could disguise the fact that you're pregnant." She was seven months along, and gloriously in bloom. With her blond hair coiled loosely in back, she made him think of a ripe peach—a particularly juicy one. He nibbled on her neck.

"You know what I mean." Did it make her look fat and ugly? As if anything ever could. She swiveled about in his arms as lightly as a ballerina. "Aubrey, let's go out tonight. I have a sudden craving for escargots swimming in butter."

"We can't. I have the Music Center tonight," he reminded her. They were doing Haydn's Symphony no. 88 in G, a particularly buoyant piece of work, too cheerful for his taste. Give him the melancholy of Beethoven's Fifth any day.

She'd looked bereft. Not so much because they wouldn't be going out, or because she'd be spending yet another evening alone, but because she wanted to be onstage, too. Poor Isabelle. She missed performing the way a race horse cooped in its stall misses the track. If her doctor hadn't insisted that the rigors of a tour would be too much at this stage in what had been a rocky pregnancy, nothing would have stopped her. She eyed her music stand in the corner as longingly as she might have a lover.

"I'll go with you then," she said.

Aubrey glanced out the window. It was pouring—the kind of deluge rarely seen in Southern California, and a reminder that mother nature always had the last laugh. Don't get too complacent, or an earthquake will come along, knocking you and your neighbors down like so many bowling pins; grow cocky and the Santa Ana winds will whip up a brush fire and send its flames racing across your path.

"You'll catch cold," he said.

Isabelle laughed. She knew he didn't take

her little ailments seriously. Hadn't he said so time and again? "I'll wear a slicker. I'll look like Pancho Villa."

He shook his head, partly in amusement, pulling her close once more and burying his face in her hair. Had he sensed then, in some deep part of him, that he would need to take in as much of her while he could, store her scent like a madman stockpiling for the imminent destruction of the world?

"I'll have Gordon take you." He'd send this driver back to pick her up.

"If there's traffic, he'll be hours." She tilted her head, her smile that of a beautiful woman used to getting her way who could afford to give in once in a while. "You win. I'll stay home."

He loved the curve of her neck. Her skin was like pearls; it shimmered, giving off a soft light all its own. All the years they'd tried for a baby, he'd wondered if the gods were denying them for the simple reason that they had too much already. Wasn't it greedy to want more? Not until later would he know it was the gods who were greedy; they'd wanted her all to themselves.

His baton had come down on the final chords of Schubert's *Unfinished,* the second of the two orchestral works on the program that night, and, in retrospect, a particularly rich piece of irony, when he received the call backstage. He remembered only snatches of it. Isabelle hurt . . . car totaled. If Gordon hadn't been at the wheel, he'd have ended up in the hospital himself . . . or at the bottom of the cliff. On the other hand, if he'd insisted on sending his driver back to pick her up, if she hadn't been foolhardy enough to drive herself none of this would have happened.

She was dead by the time he got there; he was told she'd died at the scene. Why, he wondered, do messengers of death feel the need to forestall such news? Could they possibly imagine that receiving it in bits and pieces, like shrapnel, was better than being blown up all at once?

In the elevator, on the way down to the morgue, a blessed numbness had come over him. What got him through the ordeal was knowing it wasn't really happening, in the morning he would wake up to find it had all been a terrible dream. How could that cold, blue thing on the table be Isabelle, who'd shone brighter than the sun? He'd touched her hair. It was long and fine, the color of strong ale. He wound it about his fingers. It seemed alive, clutching at him, cutting off his circulation until he was forced to let it slip from his grasp.

He calmly asked the medical examiner, a far too hearty-looking older man, for a pair of scissors. The man looked at Aubrey pityingly, as if suspecting he'd gone mad. Aubrey wished it were so, for insanity would have been a welcome reprieve from the torment he was soon to face. Scissors in hand, he snipped several strands and carefully coiled them before tucking them in his pocket. The man asked kindly if he wanted to see his baby. He declined. For him to do so, even in death, when Isabelle had been denied that joy, would have been grossly unfair. He tried to imagine her in heaven with their child—a son, he'd been told—but found he no longer believed in heaven. In fact, he no longer believed in God.

Days later, as he knelt at her grave, it wasn't to God he spoke, but to Isabelle. They were the last words he would ever speak aloud to his wife. *Je t'aime.* I love you. Now and forever. There will never be another to take your place.

And there hadn't been, until now. Were

Gerry anything at all like Isabelle, he'd have guarded against her fiercely. Yet gradually, almost without his being aware of it, she had crept past his defenses. Until one day he'd realized he was in love with her. The thought terrified him. How could he love this woman without letting go of Isabelle? Gerry wasn't the type to take a backseat. Gerry, with her animated gestures and bawdy laugh, who filled a room merely by walking into it. By her very nature she cast a shadow in which his wife's memory would wilt like a plant robbed of sunlight. It wasn't until tonight, when he'd kissed Gerry good-bye, that he'd realized he was killing any chance with the one woman since Isabelle who'd made him feel alive.

Stirring as if from a deep sleep, Aubrey brought a hand to his cheek and found that it was wet. He found himself remembering a letter Debussy had penned while composing *La Mer.* He'd written of the sea, *I have an endless store of memories, and to my mind, they are worth more than reality, whose beauty often deadens the thought.*

That's what he'd done—prized his memories over life itself. Like the music with which Debussy had captured the essence of the sea, he'd transformed something fluid into a beautiful score of fixed notes and measured tempo.

Aubrey tapped on the glass divider, and waited what seemed an eternity for it to slide open. "Take the next exit," he ordered. All he could see of the driver was the neatly clipped hair on the back of his head and a pair of mildly curious eyes in the rearview mirror.

"Sir?"

"We're going back to Carson Springs."

They arrived at the hospital without running any red lights, where the woman at the desk in the ER informed them that Mrs. Kiley was upstairs in Maternity. As they rode the elevator up, it occurred to Gerry that she hadn't been to that floor since Andie and Justin were born. She glanced at them now, Justin with an arm about his grandmother, and Andie with hers crossed over her chest. Gerry couldn't think of any two adults who'd have been more cool-headed in the face of such an ordeal, and had never been prouder.

The doors thumped open, and Gerry strode over to the nurses' station. "I'm looking for Mrs. Kiley," she said to an older gray-haired nurse built like the USS *Constitution.*

The woman consulted a chart. "Mrs. Kiley? I see here that she's on her way into Delivery. Why don't you take a seat? I'll keep you posted." She smiled pleasantly, waving in the direction of the patients' lounge just down the hall.

"You don't understand. I'm her coach."

The nurse glanced once more at the chart. "Well, in that case, she won't be needing you. I see here she's scheduled for a C-section."

Gerry struggled to maintain her composure. "Is Doctor Rosario here?"

The nurse pointed down the corridor, where Gerry caught sight of Inez Rosario, in green scrubs, consulting with one of the residents, a young man who didn't look old enough to wipe a baby's bottom much less deliver one. Thank God, Inez had made it in time. Gerry motioned to her mother and kids to wait in the lounge, then hurried over.

"Inez, you have no idea how glad I am to see you."

Sam's OB had delivered Andie and Justin, and just the sight of her now, her crisp iron hair and firm, no-nonsense manner, inspired confidence. Inez broke away from the resident, gesturing for Gerry to join her as she strode off down the hall. "Sam was lucky," she said. "A few bruised ribs, a mild concussion—but the baby seems to be in some distress."

Gerry's heart bumped up into her throat. "I don't want her to go through this alone."

Inez paused to eye her thoughtfully. "Ordinarily, only fathers are allowed in for C-sections," she said. "But I suppose we could make an exception in this case." Her brown eyes searched Gerry's, communicating the need for absolute calm.

If she hadn't looked so stern, Gerry would have kissed her. "Is Ian going to be all right?"

"It looks to be a multiple fracture, so I don't know how soon he'll be up and about. The good news is he'll be spared walking the floor at two a.m." Inez allowed herself a tiny smile. They'd reached the double doors to the OR, and Gerry followed her into the prep area with its rows of sinks. "And here's the kicker—the orthopedist told me he kept on insisting his leg could wait, that he needed to be with Sam. That is one determined father-to-be."

"You don't know the half of it."

Gerry thought of the way he'd fussed over

Sam like an Italian grandmother, nagging her to put her feet up, and tempting her with delicacies, like the pomegranates she craved. For all those doubting Thomases who'd once pegged him as footloose, Ian had proved them spectacularly wrong.

Minutes later, garbed in a mask and gown, Gerry was peering down into Sam's pale, anxious face. A kind of tent had been erected over the table on which she lay, shielding her lower half from view. Her hair was tucked under a cap like the one Gerry had on, and she was reminded of when they'd been in high school primping for dates. Right now, Sam looked all of sixteen.

"I wasn't sure you'd get here in time," she said weakly.

Gerry took her hand and squeezed it. "What good is an understudy who can't go on when the leading man breaks a leg?"

On the other side of the tent, doctors and nurses flitted in and out of view. A monitor beeped and instruments clattered against a tray. Inez, quietly issuing orders, might have been speaking Swahili for all Gerry knew. She didn't pry her eyes away from Sam until a nurse popped her head in to announce that Dr. Steinberg was on her way.

"Thank God, it's Dorothy," she heard Inez mutter.

Gerry recalled that Dorothy Steinberg, an old friend of Mavis's who had to be pushing the envelope as far as retirement was concerned, was the chief neonatologist here at Community. The baby would be in good hands. Even so, she said a little prayer.

She looked back at Sam to find her eyes swimming with tears. "I can't lose this baby," she said hoarsely. Sam, the bravest woman she knew, didn't look so brave right now.

"Hush. What a thing to say," Gerry scolded, only mildly taken aback to hear her mother's voice emerge from her mouth. "You're both going to be just fine."

"I know I didn't want it in the beginning." Sam's chin began to tremble, and a tear slipped down one temple. "Do you think God is punishing me?"

"God doesn't punish you for thoughts. And no one is as good or loving a mother." Gerry started to take a swipe at her own brimming eyes before remembering she was wearing gloves. "Dammit. *Now* look what you made me do. And here I was, saving my tears for the christening."

She was rewarded by the faintest whisper of a smile.

On the other side of the tented sheet, Gerry heard Inez instruct briskly, "Okay . . . we're cutting through the fascia . . . let's have some suction."

Sam gripped her hand. "I don't feel it. I don't feel a *thing*. Just . . . pressure. How do I know if he's okay?"

"I'll bet you ten dollars it's a girl."

"You're on."

They fell silent, gripped by the awesomeness of it all, then Inez announced with reassuring authority, "We're cutting through the amniotic sac now . . . I've got the head . . . okay, now a shoulder." She paused. "Oh, my goodness, it's a boy!"

"A boy." Sam's voice was soft with wonder.

Gerry grinned. "Looks like I'm out ten bucks."

They waited for the familiar sound that would put all their fears to rest, and when it didn't come, Sam stared at the sheet as if she could burn a hole through it.

"He's not crying. What's happening? Is he all right?" Her voice rose on a high, panicked note.

Gerry was worried, too, but she patted Sam's shoulder. "Relax. Inez knows what she's doing." Though admittedly Andie's and Justin's births had been a Sunday walk in the park compared to this.

Not like your first one.

A memory surfaced. Then suddenly, in her mind, she was being whisked down a corridor on a gurney. The pains no longer coming in waves, but gripping like a giant fist. She cried out that she felt sick, but the nurse at her side merely smiled and said it would all be over soon. She didn't understand what Gerry was telling her. When she *did* throw up, the beady-eyed woman looked annoyed.

"Where's my mother? I want my mother!" Gerry cried with the anguish of a girl barely out of her teens who'd never known sickness without Mavis's bending over her with a cool cloth and soothing hand.

"Your mother is in the waiting room," she was informed. "Now be a good girl, and stop making such a fuss."

When Gerry opened her mouth, an anguished howl emerged. The pain had ascended to new heights, not just gripping but *tearing* at her from the inside out.

A set of double doors swung open, and the gurney bumped over a threshold. A man's face, its lower half obscured from view by the mask he wore, loomed into view. All she could see were a pair of bright blue eyes netted in wrinkles and bushy white-blond brows. "How are we doing, Miss Fitzgerald, hmm?" His lips moving beneath the mask made her think of Boris Karloff in *The Mummy.*

"Who are you?" she croaked.

"Doctor DeCordillera is out of town," she was told. "I'm Doctor Perault."

Gerry shook her head. No, she didn't want some stranger. But no one seemed to care what she wanted. She was lifted onto a table and her feet placed in stirrups. Something cold was swabbed over her privates, which in the past twelve hours had come to seem like public property instead—poked and prodded and shaved, and now mercilessly on view.

It soon ceased to matter, though, for the area between her legs might have been the burning gates of hell. She writhed and screamed and begged, but God took no pity. That's when she knew for certain that He was punishing her.

"Push." The command was muffled by the roaring in her ears. "Give us a big push now. Good. Now one more. You're doing fine. Take a deep breath. Okay, again. PUSH!"

"I can't!" she screamed, feeling as if she were being split right down the middle, a ripe avocado from which the baby would be scooped like a pit.

But somehow she *was* pushing. Grunting and heaving like an animal all the while. Something warm slipped out between her legs, and the pain abruptly eased. She fell back gasping. A baby was crying, but with the sweat that was pouring down her forehead into her eyes she couldn't see it—only a blur of limbs, a thatch of whorled hair.

"A girl!" she heard a voice crow.

She held out her arms. "Let me hold her."

A swaddled bundle was placed in her arms, a pair of blue eyes peering up at her intently. A great love welled up inside her, and she instantly forgot the torment she'd been through. She watched the little rosebud mouth purse as if in anticipation of being fed, and felt an answering tingle in her breasts.

Abruptly, the baby was taken from her.

"It's better this way," she was told. In her mask and gown, the woman might have been a thief robbing Gerry of all she held dear.

"No . . . wait." Gerry started to say she'd changed her mind. How could she have known what she'd be giving up? But it was too late. The nurse, along with her baby, was gone.

A hole had opened in her chest then, and black wind came whistling through. She began to weep, and for the longest time it seemed she would never run out of tears. She wept for hours and hours, beyond all consolation, until she'd exhausted herself enough to fall into a deep sleep that was more like unconsciousness.

"What's wrong? Why isn't he crying?"

Gerry was jerked back into the present by Sam's anxious voice. She stepped out from behind the tented sheet to see for herself. What met her gaze alarmed her even more—Inez and Dr. Steinberg hunched over the table on which the baby lay, working frantically to get him to breathe. "They're suctioning him," she reported back. She didn't tell Sam how limp and blue he'd looked, and was glad for the mask partially covering her face. Sam had always been able to read her like a book.

"What's taking so long?" Sam looked like an animal desperate to reach her young. "Is something the matter with him? He's not . . ." She couldn't bring herself to say it.

Gerry had run out of reassurances. All she could do was stand there squeezing Sam's hand and hoping for the best. Where was God when you needed Him most? Hiding out like all the other men who'd let her down, leaving women to do the dirty work.

Just when she'd begun to think the worst, it came: a baby's cry. Loud and lusty and pissed off as hell.

Sam let out a whoop of joy. Gerry released the breath she hadn't realized she was holding. Inez Rosario exclaimed, "Listen to that set of lungs! You won't be getting much sleep with this one." She stepped into view, her warm brown eyes crinkled above her mask. In her arms was a bundle wrapped in a white receiving blanket.

"Sam, meet your son." Gently, she lowered him onto Sam's chest while a nurse propped her up with a pillow.

Gerry didn't know who started it, her or Sam, but all at once they were both bawling.

"He's beautiful," Sam choked, tracing a finger over the back of his head, with its tufts of damp hair like kitten's fur. His skull was perfectly formed, one of the perks of not having come into the world the hard way. "He looks like his dad."

Gerry wiped her eyes. "He's got the Delarosa chin."

"I wish Ian were here."

"He will be soon enough." Gerry half expected him to come bursting through the double doors in a wheelchair any minute.

Sam relinquished the baby to her while they finished stitching her up. "Don't worry. You'll get him back," Gerry promised, noting the hungry way she tracked him with her eyes.

She looked down at the baby nestled in her arms, and the memory once more came flooding back. Only this time it didn't hurt. She felt as if in some ways she'd come full circle. Her daughter *had* come back . . . just not the way she'd imagined.

Then, like a wave rolling out to sea, the fullness in her heart receded, leaving it bare and glistening like a shell. She thought of Aubrey, who might have been right for her if the circumstances hadn't been so wrong. Would he miss her in the months to come? Would he wonder what might have been?

Gerry pushed the thought away. She'd have enough on her mind, looking for a job, without obsessing about her love life.

"I should put Mom and the kids out of their misery," she said when the baby was once more ensconced in Sam's arms. They'd be frantic with worry, fearing the worst.

"Mmm . . . yes." Sam wasn't listening. She was too besotted with the new man in her life.

As Gerry made her way down the corridor, she had to concentrate in order to navigate a straight course. Her legs felt wobbly and her head seemed to float several inches above her neck. Anyone looking at her in her scrubs might have mistaken her for a doctor coming out of a long, complicated surgery.

She spotted a familiar figure up ahead, chatting with Mavis and the kids, and froze. Aubrey. What on earth was *he* doing here? Shouldn't he have been on his way to Brussels by now? Too dazed to think straight, she floated the rest of the way down the corridor. The only thing she was aware of was the bubble of warmth expanding in her chest, filling her with a giddy joy.

He rose to greet her. "Everything okay?"

"It's a boy." Gerry turned to Mavis and the

kids, seated on the sofa eyeing her anxiously. "He's a little on the small side, but with a pair of lungs you wouldn't believe."

"Jesus, Mary, and Joseph." Mavis made the sign of the cross. "That's fifty rosaries I owe."

"Can we see him?" Andie wanted to know.

"You can even hold him . . . that is, if you can pry him away from Aunt Sam." Gerry smiled. "She's like a mother tiger with her cub."

Justin grinned. "A boy. *Awesome.*"

"A few more and we'll have our own team," Aubrey teased.

Gerry looked at him in happy confusion. She was scarcely aware of her feet touching the ground. All she knew was that she'd never been so glad to see someone.

"How did you know to come?"

"I called him." There was a note of defiance in Andie's voice.

Aubrey smiled at her. "A wise decision, I might add."

"But your flight . . ." The sentence trailed off. Gerry couldn't think straight with Aubrey looking at her that way—as if it had been months, not hours, since he'd last seen her.

"Never mind my flight." His tone made it clear it was the furthest thing from his mind.

She met his gaze. Something had changed. He was studying her with an unsmiling frankness that was disturbing—and at the same time exhilarating. She thought of what it must have taken for him to come, the painful memories it had to have unearthed. Another man would have kept on going. The simple courage of it was overwhelming.

She groped for something familiar, something that would anchor her against this feeling that was about to come untethered, and found it in her old bantering lightness. "Well, since you've come all this way, the least I can do is buy you a cup of coffee."

"You two go on. I'll stay with the kids," Mavis urged. When Justin opened his mouth to protest, she shot him a stern look. His mouth snapped shut.

They found their way to the cafeteria on the second floor. Gerry remembered from the last time she was here, the year Andie had had her tonsils out, that the coffee was terrible. It hadn't improved in the intervening years. She took a sip and set it down to stir in another packet of sugar.

"It was good of you to come," she told him. "You didn't have to."

"Because you're strong enough to bear

the weight of the world on your own?" He spoke lightly, but his expression was serious. "I didn't come because Andie asked. I came because I had to."

"Why?"

"Let's just say I had some old business to settle."

Gerry tensed. Was he here because of Isabelle? Because of some need to put his demons to rest? "What will you tell them in Brussels?"

He shrugged. "That it's taking a bit longer than expected to wrap things up."

She felt the warmth expanding in her contract suddenly. Was that what she was, an item on his agenda to be wrapped up?

But when she looked into his eyes, it wasn't Isabelle she saw. Suddenly, she had trouble catching her breath.

"I'm not putting it very eloquently, am I?" he went on, smiling. "What I'm trying to say is that I may have made a mistake."

Gerry's heart was pounding so hard she could feel it in her cheeks, a steady hot pulsing. On this night of surprises, was she up for one more? "About me? Or leaving in general?"

"Both," he said.

She frowned. "I need you to be a little more specific."

A man nursing a cup of coffee at the next table glanced over at them with disinterest. His eyes were blank, and his jaw stubbled as if he hadn't slept in days. When she brought her gaze back to Aubrey, his eyes were the opposite—so full of raw emotion she could hardly bear to look into them.

"I realized something tonight—that I've been a fool," he said. "I imagined that if I let myself love you, I'd somehow be erasing Isabelle. But it doesn't work that way, does it?"

"You're not the only one to blame."

"Then maybe it's time we both took another look." He gestured in a way that made her think of how he looked when he was conducting, the way he'd seem to pluck a note from midair, as delicately as he might have a butterfly. "Tonight, on the way here, I was reminded of something I'd forgotten—that great music often comes from great sorrow." He smiled sadly. "I'm better for having loved Isabelle. Just as I am for loving you."

Gerry couldn't bring herself to move or even speak. She wanted to say the words beating in her head to the rhythm of her pounding heart: *IloveyouIloveyou Iloveyou.*

But something was stopping her. At last she gave up and said with a crooked smile, "We're a fine pair, aren't we?"

Aubrey reached up to tuck a stray wisp behind her ear, waiting for her to go on.

"I was thinking of Sam just now," she said. "When Martin died, she didn't expect to fall in love, but I wasn't at all surprised when she did. She's built to be a wife and mother." She idly stirred her coffee. "Me? I wasn't much of a wife, and aside from the fact that I'm crazy about my kids, I'm not even sure I'm much of a mother."

"I doubt your children share that opinion."

"What about you?" She eyed him cautiously. "Don't you want kids?"

"They wouldn't have to be mine."

Gerry felt a seed crack open inside her and send out a pale tendril. She'd always gone her own way, and had paid the price in having to shoulder the entire burden. Now here was Aubrey offering what no man before him had been able to provide: enough love to go around. Her eyes filled with tears and she angrily brushed them away.

However much she might want to, she wasn't ready to trust.

"Speaking of which, I should go see what

mine are up to." She pushed herself to her feet.

In the lounge, they found Andie and Justin sipping sodas and watching a *Seinfeld* rerun on TV. "Grandma's with Aunt Sam," Andie informed them.

"We saw the baby through the window." Justin sounded vaguely disappointed. It would be a long while before Sam's baby was old enough to be of much interest.

"I think he looks like Aunt Sam," Andie observed.

"He looks more like Ian," Justin disagreed.

"I think he looks like both." Gerry didn't have the energy to light a match, much less mediate one of their squabbles. But looking at them—Justin with his head resting close enough for Andie's hair to tickle his cheek—she thought that maybe she hadn't done such a bad job of raising them after all.

Which reminded her of Claire. She should phone and let her know what had happened. But the enormity of it all piled on her all at once, and she sank down in the nearest chair as abruptly as if a karate chop had been delivered to the backs of her knees. "I don't know about you guys," she said, "but if

I'm not home in the next half hour, you'll have to check *me* in."

Aubrey bent down, offering her his arm. "My car's waiting downstairs."

Gerry opened her mouth to decline, she couldn't just leave hers in the parking lot, when Justin popped up off the sofa, crowing, "Oh boy, we get to ride in a limo! Wait'll I tell Nesto."

"Why don't you call him from the car?" Aubrey suggested man to man. "It has a bit more cachet than having him hear about it after the fact, don't you think?"

Justin looked up at him and grinned. "Awesome."

"I'll get Grandma," Andie set off down the hall in search of Mavis, and was back moments later with her grandmother in tow.

Then they were all trooping off toward the elevator. When the doors thumped open and they stepped inside, Gerry had the strangest feeling it was going up instead of down.

Chapter Seventeen

Andie was going over the list of doctors Finch had e-mailed her when she felt the first cramp. She rushed into the bathroom and locked the door. *Please, God, let it be what I think it is. I swear I'll go to mass every Sunday for the rest of my life.* With trembling hands, she unzipped her jeans.

There it was, a streak of blood on her panties.

A wave of relief swept over her, and she sank down on the toilet seat, grabbing a towel off the rack to muffle the sob that escaped her. It wasn't until this very minute that she realized how scared she'd been. For if she *had* been pregnant, she wouldn't have been able to go through with an abortion. At the same time, she hadn't seen a way to keep it.

Like with Claire. Would her life have been any better if Gerry had kept *her* . . . or just different? It came to Andie then that very few decisions in life were 100 percent right or wrong. Claire's parents might have been the best ones to raise her, just as Gerry was best for her now. And if the family Andie had grown up in had morphed into something she hardly recognized these days—with different players and a whole new set of rules—it had started long before Claire.

The first time Andie had held Aunt Sam's baby, a little more than a week ago, she'd realized, too, how perfect it could be when everything was in place. On the birth certificate he was listed as Jacinto Wesley Carpenter, after both his grandfathers, but they were calling him Jack for short. The only boy in a family of women, he already had them twisted about his little finger with those blue, blue eyes and dimpled cheeks. Aunt Sam couldn't take her eyes off him, and Laura couldn't stop cooing. Even the coolly elegant Alice wasn't above making goo-goo noises.

And when he'd started to cry and wouldn't stop, it had been Grandma who'd put him over her knees and patted him until he let out a loud burp.

When it was her turn, Andie had cradled him as if he were made of spun sugar. He'd looked so small, though the tiny fist clutching her finger was surprisingly strong. The thing that had struck her most was the trust with which he'd gazed up at her. He didn't know yet what it was to be hurt; he hadn't learned that it was often the people who are supposed to protect you that you have to watch out for most.

She'd wondered then what it would be like to give up her own baby. In that moment she'd understood the sacrifice her mother had made—not a heartless act, but probably the hardest thing she'd ever had to do.

Andie rose on shaky legs. She couldn't wait to tell Simon. Finch, too. They'd be so relieved.

She fished a tampon from under the sink, smiling at the thought of how she used to hate her period. Her grandmother had told her that in her day it was known as a woman's "friend." Now Andie understood.

Tearing the wrapper from the Tampax was like opening the best present in the world.

Justin chose that moment to begin hammering on the door, whining, "Come on, I have to *go*! You're not the only one in this house, you know!"

She caught a glimpse of herself in the medicine cabinet mirror, cheeks flushed, grinning like a fool. She was careful to rearrange her features into a scowl before opening the door.

Her brother scowled back. "What *took* so long?"

"I'm a girl," she informed him loftily, as if no other explanation were necessary. "Why didn't you use Mom's bathroom?"

"She's in the shower."

"Face it, you're outnumbered." She took pleasure in reminding him that he was in the minority here.

"I liked it better when you were at Dad's," he grumbled, but she knew he didn't mean it. This past week he'd been nicer than usual, the other day even loaning her his Discman.

Andie brushed past him into the hallway. "I'm surprised you even noticed I was gone. You're always at Nesto's."

"Not *always.*" He grinned, looking smug.

"Okay, so you spent a day at Aubrey's. Big deal." Last Saturday Aubrey had had Justin and Nesto over, and her brother hadn't stopped talking about it since.

"That wasn't all. We went to a movie and had banana splits."

"I thought you had to use the bathroom," she said, her eyes narrowing.

"I do." He pushed past her, and slammed the door.

Andie raced into the living room and snatched up the phone. Simon answered on the second ring.

"Winthrop, Winthrop, and Winthrop. How may I direct your call?" His standard line, yet she found herself grinning as if it were the first time she'd heard it.

"Customer service, please," she played along.

"Sorry, all lines are busy."

She dropped the pretense. "Simon, you won't believe this but—"

"Great minds think alike," he broke in. "I was just about to call *you.*"

"You were?"

"There's something I want to show you."

"What?"

"It's a surprise."

"Give me a hint at least."

"You'll know soon enough. I'll pick you up in half an hour." Typically, he hadn't bothered to ask if she was busy.

When he beeped his horn in the driveway, her mother was still getting dressed for her date with Aubrey and Justin had left for Nesto's. She called good-bye to her mother through her bedroom door and headed outside.

"You missed yesterday's excitement," she told him as they rattled their way down the quiet street. "Mom picked up Sam and Ian from the hospital. She said it was funny seeing them both come out in wheelchairs."

"They're lucky to be alive. Did you ever find out what caused the accident?"

"A deer. Ian swerved to keep from hitting it." With all the excitement, the story hadn't come out until the following day.

"It could've been a lot worse."

She didn't need Simon to tell her. "My grandmother's convinced guardian angels were watching over them."

"That's crap," he said good-naturedly.

"You don't know that for a fact." Simon claimed to be an atheist, but she thought it was only because he had a hard time believing in any kind of father figure, even God.

"You don't know for a fact there are such things, either."

"No one does."

"I rest my case."

He made the turn onto Hibiscus, where Mrs. Crawford's house had been decorated for Easter weeks in advance. She'd been the kindergarten teacher at Portola Elementary for about a hundred years, and had only recently retired. Now in her eighties, she was like a five-year-old herself, plastering her front window with decals and construction paper cutouts every holiday season. Right now it was decked in Kleenex roses and baby chicks made from Popsicle sticks and fat colored yarn.

"So what's this thing you want to show me?" she asked.

"You'll see." He smiled mysteriously.

They passed the vacant lot where Andie and her best friend in elementary school, Amy Snow, had fashioned jumps out of old mop handles and broomsticks, pretending to be horses as they whinnied their way around the course. Then Simon was turning up the hill toward school.

He drew to a stop in front of the administration building, which looked to be deserted except for a janitor trundling his cart along the adjoining breezeway. Simon jingled his key ring as he plucked it from the ignition, giving her a meaningful look. Leave it to him to have the key. He'd probably gotten it from the principal himself, who considered Simon to be practically one of the faculty.

Inside, he led the way upstairs to the headquarters of the *Scribe,* where he motioned toward the chair by his desk. "Have a seat." He unlocked the top drawer and pulled out a minirecorder. "Remember last week when I took that little trip up north?"

"Monica's friend from Stanford?" Simon had missed two days of school.

He nodded, inserting a tape. "While I was in the neighborhood, I paid someone else a visit, too."

"Who?" She was in no mood for guessing games. "Simon, will you please—"

He pressed the play button. At first there was only the hissing of blank tape, then came Simon's voice. *"Okay. Got it. First time I've used this thing . . . sorry. I'm a little ner-*

vous." He sounded like a bumbling sixth grader, which she knew to be an act. What on earth was going on?

A man's low chuckle. *"Relax, son. We all have to start somewhere."* A pause. *"Now, if you'll refresh my memory, which school did you say you were from?"*

"Portola High, sir."

"Father, please. That doesn't sound like a Catholic school."

"It isn't . . . uh, Father."

"In that case, I don't know that anything I say will be of interest to your fellow students."

"Actually, uh, this isn't for the school paper." Simon's tone grew bolder. *Did I forget to mention I also moonlight as a freelancer?"*

"Really? Anything I would have seen? The voice was amused.

"There was a piece on Monica Vincent in last Thursday's Chronicle. *That was mine. It was picked up from our local paper by UPI. Not bad for my first time out, huh?"*

"I still don't see what this has to do with the archdiocese." A note of strain had crept into the voice that could belong to none other than Claire's father.

"I'm getting to that," Simon went on. *"You*

see, I'm doing this story on our local con-
vent, Our Lady of the Wayside. It started out
as a human interest piece, but when I dug a
little deeper I saw there was more to it than
that."

"I see. How so?"

"There's this woman, Gerry Fitzgerald,
who runs their beekeeping operation. Well,
anyway, her daughter's a friend of mine and
she told me an interesting story: A long time
ago her mom was a nun, but had to leave
the convent when she found out she was
pregnant." Pause. *"Father, are you okay?*
You look a little pale."

The rumble of a throat being cleared. *"N-*
no, I'm all right. You were saying?"

"Yeah, well, according to my friend, the fa-
ther of that baby was you."

A moment of silence, then came a choked
cry. *"How dare you!"* He struggled to catch
his breath. *"Get out. Now. Before I call the*
police and have you charged with . . . with
impersonating a . . . a . . ."

"A reporter?" Andie pictured Simon smiling. *"Father, with all due respect, I only*
wanted to get your side of the story. I mean,
you never know, one of the wire services

might pick it up, and if it goes national, I'd hate not having all the facts straight."

"Get out. Get out of my office! Or I'll—"

"You'll what?" All at once Simon was his hard-nosed self. *"Get the poor woman fired? Oh yeah, I heard about that, too. How does this headline sound?* PRIEST FATHERS BABY WITH FORMER NUN. *It has a nice ring to it, don't you think? I also have an interview lined up with your daughter."*

"What do you want from me?" All the anger had gone out of the man's voice. He sounded frightened.

"I told you. I'm doing this for—"

"She sent you, didn't she?"

"Ms. Fitzgerald? She doesn't even know I'm here." That was the truth, at least.

"I didn't believe it when she threatened me, but—" He broke off suddenly. *"She's out to get me."*

"Forgive me, Father, but it sounds like it's the other way—"

He was abruptly cut off.

Simon, perched on the edge of his desk, thumbed the STOP button.

For a long moment, Andie just sat there, staring at the recorder as if hypnotized.

"You're not mad at me, are you?" Simon asked.

"Mad?" She blinked, and looked up at him. "That was amazing."

Simon grinned. "I wish you could've seen it—he crumbled like day-old bread. I felt a little bad for the guy."

"My grandmother was right. She said you had moxie to burn." Andie was grinning, too. "My, God, Simon—blackmailing a priest. It could just as easily have backfired." She hadn't imagined anything like this when she'd confided in him.

"The point is, it didn't."

"You could've been arrested or . . . or gone to hell."

"I don't believe in hell, remember."

"Still . . ."

"Look, it worked. Isn't that all that matters? I made him promise to back off in exchange for killing the piece."

"You weren't really going to do it, were you?"

"No, but he didn't have to know that, did he?" Simon looked so pleased with himself, she had no doubt he *would* one day win the Pulitzer Prize.

"If my mother ever finds out, she'll be pissed." Gerry preferred to fight her own battles.

"In that case, what she doesn't know won't hurt her." He took hold of Andie's hand, bringing it to his lips. His eyes behind the smudged lenses of his glasses were large as he peered at her over his knuckles. "Which reminds me, I got the name of a doctor—Monica's."

"You told *Monica*?"

He lowered her hand. "Relax. I didn't tell her who it was for."

The tape of Father Gallagher had temporarily eclipsed her own good news, but now it came bubbling to the surface. "Actually, that's what I wanted to talk to you ab—"

"Don't worry. I have some money saved up. No one has to know."

"Simon, I—"

"It'll be all right, I promise." The tender concern in his face was almost enough to make her cry.

"I'm not pregnant," she managed to blurt at last.

He rocked back, stunned, a goofy look of relief dawning on his face. He hopped down off the desk, seizing her by the hands and pulling her to her feet. "Why didn't you *tell* me? All this time I've been going on and on . . . when did you find out?"

"A little while ago."

"You're sure?"

"Positive."

He raked a hand through his hair, making it stand up in a rooster comb. "That's great. I mean, wow, that's . . . *great.*" For once in his life, Simon was at a loss for words.

He pulled her into his arms and kissed her. If this were a TV movie, she thought, the violins would be playing, but it wasn't, and when Simon drew back to look at her, the only sound was that of their breathing.

After a moment she said, "I can't help wondering what it'd have been like."

"What?"

"Our kid."

"With our DNA? It would have been a genius." He grinned.

She shook her head, holding her lips pressed together to keep from smiling, which would only encourage him. "I hope it's a long, long time before I'm a parent."

"It's harder than it looks, believe me." He caught hold of her hand, and they headed for the door. "I have an idea. There's a Motel

6 down the road. Can't you just see it, a piece on sleazy motels from a teen's point of view? Think how it would sell. They'd be standing in line down at . . ."

He was still talking as she raced past him down the stairs.

"The most extraordinary thing." Mother Ignatius's wintry blue eyes peered at Gerry over the tops of her reading glasses. On her desk was a stack of mail, most of it unopened, as if her morning routine had been interrupted. "I just got off the phone with the motherhouse. It seems that based on Sister Clement's report, they've concluded that no drastic changes are called for. In short, we're to continue on as before."

Gerry stared at her in disbelief. She'd been so sure when the reverend mother called her in that it would be to ask for her resignation. Now goose bumps skittered up the back of her neck, making its tiny hairs stand on end. Not like a sighting of the Blessed Mother, but a miracle all the same.

She let out a breath. "Jesus, Mary, and Joseph."

Mother Ignatius removed her glasses, folding them carefully before tucking them in her pocket. "Quite honestly, I don't know what to make of it," she said.

"Could Sister Clement have changed her mind?" Even as she said it, Gerry found it impossible to believe.

"It's more likely the special mass I asked Father Reardon to say."

"You, too?" When she'd buttonholed Dan last week, he hadn't mentioned Mother Ignatius's request. She smiled. "I figured I could use all the help I could get."

And not just keeping her job. She thought of everything she'd been through these past months: a daughter coming home and another one temporarily moving out; Sam's near death and the birth of her baby (all in one night!); and, last but not least, Aubrey, who might or might not be in Carson Springs for good. It was enough to make her wonder if it was God behind the wheel—or someone learning to drive.

"I'll make the announcement in chapter, but I wanted you to be the first to know." The reverend mother's voice was calm, but her eyes shone. She extended her hand across her tidy desk. "Congratulations, my dear. I look forward to many more years of battling with you over what's best for Blessed Bee."

"Even though I sometimes win?" Gerry said with a laugh.

"I wouldn't have it any other way."

They exchanged a wry smile. Gerry was turning to go when she was brought short by an unfamiliar sound: the reverend mother chuckling softly to herself.

She hurried off down the hall, knowing that if she didn't share the good news with someone, she'd burst. She immediately thought of Sister Agnes, but a quick tour of the garden netted only Sister Henry, on her knees weeding a flower bed.

"Sister Agnes is in the infirmary," the older nun informed her. She shook her head sadly, and Gerry saw that she'd once been quite pretty before the years had taken their toll. "The poor dear doesn't have much longer." It was a panicked moment before Gerry realized she was talking about Sister Seraphina.

The infirmary was a former caretaker's cottage that had been equipped with beds and state-of-the-art emergency care. The sisters who worked there were registered nurses, and a doctor made rounds twice a week. Now, as Gerry pushed her way through the door into the sunny foyer, she was struck as always by the contrast to the exterior. While the facade retained its ancient stones and thick curtain of ivy, the interior had been thoroughly modernized—white tile flooring and a built-in reception desk with a cozy, wicker-furnished lounge just beyond. Only the security camera over the door stood as mute reminder of the community's aging population: It guarded against those who tended to wander.

"I'm looking for Sister Agnes," she told the plump-cheeked novice at the desk.

Before the girl could reply, the double doors to the patients' rooms swung open and Father Dan came striding out. Seeing Gerry, he stopped short, breaking into a smile. He looked tired, and though still handsome, was no longer the dashing young priest who'd set a new record in female attendance at St. Xavier's.

"She's at peace . . . finally," he said with a sigh.

Gerry made the sign of the cross and said a silent little prayer for Sister Seraphina. "She didn't suffer, I hope."

"I don't think so."

"Even so, it must have been a blessing."

"I don't doubt that."

They strolled into the lounge, where she

sank down in a chair facing the window. "I remember when I was a novice. She seemed ancient even then."

Father Dan sat down opposite her. "I confess I wasn't in any particular hurry this time," he admitted sheepishly. And who could blame him? "As it was, I made it with only minutes to spare."

"She'd have gone to heaven either way."

Gerry recalled how Sister Seraphina used to walk with the hem of her habit held an inch or two off the ground to keep it from wearing out. Now, in retrospect, it seemed a metaphor for her life as well: Sister Seraphina's body steadfastly refusing to wear out.

"If she didn't, I'd have grave concerns about the rest of us." He paused, smiling as if at a secret they shared. "But you didn't come to see Sister Seraphina."

She shook her head. "I was hoping to have a word with Sister Agnes."

"She's still in with Sister Seraphina. It'll be a while, I think." He didn't have to remind her that here, at Our Lady, the departed were lovingly prepared for burial by the sisters themselves. "Is there anything I can help you with?"

"Actually, it's good news for a change."

Father Dan looked intrigued. "In that case, I want to hear all about it."

She told him about the decision from the motherhouse. "It looks as if the dogs have been officially called off."

"Well, now, that *is* good news." He beamed. "But you look as though you don't quite believe it."

"You weren't there. You didn't see the look on Sister Clement's face." Gerry couldn't help smiling at the memory. The woman had gotten what she deserved. "I can't imagine her having anything remotely charitable to say."

"You're thinking our old friend had a change of heart?"

She'd told him all about her visit to Father Gallagher, leaving nothing out. Dan, to his credit, hadn't raised an eyebrow. "It's funny, because at the time it didn't seem like I was getting through to him."

"Well, he must have come to his senses. Either way, you're off the hook."

"True."

"You don't sound too happy about it."

"Right now I'm more confused than happy."

"Maybe deep down you still feel you don't deserve it," he suggested gently.

She thought for a moment, gazing out at a crab apple tree in bloom—it looked like a great pink bouquet—then said softly, "Maybe I don't." She recalled that first awkward meeting with Claire. They'd come a long way since then, but still had a long way to go. "Maybe there are some things we never get past."

"'Forgive, and ye shall be forgiven,'" he quoted from Luke. "Don't you think that might include forgiving yourself?" She turned to him, noting that his eyes were the same shade of blue as the sky just past his shoulder.

"I'm working on it," she said with a smile.

"How *is* your daughter these days?" He seemed to have read her mind.

"Never better."

"I hear that tearoom of hers is set to open any day. Just what I need, another stop on the road to temptation." He patted his middle, where the roll above his belt revealed his weakness. "Though I hear her strawberry tarts alone are worth ten Hail Marys."

"You've been talking to Sam, I see."

"I dropped in to see the baby. Fine lad. The spitting image of his mother."

"Let's hope he inherited her patience." Sam had reported that she spent more time at night walking the floor than in bed. Amazingly, even after her ordeal, she hadn't sounded as if she minded.

Father Dan's expression sobered. "He wouldn't be here if it hadn't been for you," he said. "Sam couldn't stop singing your praises."

"Keep it up, Father, and they'll soon be canonizing me." Gerry laughed to cover her embarrassment.

"Not with your record, they won't," he teased. "And speaking of the devil, I hear your boyfriend has decided to stick around." His tone imbued it with a meaning that could only have come from Sam. Gerry made a mental note to wring her neck the first chance she got.

Gerry's cheeks grew warm. "For now." She frowned. "You can stop looking at me like that, Dan Reardon. Even if I were madly in love with the man—which I'm not saying I am— happily ever after is for fairy tales. Look what happened the last time I went that route."

"I'm not buying that tired old excuse. You and Mike never should have married in the first place."

"I'm better off this way, believe me. And so is Aubrey . . . even if he doesn't know it yet." She shook her head, wondering who she was trying to convince, herself or Dan.

"What makes you so sure?"

"On top of the fact that I'm not exactly marriage material? I'd be competing with his dead wife. And, believe me, that's one contest I wouldn't win. Not even a saint could measure up."

"No one's without baggage. Especially at our age."

"I'll thank you not to remind me of my age," she said tartly.

"All I'm advising is that you not rush to judgment."

Gerry wondered if he was right. For someone who'd taken a vow of celibacy, he certainly seemed to know a lot. Did being on the outside looking in give him an unfair advantage?

"I never thought I'd see the day," she said dryly, "when my priest would be playing matchmaker."

The twinkle faded from his eyes. "What it

all boils down to is whether or not you have the courage. And I think you do. In fact, I'd bet the farm on it."

Courage? What did he know? Someone truly courageous would have found a way to keep her child. Even with Mike, she hadn't had the guts to stand up to him until the very end. Oh yes, she knew how she was perceived by those less enlightened than Father Dan. Which was laughable, really, because she was the furthest thing from being a man-eater. The reason she'd never stuck it out with any one man—Mike being the lone exception, and that was only because she'd had children to think of—was because she'd been afraid. Of getting hurt, of being gobbled up by someone's ego, and mostly of being left out in the cold. For hadn't every man in her life, going back to her father, deserted her in some way?

Now she found herself once more on the edge of that precipice. It was different with Aubrey, she knew. But just because there might be a pot of gold at the end of this rainbow didn't mean she had to go after it. Rainbows, she thought, could be slippery.

"You're lucky," she said, half envying him. "You never had to get your own feet wet."

She rose and walked over to the window. The sun was sinking, over the distant mountaintops, and the slight haze of earlier in the day had lifted. She could clearly make out the supine profile of Sleeping Indian Chief, with its jutting nose and chin.

She felt the light brush of Dan Reardon's hand against hers, and turned to find him standing beside her. "I wasn't always a priest, you know," he said softly. "I was in love once."

"Did she break your heart, or was it the other way around?"

"A little of both, I think. We just went in different directions." He looked content with the one his had taken. "She's married now. Three kids, two in college. We exchange cards at Christmas."

"Do you ever wonder what it would've been like if you'd married her?"

"I don't know that we'd have been unhappy," he said with a shrug. "But that isn't the same as being happy, is it?"

Right now what would make her happy would be an evening at home with her kids: macaroni and cheese followed by a game of Monopoly. Maybe Claire could come, and they'd see if she'd inherited the Fitzgerald penchant for acquiring hotels on Boardwalk and Park Place. Gerry could see it in her mind, the four of them gathered around the card table in the living room. Not exactly Norman Rockwell, but the next best thing.

Where would Aubrey fit in? For a delicious moment she allowed herself to imagine it: his toothbrush in the medicine cabinet, his shoes parked alongside hers. What were hotels on Park Place compared to that?

Chapter Eighteen

Easter brought more than the tolling of church bells. There was the annual Easter egg decorating contest, with prizes in every age category and the winning eggs on display in the window at Lundquists's, nestled alongside bunny-shaped cookies and loaves of sweet braided bread. The grand finale was the Easter egg hunt in Muir Park, sponsored by the Chamber of Commerce, where children from eight to eighty scrambled amid the gardenias and cape plumbago, the hostas and thyme, for the more than one hundred eggs that were hidden. Other than a few scratches, the only real casualty was when Otis and Jean Farmer's four-year-old grandson got stung by a hornet, and the only disturbance, when crazy old Clem Woolley climbed up on a bench to bellow, "Make way for Jesus!" A few took it as a tribute to the season, but most knew he meant it literally: Jesus was as real to Clem as was Reverend Grigsby, who gently escorted him over to the refreshment table, where the portly pastor treated him to two slices of Elsie Burnett's apple-plum tart—one for Clem and one for his invisible companion. (It was an underreported fact, Clem would tell anyone who'd listen, that Jesus had a sweet tooth.)

Andie and Finch, with some help from Simon—mostly occupied with keeping track of his brothers and sisters—passed out pamphlets at the Lost Paws booth manned by Laura, though the caged pets were the real draw. By day's end, nearly four hundred dollars had been raised and they had tentative placements, contingent on home inspections, for Bitsy, a four-year-old Maltese, and a big black tomcat named Cole. The mother of a little girl who'd thrown a tantrum when Laura gently explained that the animals couldn't be let out to play was discouraged from adopting, Laura saying the woman clearly had enough on her hands.

It had been Mavis's idea for Claire to advertise the grand opening of her tearoom, just a week away, with several carefully chosen desserts for the bake sale. After much discussion they'd decided to stick with classics—a triple-layer coconut cake with lemon filling, brownies, and thumbprint cookies made with homemade strawberry jam—Mavis arguing that down-home desserts a cut above the rest would make more of an impression than any fancy creations. Claire had nonetheless watched with bated breath as David Ryback from the Tree House brought a forkful of cake to his mouth. David would be a tough critic; his café was famous for its desserts.

After a tense moment, he rolled his eyes in ecstasy. "I have only one question. Do you deliver?"

Word spread and people began lining up. In less than an hour every last cookie, brownie, and slice of cake was sold. The only one who was less than pleased by Claire's success was Candace Milestrup, whose chocolate chip pound cake had been the hands-down favorite in past years.

As the big day drew near, Claire was thrown into a frenzy of activity. All the main stuff had been seen to—dishes and cutlery uncrated and put away, bulk supplies in cardboard barrels lined up neatly in the garage, the deep freeze filled with enough frozen pie shells and cookie dough for an army. But there were still a million and one details, which seemed to multiply like the brooms in *Sorcerer's Apprentice.* The curtain rods were crooked and needed to be re-hung, the dairy she'd been using had shut down due to a bovine disease, and mice had the run of the pantry.

And those were just the last-minute headaches. On her to-do list were menus (which Justin had sweetly offered to do on his computer), and ads to be placed in the *Clarion* and *Pennywise Press* for hired help. None of the candidates she'd seen so far, ranging from the sweet but slightly addled Vina Haskins to superefficient, and more than a little bossy Gert Springer, had seemed the right fit. For the time being Mavis would fill in, with Andie and Justin helping out after school.

Kitty, delayed by a flood in her basement, would be arriving any day. Kitty, whose relaxed approach and expert touch, would make it all seem easy. It would be good, too, to have someone to talk to about Matt.

Claire hadn't seen him since the evening of the party, but the other day the building inspector had pointed out an oversight—it seemed she'd neglected to put in a wheelchair ramp. With no time to waste, she'd phoned Matt in a panic. He was on another job, but had promised to take care of it after hours. It wasn't until she'd hung up that she realized what a mistake it could turn out to be. The last thing she needed right now was to see him angry or, worse, miserable. She'd end up feeling twice as guilty and torn.

But when Matt ambled in late the following day, just after Mavis had left, he was his usual laid-back self and seemed none the worse for wear. If anything, he looked better than ever: deeply tanned, just this side of sunburned, wearing a T-shirt that showed off his muscular arms.

"Thanks for making the time," she told him. "I know how busy you are." She hung back in the doorway, folding her arms over her chest. Her feet were bare and she was suddenly aware of the floor, cool and satiny against her soles. "Would you like some lemonade? You look as if you could use a cold drink."

"Sure, if it's no trouble." He sounded as relaxed as he had over the phone.

"No trouble at all."

He followed her into the kitchen, where lemons from the trees at Isla Verde were heaped in a basket on the counter. She chose three and cut them into wedges, tossing them into the blender, rinds and all, along with a cup each of sugar and water. She dumped the puree into a bowl lined with cheesecloth and squeezed out the liquid, which she poured into a pitcher. She added several more cups of water and a handful of ice.

Matt watched the process with interest. "If I'd known you were making it from scratch, I wouldn't have put you to all the trouble."

"It's no trouble." She poured some into a glass and topped it with a mint sprig.

He took one sip and said, "Best lemonade I've ever tasted."

She smiled, leaning into the counter. "People are surprised when I give them the recipe. It's as if they expect it to have been hand squeezed by Trappist monks."

"This is better." He flashed her a grin, tipping his head back to take a long swallow. She stared at his Adam's apple moving up and down the brown column of his throat. Drops of condensation from the glass dribbled over his knuckles, and she had a sudden urge to lick them off. God, what was wrong with her? Couldn't she have a conversation with the man without wanting to jump into bed with him?

Are you sure it's just sex? whispered a voice in her head.

She felt close to Matt in other ways. She could tell him things other people might have thought silly—like how her favorite pastime was watching corny old movies on TV, and that her number-one comfort food was s'mores. If Byron were here, it'd be different, she knew. But wasn't that the crux of it all?

"I can't believe we forgot," she said, referring to the ramp.

Matt shrugged. "If the inspector hadn't caught it, Monica Vincent would've reminded us in a hurry."

Claire remembered that Monica lived nearby and wondered what she was like. So much had been written about her—her tantrums on the movie sets, her countless love affairs, and finally the accident that had left her partially paralyzed. For the longest time you couldn't walk into a supermarket without seeing her on every tabloid.

"Wouldn't it be funny if she came to the opening?"

"She probably will. She never misses an opportunity to make an entrance."

"I haven't spotted her yet."

"You'll know it when you do. She's pretty hard to miss." He helped himself to another glass of lemonade. Anyone looking in the window, she thought, would've taken him for her husband, home from a hard day's work.

"Because she's in a wheelchair?"

Matt's mouth stretched in a humorless smile. "That's the least of her handicaps. Ask anyone who's had to deal with her. We all have stories."

"You know her?"

"I did some work up at her house a while back."

"What was she like?"

"You mean before or after she tried to seduce me?"

"She *didn't.*"

"Oh, I don't flatter myself. I think just about any guy in reasonably good shape would be fair game." He was quick to add, "Not that I took her up on it. Though if I had, she might have paid me for all my extra work."

"At least she's not sitting around feeling sorry for herself."

He laughed at the idea. "If anyone's to be pitied, it's her sister."

"Doesn't she work for Monica?" She recalled Andie's mentioning something.

He gave a snort. "More like indentured servitude. Anna does everything but polish Monica's hubcaps—hell, I'll bet she even does that."

"Why doesn't she quit?"

"Easier said than done. For one thing, she can't afford to. If it wasn't for Anna, their mother would be in a state nursing home."

"Why doesn't Monica help? With all her money—"

"A lot of people are wondering the same thing." He shook his head in disgust. "It's like she thinks employing Anna is enough. There's another sister, Liz, but for whatever reason, Anna does all the heavy lifting."

"Sounds pretty grim."

Claire suppressed a small shudder, thinking of her own parents. Who would take care of them when they could no longer care for themselves? "I guess I should count my blessings." Her new family wasn't perfect by any means, but they'd shown her, each in their own way, that she could count on them in a pinch.

She saw something flicker in Matt's eyes. Longing? Regret? He drained his glass, and set it down on the counter. "I should get started on that ramp while it's still light." His tone wasn't so much brusque as businesslike. "Thanks for the lemonade."

Claire could hear him outside as she washed up, the clatter of lumber being unloaded from his truck, followed by the shrill whine of his saw. Hours later, when the sun had set and the light was fading from the sky, she stepped outside to find the framework in place, its raw pine boards gleaming like x-rayed bones in the dusk.

"It's amazing. You hardly notice it's there," she marveled as she inspected it. Rather than mar the line of the porch, he'd built it off to one side, setting it back from the path.

"You'll have to extend the path a bit, but that shouldn't be a problem," he told her.

"It's the least of my worries, believe me."

"I'll send someone over with the concrete. No extra charge."

"I insist on paying. You're already out of pocket as it is."

He tugged on the creased bill of his cap, dark green with ORCHARD LUMBER printed in white across its sweat-stained band. "Pay me later."

"All right," she conceded grudgingly. "But I want it in writing."

"In that case, I'll take one of your strawberry tarts as collateral."

He flashed her a grin before bending to hammer a nail into the railing. The sound rang out in the quiet of the twilit yard. She saw a light go on across the street; that would be widowed Mrs. Gantt feeding her cat. In a minute or two the living room window would light up as well—you could set your clock by it. The old lady never missed the evening news, followed by *Hollywood Squares* and *Who Wants to Be a Millionaire?*

"I'm fresh out of tarts," she told him. "Wouldn't you settle for dinner instead?"

Claire didn't know which one of them was more surprised; the words had just popped out. When he brushed leisurely at a gnat, revealing a dark half moon of sweat under his arm, the motion seemed oddly exaggerated.

"I don't think that'd be such a good idea," he said.

"Why not? We're still friends, aren't we?" She spoke lightly, but was aware of how childish it sounded. Like wanting to believe in Santa Claus in the face of all evidence to the contrary.

"Don't take this the wrong way," he replied pleasantly. "But I have enough friends as it is."

She winced. "I guess I had that coming."

"On the other hand," he went on in the same mild tone, "if what you have in mind is more than dinner, I could be persuaded."

Claire felt something rise up in her like a wave racing into shore. She could see it clearly: Matt across from her at the kitchen table, both of them knowing the meal was little more than a prelude.

But if he stayed the night, wouldn't she be making a choice? And in choosing Matt, she'd be rejecting Byron. It was as simple as that: She couldn't have both.

"Matt, you know how I feel. But—"

He didn't give her a chance to finish. "Hey, no big deal. I'm a big boy. I knew what I was getting into. No hard feelings, okay?" He began packing up his tools.

She suddenly felt on the verge of tears. It had been naive of her to think they could remain friends. "I'm sorry. It's just . . . I *like* you, dammit. I mean, aside from . . . from . . ."

He tilted his head and smiled up at her. "It's okay, you can say it."

Blood rushed to her cheeks. "I don't regret anything."

"You just want it to be over," he said. "Well, you've got it." The lid of his tool chest clanged shut. He carried it over to his truck and hoisted it onto the bed, calling out breezily, "I'll be around sometime tomorrow to finish up."

Watching his truck back out of the driveway, she felt an impulse to run after it, an impulse that quickly faded. Face it, she wasn't the type—the craziest thing she'd ever done was quit her job and move here. She remained on the path instead, straining to see in the fading light until all that was left were the red sparks of his taillights. When they'd winked out of sight, she turned and began trudging up the steps. What no one told you about having to choose between two lovers, she thought, was that it was never a clean trade: You were doomed to long for one and give less than your whole heart to the other.

As if he'd somehow known, Byron called that night to announce that he was flying down for the weekend.

"Don't ask how I managed it," he said. "You don't want to know."

"I can't wait," she said, but the words sounded hollow to her ears.

It'll be different when he's here, she told herself. In Byron's arms, she'd soon forget Matt.

"My plane gets in at noon. If I don't run into any traffic, I should roll in around two, two-thirty."

She gave him directions to the house, saying, "It's the one with all the ivy." *And a half-finished wheelchair ramp.* "You shouldn't have any trouble finding it."

"I've missed you, babe." His voice turned husky.

"Me, too." She had, hadn't she? Otherwise, why would she have slept with Matt?

The following morning she was a nervous wreck. Would he take one look at her and *know*? She thought about phoning Kitty for a dose of common sense, but didn't her friend have enough problems at the moment? Besides, it would only delay Kitty further.

By the time Byron arrived, she was a

nervous wreck. But the sight of him climbing out of the rental car in his floppy shirt and chinos immediately put her at ease.

He wore a faintly astonished look as he wandered about the room.

"Wow! The photos didn't do it justice."

"That was Before, this is After."

Any misgivings she might have had fell away as Byron walked from room to room, admiring every detail. Though she was careful not to linger in the bedroom, never mind she'd scoured it of any sign of Matt.

"Nice," he said, not seeming to notice that the mattress was on the floor.

She showed him the adjoining sitting room, where a wall had been knocked down between two small bedrooms, an idea she'd gotten from Sam. All that was left was to wallpaper it, then she'd be able to take the rest of her furniture out of storage. The long-range plan, when she could afford it, she explained, was to convert the garage into an apartment big enough for the two of them.

Byron didn't respond. He seemed genuinely excited for her, but she noticed he was careful not to include himself in any discussion of future plans.

They returned to the sunny front room,

the only one besides the kitchen and bathroom that was complete. "Your contractor did a nice job," he said, running a hand over the wainscoting.

Claire felt herself blush. "I'll tell him you said so."

"I like the way you've decorated it, too."

She looked around, seeing it anew through Byron's eyes—the ruffled curtains Mavis had sewn, the painted tables and chairs stenciled with designs, the pine hutch with her collection of antique bottles and vintage tins from Avery Lewellyn's antique barn. The Victrola by the door was from Maude, and the quilt on the wall a gift from Olive and Rose Miller. Laura's contribution had been the oak rocker in the corner, for mothers with babies.

"I didn't do it all myself," she said.

"I wasn't expecting anything this . . . finished."

She studied him out of the corner of her eye. He looked the same, but their roles seemed to have shifted. After a lifetime of playing it safe, she'd stepped out on a limb while Byron, who'd always gone his own way, was following in the more traditional footsteps of his uncle. Gone were any references to opening a practice or doing volunteer work—subjects he'd once spoken of with passion. Lately their conversations had been peppered with mentions of his uncle Andrew, and how much he would earn a year practicing in Hillsborough.

"I was going to go with crepe paper and balloons," she answered facetiously, "but it seemed tacky somehow."

"You know what I meant." He put his arms around her, making her feel petty for misconstruing his comment. "You worked hard—you deserve to have this be a huge success."

She dropped her head onto his shoulder. He smelled faintly and pleasantly of the Castile soap his ecofriendly parents bought in industrial-size jugs and used for everything from shampooing their hair to laundering their clothes.

"Why don't we grab a bite to eat in town? It may be my only chance to show you around. The next few days are going to be kind of hectic."

"Actually, I had something else in mind." He cast a meaningful look in the direction of the bedroom.

She felt uneasy all of a sudden. "We'll have plenty of time for that later on."

"All right, if you insist . . ."

The partially completed wheelchair ramp seemed to mock her as she stepped out onto the porch. She thought of Matt and how she'd have no choice but to introduce him. Oh, God. How had she gotten herself into this? She didn't know which she feared most: Byron finding out, or hurting Matt any more than she already had.

By the time they'd walked the half mile into town, some of the tension had gone out of her. As they strolled along Old Mission she prattled on about the centuries-old oaks that were the sacred cows of Carson Springs (it had made front-page headlines last month when Norma Devane, of Shear Delight, had cut down one of hers); the lecture at the public library, given by renowned naturalist Petra Crowley, at which a red-tailed hawk had gotten loose and nearly made off with Marguerite Moore's miniature French poodle; and the post office tower with its bell that had been slated for munitions during World War I only to have been conveniently "stolen" until such time as it could be safely restored.

When they reached the end of the arcade, she took him on a tour of Delarosa Plaza, with its tiled fountain and quaint shops nestled inside bougainvillea-draped walls.

"Come on," she said, "I want to introduce you to Laura."

The bell over the door at Delarosa's tinkled as they stepped inside. She spotted Laura in back, waiting on a well-dressed older woman. Laura murmured something to her and walked over, greeting them warmly. "It's nice to finally meet you," she said when Claire had introduced her to Byron. "I hear you're a doctor. We could use a few more like you around here."

"More like a starving resident," he said with a laugh. His gaze traveled about, taking in the artful displays of pottery and weavings, hand-crafted objets d'art and one-of-a-kind jewelry. "Nice stuff. I'll bet you do a good business."

"We do all right." Laura, modest to a fault, brushed a wisp of flyaway hair from her forehead. She was dressed in dark brown slacks and a yellow silk blouse that suited her olive complexion. "To be honest, we make more money off our Web site."

"She'd do even better in a big city," Byron muttered to Claire as they were leaving.

Claire was taken aback. Didn't he get it? Delarosa's had been in the family for generations, since the days of the Gold Rush. Besides, Laura *liked* it here. At the same time, she wondered if she wasn't being disingenuous herself, her guided tour little more than a glorified sales pitch.

They wandered through Muir Park, stopping to admire the bandstand where concerts were held in summer. Clem Woolley was in his usual place by the gazebo, a tattered bundle of his self-published tome in hand. Standing nearby was burly Nate Comstock, who'd done some electrical work at her house; he was peering through binoculars at the trees overhead, *The Sibley Guide to Birds* clamped under one tattooed arm. Olive and Rose Miller, dressed in identical seersucker shirtwaists, paused to say hello before continuing arm in arm down the path.

Having skipped lunch, she was starving by the time they reached the Tree House. David Ryback, at his usual station by the door, greeted them as they pushed their way inside. "Don't tell me you're reconsidering my offer," he teased, reminding her of the job as pastry chef he'd said was hers anytime she wanted it.

"Only if it means the recipe for your ollalieberry pie," she joked in return.

"Nothing doing. I'd be out of business in a week."

When they were seated, she chatted briefly with Melodie Wycoff, who took their orders, and waved hello to one of the regulars, raven-haired Delilah Sims, rumored to be in love with David. They were tucking into their sandwiches when Byron observed casually, "You certainly know a lot of people."

"I guess so. I hadn't really thought about it." She glanced up at a little boy and girl scampering about like a pair of monkeys in the tree house overhead—they might have been her and Byron at that age—and smiled. "It's funny," she said, "but in some ways it feels as if I've lived here all my life."

He was quick to change the subject. "How's your mom these days?"

"All right, I guess."

"Are they coming to the opening?"

"They haven't said one way or the other." She felt a pang, but found that it didn't upset her as much as it once had. It wasn't that she loved them any less, just that she didn't expect so much. "What about yours? I sent them an invitation."

"Yeah, I know. They told me to tell you they can't make it. Mom's speaking at some conference. Which reminds me . . ." He dug into his jacket pocket and produced a slim paperback volume. "She wanted you to have this. It's a book of her poetry."

Claire was surprised. She hadn't known Byron's mother was a poet. "Is it any good?" she asked, leafing through it.

"Who knows?" He shrugged. "It's just the university press. I think they published it to humor her."

The old Byron wouldn't have been so dismissive, she thought. Had he changed that much? "Well, it was thoughtful of her," she said.

"She gave one to your parents, too—as a sort of peace offering." He shook his head in wonderment. "I don't know if it worked, but at least they're on speaking terms."

"There's hope for them yet." She smiled at the irony of it: Byron's parents making peace with Lou and Millie while she'd been left out in the cold. "It's funny. I used to think they needed me. But I think all I did was keep them from seeing how lonely they were."

Byron reached across the table to take her hand, running his thumb over her knuckles. "The only thing that counts is if *you're* happy."

She hadn't once heard the word *we* since he'd arrived.

"I am," she said. "But it's not the same without you here."

"It won't be forever. Just a couple more years."

"I should be in the black by then." She held his gaze, adding, "And once the garage is converted . . . "

He abruptly let go of her hand. "You know how I feel about that."

"I was hoping you'd changed your mind."

He pushed his plate aside. He was smiling at least, and she took heart from that. "Okay, I'll admit I wasn't sure at first, but judging from what I've seen . . ." He spread his hands, a look of eagerness lighting his thin, intense face. "Once this takes off, you could open branches in other places."

"It would sort of defeat the whole purpose, wouldn't it?"

If he'd caught the sarcasm in her voice, he showed no sign of it. "What would be wrong with opening a Tea & Sympathy in, say, Hillsborough."

"The land of carpooling and soccer moms?"

His face fell. "You could at least consider it."

"On the other hand, you could move here."

"Come on, Claire. Be serious."

"I *am* serious."

Byron shook his head. "Look," he said, not unkindly. "I've spent the past eight years trying to make something of myself. I'm not about to trade one backwater for another."

She felt her heart sink. There'd been a time when, like Byron, all she'd thought of was getting ahead. But she hadn't given up law to make more money elsewhere. Whether or not Tea & Sympathy was a huge success was beside the point. She was doing what she wanted, surrounded by people she liked. As long as she could make ends meet, what else mattered?

"I don't have to tell you what it was like for me growing up," he went on, reminding her that both his parents' salaries combined had barely been enough to make ends meet. "If it hadn't been for my uncle's help, I couldn't have afforded medical school. You know how I feel about my parents, but all I ever wanted was *not* to be like them."

"So you'd rather be like your uncle instead?" She was surprised by how calm she sounded. "A fancy house in Hillsborough and a Mercedes in the garage?"

"Would that be so terrible?" His face, dappled in shadow from the leaves overhead, seemed to shift with the breeze.

"I can remember when you cared more about other things."

"I still care. I just don't see why I have to starve to make the world a better place."

"You could make a nice living *here*."

But he went on shaking his head. "It wouldn't work, Claire."

Still, she persisted. "They're building a new clinic. They'll need doctors. As for volunteering, the migrant camps are full of illegal aliens who'd sooner die than go to a hospital. You could do some real good."

"Sounds as if you have it all figured out."

"All I'm asking is that you consider it."

"Will you think about what *I'm* suggesting?"

The hopelessness of it swept over her, and she shook her head. "I . . . can't."

This wasn't about Matt, she realized. Or

even her moving here. It was about the hair-
line cracks that had been widening into a rift,
so quietly and gradually neither of them had
noticed. Or maybe they'd merely chosen to
turn a blind eye. Hadn't she felt it that night
Matt had taken her to see his boat? Seeing
the love that had gone into it, she'd known it
couldn't have been easy for him to turn his
back on his dream. Yet he had, for his children's sake. Would Byron have done the
same? Once upon a time she would have
thought so, but now she wasn't so sure.

"You might feel differently in a year or two,"
he said, but she could see in his face that he
knew she wouldn't.

Her eyes filled with tears. "It's not going to
work, is it?"

It was as if a key had turned in a lock. His
face flooded with anguish, his dear face that
she'd known and loved since childhood.
"Maybe we just need some time apart," he
said in a strange, choked voice.

Claire was dimly aware of Melodie yam-
mering on and on to someone at the next
table about a remedy for hair loss that she'd
read about in the *Enquirer.* And David Ryback at the other end of the patio in intense
conversation with his tired-looking blond

wife. No one was looking at her and Byron; no one seemed the least bit aware of the seismic rupture taking place.

"Maybe so," she said.

The look in his eyes was almost more than she could bear. "When I talked you into coming here that first time, I never imagined it would turn out this way." A corner of his mouth hooked up in an ironic smile.

"Me neither."

"I don't think I should stay. It would only make it worse." Byron was suddenly having trouble meeting her gaze.

She blinked, and a tear rolled down her cheek. "You'll stay in touch?"

"Yeah." His voice cracked.

She knew it could be months, maybe years, before they'd be ready to see each other in person. She was just as certain they'd never be entirely out of touch.

When Melodie brought the check, he tossed some bills down on the table. They rose in unison, chairs scraping over the patio's worn bricks. Several people turned to glance at them but, seeing nothing out of the ordinary, went back to what they were doing. It seemed only natural, as Claire and Byron made their way toward the exit, to join hands: not as lovers, but as old friends consoling each other in a time of need.

David wore a knowing expression as he saw them out the door. He'd clearly had his share of experience in such matters.

They walked home in silence. When at last her house came into view, complete with Matt's truck in the driveway, it seemed the perfect coda to a perfectly awful day.

Matt rose to the fore with a firm handshake and friendly smile. "Nice to meet you," he said. "Claire's told me a lot about you."

"Likewise." Byron forced a smile, glancing impatiently toward the house. She could almost hear him thinking: *How quickly can I grab my things and get out of here?*

"You down for the weekend?" Matt's gaze was clear and untroubled, giving no indication that it meant anything to him one way or the other. Claire felt a burst of gratitude.

"Actually, I was just leaving," Byron told him.

Matt's face registered surprise. "Didn't you just get here?"

Claire sensed him wanting to dig deeper. "Something came up," she quickly put in.

Byron went along with it. "The guy who was supposed to cover me got sick."

"Tough break," Matt said.

"Well . . . nice meeting you." Byron was halfway up the porch steps, shoulders slumped as if with the weight of the suitcase he hadn't yet retrieved, when he turned and said, "By the way, I like what you've done with this place."

If he had the slightest inkling that much of it had been a labor of love, it didn't show. Byron couldn't know that, in some ways, she considered this house to be as much Matt's as hers.

She watched Matt amble over to his truck and begin unloading his tools. It was all she could do not to run to him, beg him to understand. But she remained where she was, gazing about at the mock cherry tree in bloom and the honeysuckle creeping up over the hedge. The old shade trees that lined the drive cast lacy patterns over the grass, and, spotting a gopher hole, she wondered about getting a cat.

Why does everything have to be so hard? she thought.

Minutes later Byron reappeared, suitcase in hand. He looked diminished somehow as he trudged down the steps, and her heart went out to him. She wasn't good with good-byes—part of the reason she'd stayed in Mi-

ramonte for so long—and for a fleeting instant she found herself wanting to run as
fast and as far as she could. Anything to
keep from having to say those dreaded
words.

She walked him to his car, where she
hugged him self-consciously, mindful of
Matt. "Drive carefully."

"Yes, Mom." For years he'd teased her
about being like Millie, though this time the
words had a hollow ring.

"I'll miss you."

"Me, too." He dropped his gaze, but not
before she saw the tears in his eyes. "I'm not
going to wish you luck with the opening. I'm
sure it'll be a big success."

"From your lips to God's ear."

He kissed her lightly on the mouth, and
ducked into his car. Moments later he was
disappearing around the corner. She
watched him go with an ache in her throat,
the light all around her suddenly too bright.
She wasn't aware of Matt coming up alongside her.

"I could come back another time if you
like."

She turned slowly to face him. She knew
what he was asking: Was he part of this, or a

mere bystander? She didn't know what to tell him. The only thing she was certain of right now was that if she tried to speak, she'd come unglued.

"I'd like it if you stayed," she said at last in a remarkably calm voice.

She saw a light go on in Matt's eyes, but it was obvious he didn't want to get his hopes up. He shrugged. "I'll be out of your hair soon enough. Give me another hour or so."

"Are you in a hurry?"

He hoisted his power saw from the bed of his truck and set it down on the grass. "Depends."

"On what?"

"If there's anything else that needs doing." He squinted up at the roof.

"I was hoping you'd stay for supper," she found herself saying. "The last time I asked, you said you'd take a rain check."

He brought his gaze back to her, his tea-brown eyes soft and considering. "I don't believe those were my exact words."

"Byron didn't leave because he had to," she said. "We decided it would be for the best."

"I figured as much."

"It's over, Matt. It has been for a while, I just didn't know it."

"I guessed that, too."

"You did?"

"If you'd really loved him, you wouldn't have been with me."

It was as if a fog had lifted. Was it too late? Had she blown it? Calmly, she asked, "So why did you ask me to choose?"

"I wanted you to know what kind of man you'd be choosing."

She looked at him long and hard. It all made perfect sense now.

There was no fanfare when he slipped an arm about her shoulders. Just the chittering of the starlings in the branches overhead and chugging of a sprinkler next door. A quiet sense of wonder filled her, the kind of acute, trembling awareness that only comes in the wake of great happiness or sorrow. She thought of the fruit trees she was going to plant—dwarf peach, plum, and nectarine—and how each spring she would look forward to seeing them blossom. Whatever happened, she would always have that: a place to hang a bird feeder, and enough fruit to fill her pantry.

And someone to share it with.

* * *

Kitty arrived the next day, filled with apologies. While the hot water heater was being repaired, it had shorted out a circuit, and she'd had to call the electrician, who kept promising to come, then didn't. Sean had offered to pinch hit, but he was studying for his finals and she hadn't wanted to disturb him. It was enough, she said, that he was taking care of Maddie. As for Tea & Sympathy, she'd left Willa in charge, with her sister Daphne taking a break from the novel she was writing to help out.

"I feel guilty, dragging you all this way," Claire told her.

Kitty had been given the grand tour and the two were enjoying a glass of lemonade on the porch, where Gerry's recent gift of a pair of wicker chairs was being put to good use.

"What kind of a partner would I be if I'd stayed home?" Kitty wanted to know. "Though it doesn't look as if you would have gotten along just fine without me." Radiant in a caftan top and trousers, her loose curls the color of ginger ale cascading down around her shoulders, she looked as relaxed as ever.

"You should've seen me a week ago." Claire rolled her eyes.

"Well, I'm all yours for the next three days."

"Believe me, you'll have your work cut out for you."

Kitty laughed as if she hadn't a care in the world. "By the way, when am I going to meet your new family?" She looked around as if half expecting them to spring from the shrubbery.

Claire told her they would be here any minute. "Mavis has a recipe for whiskey cake she wants to try out." Claire was amazed at how much lighter she felt. Last night with Matt had helped put things in perspective.

Kitty drew back to eye her admiringly. "You look different. Did you do something with your hair?"

Claire ran her fingers through it. "No. In fact, I keep thinking I should get it cut."

"That's it, you let it grow out. I *knew* there was something." Kitty smiled as if that wasn't the only change she'd noticed. "Better watch out, or pretty soon you'll be wearing a pair of these." She cast a wry glance at her Birkenstocks.

"Most of the time I go barefoot."

"You *have* changed." Kitty looked as if she approved.

They were in their aprons, Kitty measuring ingredients for oatmeal-pecan squares, which would freeze well, and Claire melting chocolate for a devil's food cake, when Mavis walked in trailed by Gerry and her kids. Without a word of introduction Mavis set down the bag of groceries she was carrying and enveloped Kitty in a hug. Seeing them together, both with the same reddish hair and Irish coloring, Claire thought they might have been long-lost relatives.

"You must be the famous Kitty Seagrave we've been hearing so much about." Mavis drew back, beaming. "The way Claire goes on, I thought you'd be walking here on water."

"I almost did." Kitty told them about the flood in her basement, and they all had a good laugh.

Gerry turned to Claire. "She's every bit as wonderful as you said."

"You must be Gerry." Kitty hugged her. "I feel as if I know you."

Gerry's eyes were clear and untroubled. "I'd like you to meet my younger children— Andie and Justin." She placed a subtle emphasis on "younger."

"Do you have kids?" Justin asked h

"One, but she's only three." Kitty
consoling face.

"Is your tearoom anything like this o.
Andie wanted to know.

"In spirit," Kitty said. "That's the secre
actually—every place should have its own
personality."

Soon they were chattering away like old
friends. Kitty regaling them with tales of her
regulars. Mavis reminiscing about the Carson Springs of her girlhood. Gerry filling
them in on the latest goings-on at Our Lady.

Before long Mavis was elbow to elbow
with Kitty at the counter and Andie peeling
apples at the table, while Justin cored and
sliced. Gerry, a self-professed kitchen klutz,
made herself useful ironing napkins.

She was refilling the iron at the tap when
she spied the note tucked inside the pot of
African violets on the sill. "'Looking forward
to the big day. Love, Aubrey,'" she read
aloud, flags of color appearing in her
cheeks.

"For a man with his suitcase packed, he
doesn't seem in too big a hurry," Mavis o
served dryly.

"He's coming to the game on Sat

ustin tried to sound as if it were no big deal, but the look on his face was a dead give-away: that of a boy who'd scanned the bleachers once too often in search of a father who wasn't there.

"Which is more than I can say for *some* people," muttered Mavis, who clearly had no fondness for Gerry's ex.

Andie surprised everyone by blurting, "You should marry him, Mom."

Gerry's head jerked around. "What?"

"He's just your type." Andie ticked off all the reasons on her fingers. "Mysterious and unavailable . . . till now, that is. And he's never, ever going to bore you. Not to mention he's crazy about you."

"Crazy is the word for it," Gerry joked. "He doesn't know what he'd be getting into." But from the deepening color in her cheeks she'd obviously given it some thought.

"Oh, I think he has a pretty good idea," Claire said.

"Why don't we take a vote?" Kitty spoke as if she'd known Gerry all her life. "Let's see a show of hands for all those in favor."

Three hands went up. Only Kitty, who had to meet the man, abstained. Claire knew scored a direct hit when Gerry let out a little yelp: She'd scorched the napkin she was ironing.

"I have a better idea," she said. "Why don't I mind my business, and you mind yours?"

"I guess that means Simon and I can elope after all," Andie deadpanned.

"Over my dead body," Mavis shot back, wearing a look of mock outrage.

"When you're my age and your life is already ruined, you can do as you please," Gerry said.

Listening to them, Claire probed for the secret envy she'd once felt as gingerly as she might have a sore tooth. But somewhere along the line it had gone. She would never be as much Gerry's as Andie or Justin, but they had a different kind of bond: They'd chosen this as surely as Lou and Millie had chosen her.

If only Mom and Dad could see it that way. She felt sorrow well up in her, but it was more of a phantom pain. She still hoped they'd make it to the opening, but if not . . . well, it would be their loss.

"It just hit me," she said. "In less than forty-eight hours, we'll be officially open for business."

"That calls for a drink." Mavis hoisted the bottle of whiskey she'd brought for her cake. She took down six glasses from the cupboard and poured a splash into each one, including Justin's.

"Long live Tea and Sympathy," Kitty toasted, lifting her glass.

"To second chapters." Mavis tossed a meaningful glance at Gerry.

Justin sipped his and made a face. "Ugh."

"It's an acquired taste." Andie spoke with an air of experience.

Claire looked about the sunny kitchen filled with the familiar faces of the people she loved. Was it only a few months since she'd moved here? It felt like aeons. The future no longer seemed so scary. She'd taken the biggest leap of faith in coming here, and look how it had turned out. Everything else was just encore.

"I couldn't have done this without your help," she said to no one in particular.

"Nonsense. What are families for?" Mavis walked over and hugged her. She smelled faintly of whiskey, but in a good way—like medicine to make you feel better.

"Not to mention friends," Kitty chimed.

"I think I'm going to be sick." Andie made a gagging noise.

"Don't move anyone." Gerry reached into her bag for her camera and, ignoring Andie's and Justin's groans, snapped off several shots.

"I just hope they don't make me look fat," Andie said.

"You don't need a camera for that." Justin looked pleased at having scored a direct hit.

"Cut it out, you two," Gerry scolded, though it was obvious her heart wasn't in it.

Claire just stood there, smiling. In her mind, she'd already picked out the spot on her bedroom wall where the photo would hang.

Sunday, the day of the opening, it poured for the first time in weeks. Gerry was in a cold sweat that morning as she dressed. Of all the days for it to rain! Poor Claire. An image flashed across her mind: an array of cakes, pies, tarts, and cookies with no one to eat them. For in Carson Springs, where the sun shone year round, the rare shower might as well be a monsoon. People stayed home for the most part, and those who happened to be out and about went racing for the nearest shelter, their collars pulled up around their ears. Some might end up here, but most would opt to come another day.

Tea & Sympathy wouldn't go out of business, but the wind would go out of its sails. And Gerry wanted so much for it to be a success. They all had something invested, not just in this venture, but in this family patched together out of odds and ends. She paused to smile, as she was tugging on her jeans, at how little she'd understood when she was young. She'd imagined miracles to be visions of the Blessed Virgin, and signs from God on the order of the burning bush . . . but the miracles of everyday life were what she marveled at now: a lost daughter reclaimed, a new baby born to an old friend, unexpected love in the unlikeliest of places.

The thought of Aubrey surfaced once more. She brought a hand to her cheek, which felt warm. Yesterday after the game— which Justin's team had won with a home run in the final inning—she'd spent the evening at Isla Verde, but something had been different about their lovemaking this time. Though Aubrey had always been considerate, there was a new tenderness in the way his hand lingered on her cheek and his mouth seemed to drink her in. He hadn't told her he loved her, but the endearments whispered in her ear seemed to convey much more. At one point, for no reason whatsoever, she'd nearly burst into tears. Afterward, spooned up against him, she'd drifted to sleep thinking, *I could get used to this.*

She frowned now as she zipped up her jeans. Why couldn't they just go on like before? She remembered what her father used to say: If it ain't broke, don't fix it. If she gave into what her heart was telling her, she could risk ruining a perfect thing.

She was on her way out the door when the rain abruptly ceased. She paused on the stoop, looking up at the blue sky peeking through the clouds, and mouthed the words *thank you.*

Andie and Justin had caught a ride earlier with Finch. They'd all signed on as volunteers for the day. The girls would wait tables while Justin and Nesto bussed. Mavis would help out in the kitchen. The only thing left for Gerry to do was to pick up Sam and Ian. Sam was understandably nervous about driving and Ian restricted to the passenger seat until his cast came off.

Pulling into their driveway, she spotted Ian on the porch with the baby. She smiled at the picture they made: little Jack in his pouch strapped like a baby kangaroo to his father's chest, both equally content. Ian waved to her as she got out.

She stepped lightly up onto the porch, greeting him with a kiss on the cheek. "Just promise you won't get his ear pierced," she teased, giving the silver stud in Ian's ear a little tug. She nodded toward his cast in its blue nylon brace, every inch of it covered in writing. "Looks like you've had company. Is there anyone who *hasn't* been by?"

He kissed the fuzzy top of Jack's head. "I'm just the warm-up act. This little guy's the main attraction."

Gerry, who never in a million years thought she'd envy her best friend, looked into the baby's bright blue eyes and felt a rush of . . . what? Not longing, more like wistfulness for what was past. Oh, for the chance to do it over again, and this time get it right!

Sam was dressed and ready to go when she walked in. Gerry took one look at her in her form-fitting silk dress and said, "I hate you. How can you fit into that so soon?"

"Easy. It's a wrap-around." She twirled around to show Gerry the ties in back. "You want to grab that?" She gestured toward the diaper bag while she went in search of the car seat, calling over her shoulder, "I'd forgotten how much paraphernalia there is. Getting out the door with a baby is like a trip to Europe." She didn't sound the least bit perturbed that, at her age, she *could* have been vacationing in Europe instead.

They arrived at Tea & Sympathy to find everything in place . . . and everyone in a high state of tension. It was shortly after ten-thirty, with the opening scheduled for eleven. The room shone from the scrubbing Claire and Kitty had given it the night before, and the shelves of the display case were lined with jewellike tarts, pillowy buns and muffins, cakes and cupcakes, fruit pies and tarts. A vase of yellow roses stood on the Victrola by the door, and on each table was a bud vase with a sprig of clematis.

Maude Wickersham, in a lilac silk gown more suitable for an Edwardian high tea, had positioned herself at the front door. "You missed all the excitement," she said, her periwinkle eyes aglow.

"The smoke alarm went off, and the firemen were a little overeager in getting here," Laura explained.

"I think they wanted first crack at the goodies." Alice, in tapered slacks and sleek turquoise top, stepped up alongside her sister. "Claire sent them off with a sack full of sticky buns."

"How's my favorite grandson?" Wes tickled the baby, who stared in fascination at his big, bearded grandfather. He might be on the fence about having another child of his own, but he was clearly smitten with Jack. "Want me to take him?" he asked Ian.

"Just remember, if his diaper needs changing, he's all yours." Ian's smile, as he gently lifted Jack from his carrier, was laced with irony. Wes hadn't been the most attentive of fathers—too busy empire building—but now that Ian was a father himself, he'd gained a new perspective.

Gerry envied Ian. Why couldn't she do the same—let go of the past and look to the future? *Face it, you're a fake, a phony.* Forever encouraging her friends to take the leap while she herself held back. No wonder she and Aubrey were a perfect fit: They were both hobbled in some way.

Claire poked her head out of the kitchen

to announce cheerfully that if one more thing went wrong, she'd shoot herself, while Kitty stood serenely at the counter piping last-minute rosettes onto a cake. Mavis was making the rounds, checking to see that every sugar bowl was filled and every napkin neatly tucked in its ring. She'd had her hair done yesterday at Shear Delight, a softly swirled upsweep that made her look years younger. Gerry couldn't remember when she'd last seen her mother so vibrant.

Shortly before eleven, people began to trickle in. Rose and Olive Miller in flowered dresses and hats, accompanied by Rose's flaxen-haired granddaughters. They presented Claire with a vintage relic from when the Blue Moon café had been their father's: a tabletop jukebox. Coming in on their heels were Reverend Grigsby and his petite wife, Edie, followed by Carrie Bramley, First Presbyterian's pretty new organist.

Head librarian Vivienne Hicks arrived arm in arm with Tom Kemp. Gerry was pleasantly surprised; she hadn't known Tom and Vivienne were dating. She saw now that they were a perfect match: both angular and bookish, with a tendency to redden easily—as they were doing now. When Sam drifted over to greet them as if Tom were no more than an old family friend, Vivienne looked relieved.

Tom peered at the baby nestled in Wes's arms. "Will you look at all that hair!"

The downy fluff Jack had sported at birth had grown into a Kewpie-doll swirl. Wes looked as proud as if he'd been personally responsible. "He's a Carpenter, all right."

"I think I may have had something to do with it," Sam said mildly.

"Congratulations, Sam. He's beautiful." Vivienne seemed to take a special interest, and Gerry was reminded of how she'd stood up for Sam last year when Marguerite Moore tried to have her ousted. Who knew? Maybe this time next year they'd be congratulating Vivienne.

Myrna McBride, from The Last Word, showed up with a cookbook for Claire. "From the looks of it, you won't be needing this," she said, surveying the display case with delight.

Claire thanked her anyway.

Myrna's ex-husband arrived a few minutes later. Perry McBride, a slope-shouldered, slope-chinned man who brought to mind Ichabod Crane, had clearly been thinking along the same lines: He presented Claire with a handsomely photographed book on collectible teapots. Gerry saw him cast a smug look at Myrna as he handed over what he clearly thought the more fitting gift.

Lupe and Guillermo walked in next, hand in hand like teenagers—never mind they'd been married fifty years—accompanied by crusty veterinarian Doc Henry and portly, white-bearded Avery Lewellyn, who, even without his red suit, was a dead ringer for Santa Claus.

More than half the tables were filled by the time Fran O'Brien blew in the door with her strapping teenaged sons. Though dwarfed by them, the feisty redhead nevertheless wore the air of a lion tamer with the upper hand. Gerry recalled that it was Fran who'd first told her this place was for sale.

"Checking out the competition?" she teased as she escorted them to a table.

"I can already see I'm in trouble." Fran, her frizzy red hair sprouting from her topknot like sparks from a Roman candle, glanced about at the trays sailing by.

David Ryback arrived solo, explaining that his wife was home taking care of their son.

Gerry thought there was more to it than that: Rumor had it their marriage was on the rocks. Melodie Wycoff claimed he spent after hours with Delilah Sims, with whom he shared a passion for literature . . . and maybe something more.

But it was Monica Vincent who stole the show when she was wheeled in, swathed in layers of diaphanous red silk. It was a moment before Gerry recognized that what she had on was a sari. Since when had Monica gone native? In comparison, her sister Anna looked even dowdier than usual.

Matt ambled over to greet them. "Anna . . . Monica. Any trouble getting up that ramp?"

"Did you build it?" Anna was really quite pretty when she smiled.

"With my own two hands." He held them up as if to remind Monica of the work for which she still owed him.

But if Monica remembered, she gave no sign of it. "I could use a pair of those around my house." She hesitated just long enough for the double meaning to sink in.

Ignoring her, Matt turned to Anna, asking, "How's that pipe holding up?"

"Fine . . . thanks." She blushed, explaining to Monica, "The one under the kitchen sink

was leaking. Matt was nice enough to fix it."
Anna was obviously referring to the house
she shared with their mother.

"How sweet," Monica said insincerely.

Gerry showed them to a table by the window, where Monica would be in the harshest
light. Anna, beside her, unexpectedly glowed
in comparison, her creamy complexion taking on a rosy hue.

When she finally got around to checking
her watch, Gerry was surprised to see that it
was almost noon. What was keeping
Aubrey? Had something come up? It was a
good thing Justin, ferrying plates back and
forth, was too busy to notice. The last thing
her son needed was another disappointment in his life. She, on the other hand,
would be grateful if Aubrey didn't show.
Wouldn't it solve everything if he were to
jump on a plane, saving her from having to
decide what to do?

The thought brought no comfort.

Moments later she forgot about Aubrey
when Kevin and Darryl breezed in through
the door. Gerry darted over and flung her
arms around her brother. "Kevin! I was beginning to think you two weren't going to
make it."

"Car trouble. Never trust a fairy with tune-ups." Darryl winked, and she remembered that he and Kevin had decided to make a minivacation out of it by driving down the coast.

Kevin stepped back to give her the once-over. "You look good, Ger. New man in your life?"

"As if you didn't know."

"He still playing hard to get . . . or is it the other way around?"

"I refuse to answer on the grounds that it may incriminate me," she said with a laugh. "What have we got here?" She peered into the shopping bag Kevin was holding.

"Spices from the Orient." In his Armani sport coat, her brother stuck out like a sore thumb in the sea of denim. He glanced about the crowded room. "Where's Claire?"

"In the kitchen. Where else?"

"I'll see if she needs any help." Kevin was already taking off his jacket and rolling up his sleeves. "Darryl can entertain the ladies while I'm gone." It was a private joke that his boyfriend, a young Al Pacino look-alike, hooked them every time—even the ones who knew he was gay.

Gerry was showing one of the new moms

from Sam's Lamaze class to a table when Father Reardon appeared. He gave Emma Pettigrew a hand with her two younger boys while she freed the baby from its carrier. Emma thanked him profusely, taking the opportunity to ask if she could stop by the rectory later on to discuss baptism dates.

Gerry took him aside. "I'm glad you could make it." She felt honored, knowing he'd left today's noon mass to his friend Father Hurley, visiting from Seattle.

"You know my weakness." He glanced longingly at the display case.

"I saved you a piece of whiskey cake," she confided in a low voice.

"As long as it's our little secret." With a twinkle in his eye, he glanced over at Althea Wormley, president of the altar guild, tucking into a strawberry tart lathered in whipped cream. "If Althea gets wind of it, she'll have me following in Father Kinney's footsteps." He was referring to his predecessor, who'd gone into rehab.

"I'll bring it in a brown paper bag," she joked, though her heart was heavy. Where the hell was Aubrey?

She'd just about given up hope when as suddenly as the skies had cleared, he strolled in through the door. Heads turned, and people looked up. Aubrey might have been conjured from the steam rising genielike from the teapots. It wasn't just that he was famous: The party didn't start until he arrived.

"You're out of luck," she told him, her heart beating much too fast all of a sudden. "I just gave away the last table."

She looked about in amazement: The opening was a success. Every muffin was gone from the case, and only a few tarts remained. When Kitty sailed in with a tray of apple turnovers fresh from the oven, they were snatched up at once. Gerry wondered if Claire, who popped in from the kitchen every now and then wearing a harried look, had had a chance to let it sink in. Probably not. Later, when the dishes were washed and stacked, she would savor it.

"I don't mind sitting on the porch," he said. "Will you join me?"

She hesitated, not wanting to abandon her post. It wasn't until Sam, seated nearby with the baby on her lap, caught her eye and gave a nearly imperceptible jerk of her head that Gerry reluctantly gave in. "All right," she said. "But only for a few minutes."

On the porch, the wicker chairs creaked as they settled into them. The hubbub inside was a pleasant hum. Gerry saw that the morning glories planted only weeks before were already climbing up the railing. In no time at all they'd need to be cut back.

"I'm delighted for Claire," he said. "It looks as if it's all working out as she'd hoped."

"It wasn't just luck."

"Of course not. You had a hand in it as well."

Gerry turned to him in surprise. "What did I do?"

"If you hadn't gone with her to see her mother, this might have had a very different outcome."

"I didn't think it through at the time," she said with a shrug, "I just did what seemed right."

"Spoken like a mother." He smiled, and reached to take her hand.

"They sent balloons," she said. "Do you believe it? With a card that said 'Best of luck, from Mom and Dad.' Claire tried not to show it, but I know she was hurt. And you know something? I wish they *had*, come. It just seems so . . . unfinished."

"Speaking of unfinished." Aubrey's fingers

tightened. "There's something you should know."

Gerry felt her heart constrict. That night at the hospital had been nothing more than chivalry, and now he was growing restless. She could see it in his eyes: the need to move on. And though it was what she wanted—or so she'd been telling herself—it felt like a door about to slam shut in her face.

"I'm all ears." She tried to sound light-hearted, but it came out like a dropped rock instead.

Aubrey hesitated, a silence filled by the roaring of blood in her ears. Then he said in a soft voice, "I know we promised each other in the beginning that we wouldn't let it get out of hand. Fuck buddies, I think that was your term for it." He smiled. "But I meant what I said the other night—I think it's time we took another look."

She couldn't keep from blurting, "What about Isabelle?"

His gaze was clear as he answered, "I won't make any promises I can't keep—I couldn't forget her if I tried—but there's a difference between cherishing someone's memory and, as you so quaintly put it, throwing yourself on the pyre." He paused, his eyes searching her face. "What about you, my dear? Will you stay for the second act?"

Gerry could feel the tight ball that had been her heart unfolding like petals. "I always felt there was something noble in not needing a man. Like I deserved some sort of medal." Her mouth curved in a rueful smile.

"Would you settle for a ring instead?" Aubrey fished something from his pocket: a small velvet box.

Gerry stared at it, a rash of goose bumps spreading up her arms and neck.

"It's the reason I was late," he went on. "I had it sent over by courier from London." He opened the box, and a perfect emerald-cut diamond caught the light in a dazzling burst that made her gasp. "It was my mother's. She'd have wanted you to have it."

"What . . . what about Isabelle?" Gerry immediately wanted to bite her tongue. What a way to spoil the moment.

But Aubrey's face was relaxed and his gaze steady. "The truth is, my mother didn't much like her," he said with a shrug. "I never quite knew why—maybe they were too much alike—but you, on the other hand, she'd have liked you." He regarded her tenderly.

"Mother had absolutely no sense of humor, but she appreciated it in others."

"I can't think of a single clever thing to say right now." Gerry began to tremble.

"In that case, don't say anything at all." Aubrey slipped the ring onto her finger. Not surprisingly, it was a perfect fit.

Gerry held out her hand, turning it this way and that. The ring flashed as if signaling in Morse code. What would its message be? She eyed it for a long moment before giving up and listening to her heart instead. The words came then, spilling from her effortlessly.

"I hate big weddings," she said.

"My sentiments exactly."

"There's always Vegas."

"Your family would never forgive us." Family. Oh, God. Did Aubrey have any idea what he was taking on? Her fears vanished at once when he added, "I know a certain young man who'd be delighted to walk you down the aisle."

"With Andie and Claire as bridesmaids."

"And Sam as matron of honor."

"Holding a baby instead of a bouquet." She laughed.

There, that wasn't so hard, she thought.

Just a matter of putting one foot in front of the other. Before you knew it you were there. She squeezed Aubrey's hand, a sense of peace stealing over her. It wasn't about a knight riding up on his white charger. She'd rescued herself . . . and salvaged something important along the way: the courage to love again.

She smiled at Aubrey through her tears. "We should go back in. They'll wonder what's keeping us."

"In a little while," he said.

For once, she didn't argue.

I love hearing from readers. For those of you who'd like to get in touch, either to tell me what you thought of this book or to find out about the next one, I'm only a pen stroke, or mouse click, away.

Here's how you can reach me:

www.eileengoudge.com
direct e-mail: eileeng@nyc.rr.com

or

Eileen Goudge
P.O. Box 1396 Murray Hill Station
New York, NY 10016